Explosive

Explosive

CHARLOTTE MEDE

BRAVA

KENSINGTON PUBLISHING CORP.
http://www.kensingtonbooks.com

BRAVA BOOKS are published by

Kensington Publishing Corp.
850 Third Avenue
New York, NY 10022

Copyright © 2008 by Charlotte Mede

All rights reserved. No part of this book may be reproduced in any form or by any means without the prior written consent of the Publisher, excepting brief quotes used in reviews.

All Kensington titles, imprints and distributed lines are available at special quantity discounts for bulk purchases for sales promotion, premiums, fund-raising, educational or institutional use.

Special book excerpts or customized printings can also be created to fit specific needs. For details, write or phone the office of the Kensington Special Sales Manager: Kensington Publishing Corp., 850 Third Avenue, New York, NY 10022. Attn. Special Sales Department. Phone: 1-800-221-2647.

Brava and the B logo Reg. U.S. Pat. & TM Off.

ISBN-13: 978-0-7582-2365-4
ISBN-10: 0-7582-2365-X

First Kensington Trade Paperback Printing: January 2008
10 9 8 7 6 5 4 3 2 1

Printed in the United States of America

For K., as always

Art! Who comprehends her? With whom can one consult concerning this great goddess?

—Ludwig van Beethoven, 1810

Chapter 1

London, May 1818

A murmur cut through the smothering darkness. The Marquess of Blackburn kept his eyes closed, heavy lidded from the streams of opiate coursing through his veins. The voices moved nearer, the blend of French syllables mingling with the blood throbbing to the rhythm of his heart.

"He didn't offer much resistance—that alone is suspicious." The words were muffled, as though coming from the other side of a heavy door or thick wall.

Aware of dampness seeping into his bones, Blackburn fought the lure of sleep, lulled by the numbness of his body. Only the voices pierced through the haze clouding his mind.

He rose through layers of consciousness, carefully turning his head from side to side, planks of wood grinding into his spine. In a corner, water dripped slowly and, inexplicably, he sensed the Thames nearby.

He was parched, the back of his throat as dry as sandpaper. His limbs remained leaden, his soul pitiless and emptied. Gray Dalton, Marquess of Blackburn, was a patient man not by nature, but by hard-won experience. In this dark prison he would lie in wait.

"If I could say so, guv'ner, there was the four of us, guv'-

ner. He didn't have much of a chance. And drugged, he was, too."

"This isn't your usual dupe, you fool. He would never let himself be taken prisoner unless it suited his purposes."

"But the Lady Treadwell drugged him, guv'ner. And we was right there, waitin' fer him, outside."

Clarity slashed through a layer of his physical numbness. A Frenchman and an east Londoner, judging by their accents. The rasp of his breathing was shallow and steady and he could feel the dry grit of blood crusting his knuckles, hours old, he guessed.

Forcing himself to remember, Blackburn pushed aside the shadows clouding his thoughts and recalled Susannah Treadwell and their interlude after the ambassador's reception. Everything had gone according to plan, his and hers, he recalled with a cynicism that ran miles deep.

That cat-and-mouse game they played so well together. He didn't know who was the more ruthless: Susannah with her abundant allure which she used to feed her bottomless appetite for money and intrigue. Or perhaps he was the more cold-blooded, armed with a brutal and callous disregard for anything and anyone who stood in his way.

He was tired of the game, bone weary, but he had convinced himself that the next round would be his. *Just one more time.*

The thought brought with it a burst of energy. He moved his arms experimentally, the stiffness in his broad shoulders easing. Threads of sensation began flowing back into his muscles as his eyes opened to a windowless cell.

Pitch blackness met his gaze except for the scarcely lighter shadow along the bottom of what he perceived was the door. No way to know whether it was day or night, yet again his instincts told him it was late—close to midnight. He was lying on a hard wooden bunk with his hands expertly bound, the situation an echo of the past, insistent and strangely welcoming. Damned if he didn't feel vaguely nostalgic.

The sound of footsteps on flagstones scraped closer. A new voice this time, low and female, just outside the cell.

"He's still useful to me, I trust?" the woman asked, words like chipped ice. There was a shuffling of feet, the jangle of keys.

"Somewhat bruised you'll discover, Mademoiselle," said the Frenchman. "But I'm certain neither you nor Le Comte will be disappointed."

Le Comte and his bait, thought Blackburn in the darkness. He began to work the ropes around his wrists and ankles, the cords burning into his skin like a physical memory. He'd escaped from far more dangerous situations and, after all, this was one scenario he had planned himself.

The voices ceased abruptly, and he could hear nothing but a faint whisper to his left, the door opening quietly. With the smooth movements of someone in absolute control of his body, he twisted his upper torso a fraction, ignoring the jab of pain slicing through the back of his head.

He saw clearly now, with the kind of detachment that comes only once or twice in a lifetime, a pale nimbus of light surrounding a figure on the threshold. Dark red hair, alabaster skin, the sensuous rustle of black silk and the muzzle of a silver-mounted pistol aimed straight and unwaveringly at his heart.

The woman he'd been waiting for.

Chapter 2

Blackburn stared hard, hard as the head-splitting pain on his right side allowed.

She was beautiful, his angel of death, sporting a small lady-like pistol in an admirably steady grip. Silhouetted in the light of the open doorway a few feet away, he could see that her eyes were the color of the North Sea and just about as cold.

"Sit up." She left the door partially ajar, her glance quickly appraising.

"I suppose it would make for an easier target." He struggled to an upright position, the pain giving way as the room slowly stopped spinning. The light from the outside hallway lit the small space, bare except for his bunk and a wooden stool in the opposite corner.

Like a general surveying a battlefield, she walked toward him out of the dimness, taking dispassionate note of his physical condition, his securely bound hands and legs. "Such wit." Her soft low voice dripped contempt, strangely enticing given the circumstances. "You probably should not have put up such a struggle, Blackburn. Three men to one are hardly in your favor."

"The opiate did help those in your camp," he said. "And I'm assuming my attackers were your emissaries." The footpads had posed very little challenge as a matter of fact. But then if he hadn't let them wrestle him to the ground and into this small corner of hell, he would not be facing Devon Caravelle at this moment, a critical link to one of the most dangerous men in Europe—and a most convenient outlet for his own plans for vengeance.

"Now I suppose you're here to tell me how I might be of help?" He scanned her face with a professional expertise, searching for something he couldn't yet define.

She refused to be pushed into any quick answers. "In good time."

The diffuse light cast a sheen on her dark auburn hair and threw into sharp relief the delicate planes of her face. Her English appeared perfect and unaccented. And she was clearly accustomed to brandishing revolvers. Without lowering her pistol, she moved in closer. Her cloak was brown, deliberate camouflage for physical assets tempting enough for a Jesuit. Every time she moved, he heard the unmistakable shimmer of the silk she wore underneath. He knew her type—and her world—all too well.

She shrugged in his direction, her brow raised in reproof. "For your own sake, I caution you. I can and will use this revolver should the situation dictate."

Blackburn didn't doubt it. "What threat do I possibly present?" He held up his bound hands for her inspection. His jaw must be sporting at least a few bruises as well, now dark with two days' stubble. De Maupassant's henchmen weren't known for their subtlety, causing Blackburn to wonder if this beautiful ambassador knew the extent of their cruelty. He expected at least a flicker of revulsion, but her eyes remained unmoved.

"True—but you do seem to look after yourself remarkably well." Her lips curled over the last word as she took a few steps away from him.

Blackburn accepted the backhanded compliment with a small smile, waiting for her next move. Seated on the bunk, held immobile by thick ropes, he felt a strange euphoria, a coiled tension that he hadn't felt in a long while, an edginess that perversely cut through some of the guilt and darkness that marked too many of his days. Devon Caravelle was not exactly as he had expected.

He watched the slow pulse at the base of her slender neck above the rise of rounded breasts no amount of brown wool could conceal. She did an admirable job of hiding her thoughts, those wide compelling eyes revealing little except a penetrating acuity. She was her father's daughter, there was little doubt.

Yet there was a strange vulnerability about her as she stared at him over the gun, her expression a closed prison door. "I'm going to tell you what I want from you, Blackburn. I trust you're ready to hear it."

Bloody hell, he couldn't wait.

But keeping his face expressionless, he merely shrugged. "A cynic would conclude that everybody wants something. It's an unfortunate aspect of human nature I've learned."

"Indeed." Devon Caravelle's delicately rounded chin lifted higher.

He smiled inwardly. This was exactly what he and the Duke of Wellington had planned—for Devon Caravelle to come to them. They both knew how useless her father, Brendan Clifton, had turned out to be, refusing to be of help to St. James's Palace, throwing his lot in with neither the English nor the French. And how convenient it had been for him to send his daughter away to the music conservatory that last year, as the dangerous currents of the war between England and Napoleon swirled about him. Right before his murder.

Blackburn felt his gut tighten like a bow. Despite those measures, Clifton had left his daughter with a highly volatile and explosive legacy.

She was the only person alive who had a chance of accessing the dangerous truth embedded in Beethoven's Eroica score.

With that thought, the pounding in Blackburn's head resumed. In response, he attempted to stretch the cramped muscles in his shoulders as Devon Caravelle instantly retrained her pistol, aiming precisely for his heart.

"I'm just getting comfortable," he reassured her, surprised at her nervous reaction, the tightening of her lips as she concentrated her gaze on him.

"That's precisely my concern. The last thing I want you to feel is comfortable." The words dripped acid.

She stood limned in the dimness, and he focused on the slender but strong gloved hand that gripped the pistol.

"You're not going to kill me—at least just yet," he played along with the game. "Are you preparing me for another bout with those henchmen? I suppose I should be trembling in my boots." What he really wanted to ask her was why she had aligned herself with a man as cruel and dangerous as de Maupassant.

"It can be arranged," she said dryly, seemingly secure in her position as the Frenchman's mistress and musical protégée.

"For Christ's sake, put down the gun and relax. I'm not going anywhere," he ground out. Blackburn saw her eyes widen in momentary surprise but the pistol didn't waver.

"I'll relax when this is over, thank you." She wet her lips seemingly unaware of his gaze following the sensuous curve of her mouth.

He tried to keep the grimness from his tone. "When what's over? You're taking a rather long time to get to the point."

"That's my prerogative given the circumstances."

"Circumstances can change quickly." Blackburn watched her remarkable eyes darken at his comment. He would probably bed her, he thought cynically, but with *purpose* in mind. Here was just another link in the chain of de Maupassant's machinations, another weapon to get to the *Eroica* and the cipher that was the ultimate prize. A beautiful, sensual package that possessed the secrets of untold power and of England's and Europe's potential devastation.

"There is a chair available." He gestured with bound hands to the stool in the corner.

"I prefer to stand."

"You have the pistol, so naturally, whichever you prefer." They eyed each other. Blackburn shifted slightly on the bunk and sensed the apprehension in the tight set of her shoulders.

He itched to get his hands on her. "You're probably not going to shoot me, or you would have done so already. What is it that you want?" he asked instead, lowering his gaze, completely at ease staring down the barrel of a gun.

She made a small sound, a clearing of her throat, giving his question some consideration. "I sense that like most men, you have little patience." The words were said in a low contralto in the gloominess of the cell. "And yet, I have my suspicions that you already know what I want."

There it was, the gauntlet, thrown down in challenge. He regarded her impassively, all the while wondering how she would go about asking him—forcing him—to work with her on deciphering the score.

Without turning her back to him, she walked slowly toward the stool in the corner and dragged it to the center of the room before sitting down and carefully arranging her skirts as though the action was the most important thing in the world at the moment. She was a fine actress. And why wouldn't she be? He was in the presence of the daughter of one of Europe's most accomplished mathematicians and cryptologists. As a worldly woman who had traveled among Europe's most bohemian revolutionary circles, she was certainly no innocent waiting here in this cell for his reluctant cooperation.

And her eyes were spectacular, as compelling as gathering storm clouds, he noted distractedly, while continuing to work surreptitiously to free his bound hands and legs.

"You've gone to considerable trouble to have me transported here—what with the drama of opiates and ruffians, so you'll forgive my impatience," he said trying to get her to say the words he wanted to hear.

She looked at him carefully, smoothing the leather of her gloves as though the motion helped her come to an important decision. "I believe I'll explain what you *need* to know later," she said slowly and unpleasantly. And with her free hand pulling her cloak more closely around her she made a motion as though to rise from her seat. "In the interim, you're coming with me."

"Just like that?" He raised a brow speculatively. "This is becoming more and more diverting, so much so that I can almost forgive the brutality of the previous evening. Now tell me," he leaned forward slightly as though being asked to raise the stakes in a polite game of whist, "why should I?"

"I have something you want."

"You *are* an attractive woman . . ."

Anger steeled her voice as she rose from the stool in a swirl of wool and silk. "Don't be obtuse. There's much more at stake here which I'm sure you know."

Blackburn shrugged, feeling implausibly relaxed in his rumpled evening clothes. Despite an urge to destroy the woman in front of him, along with the man who sent her, he was actually enjoying himself. "Why don't you tell me what it is, then," he asked almost gently, as if he'd ever been denied anything in his life. "I'm getting rather bored. I should like to think you'd get to the point in the next minute or so."

"You actually believe there's cause for humor here?" She cocked her pistol for emphasis, the silver glinting in the dim light. "I suggest that you take this meeting quite seriously, Blackburn, because you have a critically important decision to make. You either go with me willingly tonight—or I leave you here to languish indefinitely. I somehow suspect these accommodations are much too damp and dark for your liking."

"I'm truly intrigued now, Mademoiselle." She couldn't mistake the mockery in his voice.

"Introductions are hardly in order," she conceded, her full lips tightening, as though preparing herself for an unwelcome task. "I know who you are. And you, no doubt, know who I am. More important, we're after the same thing."

"And that might be what exactly?" If Devon Caravelle had been watching more closely, she would have noticed that his smile didn't reach his eyes.

"Beethoven's *Eroica* score. I know who has it."

The *unspoken* name swung between them like a noose.

Le Comte Henri de Maupassant.

His eyes never left her face, but his expression was deliberately indolent, almost careless of the situation. "So you may be aware of the *Eroica*—but why should I be impressed? First off, you're Brendan Clifton's daughter, Devon Caravelle. And second, it should be easy for Le Comte's current mistress to ascertain its whereabouts."

"I expected that you would know who I am," she countered, not bothering to deny or confirm her position of mistress to the Frenchman.

It wasn't as though he was expecting her to blush or demur, for God's sake, yet Blackburn fought back a sense of irrational disappointment, as though her association with de Maupassant should in some way matter to him.

"The fact that you're his new mistress is widely known— no news there," he said harshly, giving himself a mental shake. "I also know that you're probably with the Frenchman because of the score." Surprisingly, the words left a bitter aftertaste.

She rose from the stool, switching the pistol to her left hand, her eyes guarded, her shoulders braced. "Those details are unimportant." Each of her words was as hard as diamonds. "What is important is that you are—unfortunately for you— integral to discovering what lies entangled within some of the most beautiful music ever composed."

"I think I'm beginning to understand now," he interrupted. "You and Le Comte need me." In this strange conversation, they had come to an impasse, the air between them crackling with a strange and uncomfortable current.

"That's probably a fair assessment." She kept a firm grip on the pistol and he knew that this encounter was costing her some effort. He could see it in the rigidity of her spine, the resolute set of her chin. Her every move was calculated, controlled and yet something about her suggested emotions, and a bold sensuality, held closely in check.

Her eyes pinned him to his place on the bunk. "I will secure the *Eroica*—which you have been unable to do so far— and then under my direction, at an undisclosed location, we will discover what secrets the score holds."

Just like that.

Inwardly, Blackburn shook his head, amazed. The idea of supervision held little appeal for him, reinforcing his growing suspicion that Devon Caravelle was either arrogant beyond belief, reciting from a prepared agenda, or unwilling to recognize exactly whom she was up against. In response, he assumed his best imitation of the dissipated rogue, shifting his long legs out in front of him while loosening the cords binding his booted feet—as if he had all evening to discuss his options.

"But why should I?" he murmured insolently. Then lying through his teeth, he added casually, "Le Comte and I move in some of the same circles, though I can't claim any direct association with him. And forgive me if this question is crude, but quite frankly, what do I get out of this?"

Devon Caravelle smiled without humor. "From what I understand, you've been after the *Eroica* for some time. So now's your chance. And once our work is done, you can report back to your Wellington that all is well for all I care. What could be more straightforward for somebody like you?"

"Hardly straightforward—for somebody like me," he said in a warm gravelly voice inviting confidence, yet at odds with the frost in his gaze. "Theoretically, if we were to do it your way, I would help you decipher the code and then have you relinquish the results to de Maupassant." Blackburn's gaze was mocking. "Doesn't make much sense to me. And more important, why should I trust you—and the Frenchman?"

"Because you have no choice." Her voice was steady, her

stance arrogant. And suddenly, it was enough for Blackburn. He sat absolutely still, but his body thrummed with intensity.

"You clearly don't know me very well, Mademoiselle." His gaze fastened on her. "I always have a choice."

The words held a veiled threat and, for the first time that evening, she backed away from him turning toward the door. Blackburn stopped thinking and surged from the bunk. He moved quickly, his next actions a blur as the loosened ropes binding his hands and legs were kicked aside. He spun her around so quickly that her feet left the ground as she was shoved roughly up against the door, slamming it shut, her pistol clattering uselessly to the floor. The room plunged into darkness.

Damn, it felt good.

He could sense every inch of her body stretched next to his. It would be far simpler to kill her now.

Holding her wrists high above her head, he heard her breath catch in her throat, a sound of vulnerability that he knew well. She was frightened, as well she should be. In the frozen silence and aware of how easily he could crush the life out of her, Blackburn took the time to examine his abductor at his leisure.

As his vision adjusted to the dimness, he could make out large gray eyes fringed with dark lashes gracing a face that was as unusual as it was lovely. His practiced look took in the defined cheekbones, the translucent skin that was a perfect foil for richly hued tresses and a mouth whose soft fullness suggested an ardent sensuality. And she had the enviable good sense not to scream. He could snap her neck in a heartbeat and she knew it.

He said in infuriatingly measured tones, "Now back to choices. You mentioned earlier that I have two. But let me amend your proposition by adding a third."

"I shall scream for help." Her eyes glittered in the darkness.

"No you won't. You know that I can silence you and manage those two fellows hovering outside. Besides which, you wouldn't get what you want. And neither would I."

Blackburn knew she could feel his hard thighs and hips outlined by his tailored breeches. Deliberately, he moved even closer, enjoying her barely contained panic in the darkness— and something else. He was adept at recognizing a sensual response. His large hand held her two wrists as easily as a child's. Her eyes moved to his wide mouth, his lips curved in a knowing smile.

"Let me go this instant," she snapped, rigid as a washboard. "Get your hands off me."

He smiled tauntingly. "I'm no longer holding on to you, Mademoiselle." He offered strong beautifully shaped hands for her view. She flushed under his gaze, unable to move away, still blocked by his body and considerable height.

"Let me tell you about that third option," he said looming ever closer, dispassionately aware of his own reaction, the swelling in his breeches that started the moment she'd walked into his cell.

Her full lips parted in expectation, agitation, or passion, he couldn't tell. Devon Caravelle's breaths came in shallow gasps as she was clearly unnerved by his nearness and the danger he represented. Blackburn didn't envy her—positioned as she was between himself and Le Comte.

He said, "You get me the *Eroica*. We work on the score together. I decide what to do with the contents."

"That's impossible."

"Nothing's impossible."

"You don't trust me."

"Why should I? You're Le Comte's newest bauble. It stands to reason your loyalty rests with him. No doubt he's compensating you handsomely. And no doubt he sent you to secure my cooperation," Blackburn said brutally, wondering what securing that cooperation might entail. His erection lengthened at the thought, primed as a pistol. "I will quadruple whatever he's offered you." It seemed to him that she flinched.

But she maintained a mutinous silence, thick lashes at half-mast over her spectacular eyes.

"While I find your antics charmingly cloak and dagger," he continued, forcing himself to ignore the heaviness in his groin, "I have neither the time nor the patience to work under your *direction*, as you charmingly suggested earlier. Now you're the one who hasn't a choice."

Her face paled from cream to alabaster. "Look, you don't understand."

"Of course I do, Mademoiselle," he said callously. For some reason he didn't fight the urge to touch her and flicked a careless finger along the smoothness of her cheek. Her breaths came even faster. "It's quite simple. You work for me against Le Comte."

"And if I refuse?" She suppressed a shiver as she felt his caress.

In response, he forced her against the door, resting one hand casually over her head and effectively caging her with his body. One fraction closer and she would feel another kind of physical threat. "I don't think you will, Mademoiselle. I'm sure a damp prison cell is as much to your liking as it is to my liking, wouldn't you say?"

"You mean to throw me to the magistrates?" She was so close he felt the warmth of her breath in the dark.

"Yes, I would—tonight, as a matter of fact. They'd be more than pleased to *stretch your neck.* Capturing the daughter of an infamous traitor; moreover, a daughter who was involved in her father's rather important work? And of course, I would be available to testify that you had me abducted in order to help you with your treasonous plans."

It was as if he had cracked her veneer, hit a nerve. "Get away from me." Her voice filled with pain and an odd undertone of protectiveness. "Don't dare ever mention my father again."

"As you wish." He turned to block the door with his back, arms crossed over his chest. "But I believe I have your answer. And don't worry, Mademoiselle. De Maupassant will never know you're working against him, rather than for him—as long as you cooperate with me, of course. And for this deception you will be reimbursed handsomely. Don't look so shocked," he added, watching her rooted to her spot in the gloom. "I'm sure you're accustomed to treachery for the right price. So—you will have the score for me tomorrow evening at the recital your generous benefactor is hosting to showcase your considerable charms."

Devon Caravelle took a breath and raised her chin. "What if he refuses to relinquish it to me?"

Blackburn's expression was derisive as he deliberately surveyed her form, from her glorious hair and mobile mouth to the slender body alluringly hidden beneath swatches of brown wool.

His voice was rough, his breath soft on her ear. "Seduce him—what else? Return to your lover tonight and beguile, captivate, and lie as fluently as I'm sure you can. Simply pretend all is going according to plan."

His smile was distinctly unpleasant as he pulled himself away from her. "Now go—because I'm sure he's expecting you."

It was as though the impossible had occurred and he had shocked her, her profile frozen ivory. "You disgust me," she whispered, gathering her cloak and grabbing the latch of the door to pull it open.

"Don't forget your pistol." He picked it up from the floor and held it out to her. She quickly snapped up the weapon with a gloved hand, afraid to touch him. But Devon Caravelle didn't call for the guards.

"Tomorrow evening," said the Marquess of Blackburn throwing her an indifferent glance, as though getting ready to depart from an unexpectedly tedious reception rather than walk out of a prison.

For the briefest of seconds he wondered whether he should

let her go back to Le Comte. The thought of their being lovers did more than usual to fuel his natural cynicism. *Bloody hell,* he wanted a drink, wanted to sit by himself and cool his response toward a woman who could easily destroy him. It was time for his exit as he obviously needed a brandy to clear the pounding in his head.

He stepped over the threshold into a narrow hallway, consciously leaving the shadow of Devon Caravelle's disturbing presence behind him.

"And do whatever you have to do to get the score—to keep the magistrates and the hangman at bay, of course," he said by way of a parting shot. "I'm sure you know how, Mademoiselle. All too well."

Chapter 3

Devon Caravelle's hands shook as she shrugged out of her cloak. Her suite of rooms at Le Comte's lavish town house in Mayfair was already lit by one of the many servants the Frenchman kept in dancing attendance. The illusory comfort of the flickering wall sconces did little to allay her anxieties.

They'd be more than pleased to stretch your neck.

The richly patterned wall, draped in watered silk, danced before her eyes.

She didn't have the score.

Worse still, she hadn't any idea where it possibly could be found in Le Comte's town house and she'd been surreptitiously searching for weeks. She shivered, missing the warmth of her cloak just as she heard the knock. Walking to the door and turning the handle, she felt every nerve standing at attention.

Le Comte was already lounging in the hallway, taking in the young woman displayed before him like the finest jewel amid the sumptuous luxuriance of the boudoir. He stepped into the room adorned in the palest cream and amethyst fabrics and raised his eyes to a baroque mirror that reflected the perfection of creamy skin and dark red hair.

He smiled thinly at her reflection in the oval above her

vanity as he began to remove one of his pristinely white evening gloves.

"You look somewhat disheveled, *ma chère*. I hope the Marquess did not give you any undue trouble. Where is he—still rusticating in that cell I arranged for?" His voice was reedy with mockery, his face appearing next to hers.

She saw herself in Le Comte's gaze, a worldly woman, an intellectual who had the key to something he wanted desperately. Her vision blurred and all she could see was the image of the Marquess of Blackburn. The most strikingly beautiful man she'd ever encountered, a portrait of contrasts, a combination of overwhelming physicality and concentrated intellect. Focused on her.

He was too tall, his shoulders too broad, the jaw too strong for fashion. And it had taken all her control to keep from reacting as he'd surveyed her with those midnight blue eyes. Her pulse raced at the memory of an indefinable energy permeating the cell, pulling her closer to him against both her reason and her will.

Devon dragged herself back to the present, aware of Le Comte's image in the mirror beside her and all too aware that lying and deception was the only way out.

"I believe you'll find everything proceeding to plan." She kept her voice low, infusing resignation and desperation in her tone. "The Marquess, under duress, committed to working with me."

To distract herself from the lie, Devon picked up a silver comb on the vanity. For a moment the room's opulence shimmered in the mirror; the door of her dressing room opened to reveal the spill of silks and satins, gifts from de Maupassant, every last one given with a purpose in mind, a small voice reminded her.

"My dear Devon, I am so pleased to hear the good news." Le Comte began casually to remove his other glove before tossing both aside and lowering himself into a flounced and beribboned chaise. "Although I also heard that you allowed him to waltz out of the prison I so thoughtfully arranged for him, or so my men have informed me. And I take it he's not waiting for us at the apartments I'd organized for the two of you on Grosvenor."

Devon improvised. "I needed more time; besides which, the Marquess is as good as imprisoned." One lie led effortlessly to the next. "He wants access to the *Eroica* score and to have it deciphered as much as you do and he recognizes that this is—and I am—his only opportunity to do so."

"Indeed—all of which I knew well in advance," mused the Frenchman with a superiority that was second nature. "He dearly wants the music and he clearly wants to work with Clifton's daughter—you—Devon Caravelle. He knows that the two go hand in hand." Le Comte paused for emphasis, his gaze sharpening. "You worked with your father to the end. You understood—*understand*—his world. His talents are your talents. His secrets, your secrets."

If only Le Comte were not speaking the truth.

Glancing down at the open cameo on the vanity table, she could distinguish the faint but indelible images of her parents. The past was becoming for her a series of faded portraits. Their small cottage at Blois. Her mother dying from a fever. Her brilliant and lonely father. His urgings that she continue her study of music, that she play her mother's pianoforte, although she knew each note and chord she struck was bittersweet for them both.

The terrifying implications of his work and his obsessions.

"I was his assistant, nothing more." She put down the comb carefully and turned around to look directly at Le Comte.

"Of course, of course, my dear," the Frenchman mocked her earnestness. "All the more reason I want you to work with Blackburn. Your combined knowledge will prove most useful. I'm certain he will help you, *help us*, make the most of what little you claim to know."

"And if I refuse?"

"Come now, I expect better from a woman of your intelligence. Certainly, there's no need for any more of the high drama and coercive strategies I was forced to use with Blackburn to bring the two of you together." Le Comte paused significantly, crossing a stockinged leg and absently admiring a silver buckle on his shoe. "And even if you were to refuse," he reflected philosophically, "I would hand you over to the authorities in France as a traitor. The daughter of a traitor, to be more specific. Or perhaps I'll turn you over to England. It's actually difficult for me to choose. Your father changed sides with alarming regularity, as you may recall."

Devon's eyes burned at the insult as she dug her hands into the marquetry of the vanity table behind her. "My father was not a traitor. He was a genius."

Le Comte sighed theatrically. "You are being tedious, Devon, as well as decidedly ungracious. I made a very generous offer when I first came to you at the Conservatoire—and it still stands. Discover what the *Eroica* score holds and I shall ensure your freedom from prosecution. Even at your most cynical, you must admit the proposition is sound. After all, what better guarantee? You will have as much knowledge about my motives as I will have about yours."

A pact with the devil. Simple enough. Just sell her soul and spend every day under Le Comte's watchful eyes, tortured into giving away her father's dangerous secrets, at every turn threatened with having her father and herself exposed as traitors.

She closed her eyes against the onslaught of panic, conjuring the image of the man she had met at Blackfriars Bridge just hours before. The gaze that missed nothing, a cold hard blue. He even smelled of danger, a scent that overpowered her senses until she couldn't think.

Her mouth was dry with desperation. Clenching her hands into fists, she charged headlong into the breach. "You promised to give me access to the original score. Blackburn and I will need it to unravel the formula."

"You're quite right. Time is running out." Le Comte settled more comfortably into his chair. "But before I relinquish the score I want to be sure that you have *entrapped* our Marquess as surely as Delilah ensnared Samson. You do remember the story, Devon?"

A powerful man who was brought to his knees by a dangerously sensual woman. She swallowed the panic in her throat.

"Blackburn will surely find you a beautiful, intriguing woman. More important, he will like nothing more than to think he could steal not one, but two of my prized possessions, the *Eroica* and my valuable protégée." Le Comte made a minute adjustment to his extravagant cravat before adding, "Let us just say that the Marquess and I have a certain shared history that adds a piquancy to this situation."

There was something more to the relationship between the two men, Devon was beginning to suspect, an enmity, a bitter rivalry that transcended mere ideology.

Something Delilah could exploit.

"Is that the reason you're hosting these recitals? To make very public your newest, shiniest, liaison?" she asked, biting back the urge to say more. She momentarily caught sight of her profile in the mirror, her eyes glittering feverishly.

"It does add a certain drama," the Frenchman conceded, toying with the crystal stopper of a perfume bottle beautifully displayed on the pedestal table by his chair, the sweet cloying scent instantly filling the room. "I want to keep you and the *Eroica* dangling just out of Blackburn's reach—for now. It will only whet his appetite and bring him under my control—and trust me, he is a difficult man to control."

As though she had any doubt.

Le Comte continued pompously, "Understand this, if nothing else. Together you and Blackburn form two halves of a whole and that whole is what I want. Together you have the ability to give me what I've been after for years." His lips thinned and his eyes narrowed. "Let me emphasize one more thing, Devon. I've waited long enough. And I'm expecting you to perform. I trust we're clear on that point?"

Le Comte continued, digging the knife in deeper. "One must admit that the *Eroica* is a symphony of incredible beauty and, thanks to your father, it carries in it the seeds of humanity's destruction. Quite the horrific irony, no?"

Soulful, majestic, heartrending, Devon could hear the strains of the melody, a composition dedicated to the courage and folly of Napoleon Bonaparte and the Revolution.

"And it led to my father's murder, leaving in its place an ineradicable stain of blood." Her words were a whisper in the room.

"Unfortunate for you, isn't it?" Le Comte eyed her speculatively.

"And that's why I'm here, Le Comte," she concluded bitterly, ultimately a realist.

Even if she had the *Eroica* in her possession, to wrestle with the code alone was impossible. Even her highly vaunted proficiency was limited when it came to the complex cipher that her father had a part in creating.

She needed Blackburn. And yet he could just as easily toss her to the magistrates as a spy or traitor to the British cause once he had what he wanted.

Her blood warmed in anger as she remembered his words, his touch, his *threat.*

Seduce him . . . what else?

The words appalled her, and again she felt Blackburn's hot breath on her skin, the hard hands enclosing her wrists. In the eyes of the Marquess, she was entirely disposable, a mistress as easily manipulated as a rag doll, her body to be used as currency.

Devon felt the unblinking cold of Le Comte's stare on her skin, shocking her back to the present.

His face was a sly mask, barely disguising his pleasure at his own machinations. She was freezing again. In spite of the hothouse confines of the room, her blood ran like ice. Unable to hold his gaze, Devon once more conjured the specter of Blackburn, forcing herself to admit that the Marquess represented the biggest gamble of her life, and she was more than familiar with the laws of averages.

"You seem fatigued, ma chère." Le Comte interrupted her thoughts with false concern. "Shall I ring for your maid?" His eyes were sharp and she shivered again at the thought of those pale, white hands on her body.

"No need—I'm quite all right." She knew it was useless to inquire about the whereabouts of the score, as Le Comte was a man who never changed his mind once it was set upon its course.

"Do get some rest, then. You have a challenging few days in front of you, Devon, keeping our Marquess primed like a rutting stag, no?" Without bothering to watch for her reaction, he moved languidly from the chaise to ring for a footman before adding, "And by the way, you never did recount the *details* of your meeting with Blackburn. Did the Marquess have a message for me, perhaps?" His look was as anticipatory as a fencing master waiting for the next thrust and parry.

A film of perspiration dampened her palms and she had a mad impulse to turn around and simply run out the door. Instead she answered abruptly, "He expects to be given the score tomorrow evening at the recital."

Le Comte looked slyly triumphant. "Ever arrogant, our Marquess." His eyes lingered on the Meissen clock over the fireplace, as though counting the minutes. "Yet he'll learn, once again, that there's a price to be paid for everything."

The Frenchman was right. Loyalty, integrity, honesty— Devon had learned all too recently that they could be bartered for a price, or for a cause. As the door closed behind Le Comte all she saw was a swinging noose and all she heard was the mocking voice of the Marquess of Blackburn.

Do whatever you have to do to get the score. I'm sure you know how, Mademoiselle. All too well.

Chapter 4

Blackburn listened to the crescendo of violins, distant and lilting, wafting into the candlelit boudoir just as the woman draped over the satin and lace-strewn bed peaked for the second time. He felt her body tense, the lush, extravagant curves fill his hands moments before he, accommodating as ever, lost himself in her dark depths.

Several heartbeats later dusky eyes framed by a profusion of ebony curls opened lazily. "You may love me to death," breathed a satiated Susannah Treadwell, "anytime." Her intense gaze—supremely satisfied and simultaneously carnal—devoured the man whose lean powerful body had just given her an encounter with Eros she would long remember. She arched her back in languid contentment, a smoothly curved arm supporting her slender neck.

"My pleasure." He moved away with economic grace to stretch his tall frame, nakedly confident, alongside the bed. Magnificently male in a casual sprawl, his broad shoulders were an incongruous match for the fragrantly tousled ivory sheets and lace-embroidered pillows.

The Lady Treadwell was in a class by herself, a woman whose lack of inhibition and insatiable proclivities matched his—stroke for passionate stroke.

Exactly how involved she was with Le Comte and the *Eroica* score was, of course, another matter and did absolutely nothing to keep him from enjoying the scarlet-tipped hand which lingered so effectively on his hard torso. The hand stole upward, infinitely slowly from the indentation of his navel, to caress the sculpted chest.

"Must we attend this tedious recital, Gray?" Lady Susannah pouted prettily, intent on her pleasurable exploration of a well-delineated pectoral. "I can think of far better ways to spend our time than waiting interminably for this pianist. I do believe Le Comte has temporarily lost his mind. All this excitement over a woman playing Beethoven. I saw her just the other day riding on Rotten Row. A shriveled bluestocking. Only wonder why Le Comte has taken an interest!"

Blackburn suspected the Frenchman had told Susannah very little about Devon Caravelle. He rarely supplied details, only money, aware that her elderly husband had run through his fortune long ago. The Frenchman had paid her well to offer him up to his abductors, he was sure of it.

Blackburn's expression revealed nothing but amusement as he settled his long frame more comfortably on the overstuffed softness of the hastily commandeered bed.

"Quite the sensation from what I've heard. Could it be that you're afraid of a potential rival? The way you propelled me out of that crowded hall tonight and up those stairs was nothing short of brazen," he said with mock amazement, shaking his dark head while noting with an expert's eye the heavy fullness of her impressively displayed breasts.

A husky laugh punctuated his remark as her warm, spicy scent formed a web around them. "Well, darling, I knew this guest room was unoccupied," she purred convincingly, tracing the outline of a bruise on the left side of his jaw with delightful concentration. "I must have my pleasures. You know what a bore old Treadwell can be. How can you blame me?"

"The things we do for money, like marrying well in your case, seldom come easily I suppose." Blackburn petted Susannah's sumptuous behind lingeringly, philosophically flexible about such comparatively trifling moral issues. His life's experience had made certain judgments impractical.

"I'm not pleased, however, that those beastly cutthroats were working on the behest of old Treadwell," she lied effortlessly. She made a moue of distaste. "To attack you outside my town house the other night! I'm afraid that my husband has finally seen through the haze of his senility and realized what a ridiculous cuckold he's become."

"Many thanks for your overwhelming concern," murmured Blackburn with considerable irony. "Mercifully, I recover quickly."

"I have noticed that your recovery time is enviable." Susannah turned onto her back in one calculated seductive move. "Which has more to do with my eagerness to escape with you this evening than anything Le Comte's new mistress could possibly have to offer."

"Those who have heard her play maintain she's impressively talented. Her interpretation of Beethoven is said to be masterful."

"Since when have you developed an interest in music?" Susannah asked sharply.

Since his encounter with an icy, fiery-haired woman in a dark cell by Blackfriars Bridge.

In the next instant he was beset by the image of Devon Caravelle emerging triumphantly from the Frenchman's bed. He stretched his arms over his head and steeled himself. It wasn't anything he wanted to think about—who she'd sleep with and what she'd do to keep the noose from tightening around that beautiful neck. Instead of the elation he expected to feel at upending de Maupassant's plans, he found himself sinking into a cynical torpor. He shifted away from Susannah, her physical presence suddenly cloying.

"Anything I can do, darling?" He'd forgotten how perceptive Lady Treadwell could be. "You seem preoccupied suddenly."

He smiled distractedly. "I think we should get back to the concert."

Every muscle in his body felt tight, his jaw locked, his mind in turmoil. The intriguing and dangerous Devon could just as easily be playing him for a fool. Money was more often the motivator than loyalty to a political cause. Or the motives might well be political in nature. He drew a long breath.

The gloves would then come off. He'd never again risk a disaster like the one involving his murdered brother.

With heavy lids and darker intentions, he observed Susannah carefully. Much as it would wound her overdeveloped sense of vanity, he thought, wrapping his wrist in a swathe of her jet hair, this seemingly spontaneous seduction had been welcomed not the least for the sexual interlude as for the information he always gleaned from their postcoital conversations.

"A female virtuoso, it's unusual, you must admit." He pushed carefully, positioning a pillow behind his head.

Pouting her disappointment as the subject matter turned from her, Susannah tugged away her hair with small teasing gestures before inching closer to Blackburn. "Her mother, they say, was French, one of those horrid women who became involved with the radicals during the Revolution. Her father was English but nobody seems to know anything about him. They divided their time between London, Paris, and some absurd little cottage," she revealed cattily. "I suppose she was born on the wrong side of the sheets, hence her French surname. Some men find that sort of thing attractive, particularly in a mistress."

"De Maupassant and she met in Paris?"

"You've been listening to the same gossips as I have, darling," Susannah scolded mockingly. "One hears that Le Comte's son was taking music lessons from her at the Conservatoire. I presume, like any other woman with very little to trade upon, Mademoiselle sensed an opportunity and planned to make herself indispensable to Le Comte, *in every way.*" Susannah's dark eyes suddenly turned feline before she said in a throaty voice, "You seem very interested, darling."

And Susannah seemed overly informed.

He shifted to a sitting position on the side of the canopied bed, the corded muscles in his arms flexing. "Interested enough that I recommend we return to the reception before the recital begins. And more important, I wouldn't want to deprive your legion of admirers of your company."

Susannah replied by snaking one arm around his abdomen pleasured by the sensation of finely tapered muscle. "Just five more minutes," she whispered beguilingly, smolderingly confident that her seductive pose would have the desired effect.

Blackburn felt the sway of her pointed nipples against his back as moist lips and tongue traced a path across his broad shoulders. "Blackburn," she growled low in her throat, "don't ever think another woman would be any match for me."

"I think we've had enough talk," he circumvented the possessiveness in her voice, leaning over her lazily, "of Le Comte and his mistress."

Yet her image wouldn't leave him alone. The wide gray eyes as she faced him in the dark cell at Blackfriars Bridge, the generously expressive mouth, the controlled sensuality evident in every motion of her body swathed in brown wool. The sensuous whisper of rich silk.

Unaccountably annoyed, he shunted the memory and one of the abundant pillows aside. His hands, equally familiar with intrigue and seduction, continued to caress the silken skin of the eager Lady Treadwell, skimming over her abundant curves. He felt her lips snake persuasively over his taut stomach, narrow hips, until he forgot everything except the spasms of pleasure that racked his body—all the while de Maupassant's concert proceeded circumspectly below.

Le Comte Henri de Maupassant barely contained his excitement behind his habitual mask of hauteur. His eyes swept the ballroom of his town house, a massive hall that had been recently regilded without thought to cost. On this night he had made sure that one thousand candles cast incandescent light over jeweled and silk-clad guests who were all holding their collective breaths between sips of the finest champagne.

All the better for him to see the Marquess of Blackburn snap the first trigger of an elaborate, and deeply satisfying, trap.

"It's truly shocking and should not be countenanced," he heard Lady Hester Bankfort intone, as she pursed thin lips and tapped her meager bosom with a fan for emphasis.

"And that's precisely why we've all decided to attend," reminded her daughter-in-law Belinda who, along with the two hundred or so of the cream of London society, filled the ballroom of Comte Henri de Maupassant.

"Even if she *is* his mistress," allowed Lady Bankfort while giving a brief nod to Le Comte and to a knot of gentlemen already arranged in a row of exquisite Louis Quinze chairs for what was to be the London Season's most scandalous recital. "But to parade her about shamelessly, like some kind of odalisque . . ."

Le Comte heard her voice trail off in a huff of disapproval. "Public performances given by a woman! The French take simply too many liberties."

Le Comte knew the slight was intended for him, a host whose aristocratic lineage, far superior to Lady Bankfort's, quite frankly rankled. He also knew that Lady Bankfort and the rest of his guests were conveniently forgetting the moral and material excesses of previous decades when enmity with the French loosened both fashions and mores.

He circulated with an air of entitlement among his guests, his expression faintly patronizing. Relinquishing his glass of champagne to a passing footman, he went to stand within a few feet of a gleaming mahogany Broadwood pianoforte. A hush descended as the candlelight flickered around the man for whom, gossips liked to say, libertinage was a religion. With a string of mistresses, one more beautiful than the last and, conveniently, a wife and requisite heirs permanently traveling abroad, Comte Henri de Maupassant lived as if the *ancien régime* had never gone the way of the guillotine.

The family history was well known, the lives lost to the Terror, and the quick escape to England with a cache of gold and jewels dating back to the Middle Ages. Le Comte had all but been raised in England save for forays to the continent to reclaim gradually the ancestral lands in France.

"That's where he found her," someone in the front row of the assembled guests whispered, "at the Conservatoire in Paris."

Le Comte smiled faintly in acknowledgment of the remark, his face the detached mask of the polished host. He raised a white-gloved hand for silence and turned to the fashionable crowd who were having trouble dissembling their unfashionable excitement.

Ah yes, the right combination of scandal and titilation always served as the most delectable kind of enticement.

He was certain that Wellington, Whitehall, and the Marquess of Blackburn were all too aware of whom he was dangling right in front of their noses. What delicious irony, ensnaring England's master spy to do his bidding at long last— and in the most banal way possible. Through the seductive allure of a woman.

"Dear Ladies and Gentlemen," he began. The sibilant tones carried just a charming hint of accent. "My most heartfelt thanks to all of you for granting me this opportunity to introduce a remarkable sensation." Le Comte paused deliberately for a moment, lingering on the syllables of that last word, relishing the palpable tension in the room.

"I know that many of you are truly devotees of music, worshippers at the shrine of Apollo, loyal disciples to the world's greatest composers," he continued with the barest trace of irony. His words drifted over the candelabra bracketing the footmen who were positioned around the alcoves of the ballroom. Only the fine murmur of expensive fabrics and hushed breaths punctuated the absolute stillness.

"And to do justice to this great devotion, I have the honor of introducing to you this evening my most recent protégée, a young woman recently arrived from France whose talent at interpreting the work of one of our greatest composers is, I submit to you, unparalleled."

A few nervous coughs as the audience shifted in their chairs and several of the men endeavored not to lean noticeably forward, monocles raised in anticipation.

De Maupassant turned expectantly to the back of the ballroom and began again: "Dear Ladies and Gentlemen, I present to you, Mademoiselle Devon Caravelle."

As though perfectly choreographed, a figure emerged into the light from under one of the alcoves. As lorgnettes and monocles were raised to catch a glimpse of Le Comte's latest paramour, she glided toward the pianoforte silently, a column in a swathe of silver tissue. Her slender neck was set off by a square bodice unadorned except for a single choker of emeralds, a deliberate sign to all society of her protector's possessiveness. Walking gracefully, she held her head high.

Le Comte watched as she reached the small podium which had been positioned in the center of the ballroom. For a moment, she stood facing her audience, her white expanse of shoulders posed against the rich brown of the Broadwood, her expression giving no ground. Her luminous gray eyes regarded her audience almost brazenly, radiating an intelligence and bravado that were shocking in the rarefied elegance of the room.

He bowed slightly as Devon sat before the pianoforte, her dark red hair a halo of fire against the purity of her profile. A few men in the front rows shifted in their evening finery, Le Comte noticed with satisfaction, hardly immune to the strikingly sensuous figure Devon Caravelle presented. She paused, hands held quietly in her lap, her slender legs still. Le Comte took his seat, pleased beyond measure as the first chords of Beethoven's "Appassionata" were struck.

Strong, wild, and tempestuous, the notes filled every corner of the great space, feeding the growing excitement and disapproval of the assembled guests. It was astounding, scandalous, a woman playing Beethoven when everyone was expecting, at best, Bach. And the choice of music, the "Appassionata." Everyone knew it had been inspired by the composer's young mistress.

A totally inappropriate selection, yet how astonishingly and ardently she played. Her supple hands coaxed from the instrument emotions both voluptuous and controlled, her beautiful gray eyes closed to all but the music within her. Dynamic chords set the finale, dissipating to a subtle and haunting conclusion.

She finished to a stunned and thundering silence before launching into the first movement of the Waldstein, an unleashing of demoniac forces that swept the ballroom like the strongest gale. She played with an abandon immodest in its intensity and no man could tear his eyes from the young pianist, her movements a seductive invitation into a world mysteriously closed to them.

Devon played with no respite until the last echoes of the "Sonata in C Major, the Waldstein, slowed to greet another astonished silence from the audience. The lit tapers had burned down with the approach of midnight and Le Comte watched as Devon rose from the bench as if awakening from a deep reverie. The slightest pink tinged her cheekbones, and the emeralds around her throat winked in the candlelight. Her gaze swept the ballroom briefly, but she acknowledged neither her benefactor nor her audience. Cool and distant, without saying a word, she rested a pale hand on the gleaming rosewood of the pianoforte. Then a small, enigmatic smile tilted the corner of her full lips as she stepped away from the instrument and dissolved from the ballroom like a goddess slipping into the night.

But Le Comte knew better. Devon Caravelle was no goddess. She wasn't slipping away into the night's ether but toward a hard and inescapable reality in the form of the Marquess of Blackburn. Not even the threat of a torturous death for his brother had brought the proud and incorruptible Marquess to his knees, his self-control and iron will impenetrable.

The Broadwood piano gleamed under the light of the flickering candelabra. He now had the Marquess exactly where he wanted—under the spell of Devon Caravelle. Together they were an unmatchable combination, the only combination that would deliver into his hands the formula for a weapon that would make him the éminence grise of the most powerful emperor the world had seen since ancient times—Napoleon Bonaparte.

By resurrecting Napoleon from St. Helena and by unleashing the terrifying prospect of destruction upon Europe and beyond, Le Comte would reclaim a hundredfold the power, riches, and prestige lost by his family during the Revolution.

Just bring him to me, Devon, the one man who stands in my way.

His fingers gripped the fine stem of his crystal glass in obsessive anticipation.

Devon glanced over her shoulder in the shadowy hallway outside the ballroom, looking for Blackburn—before he came looking for her. The corridor stretched in front of her like a board game with its neatly formulated black and white marble tiles. She stifled the urge to run from all of this, damning the thinness of her gown, the delicacy of her slippers, the parody of a recital. Unlike the usual feelings of euphoria that floated over her after a concert, she felt ready to jump out of her skin. From the sense that the Broadwood was tuned slightly off-key to the loose piano pedal that had vexed her like a pebble in a shoe throughout the concert, she was relieved that at least one concert was over for the night.

Act Two involved a performance for the Marquess, albeit from a script that she had yet to compose. Feeling uncharacteristically agitated, her nerves on alert, she could sense somehow that he'd already arrived. She pictured him in her mind's eye, his broad-shouldered form moving through the crowd, his dark blue eyes hunting her down. Hunting her down for that elusive, potentially explosive score.

Which she didn't have.

Seduce Le Comte, Blackburn had ordered. Leaning onto the cool wall for support, she squeezed her eyes shut at the horror of the thought, her throat constricting in panic.

But then again, what would it feel like to hang? Unconsciously fingering the emeralds lacing her neck, she cursed both the Marquess and Le Comte for the tenth time that day.

From the top of the stairs, the cringe of hinges and a door opening and closing. She made herself deliberately small, observing from the corner as a tall man strode down the stairs, his face thrown into sharp relief by the glare of light from the crystal chandelier overhead. Devon would have recognized that strongly etched profile anywhere and, pulse accelerating, she grabbed the gossamer of her skirts, holding her breath, wondering if he would pass by. It was as if, ridiculous notion, they had somehow catapulted into one another's orbit, destined to collide.

The flicker of recognition was immediate, a lightning charge in the quiet corridor. Dark and supremely elegant in his evening clothes, Blackburn unerringly found his way to her side, like a bullet to a target. His hair was disordered, slanting over his ears and forehead, and his formal dress did absolutely nothing to conceal the breadth of his shoulders, the lean musculature of his body. Her nerves rattling, Devon tried to deny that in addition to being lethal, the man was stunningly, disastrously handsome.

"Mademoiselle Caravelle." The low words were a growl.

His smile wasn't a nice thing and sent fingers of awareness tripping up her spine.

"I was searching for you," she tried, her voice a low whisper. Her blood pumped fiercely at the prospect of his dragging her from a London ballroom to a prison when he discovered that she didn't have the *Eroica*. "I thought that I might find you here."

"In a shadowed hallway?" His eyes were a cold blue and locked into hers. He was standing so close that she could breathe in his warm scent. It was an outrageous thought, but if she reached out she could trace the faint lines bracketing his wide mouth, stroke the hard line of his jaw. She was mesmerized, on the brink of a strange madness.

"You do have a marked preference for the dramatic I've noticed in our brief acquaintance, Mademoiselle."

"Believe me, not by choice." She tried to keep her voice calm, and as an outlet for her nervousness, she took a look over his shoulder and down the still deserted corridor.

"I don't believe you. In any case, the truth is rarely helpful in these instances." His eyes skimmed her body. "Although I'll admit you've chosen well—an out of the way spot to hand off the score." His glance took in her scantily clad form, lingering on the emerald choker around her neck. "But it's obviously not on your person."

"A brilliant deduction," she said defensively, studying the blinding whiteness of his cravat to slow her pulse. They were entirely alone and it would take nothing to have him haul her off to some dank cell at Newgate to await the hangman. She was seconds away from full-blown panic.

Swallowing the lump in her throat, she had to remind herself to keep breathing, the air was so thin between them.

"Look, I don't have the score . . ." The words left her lips in a rush and she wished desperately that he wouldn't stand so close to her. She felt his incredible heat as he leaned in toward her, saw his nostrils flare, and heard his indrawn breath. She found herself staring into his dark eyes and, inexplicably, a sense of female boldness filled her, a form of insanity, she was convinced, almost obliterating her panic.

Blackburn crossed his arms, his face wiped clean of expression save for a cynical curve to his lips. "That's not what I came to hear. You really leave me with no choice." His voice was dark and Devon waited, shivering with dread and a strange, unwelcome desire.

"I tried . . ." she said, turning away.

One step and he had her, pulling her up rough and hard against his chest. "Trying's not good enough, Devon." His intense scrutiny was a slow burn on her skin. Shadows glanced across the bridge of his nose, his wide mouth, and the angle of his jaw.

"Give me more time, then."

"Time was never an option."

She was unyielding, stiff in his arms and he waited a moment to see what she would do. From what seemed a long distance away came the chime of crystal and laughter. Devon glanced furtively over her shoulder, the black and white tile swimming before her eyes, before she returned to Blackburn's suffocating gaze and embrace. "This isn't the right time or place for this discussion," she said pushing away from him.

He let her go, but she could see the effect of her words in the darkening of his eyes, his mood dangerous. "I'll make myself clearer, then. I'm not interested in further discussion and there's no use putting off the inevitable, Mademoiselle." His smile was deadly as he took her by the bare arm as if they were about to engage in a quadrille. His hard palm burned her bare skin and she sucked in a startled breath in response, attempting to pull away. A moment later he thrust her under the light of a wall sconce, his gaze ruthlessly searching her face.

"You may not have the *Eroica* in your possession right now, but you damn well know where it is." In an insulting glance, he took full stock of her trembling form in her wretchedly revealing dress. His eyes locked onto hers, refusing to let her look away. "You're a beautiful woman—there's not much Le Comte would deny you."

"I already told you that I don't have it." She was exposed to his merciless gaze in the unsparing glare. His long fingers didn't tighten on her arm, but they didn't have to.

"Then we're going to have to do something about that—but not here."

Devon braced herself against the wall. Protest was stillborn on her lips as Blackburn's hard palm slid from her arm to around her waist, his long fingers spanning her hipbone through the thin fabric of her dress. She tried to retreat backward, but that only brought her once again flush against the hardness of his chest.

Very deliberately, his hand slid around her neck, the contact squeezing her heart. His gaze caught hers and held. "Such a lovely, slender throat." He stroked her softly, feeling the coolness of her skin against the contrasting heat of his palm. "What a shame it would be to see you hang, Devon." The caress stopped for a moment before he resumed the mesmerizing rhythm again, and then his hot hand slid down her neck to rest on her back, an inch away from her breast.

Devon stopped breathing, a new, wilder rush of dread invading her senses. "What do you want me to do?"

The words were a strange combination of boldness and vulnerability.

He didn't answer, his hand burning through her rib cage, the pressure searing and light at the same time. Devon couldn't breathe as he studied her with the intensity of a wild animal before he lowered his head toward her, obliterating the world around them.

She closed her eyes—just as a sultry voice floated toward them.

"There you are, darling," gushed Susannah Treadwell emerging in a fragrant cloud of burgundy damask and heavy musk.

Devon's eyes snapped open, Blackburn's face a fraction from her own.

Over his broad shoulder, she watched as Susannah took the last steps of the stairs with sinuous grace before tucking an errant black curl into her elaborate chignon. Her eyes narrowed with disapproval as she absorbed the intimate scene.

Recovering herself immediately, she cooed, "So sorry we missed your little concert, Mademoiselle Caravelle. Time just seemed to slip away for the Marquess and me as we managed to find vastly more amusing entertainment elsewhere. Didn't we, darling?" she asked, draping herself around Blackburn before confidently placing a possessive hand on his arm.

In what seemed like slowly infinite degrees, Blackburn relinquished his hold on Devon, transforming it into a light caress. Which wasn't lost on Susannah.

He flashed her a tight smile. "I'm surprised you haven't made your way to the ballroom, Lady Treadwell. You wouldn't wish to miss the evening's many diversions."

Devon's stomach pitched at her narrow escape. And yet looking at the Marquess and Lady Treadwell together, her fear coalesced into a flare of outrage.

England and Europe could disappear in an apocalyptic conflagration, her father's work could be exploited for malevolent purposes, and she could hang—all the while Blackburn disported himself in bed with one of London's most amoral and avaricious women.

He seemed quite comfortable with Lady Treadwell who had nestled herself beneath his shoulder and he had the arrogance to look completely unaffected by her coyly delivered revelation about their earlier encounter.

For a moment she thought she couldn't move. Her body was stiff, her thinking scrambled. *Blackburn's hands on her body, and around her neck.* Her defenses were wearing thin.

She turned to Lady Treadwell, but the words were meant for Blackburn. "I believe we've concluded our discussion." Her voice echoed along the corridor.

"Of course, you're *finished*," agreed Lady Treadwell in dulcet tones.

Another heavy silence before Blackburn stepped back, the shadows in the hallway hardening the lines of his face.

"*Discussion* is not on the agenda, Mademoiselle. It never was."

They waged a silent battle, a contest of wills. But he made no move toward her.

"My apologies for intruding on your interlude." Devon deliberately addressed Lady Treadwell. She refused to meet those dangerous eyes, her arm still tingling from his large hand at her throat, her body resonating shamelessly from just being near him.

Squaring her shoulders and lifting her chin, she simply turned and walked away, Blackburn's gaze scorching her bare back.

Opportunities for escape were narrowing, the noose slowly tightening around her neck. Her tightrope walk had just become more dizzying.

When Blackburn moved in for the kill—and it would be tonight—she had a long way to fall.

The ballroom was ablaze with candles and loud whispers.

"Good riddance! I think that instrument is one of those monstrosities that Broadwood had designed expressly for Beethoven, for extra volume, in the hope that the deaf musician might be able to hear it better," sniffed Lady Hester. "Furthermore, women's finer sensibilities do not equip them for such indecorous public displays," she added, eagle-eyed, as the Broadwood pianoforte was moved into storage by several of Le Comte's blue liveried servants.

"Never knew a woman to be either particularly sensitive or sensible," groused Lord Treadwell, raising his quizzing glass to better see his much younger wife, Susannah, surrounded by a clutch of admirers. She hung possessively from the Marquess of Blackburn's arm who, it soon became patently clear, was having no small difficulty keeping his intense gaze from Le Comte and his mistress.

"I trust there won't be a scene." Lady Hester raised her

own lorgnette to take in the view. "The whole situation is unsavory to begin with. Let us not have to witness a contretemps over some ridiculous foreign creature." She surveyed
the Marquess critically. "I simply do not see what either Le
Comte or the Marquess might find attractive about this
Mademoiselle Caravelle.

You would if you were a man, thought Lord Treadwell,
leaning heavily on his cane. Devon Caravelle had every gentleman in London under the age of eighty smoldering, while
rendering every other woman in the ton all but invisible.

"I do believe the Marquess is hoping to see if her dance card
is filled," Lady Hester huffed in disapproval. "The rogue—as
though half of London's eligible and ineligible women were
not enough."

Lord Treadwell did not seem to take offense that his wife
was included in the latter group.

The violin ensemble, pressed into service once again, began
with a lively gavotte just as the Marquess disengaged himself
from Susannah.

"The effrontery," Lady Hester said to no one in particular.
"This will certainly not endear Blackburn to our host."

"I don't think he's worried on that score," added Treadwell, watching, along with at least half of the other guests, as
the Marquess of Blackburn offered Devon Caravelle his arm
to lead her onto the ballroom floor.

Across the room his wife's face darkened like a thunder-
cloud, a beautiful woman supremely unaccustomed to such a
blatant show of male indifference. Tossing back her champagne and with a swing of her hips that had seduced scores
of men, Susannah sauntered toward Le Comte who stood
momentarily alone, an island in a sea of tulle and silk.

The Frenchman's pale eyes narrowed at her approach and
he bowed cursorily over her hand before Susannah flicked
open her fan and plunged in without preamble.

"What are your plans for the Marquess and that French

tart, Monsieur, if I may ask?" Her usually sultry tone was strained despite the coquettish tilt of her head.

"As a matter of fact, you may not ask, Susannah." Le Comte clasped his hands behind his back as his eyes followed the couple in question on the dance floor. "And please don't tell me that you're actually jealous. You're far too old and experienced for that sort of thing."

Susannah's eyes flashed fire at the multiple affront so casually delivered. Her smile tightened as she saw old Treadwell look their way over the heads of swirling couples entranced by the strains of Scarlatti. Useless codger. She wondered, uncharitably, why she couldn't have Blackburn sharing her bed permanently rather than a man three times her age.

"Quite right, Henri, I have become older and more experienced under your tutelage," she admitted, closing her fan with a decisive snap. "I also learned from your example never to forget an insult, although for just this moment I shall try."

Infuriatingly, the Frenchman kept his eyes glued on the dance floor.

Throwing back the last drop of champagne, Susannah suddenly found it bitter. She followed Le Comte's gaze and watched Blackburn and Devon trade partners twice before the two of them were brought together again by the music. She was unwilling to account for the instant and insistent desire for the Marquess, the one man she was learning she couldn't live without. There was absolutely no way she would allow Devon Caravelle to become a problem and, quite definitely, that little scene she'd tripped upon in the hallway still galled.

"I can imagine why our Marquess would be of use to you, Le Comte, but that French slattern? Why are you so intent on bringing these two together?"

Still surveying the ballroom floor, Le Comte's thin mouth tightened at her venomous tone. "It's not for you to know, Susannah, alas." His tone was dismissive.

"Condescension has always been your strong suit, although increasingly, I find that you don't always apply it wisely, Monsieur."

Reluctantly, Le Comte turned to her with an assessing glance. "I wouldn't become overly involved, Susannah."

"You mean with your plans or with the Marquess?"

"Either—because if you do, you will be interfering in something of the utmost importance to me. And that wouldn't be prudent, would it now?"

Not easily dissuaded, Susannah raised her now empty glass to her lips, showing sharp, white teeth. "It all depends on your definition of prudent. What I do know is this—that you and the Marquess are after the same thing, and I'm not talking about that shriveled pianist. She's simply a convenient pawn." She tilted her glass in imitation of a toast, suddenly confident. "This situation has everything to do with that episode concerning Blackburn's brother which didn't turn out well for either of you, as I recall."

Le Comte's response was sharp. "I wouldn't believe every bit of information you pick up on your *travels*."

"Indeed, pillow talk is a wonderful thing. That's something else you taught me, Le Comte, remember?"

Only Susannah knew that the almost imperceptible tic below the Frenchman's left eye signaled his intense displeasure with her. "I'm warning you, Susannah. Leave off. This is a race to the finish involving only the Marquess of Blackburn and myself."

Susannah smiled slyly. "And may the best man win, naturally."

"I *shall* prevail." Le Comte dismissed her with a wave of his gloved hand and a curt nod. "Very soon you will see your Marquess following my every command slavishly."

Susannah raised her perfectly plucked brows in astonishment. "Come now, I find that difficult to believe. Blackburn is his own man if nothing else."

"That's a luxury he will soon discover that he can ill afford." He fixed the lithe figure of Devon Caravelle in his crosshairs. "I'll give the Marquess three days. After which, if he and I can't come to an understanding, he will find himself reprising that unfortunate business with his brother. Except this time, it will be our lovely pianist who will serve as the sacrificial lamb."

Le Comte gave a small nod to a passing trio of acquaintances before adding cavalierly, "That should keep you happy, Lady Treadwell, *non?*"

"He is looking at us."

Blackburn gazed down at the woman he held in his arms, a woman who was playing a dangerously unwise game with him.

"That's the least of your problems right now, Mademoiselle." He executed a required bow before taking Devon Caravelle back into his arms. The high curve of her breasts rose out of a layer of exasperating silver ruching, her fine profile turned deliberately away from him.

"Why don't you just waltz me right out of this room and into Newgate, then?" she challenged coolly.

A short silence. "I won't ask you again for the *Eroica*, Devon."

She lifted her chin. Bravado was all she had left. "What good would I be to you imprisoned or dead? You need me, Blackburn."

His expression was grim. "I wouldn't make that mistake." He was a man who'd never needed anyone in his life.

"You *threatened* me." She returned his bow with a low dip. "My goal was simply to secure your cooperation in deciphering the score."

"Your definition of cooperation is a curious one. I didn't think opiates, violence, and a prison cell exactly constitute persuasion."

"I have no control over the behavior of Le Comte's men."

"I'm pointing out that you set the tone of our association."

"Which gives you the right to threaten me with *hanging?*" Her voice was ragged. Glancing up at him from beneath a sweep of thick eyelashes for the benefit of onlookers, she made certain that her words belied her flirtatious expression. "You are asking me to take on a deception of monstrously dangerous proportions—with no guarantees."

"I never offer guarantees when there's enough money involved to mitigate the dangers."

Devon looked as fragile as blown glass and yet he suspected he was holding finely tempered metal in his arms, a woman fully capable of bartering what was left of her integrity, of selling herself to the highest bidder. His hand tightened on her waist, reminding himself that, in the end, he was hardly any better.

"There are no guarantees for me either, Mademoiselle, not that you should give that thought any consideration," he said as his hand joined hers briefly. He felt the cold fingers through the fine silk of her gloves. "Your loyalties, if you have any, are hardly transparent, and it's probably not particularly auspicious for me to be dealing with a woman who plays the roles of mistress, pianist, and spy with such remarkable ease. You are without doubt an unusual woman."

"I won't take that as a compliment."

"None intended."

"And I'm not an agent—no matter what you've been led to believe."

Not for the first time, Blackburn resisted the inexplicable urge to pull Devon closer. Too tempting, too erotic, the connection between them a lightning rod. His hand brushed her shoulder, the silkiness a potent reminder.

"Is Le Comte still looking our way?" she interrupted his thoughts, whirling into his arms and then away again.

Blackburn glanced across the room where the Frenchman

was holding court, bowing gallantly over Susannah's small plump fingers, so different from Devon Caravelle's slim, talented hand. Blackburn noted the strange expression passing over the Frenchman's face, one that he knew far too well.

"You're better off taking your chances with me." His arm tightened momentarily around her narrow back.

"You mean risking the gallows?"

He ignored her question. "What exactly is the nature of your agreement with de Maupassant? Is it money? The promise of notoriety?"

Devon turned her head sharply to look up at him, absorbing the stark lines of his face, the wide mouth above the strong jawline. She pivoted gracefully in his arms, holding herself stiffly as though more conscious than ever of a confused upsurge of unwelcome sensations, of fear and desire. Blackburn felt her invoke her steeliest reserve.

"My relationship with Le Comte has nothing to do with us."

"He has everything to do with us," Blackburn muttered. "He's thrown us together quite deliberately. And he's prepared to give you access to the *Eroica*, despite your denials," he said just as the orchestra struck up a lively minuet.

"It's not that easy." Her mouth was set in a firm line. "I don't want or need your offer of money, or anybody else's for that matter."

"Don't take me for a fool, Mademoiselle. And I won't take you for the innocent that you pretend to be," he said in a softly uttered threat. "You know how to play Le Comte for a puppet, and you know exactly how to convince him to relinquish the score to you."

The confusion and embarrassment clouding her eyes was a fine bit of acting, he thought, looking at her drift away from him a few steps, in perfect time with the music's rhythm.

"Tell me, is Le Comte sparing with the purse strings?" he continued ruthlessly as his strong arms propelled her back toward him. "One should think those emeralds around your lovely neck would keep you satisfied. Or are you trying for diamonds?"

"Stop it," she whispered under her breath, then in the next instant lifted her gaze to him boldly as though changing her mind. "Rubies, actually," she said with a brittle voice. "I'm trying for rubies, if you must know."

He didn't like the answer or her bravado. "Then perhaps we should turn up the heat."

She gave him a mockingly sweet smile, for his benefit or for their audience, he wasn't sure. "And how do you propose we force Le Comte's hand?" she asked.

"With the utmost discretion, of course," he said, fooling neither her nor himself. "As strategies go, you of all people must know how potent the combination of seduction, jealousy, and deception can be, Mademoiselle," he explained, his voice rough velvet as he led her from the center of the ballroom to the protective shadows of a grouping of leafy plants.

She was a tall woman but he still towered over her, backing her into a corner. In the wavering candlelight, he thought he glimpsed uncertainty and fear in her eyes as she refused to lower her gaze, staring steadily, courageously into his face. Vulnerability was difficult to feign and for a moment, Blackburn questioned his own powers of observation. He watched the tip of her tongue slide from her lips, the gesture deliberate, which he didn't know. All he knew was how his body reacted with a blast of heat.

As though to make it easier for her, his shadowed face moved fractionally closer as he slid his fingers deep into the mass of her hair to tilt her face upward. It was just one way to fight the battle, he persuaded himself, before taking her face in both palms. Her mouth trembled beneath his, moist, pliant, and intensely female.

The tension eased out of her by slow degrees as his lips brushed lightly against hers. Instead of drawing away, Devon drew unconsciously closer, her lashes lowered, closing her eyes. He teasingly nipped her lower lip, his tongue licking inside. She surrendered her mouth, opening to the voracity of his deepening kiss while the strains of violins and the protective covering of fronds receded in the distance.

More insistent and demanding, the pressure of Blackburn's lips increased in a velvety heated stroking as his tongue suggestively explored, caressing her sweetness, tasting her mouth with a lazy greed. Slow and inexorably consuming, his mouth devoured hers until she gasped for breath. He heard her groan as she pressed her breasts against him, oblivious to the sharp edges of the pilaster biting into her back, sighing against the succulence of their hot, ravenous play.

"We should have done this from the very first," Blackburn whispered roughly, and plunged again for her pliant tongue as his hands stroked their way down her back and to the sides of her breasts.

Against his mouth, she whispered, "This makes no sense . . ." But she wound her arms around his neck, shuddering at the feel of his palms molding her breasts. She sank into his kisses, long, leisurely, wet incursions that left her so weak he had to hold her up in his arms.

As if he had all the time in the world, and as if a good number of Le Comte's guests had not spied their impromptu rendezvous, Blackburn traced a voluptuous trail along her parted lips, her smooth cheek, the curl of an ear, the highly sensitive, he discovered, curve of her neck. He moved his mouth to the softness of her shoulder and felt Devon shiver at the touch of his mouth, his teeth, the soothing stroke of his tongue.

No longer distant nor in complete control of the encounter, Blackburn felt himself become harder, tauter, his body contemptuously mocking his attempt at detachment. Her skin was like rich cream beneath his lips, her body sinuously lush as it melted into his. She drew a shuddering breath and, against his will, his hard fingers slid from her breasts to the back of her head where they tangled in her thick hair. His mouth, a hot brand, closed over hers once again.

His eyes closed in self-defense and he immediately saw her naked beneath him, warm and soft and ready. He groaned against the tidal wave threatening to overtake them both. Her open and ardent sensuality startled him like nothing had in a very long time, and he had drunk from the very depths of decadence, manipulating, controlling the most sophisticated of carnal games.

He forced his eyes open, pulling back and releasing her by slow degrees with small kisses, erotically tugging at her lips, willing himself to ignore the clamoring of his heated blood, willing his erection to subside. She was just another of de Maupassant's women. His pulse slowed, he tensed and ice water began to replace the blood in his veins.

The objective was to have her secure the *Eroica*, at whatever cost.

Blackburn looked at the woman in his arms, his body responding all out of proportion to those full lips, ripe and parted in longing, at the eyes widening in alarm as she intuitively realized his intent. She made a small sound at the back of her throat.

This was a woman who could destroy a man.

He felt the iron rod of his erection mocking him.

He would give her one more night with her lover.

Blackburn's hands tightened on her waist, struck from nowhere by the thought that he would not be able to pry his hands from her body. He couldn't let himself imagine her lying naked beneath him, open to the incredible pleasure he'd give them both.

Anger washed over him, fresh and raw. "Go to him, Devon," he growled softly.

Devon spared him a frantic look, allowing him to remove her clutching hands from his shoulders. He firmed his resolve, blocking out any feelings bleeding around the edges. With this woman, he needed every advantage he could get.

"I'll give you one more night." His tone was simultaneously ferocious and cold and, sensing her shock, he wanted to make sure there were no more misunderstandings.

Her hands fisted by her sides, her body taut in rebellion. "This is absolutely barbaric," she whispered, searching his face for explanation.

"Dispense with your pretense of bourgeois morality, Devon." A slow burn ignited in his stomach. "You clearly have no problem sharing your favors with me, so what's your problem with de Maupassant? The fate of Europe and England hangs in the balance while you're busy playing ingénue."

"I am fully aware of the implications," she said, her voice quavering slightly. "It's not that simple . . . you don't understand." She drew a breath, diverting his attention to the smoothness of her shoulders and to the perfection of her breasts rising like offerings from the shimmering fabric of her dress.

The need for her was strong. His erection strained against his breeches and he swallowed, giving himself a hard mental shake. "Tonight, Devon."

She licked her lips, her eyes wide and vulnerable, testing his resolve. Then she wrapped her arms around herself.

Before he could respond, he heard the voice, as he expected he would, the sibilant tones of Le Comte de Maupassant.

"My, my—what an intimate scene." Aware of the frozen tableau of people behind him, Le Comte impaled Blackburn and Devon with the aristocratic hauteur of eight generations. His look was pure triumph—and something else.

Blackburn knew that he'd just raised the stakes in the contest that Le Comte had started years ago. Well, so be it. He'd just thrown Devon Caravelle to the wolves, the most vicious of the lot.

And he couldn't afford to care.

Susannah seethed. That French bitch had simply brazened it out after launching herself at the Marquess of Blackburn.

She'd probably enjoyed the stares of Le Comte's guests who were this very instant digesting the incident with their usual salacious appetites.

Susannah surveyed the banquet hall glittering with crystal and silver, the air redolent of rich delicacies. No sign of Blackburn, Le Comte, or that little trollop. Her sixth sense told her that Devon Caravelle seemed to have gotten under the Marquess's skin. And Susannah didn't like it. The Marquess was hers, she decided with haughty fiat, secure in her beauty and seductive prowess. She felt the warmth of the room close around her and her bones melted, her breasts straining simply at the thought of Blackburn. Her unparalleled lover, and she had sampled many.

Cooling herself with her lacquered fan, Susannah thought about their interlude just a few hours before. What had first started as just another bout of intrigue, for a handsome pay packet of course, had developed into a gnawing need, a fire in her womb. How could the Marquess remain impervious to her charms and leave her stranded in the middle of a soiree to consort with that Frenchwoman, and so publicly?

She pursed her lips. The situation was positively humiliating. And frankly untenable. It was a wonder de Maupassant didn't call Blackburn out, the ton would probably say tomorrow afternoon as they gathered at their clubs. Probably had less to do with the fact that it was bad form to defend the honor of one's mistress and more to do with the fact that the Marquess could drill a sovereign at twenty paces. And as rumor had it, the two men already shared a bad history.

What Susannah desperately needed was another drink. Her mouth was parched from all the drama, she thought sourly. Just in time, she spied one of Le Comte's factotums, standing alone staring morosely into space, oblivious to the dull roar of chatter around him.

She strolled over to the tall, thin man who reminded her of a scarecrow or, on better days, a particular species of undertaker. Fortunately, his demeanor didn't mean that he was immune to her charms.

"Bertrand, *mon amour*, you look entirely too preoccupied," she trilled at his side, one hand splayed over her capacious bosom. "You look in need of fortification, as a matter of fact. Le Comte has a way of enervating one, would you not agree?"

Deep in thought, his brow furrowed, he blinked twice before finally recognizing her. He gave her a belated bow. "Lady Treadwell. What a pleasure. But of course, refreshment, immediately."

Moments later Bertrand Lacan was staring moodily at her décolletage in between sips of champagne and deepening sighs. Guests were beginning to drift from the room like colorful autumn leaves and Susannah shrewdly used the opportunity to create a feeling of burgeoning intimacy. It was almost one in the morning, but a man could still dream that the night was young, she thought strategically, trailing her fingers over the deep valley of her bodice for added impact.

"So tell me, Bertrand, you who know *everything*," she encouraged with a little pout. "Do explain for me the main performance of the evening: That Frenchwoman throwing herself at the Marquess of Blackburn."

Lacan raised his watery blue eyes to hers and in their depths was a flicker of anger. "It is an ugly situation, Madame." His mouth snapped shut as though unwilling to say more.

"Precisely how *nasty*, Bertrand?" cajoled Susannah, linking her arm with his encouragingly.

Lacan was reluctant to be swayed, holding himself stiffly away from temptation. "I do know some details," he supplied, trailing off and nervously catching the eyes of several guests making their way from the banquet hall to the ballroom.

Susannah awarded him with a brilliant smile designed to recapture his attention. "I'm sure you do, Bertrand. You are so close to Le Comte, after all. But *what of* his entanglement with that Frenchwoman?" Susannah could be like a pampered terrier with a bone.

The late hour and more than a few drinks contributed to Lacan's lowered defenses. He straightened contemptuously, his face mottling with resentment. "Bah," he spat dramatically. "Frenchwoman! Devon Caravelle is a traitor to France, like her father and mother before her, fomenters of the Revolution and the overthrow of the king."

"A rather nasty piece of work by the sound of it."

"More than you could ever imagine, Madame!"

"My imagination is quite fertile, Monsieur; not to worry."

Susannah had clearly hit a nerve. Requiring less prompting now, Bertrand Lacan continued on his rant. "And yet, Le Comte is willing to reward her for her disloyalty."

" 'Reward her for her disloyalty'—I don't quite understand."

"Devon Caravelle has many talents that Le Comte is willing to put to use," Lacan pronounced, his disaffection boiling over. He gesticulated for emphasis. "Not for the *gloire* of France, *malheureusement*, but in the service of that tyrant, Bonaparte."

Susannah tilted her head closer, prepared to be the beneficiary of Bertrand Lacan's simmering discontent. "But you were more than willing to set her up with the Marquess of Blackburn the other evening, Bertrand," she reminded. He was the one who had given her the opiates and the directive to lace Blackburn's drink.

"I had no choice," he said, with a shake of his head.

Susannah nodded understandingly, patting his arm. "But what service could the Marquess and the Frenchwoman together possibly supply?" she pushed gently, keeping her voice low.

Only a few guests remained, despite the fact that the banquet table still groaned under the weight of artfully arranged delicacies that footmen continued to replenish. Le Comte had reveled in the lavishness of the display, no doubt, thought Susannah.

She turned her attention back to Lacan, her eyes narrowing seductively at her quarry. Suddenly suspicious at being the focus of Susannah's undivided attention, Lacan momentarily blocked out both her obvious bounty and his acute displeasure with Le Comte. "I can't possibly reveal that," he said. Relinquishing his glass on a table behind him, his hands twitched nervously at his side.

"And why not?" Susannah asked prettily, trying to keep the sharpness from her gaze, aware of the fact that the room was emptying quickly, with couples sailing from the hall to find their generous host. "You are loyal to Le Comte, no matter what. And I am loyal to Le Comte, no matter what. There's absolutely no problem with your unburdening yourself to me, Bertrand." She gave a throaty chuckle. "We are, after all, comrades-in-arms, are we not?"

Lacan ran a hand through his rapidly retreating hairline before sighing. "I don't understand why Le Comte would do anything to support that *bâtard*, that *tyran*."

"Indeed," concurred Susannah. "Le Comte comes from one of the oldest families in France. It makes no sense that he would throw in his lot with Napoleon, defeated and exiled on St. Helena, a man with nothing left . . ."

"We can only hope that he has nothing left," Lacan mumbled, crossing his arms defensively. "Unless, that is, Le Comte *gives* him the power that he needs, that the tyrant craves!"

"Truly all this intrigue—it's quite exciting." Susannah's cheeks flushed pink and she edged in closer. "What could the source of that power be, do you suppose?"

Finding his anger dissipating in a miasma of musk, Lacan's shoulders descended two inches as he breathed in her intoxicating scent like a drowning man. Susannah raised her heavy lashes and looked deeply into his watery eyes. "You always know *everything*, Bertrand." She pretended to adjust the neckline of her dress, pushing it a fraction lower. Political intrigue forgotten, Lacan was mesmerized.

"I really shouldn't, Madame."

"Whyever not, Bertrand?" Susannah was at her coaxing best, a skill honed by years of whispered conversations in darkened boudoirs. "Our discussion will go no further. And besides, what harm could there possibly be? For some time now Le Comte and I have shared just about everything, as you well know."

Her sultry murmur offered him all manner of possibilities. At that moment, with his nose a whisper away from her cleavage, he could withhold nothing. The dam burst forth. "It's all about the cipher, in the *Eroica*," he muttered, as Susannah placed a delicate hand on his chest, playing with his cravat as reward.

"The *Eroica*?"

"Beethoven's symphony, the original manuscript."

"But I don't understand, Bertrand," she mewed, her fingers making dizzying patterns that burned through the fabric of his shirt. "How does that involve the Marquess and the Frenchwoman?"

"Together, they're the only ones who know how to decipher it." Bertrand didn't dare move for fear of losing his superb view of Susannah's trembling breasts.

"And why is that of such importance to Le Comte?" she whispered with an intimacy that held Lacan in thrall.

He hesitated for just a moment. Reading the signs of capitulation like the seasoned warrior she was, Susannah closed the gap between them, her breasts brushing Bertrand's shirt front, achingly close, but not close enough. His hiss of indrawn breath was her reward.

"There is great suspicion that it is a new type of explosive." The words tumbled from his mouth as he closed his eyes at the sensation of pure Susannah.

"You mean like gunpowder?" Her tone was still entirely provocative.

"Only more powerful—a thousand times more powerful."

"I see." She slid a hand down between Bertrand's shirt front, a teasing barrier. "But what makes Le Comte so sure that once the Marquess and the Frenchwoman have decoded the cipher, they won't run to Wellington with what they've discovered—before he has a chance of getting it to Napoleon's supporters?"

Susannah could see Bertrand's prominent Adam's apple bob up and down as he swallowed hard. "He has a letter which contains the final piece of the puzzle. Whatever they discover is only useful if all the pieces link together."

"You are *so* clever," purred Susannah, allowing herself to sink into his chest. She could feel the shallow breathing inspired by pure lust. "But there's just one last question bothering me . . ."

Aware that they had been entirely alone for the past five minutes, save for several footmen, Susannah took Lacan's silence for complete surrender. "Why the urgency? Why does Le Comte need this resolved in such a short time?" As added incentive, she stroked his chest sinuously, promising better things to come.

Susannah felt the shudder travel from the cavernous torso to the soles of his boots. As though he had no control over his movements, Lacan lowered his head to hers. "Napoleon's escape from St. Helena depends on it."

At that moment, and with those words, Susannah Treadwell knew that she was the most seductive, beautiful woman in Britain and on the continent combined.

She had the *power* and she would guarantee that it was only a matter of time before the Marquess of Blackburn and Le Comte knew it, too.

"My, my—that is urgent," she breathed into his chest before staring up into the rheumy eyes. "I'm sure we'll be able to help each other in the near future, Bertrand."

She smiled up at him brightly. "In the interim, will you keep your sights on the Frenchwoman for me, *mon amour*? I don't want her getting too close to the Marquess and, as it turns out, neither do you."

Chapter 5

Breath caught in her throat, Devon woke with a start, grasping for her small pistol secreted beneath the pillow. It was gone. Panicked, she shot up and, heart frozen, stared at the man sitting calmly at the side of her bed.

Blackburn, still marvelously turned out in evening attire, was leisurely examining her small silver-mounted revolver. A dark specter in the moonlight, he held the pistol in his large hands, removing the bullets from their chamber with seasoned expertise.

"A lovely piece." He tossed the pistol onto the rumpled bed. "A gift from de Maupassant?"

She was scared and she had every right to be. His height, the breadth of his shoulders—he took over the entire room, a menacing threat that had formed out of the shadows. Refusing to cower, she let the bedclothes fall from her shoulders, quickly reappraising the situation.

"I insist you leave," she challenged with an arrogance that, if he had been a man, would have given Blackburn pause. Vulnerability was not her strong suit despite threats of a hangman's noose. Her expression was at odds with the luxurious spill of her hair and the revealing lace of her nightdress.

"That's unfortunate." He glanced at the rumpled covers and the dent in her pillow. "So where's your lover? You have only a few hours left to secure the *Eroica*."

She shot him a cold look without moving from under the heavily brocaded duvet. "I asked you to leave. This is neither the time nor place . . ."

"So you keep reminding me." Blackburn made himself more comfortable on the edge of the bed. "As I recall, we have some unresolved business between us."

"As I recall, I told you that I don't have the *Eroica*. And in response you so generously gave me the evening to persuade my *lover* to relinquish the score to me, remember?" Her anger mounted, overriding her fear and the fact that only the fine silk of her night rail stood between them.

He shrugged off her comment easily, moonlight slanting across his face. "I had a feeling that you weren't taking my exhortations seriously enough, Mademoiselle."

"Your threats, you mean."

His dark glance swept the room in response. "I don't see Le Comte here."

The words were intended to pierce her veneer. He had succeeded earlier that evening, and she wondered if he was as easily aroused as she was at the thought of that explosive intimacy. That clever mouth of his, his hands molding her breasts. She flushed at the memory. Her behavior was nothing to be proud of nor could she entirely account for it, as if her entire life's experience, her faith in rationality and logic, simply melted away whenever he wanted it to.

Well, the battle of wills was just beginning. "I said I needed more time."

"I no longer believe you, if I ever did. You are the man's mistress and you have the opportunity to manipulate him sexually. And yet you are reluctant to do so. Why? My patience is wearing thin."

"You were expecting me to run from your arms to his tonight?" Devon threw back the coverlet and rose boldly from the bed to slide into her slippers. Despite her all but transparent gown, Blackburn seemed unperturbed by her near nakedness.

"I'm certainly not asking you to do anything you haven't done before," he said with infuriating nonchalance. He had absolutely no idea that she was immobilized by the hideous choice that he was forcing her to make.

Furious, she stalked past him to the foot of the bed. "And you thought that the damn scenario you created in the ballroom this evening would somehow help. Did you think that Le Comte, maddened by jealousy, would calmly hand over the score to you in exchange for my undying devotion, once I came to his bed from yours?"

Two seconds passed and his dark gaze did a slow burn down the length of her body.

"You weren't coming from my bed."

The words were said in a barely audible growl and she felt an awareness as intense as a stroke of flesh on flesh. Her knees weakened as heat pooled between her legs.

In self-defense, she reached into a wardrobe and jerked out a satin robe.

"That garment is not suitable for where we're going."

"We, Blackburn, aren't going anywhere," she said with finality, shrugging into the robe and tying the narrow sash firmly around her waist. "All you have to do is give me more time and I'll get the damn score."

"I don't see de Maupassant nestled between your sheets. So let's just say your time has run out." Blackburn lounged on the bed, watching his quarry frantically looking for ways out of her maze.

"I don't need another ultimatum." She firmed her jaw and motioned toward the door hoping to usher him from her room. "Tomorrow we'll see if that public charade you orchestrated has had the desired effect on Le Comte. Maybe he'll present us with the score on a silver platter. Though I doubt it," she ended caustically.

"For once we're in agreement." Blackburn slipped her revolver neatly into his waistband. "And that's why you're coming with me."

How could she have forgotten just how sleekly he moved, lethal and quiet, as he closed the distance between the bed and the door in the space of a held breath? She steeled herself for his touch, feeling like a ripe fruit about to burst. His scent, a faint hint of sandalwood. Then a strong hand enclosed her wrist like iron, convincingly stalling her escape.

His voice was rough, his breath soft on her ear. "I don't like it when people renege on their promises, Mademoiselle. And I don't make idle threats. You failed to produce the *Eroica* this evening—there are consequences."

A heady combination of barely restrained desire, fear and mistrust scented the air. She tried to pull away, a jolt of streaming pleasure mixed with panic rising like a tide.

"Surely you don't mean to hand me over to the authorities tonight." She stared at him, barely comprehending. "What use would I be to you then? You'd be no further ahead, no closer to getting the score."

"Didn't you think I might have my own motives for participating in this drama of yours, Devon?" Blackburn continued, his question purely rhetorical. Her name fell from his lips and lingered tantalizingly in the hostile air between them.

She held her ground. "Your motives are of no interest to me."

His smile was more taunting than comforting. "Probably your first mistake." Without releasing her wrist, he quickly searched the cavern of her wardrobe and withdrew a dark green pelisse.

"So, go ahead—throw me to the authorities." Despite the brave words, Devon now tried to shrug away from him. She watched in disbelief as he silently threw the garment over her shoulders and propelled them both toward the window. Opening the shutters and then the casements, he lifted and then deposited her effortlessly outside on the small balcony overlooking the interior courtyard twenty feet below.

The night was soft and she found herself pinned against a

frame as hard and unyielding as granite. She waited, this time hanging on desperately and with a sinking in her stomach.

She couldn't see his face but felt his mouth touch her temple, her ear. "*I am the authorities*, Devon—as you'll soon learn."

Her heart shuddered and then began a nervous staccato. *Dear God.* She pictured a dark, damp cell and worse, torture, the rack, bread and water . . . Her thoughts careened out of control. Hanging would be preferable.

"I shall scream," she warned in a small voice, trying hard to ignore the rise and fall of his warm chest against her back.

"No you won't. Somehow I don't think you'd like to attract your lover's attention at the moment."

Damn. She hated it when Blackburn referred to Le Comte as her lover. Tamping down her anger and fear, she focused on what was sure to be a hard landing on the flagstones of the courtyard below. The Frenchman's concert festivities had concluded and not a creature stirred in the almost preternatural silence of this wealthiest section of London.

Blackburn's quiet, deadly calm was more terrifying than what could possibly wait beyond the courtyard and yet she fought the disconcerting urge to turn around and cling to him. He held her patiently as though expecting a struggle and then, taking advantage of her surprising docility, levered them both over the ironwork balustrade to dangle for a dizzying second ten feet over the flagstones below.

They landed soundlessly alongside clinging ivy.

Ready to run, she kicked backward and felt her slippered foot make contact with his shin.

"Not good enough." His words caressed the nape of her neck, as sensuous as the inky air surrounding them, and she answered with a rebellious but hopelessly futile jerk in his arms. She could feel his smile in the dark.

Fury boiled to the surface. This escapade of his was going to cost. "This is positively medieval. Where are you taking me and why? Why even bother with a parody of justice?

Why not just kill me here on the spot?" No answer except for his unyielding force, dragging her toward the back garden of Le Comte's luxurious town house.

Slipping by the deserted servants' entrance lit by a single torch, they rounded a corner where the fine gravel stone gave way to a meticulously manicured lawn. In the darkness and only for a moment, Devon thought they had stumbled upon a bronzed colossus, but with a flick of its proud head at the sight of its master, the horse came to life.

Blackburn was past listening to her. Instead he heaved her up into the saddle and mounted behind her while, as though accustomed to such nightly adventures, the huge steed, rooted to the spot, waited for its master's signal. Enveloping them both in the caped greatcoat that had been secured in one of the saddle pouches, Blackburn pulled Devon firmly against him. She could feel the steady beat of his heart through the fine fabric of his evening clothes.

They rode hard, a half ton of steaming horseflesh devouring the miles as the moon-saturated night unfurled before them. Blackburn chose a bridle path through Hyde Park and then headed north to leave London behind in a thunder of hooves and flying mud. Devon had no choice but to cling to his waist, the friction of his greatcoat barely concealing the hard, moving muscles beneath. All she could do was fight her awareness of him, of his scent, the strong curve of his back shielding her from the night.

It must have been an hour before they slowed, the horse's hard breathing the only noise in the night's stillness. The animal skidded around a corner, slowing to a canter as a manor house appeared on the still-dark horizon, illuminated only by moonlight, a rustic stone pile surrounded by tall hedges and a curved driveway. Devon took a deep draught of the moist night air, calculating the hour to be three or four in the morning.

"Don't move—trust me, you have nowhere to run," Blackburn said as he reined up. The curve of his mouth indicated the futility of any escape plans she might entertain.

He would get nothing from her, Devon swore moments later, feeling vulnerable and ridiculous in her nightdress, robe, and cape in the chilled front hall of what was clearly, in centuries past, a hunting lodge. They were alone except for an ancient man who emerged from the darkness to light a fire in the cold grate of the front drawing room. In a few moments the kindling turned to flames, lighting up a simple paneled room lacking the florid carving of more sophisticated country manors. A curving staircase in the front hall and stone floors cut from local granite formed the backdrop for decidedly masculine furnishings. Only a dark red Aubusson carpet added any softness or warmth.

"Nothing as luxurious as what Le Comte has to offer, but you'll find it comfortable enough," said Blackburn, reading her thoughts. He joined her in the drawing room, incongruously formal in his white cravat, tailored cutaway jacket and breeches, his stark looks an unwelcome intrusion.

"I'm surprised you haven't lowered me into a dungeon."

"The night's not over yet."

The room was cold enough and Devon hunched further into her pelisse.

"Would you like something to eat or drink?" Blackburn asked neutrally, unconscionably vital and as if he'd not just spent the last twenty-four hours without sleep. "And you may as well rest."

Before what? An interrogation or worse?

Devon turned to sit on the proffered divan, determined not to let the man detect her fear which sat like a heavy stone in her chest. "I don't know where all this is going," she said, trying to keep the tremor from her voice. "Neither of us has the score, so what do you hope to accomplish here? Or is this simply your idea of revenge, a salve for your wounded male pride at having been abducted by Le Comte's men and dragged into this affair?"

He dropped into a wingback chair opposite her, his expression inscrutable. "When you come to know me better you'll realize that I seldom allow pride to get in the way of anything I do."

"I don't intend to get to know you better," she answered huffily. "I shall return this instant to Le Comte and insist that we proceed without you."

It was a feeble bluff. The best she could do at the moment up against cold-blooded reality.

"Somehow I doubt it," he said, reading her mind again. He stretched out his long legs and sank further into the chair. "Instead, I think de Maupassant will come for you. As a matter of fact, I'm counting on it."

She sucked in a startled breath. His dark blue eyes met her own. "You believe Le Comte will want me back badly enough to give you the score? That's ridiculous!"

He leaned forward in the chair, his gaze predatory. "You underestimate your value to him, Devon. Of course mistresses are plentiful, that's not what I'm referring to."

"What are you referring to?"

"Access to what you know—he wants what's in your head."

Devon catapulted to her feet, nearly stumbling over her pelisse. She was overtired and on the brink of overplaying her hand, ready to shout at him that she was *not* the Frenchman's paramour.

She stopped just in time when she noticed how he searched her face, his dark eyes almost black in the firelight. He was thinking, calculating, manipulating—and it infuriated her.

"I would rather hang."

The look he shot her was skeptical. "That can be arranged, all too easily. So sit down, I'm not finished."

Her eyes blazed fury.

"It's your knowledge that de Maupassant is interested in and your relationship with your late father."

Of course, her father. The traitor. The man whose work and reputation she was trying to vindicate. If it killed her.

She made a small sound of contempt, perching herself at the edge of the divan. "Do you intend to hold me hostage then?" She made herself fold her hands calmly on her lap while drawing from her rapidly dwindling resources.

Blackburn gave her a considering look. "It's your doing. You failed to secure the score from the Frenchman as required. This is simply another way of forcing de Maupassant's hand—he needs the two of us. And I need the *Eroica—now*."

Bloody hell, the man was high-handed. Devon's resolve hardened like stone against his arrogant stance. "And I'm simply to acquiesce to either your or Le Comte's request, just like that?" She snapped her fingers in his face. "And as I said to you before, don't bother offering me money."

Devon braced herself as Blackburn rose from the chair and walked to the fireplace. He leaned against the mantel and folded his arms over his chest. "What would you have me believe, Devon? That you failed in your bid to *charm* the *Eroica* from the Frenchman's grasp? I'm beginning to think that you're playing me false. As a matter of fact, I wonder whether you're as politically neutral as you pretend to be. It wouldn't surprise me at all if your sympathies lay with Bonaparte, given your familial history."

The implication of his words sank into her bones. In order to manipulate, to subdue—Blackburn had to trust her. "My only interest is in my music," she equivocated, raising her chin aggressively. "De Maupassant was the only avenue open to me, the only opportunity to continue my study. In exchange, Le Comte forced me into securing your cooperation."

Gaze pinning her, he stalked forward. She felt his hard fingers tip up her chin. "You're lying," he said simply.

Devon held herself perfectly still, afraid she'd fall apart if she moved a single muscle, her silence the only answer. She hated him. She hated the situation they found themselves in. And she hated the fine trembling suffusing her body as he wrapped one large hand around the back of her neck.

"You're very beautiful." He stared at her hard and she couldn't look away.

Her breath came faster.

He tilted her head, exposing the vulnerable column of her neck, holding her immobile between his warm hands. Very quietly, he murmured, "I know what you want, Devon, and I can give it to you."

The air left her lungs in an instant and she felt herself retreating into herself, away from that touch that managed to obliterate all thought. She wanted to close her eyes, shutting him out, but she couldn't. He shook his head and the world came to a standstill.

"I can make this easy for you. If you let me."

"That's impossible. You don't know." Her voice broke. "You can't know."

His gaze hooded, he watched the emotional struggle reflected in her eyes. As if he had all the time in the world to bend her to his will. It was worse than any threat, hearing that velvet voice saying the words she so desperately needed to hear.

"It's your father, Devon. You want to discover who murdered him and why, don't you?"

Chapter 6

With her body inches from his own, Blackburn could feel waves of shock pulse through Devon. It would be so easy to take advantage of her vulnerability, but he let his arms drop to his sides.

She sat stiffly with straight back, her hands clenching into fists. "I shouldn't be at all surprised that you would be involved in such a dirty business as murder."

Blackburn shoved his hands in his pockets, smiling congenially. "I thought you might say that."

She wrapped herself more securely in her pelisse, closing the opening at the slim column of her neck protectively. "What do you know about my father's death?"

"We'll get to that in a moment."

"Don't play with me, Blackburn."

"I'm not playing at anything, Mademoiselle. You just don't like it when you're not in control, do you?"

He could tell that she was beginning to detest it when he called her *Mademoiselle*—with all its unsavory implications.

"Isn't it the other way around," she taunted recklessly. "The idea of a woman in control is clearly not to your liking, is it?"

"I believe that's a moot question given the present circumstances," he pointed out in measured tones, still looming over her, ready to intimidate if necessary. The crackling of the burning logs did nothing to edge out the tangible and mounting tension between them, a volatile mixture of high-stakes emotion and guardedness. Blackburn watched Devon carefully as if everything about this woman affected him immoderately, the feel of her in his arms, the pliancy of her soft mouth and lush body.

No, it did not bode well, his intensifying fixation with de Maupassant's young mistress. He was breathing hard at just the thought of having her all to himself, here deep in the country. Where he could do anything he wanted with her.

He always knew that he would bed her. But he couldn't let this get out of hand.

Unless he used it to his advantage.

How very tidy, the concept of self-indulgence not entirely foreign to his nature.

She was waiting. Her hair was in disarray, pins lost somewhere between London and Armathwaite; her body, that slender yet voluptuous form, still enveloped in her voluminous pelisse. His response was immediate and undeniable, an erection that could kill and that managed to mock his well-ordered strategy.

"A moot point?" she asked with false bravado, her own dread fascination with their currently intimate situation clear in the unsteadiness of her voice. Blackburn sensed that she was unaccustomed to operating on instinct, that she hated the conflicting emotions he aroused in her.

He sauntered toward her slowly, his smile wolfish, his voice low as he leaned over her, his lips a fraction from hers. "All those revolutionary values, where are they now, Devon? You're not out to save the world, to defuse what could be the worst weapon the world has ever seen. You're just worried about your own beautiful hide." She shrank into the settee, his dark blue eyes imprisoning her as powerfully as his arms ever could. "Find out who murdered your father, why don't you, and you may have a chance of clearing your name. While the rest of the world goes to hell, for all you care."

Devon glared at him. "As though your motives are so pure, sir."

"You never thought to ask, did you?"

She ignored his question with one of her own. "And why would I?"

Blackburn smiled cynically. "What I can't quite understand is your seeming reluctance to crawl into bed with Le Comte and do what's necessary. Your own neck is at stake, Mademoiselle, lest you forget."

A fire ignited in her eyes. In her anger she leaned forward and clutched the front of his shirt. "I decide when and with whom I *crawl* into bed, Blackburn. Don't ever forget that!"

He covered her hand with his own, holding it tightly against him. "I love these moral dilemmas, Devon, I truly do. So the question must be asked—what would you do to gain the information you want concerning your father's murder?"

His patience was at an end. He entangled his free hand in her hair, fire that rivaled the flames crackling on the hearth. The gesture was entirely his, practiced and assured, a deferral of everything but the face and body he suddenly needed to possess. He knew how to get what he wanted, how to cajole, persuade, and please a woman.

He drew Devon to her feet until he could feel every rapid breath she took against his chest. She jerked once in his arms and gasped at the same time, giving him the opportunity to delve into her open mouth, his tongue slow, latent and abandoned. He traced her upper lip leisurely, getting to know her mouth's contours and susceptibilities.

"I don't want to do this," she managed to whisper, a slender hand in the sleekness of his hair. She breathed him in as his scent detonated a chain of small explosions, right before all reason and logic fled.

Blackburn brushed her jaw lightly with the back of his hand. "Don't think so much."

And then plans momentarily forgotten, schemes abandoned, Blackburn concentrated on plundering Devon's mouth. He lingered tasting the fullness of a lower lip, tempting, teasing until her breathing quickened and he felt her small tongue dance over his, asking for more.

His hands moved slowly over her back, pushing away her cape and tugging loose the satin belt of her dressing gown. His fingers ran up the hollow of her spine, the shoulder blades drawing together and thrusting her breasts outward through the delicate Valenciennes lace of her night rail. Blackburn felt her stiffen slightly, as though she should stop the madness, a whisper of doubt quickly extinguished by his persuasive hands caressing soft skin.

He pulled her toward him to the Aubusson carpet until they were kneeling in front of the fire. Drawing down the neckline of her shift, he left a trail of soft kisses along her neck to the satiny crevice of her shoulder. Full and round, her breasts, erotically revealed to the firelight, begged for his mouth. He tested the skin, finding it as pure as taut silk to his touch, the cresting tips of large peach-tinted nipples made for his lips. He could feel her let go, her muscles beneath his hands relaxing. She murmured her pleasure, her arms languidly lacing around his neck, eyes closed in sensual intemperance.

His chest expanded on a sharp breath. Her breasts were exquisite and his hands came up roughly to cradle them. She immediately arched into him, and his control nearly snapped, his need rock hard. He felt her feverish hands at his neck, burrowing beneath the crisp cambric of his shirt as she impatiently tore at the ivory fastening to find bare skin and muscle.

Blackburn's lingering fingertips hovered at her narrow waist, coaxing material over her hips as his lips left her breasts reluctantly and traced a path along her jutting hipbones and smooth stomach with its delicately indented navel. Lost in her own tumult of feeling, Devon allowed him to pull her inexorably to the floor until she was splayed out in front of him. The burnished triangle of curls awaited his exploration, and spreading his hand flat against her stomach, he spread her wide. Like dampened silk, the pale velvet of her inner thighs moved impatiently beneath his hands, urging his touch upward. A flawless judge of flesh, he was shocked at the intensity of his response to the slender body, the fragile lace next to fragrant skin an unparalleled aphrodisiac.

"Please . . ." she murmured, her face a flush of desire in the grip of his maddeningly long and slow strokes. When he slipped a hand over her silken mound and eased two fingers inside, she cried out. She was wet and so hot that her muscles clamped down on his fingers. Through the haze of sharp longing his gaze swept the naked woman lying beside him, her hair a riot of loosened curls, the twin peaks of her aroused breasts gleaming in the firelight.

He took a ragged breath. He felt her shiver and heard her groan deep in her throat as he tantalized each breast with his teeth, lips, and tongue relishing her long, shuddering breaths. She filled her hands with his hair, drawing him closer to the crested peaks and her desire. Murmuring something indecipherable, she urged his face to hers with a kiss that threatened to unman him. Blackburn's hand moved through her moist heat, the lush folds, as she writhed against him, against the experienced stroking and the mouth and tongue on her breasts. He felt the frantic movements of her hips against his persistent caresses until the heat reached its zenith.

Blackburn drew away. His erection was stiff against his groin, pulsing with blood, a hellish reminder of how much he wanted her.

It was too damn good. Dangerously good.

He felt the weight of the nude pliant woman lying in his arms. He never liked relinquishing control, and he liked it even less when it came to Devon Caravelle. She was like a thorn in his side, pleasure, pain. If he couldn't maintain command when he was with her, he would soon find himself strolling into de Maupassant's trap.

The thought robbed inches from his erection.

For one moment he allowed himself to press his face to

Devon's throat, inhaling the scent of her body, her hair, her essence. She stirred against him, deliberately arousing them both further by moving her nipples over his chest, her lips on his mouth, his chin, his shoulder.

He was sweating blood, his breaths coming in gasps. Doing his best to ignore his own hammering need, he rolled away from her.

She was just another woman, like hundreds of others playing the second oldest game on earth. He was too experienced, too jaded—a veteran, *bloody hell*—to be trumped by a willing body and a hot mouth.

He took three deep breaths until he trusted himself to touch her again.

She lay curved toward him, eyes half closed. His voice, hot as a lover's, was meant to punish. "Who's in control now, Devon?" He trailed a hard hand over the arc of her lower back.

He punctuated his question with a caress intended to scorch them both.

Chapter 7

Devon's eyelashes slowly drifted upward at his touch. She felt the languorous heat of arousal slowly seep from her body as she focused on the face a pulse beat from hers.

She felt liquid, breathless. Her body was feverish with heavy longing and she could still feel his wild wet tongue on her neck, on her breasts, his hands everywhere. Not saying a word, she leaned away from him, then stood up and silently gathered her robe and cloak to hide her nakedness. With a nonchalance she didn't remotely feel, she returned to sit by the fire, its glow undiminished.

How desperately she wanted to look away. Blackburn was playing her with consummate virtuosity, leaving her brutally disoriented, her emotions strung to a fever pitch. Feelings surged within her like a cacophony of discordant notes.

"That was a mistake," she said shakily.

"You think so?"

"We were talking about murder." A return to reality began to cool her heated skin. Never let Blackburn believe he was sailing the ship. If she was going to manipulate and manage the man, she had to do better than this.

"Now that you've adequately demonstrated your highly vaunted *control* over this situation, you should feel entirely confident about telling me what you know." She took a shallow breath. "About my father's murder."

"Nothing's ever quite that easy, Devon." He sat in a relaxed sprawl on the rug, observing her with a calculating indifference she was beginning to hate. "I'm not prepared to tell you anything until I ensure your cooperation. And that has to occur before Le Comte comes for you."

Devon jerked as if she'd been slapped. "I'm not a package of goods to be tossed about. And you may think you're good, but you're not that good, despite what you may have been led to believe by the many women of your acquaintance."

"I can't say that I've had any complaints before. But then again, you've probably had ample opportunity to compare and contrast." He rose, walked toward a low drinks table and poured two brandies into square cut-crystal glasses, handing one to her.

"Gallant of you to point that out." *The bastard.* She took a sharp draught of the liquor. It cut a fiery path down her throat. "I'm waiting with bated breath for you to explain how seduction will ensure my cooperation."

He shrugged and she remembered the feel of those muscles under the fine linen of his shirt. And again she fought the corresponding warmth between her legs. Blackburn had a purpose in seducing her, a coldness of purpose that was so important to him that he would rather not take his pleasure in order to succeed at his own game. She would be wise to remember that.

His thick black hair gleamed in the light of the fire as he sank into the high-back chair, legs outstretched, his head resting against the padded leather back.

"Let me frame the situation another way," he said. "What is it that the Frenchman can do for you that I can't?"

"He has the *Eroica*—you don't."

"But I also have something you want."

Devon's gaze lingered on the strong hands that cradled the brandy glass, hands that had brought her such pleasure moments ago. "Information to clear my late father's name and my own, you mean? So far you haven't offered me anything remotely solid in that regard."

"That's because I'm not a gambling man. As I said earlier, I don't care for those who renege on their commitments. You failed to produce the *Eroica* so I decided you needed extra inducements."

"Inducements? You mean the threat of hanging? Or do you mean a quick tussle on a rug in front of a fire?"

Devon watched Blackburn's eyes hood over. There was hunger in those eyes. "You want more information?"

"I do." The words came out with more desperation than she wished.

"And in exchange I get your cooperation?"

"It depends on what you have to tell me."

The fire popped, sending cinders into the air, the acrid smell of burnt wood. Blackburn turned to the flames before saying tersely, "Very well, let's start with Beethoven, a friend of your father's."

Devon bit back the urge to interrupt, her stomach tightening for what was to come, what she didn't want to hear.

Blackburn's tone was carefully neutral. "He composed the *Eroica* in 1803, recalling a Bonaparte as first consul, as I'm sure you know. At the time, Beethoven had the highest esteem for him and compared him to the greatest consuls of ancient Rome. But we also have it on good authority that when Napoleon had declared himself emperor, Beethoven broke into a rage, discovering that his hero had turned tyrant."

Memories flooded over her. "My father was disillusioned to see the successes of the Revolution turn to dust."

"It was more than disillusionment." Blackburn paused and looked away from the fire as though on the precipice of some revelation. He sent her a flicker of compassion that just as quickly disappeared with another fortifying draught of brandy.

"Your father was wracked with guilt," he continued, draining his glass, "because he did much more than simply support the Revolution."

A lump suddenly lodged in her throat. She nodded for Blackburn to continue.

"He wanted to ensure its success by embedding a powerful code in the score of his friend's Third Symphony. But what happens when the Revolution doesn't turn out the way you'd planned?"

Devon blinked up at him, confused. "That's where you're wrong. His intent was to *decipher* the code when he was murdered."

"Why didn't he simply destroy it?"

"I would stake my life on it—he didn't have anything to do with embedding the code originally. He knew nothing of explosives!"

Blackburn smiled humorlessly before rising to walk over to the drinks table with its decanter of brandy. Liquid sloshed into his glass. "We all want to believe the best of our family," he said.

Devon surged from her seat, her exhausted mind racing. "I won't have you patronizing me. I refuse to believe that my father had anything to do with the original code. Music and mathematics are related sciences—Beethoven was more likely to have been the one, as a composer for God's sake, to embed the original cipher."

Blackburn pushed out a disbelieving laugh, gazing at her with pity. "You don't want to see, do you, Devon? Both Beethoven and your father were looking for a guarantee to secure the gains of the Revolution."

"You're making no sense," she said, turning away from him, her eyes feeling gritty with tears.

"You don't want to see what's right in front of you," he persisted. *"The potential to change the face of warfare for centuries to come.* We're talking about a formula for the ultimate weapon. A weapon so lethal that whoever has it— whichever side has it—is destined to win."

Devon rubbed her eyes, so weary she couldn't think. Then she sat back down slowly in a show of calm. "We obviously can't agree on this point," she said steadily. "And you've also failed to convince me as to why I should excise Le Comte from this arrangement."

He paused for effect before folding his tall frame back into the wing chair. She forced herself to lean forward to meet the challenge in his gaze.

His eyes locked with hers. "Whatever your arrangement with de Maupassant, I'll multiply it ten times," he said abruptly. It was a small price to pay, and one he could easily afford. To own her—and everything she knew about the *Eroica*, beginning with where to find it. "And I'll tell you what I know about your father's murder."

The silence was deafening, even the fire a muted simmer. There was an unassailable glitter in his eyes. He wanted something desperately.

"My—how generous. But how can you be sure I'm worth it, Blackburn?" She regained a measure of control and pulled the lapels of her pelisse together despite the growing warmth from the fire.

"My instincts are never wrong."

His experience with far too many women taught him that, she thought edgily, leaning back into the divan. "And what exactly would this liaison entail?"

"You do what you have to do to get the score from de Maupassant. And then we proceed from there." She watched his strong elegant hands trace the patterns on his crystal tumbler.

"You're still being deliberately vague."

Blackburn didn't respond but he seemed to be enjoying the moment, sensing her capitulation.

"I don't see how this differs from your earlier offer at Blackfriars Bridge. What's changed?"

"You're here with me for a start."

"Not for long if I can help it."

"You can't help it," he said, ruthlessly shoving the brandy aside on an end table flanking his chair. "When do you think Le Comte will discover you missing and decide that it's worth his while to get you back? And what do you think will happen if I tell him that I've learned you're entirely useless to me and to this whole enterprise?"

A red haze clouded her vision. "You wouldn't dare."

"Wouldn't I? You know what would happen to you if Le Comte believed you weren't essential to me or this plot? If he thought you were nothing but a huge risk offering no chance of returns?"

Devon didn't have to answer. Whether it was a prison in France or the tumbrils in England, she realized that holding on to Le Comte was her only chance to bury the *Eroica* and loosen its grip on her family.

Her face felt hot and her eyes stung. "You realize how important my father is to me and you're using that as leverage. And you don't care what I have to do to get the score." Why was she even asking such a question when she knew all too well what his response would be.

"Get the *Eroica*. Bring it to me. Then I'll help you avenge your father's death. I'm very good at vengeance by the way."

His expression said it all and she turned away from him to stare into the fire, mastering a flood of emotions, contradictory and unruly.

"What if I told you I've already tried everything at my disposal to convince Le Comte to relinquish the score?"

"Then I'd say you haven't tried enough. Or perhaps you lack imagination. It certainly can't stem from a dearth of experience." She found it hard to breathe. "How much do you really want to clear your family's name, Devon? What's it worth to you?" he asked in a voice that was pure silk belying the ugliness of his words.

She said quietly, "It means everything to me."

The firelight danced around them, enclosing them in its false embrace. Devon felt exposed, more exposed than moments before when she had lain half naked in his arms half mad from pleasure.

He sat still in the chair, and only his eyes moved as he looked her over, slowly, as if he'd never seen her before and needed to commit her to memory. "You asked me a question earlier this evening." His voice was low and deep. *"What makes you think I'm worth it?* I'm beginning to wonder— perhaps you're losing your grip on de Maupassant too soon?"

"What's your point?" She wanted to fling her glass at him, but instead placed it carefully on the polished floor beside her.

He shrugged and she followed the line of unambiguous muscle, from shoulder to ridged thigh to long length of calf. "Perhaps Le Comte requires rather more innovative diversions than you are prepared to devise—or deliver." His look was speculative. "You're a beautiful woman—but then, sometimes that's not enough."

"You don't think I can hold his attention?" The words were out of her mouth before she knew it, the brandy lingering on her tongue. "You're wondering whether I'm capable of securing the *Eroica* for you. And you're also wondering whether you're wasting your time."

"Are you worth it, Devon?" His smile was as cold as it was mocking. He picked up his glass from the side table and drained the remains of his brandy in one fluid motion.

He caught her in a moment of stunning vulnerability. She forced herself to breathe normally, although the irony almost choked her. She wanted to wipe the world clean of the *Eroica.* She wanted to clear her father's name.

"You're asking me to be your lover." Devon watched for his reaction as her pulse throbbed, dull and heavy in her veins.

His blue eyes were simultaneously amused and distant. "I knew you were clever. Clearly you're accustomed to such arrangements, offering favors in exchange for something you truly desire."

"You are contemptible."

"We're playing the ingénue again. Let's try honesty for a welcome change. I'd say, judging by your response earlier this evening, you want me as much as I want you." He saluted her with his empty glass.

Devon listened to the crackle of the fire in an attempt to drown out his words. Her choice was anything but clear, her strategy lost in a murky brew of uncontrollable desire and fear.

"How do you propose we proceed?" he asked, the answer to his question suspended in the air between them.

Devon shivered, not against the damp, but something else. The web they were both spinning was dangerously intricate, an elaborate skein with the potential of entangling them both.

Her storm-gray eyes lowered, she picked up her glass from the floor and took the last dregs of the brandy, false courage, before moving from the divan toward him, until she was only an arm's length away. Resting her hands on the heavily braced sides of his chair, she leaned over the unresisting man in a rustle of rich fabric, aware of the heat from his body, his scent, clean and sharp. She took in the defined line of his jaw, the taut skin that had felt exhilarating to her touch, allowing herself to revel in those remembered sensations. Very slowly, her lips tentatively swept over an angled cheekbone, a high bridged nose to land experimentally on a wide firm mouth.

Blackburn had his answer.

The sensation of Devon's warm breath acted like gunpowder to Blackburn's nerve endings. Despite all reasonable arguments, he wanted her with a hunger that defied all the lies between them. He wanted to jam into her, feel the pull of her lips and tongue, grind his body into hers. The *Eroica*, Le Comte, discipline, and control evaporated in the heat of that first contact.

Stroking the delicate wrists straddling the arms of his chair, his hands slid slowly upward to push back the cloak and lace sleeves and to glide over the tender skin of her shoulders. Her mouth tasted, wavering and unsure until he, shifting forward, pulled her down onto his lap, his penis huge and hot, flexing against her. His erection, seemingly omnipresent around Devon, gained another few inches as he began a savoring kiss that ate at her lips and importuned the moist interior of her mouth. He sucked at her deeper, harsher as his hands wrapped themselves in the flow of her hair veiling them both in a tumble of auburn silk.

He wanted to trap her in a vortex of sensation, in the languidly deep kiss that probed and enticed and chased away the last vestiges of rational thought. He wanted every fiber of her being awakened, for her to revel in the feel of his hands as he deftly drew aside lace to linger on her bare leg, stroking persuasively higher. Blackburn savored the velvet flesh, the long limbs, taking his time to touch, massage, and seduce. She was well named, like Devon cream, sweet and delicious. His tongue enveloped her, probing, stroking, continuing to claim her mouth with a flawless combination of delicacy and recklessness that was terrifying in its proficiency.

He moved to her breasts, the tips tingling and hard for his touch. He remembered their shape and texture without yet caressing them, the highly responsive mounds of flesh made for his hands and mouth, made to entrap a man. The smooth flesh slipped under his palms, the nipples covered by silk and lace hardening into long tips, eager for his lips. He tugged at them, stroking and suckling while his erection thrust hard and urgently. Devon was eager, writhing and arching into him so that he couldn't relinquish the pressure on her nipples, simultaneously passionate and curiously artless.

He breathed in her scent—the delicacy of freesia combined with her strange aura of innocence—and was instantly beset with an image of her with de Maupassant. He cupped her breast and slid his thumb back and forth across the taut skin.

So voluptuous. So responsive. This exquisite, sumptuous body in the hands of a man he loathed.

A surge of anger fueled his lust, and suddenly he stilled.

Her lips were swollen, her nipples hard and dark beneath the silk of her nightdress, her cloak a sinful disarray as she lay across his knees.

De Maupassant's mistress.

He had never felt possessively about a woman before. Juggling truth in its many permutations was what he did best, the labyrinths of intrigue negotiated with instincts as finely tuned as a poet's ear or a marksman's eye.

Right now he couldn't control anything. Not Devon Caravelle, not sex, and not his rampaging iron rod that threatened to explode.

Control. He closed his eyes away from the sight of that erotic mouth, those taut-tipped breasts. He made his mind blank, balancing himself on the precipice of hot lust, listening for the voice of temperate logic to call him back. His self-discipline seldom failed him. He hoped it wouldn't fail him now.

Seconds later he became aware of the room around him and heard his own words seeming to come from a distance, a lazy murmur designed to right the balance of power.

"Perhaps you're correct, Mademoiselle." The coldness of his voice startled even him. "Let's see if you're worth it. If you have what it takes to seduce Le Comte." It took every ounce of strength he had to thrust her away from him. Blackburn saw the startled flash of surprise in her eyes.

"So seduce me, Devon," he continued, leaning back into the chair as she slid from his knees. "I want to see what I'm stealing from de Maupassant. And I want to see whether you can do a credible job at seducing him for the *Eroica.*" His hand on her arm was unequivocal, as if awaiting a performance, the prince and his subject.

Eyes wide with confusion, she actually seemed uncertain of what to do next. "Blackburn . . . look . . . I'm not quite sure what you mean . . ."

His answer was to slide his hand around the smoothness of her waist, to the heat of desire under her skin. Blackburn wanted to make sure that his hold felt like silken shackles tying her closer to him.

She licked her lips anxiously and said softly, "What would you have me do?"

Blackburn hardened instantly at her words, bracing himself against the chair. "Tell me you want it." With those words he was testing her. And he wanted her to know it.

She hesitated, shivering. "Fine," she whispered and he could see the dark pupils of her eyes dilating in desire. "I want it."

"Tell me again." Blackburn tried not to show his surprise at her ready acquiescence, agonizingly aware that this seduction was what de Maupassant had in mind all along. Devon was primed for sex like some ripe fruit, offered to him on the proverbial silver platter, a sweetness concocted to trap and ensnare. He was tempted all right, and he would succumb, but only with eyes wide open.

"I want it . . . But I'm not sure." He could feel her quick and shallow breaths beneath his hand, her skin burning through the thin silk of her shift.

"You're an experienced woman," he said, deliberately cruel. "Use what must be your considerable imagination."

Devon's gray eyes darkened in anger and frustration, but she held his scorching gaze. Blackburn had to give her credit. After hesitating the merest of seconds, she scrambled to her feet, head bent, and began playing with the sash and the tiny buttons of her robe.

One, two, three gave way to the creamy smoothness of her neck before, with a soft shake, the fabric landed in a ripple of white on the floor. Lithe and slender, she emerged, the light covering of her gown baiting him with its transparency. She stood perfectly still, chin raised and her hair a dark flame against the perfection of her skin, as though unsure of what to do next.

"You have my undivided attention." He was intrigued by her game of ingénue. He felt himself swelling, impossibly huge, against the cashmere of his breeches. "Continue," he ordered, a roughness to the texture of his voice.

She almost said something, her lips parting in an inchoate whisper as she fought the slow drift of desire, magically lifting her hands to the ruching of her shoulders. In a seemingly unconsciously seductive motion, she pushed the material down over her arms, the full high breasts, the slender waist, gently curved hips and down a graceful length of leg. Blackburn felt the pounding of his blood like a low drumming in the distance.

His gaze swept her form, those incredible breasts suspended enchantingly high and tipped with large peach-tinged nipples hardening in the cooling air. A long slender waist nipped by a smooth stomach taunted him. The hint of tightly curving buttocks turned away from his sight fired his suddenly savage desire.

Blackburn wanted Devon Caravelle with an uncontrollable and frightening greed that defied even his experience. He was ready to explode. He needed her *now*.

"Come here," he exhaled, his voice dark persuasion.

As if he were a mirage, a smoldering illusion, Devon floated toward him to stand weak with desire between his iron hard legs. The black cashmere rubbed at her body, heightening the eroticism of the moment. The powerful, fully dressed man and nude, pliant woman.

Her mind reeled wildly, miles away from reasoned thought as a cyclone of emotions blotted out all and any rationality. Blackburn's hard palms tested the round firmness of her buttocks before trailing to encircle her waist and caress the outer curves of her gleaming breasts. The blue eyes glittered with passion as he laved first one nipple then the other. He blew lightly on a dampened crest, feeling her body vibrate in his hands. Then his palms cupped both breasts, thumbs running over the raised peaks, and she gasped. Drawing upon years of erotic encounters, he teased the swollen crests mercilessly, trying to ignore the frantic movements of slender hips.

Almost against his will, the fragrant flesh beckoned as his lips left her breasts and trailed the length of her narrow waist to coax open her thighs, positioning one of her legs on the seat of his chair. Purposefully removing her hands that, in a game of what was surely false modesty, blocked his way, he encountered the moist heat of her cleft. The textures were exquisite, overpoweringly female and, bending his dark head, he couldn't resist running his tongue over the pearlescent flesh.

"Please," Devon moaned, breathily begging with small panting whispers for him to go on. Her fingers tangled themselves in his hair, holding on as if the shattering craving would sweep her away.

"Pleasing's the idea," he laughed softly, not missing the rhythm of his ministrations and returning to linger at the peaking juncture of her thighs. His wicked tongue traced heated patterns, swirls of sensation, branding her. He wanted her to lose control, to set her on fire and to transform her into a malleable woman locked in his arms. She was holding back the cries that welled in her throat, focused on his hands on her thighs, her buttocks and his burning eyes. His manhood jolted and right before she crested, her body tensing in his arms, he drew away.

Suspended on the edge of an erotic zenith, Devon allowed herself to be lifted in his arms and arranged carefully on the floor by the fire. The dark Aubusson carpet was rough against her overheated skin as she lay still, watching him through heavy eyes as he made short work of his clothes. The firelight cast a red light on his hardness, all bone and muscle, a shadow of broad shoulders and a powerful length of leg. Her eyes closed, seemingly daunted at the size of his erection.

Her virginal response was unexpected, just another of her travesties that belonged in her considerable sexual repertoire and one that was just as unexpectedly arousing. It was not a game Blackburn often played, preferring his women seasoned in the sexual battlefield. Nonetheless her body drove him to a frenzy of desire, drawing him toward her once again in front of the fire an instant later, soothing and cajoling with hands and tongue. Teasing delicately, he brushed her lips, the crest of a cheek, the sensitive length of her outstretched neck. She couldn't wait any longer, her motions told him, her eager mouth biting at his lips until they were swollen and bruised, her fingers locked in his hair. Fitting her body to his, she ground her hips brazenly into his arousal and offered her painfully stimulated breasts to his wandering mouth.

Searching the lust-hazed corners of his mind, Blackburn pushed away the unfamiliar emotions threatening his actions. This was simply a dance or an exchange of goods, a settling of accounts. Devon Caravelle was surely no novice when it came to the delights and uses of seduction, despite this evening's role of ingénue. She was a courtesan, a mistress, a spy, without soul—as he was. Only the best could play so confidently with two dangerous men.

He smoothed a swathe of hair and trailed the curve of a cheekbone. Parting her thighs, he found the softly swollen flesh eager for his touch. Her breath caught on a deep moan and all he wanted was to ram into her, rigid and thick, aroused beyond all limits. The games, the carnal subtleties that were his stock-in-trade—all lost in the primal urge to feel his manhood flexing between her thighs and then in her wet, tight sheath.

Sliding past the entrance, he penetrated the slippery warmth with supple fingers that stretched and prepared, the folds redolent of female arousal. Tossing her head against his arm and seeking to end the sweet torture, Devon arched upward against the strong fingers moving in and out and brushing against the apex of her core.

Seduced by creamy hot dampness, he moved over her to kiss her again, his mouth devouring, her nipples brushing his chest. Trapped, she was spread beneath him, her stormy eyes heavy-lidded. Blackburn shifted excruciatingly slowly into her tight opening, moving his rock-hard erection in small motions, intent on building the sensation in a combination of masculine pride and desire to conquer at all costs. Alternatively thrusting and brushing expertly against her center, he felt the cadence of her breathing increase and her long legs grip more tightly. He slid over her moist cleft in an intoxicating rhythm, deliciously prodding, probing, pushing until his shaft buried, increment by increment, into her sheath.

He usually prided himself on his control but her unexpectedly slick narrowness nearly sent him over the edge. He was a breath away from ejaculating; she was so tight, so wet—

It was then that he felt the thin barrier. And for a moment there was nothing except the rush of blood in his ears.

It was impossible. A thin sheen of sweat stood out on his forehead as he battled with questions and contradictions. He couldn't think. His head throbbed and his vision blurred and all he could do was feel, smell, and taste Devon Caravelle.

He felt her undulating hips against his groin. And for the first time in his life he lost control, a convulsive ferocity blotting out all rational thought or argument. Need for her overwhelmed him, driving him on with hot agitation in his bid to control her absolutely and irrevocably. She was his for the taking, her small moans urging him on as he took a ragged breath and plunged forward, until his painfully rigid shaft was buried to the hilt.

He pulled back and thrust again, feeling her tense as sharp pain enveloped her and then eased in the wake of holding him deep inside her. Filled with an unbelievably exquisite expansion of pleasure, Devon pulled him to her as he nudged and stroked, making long and leisurely, short and luscious, incursions into her tightness. He wanted her to feel it, know it, his power and his possession.

Everything was forgotten, complexities and opposing circumstances ignored in the explosion of carnality that threatened to obliterate them both. Panting, her eyes closed in passionate concentration, Devon felt a wild and urgent fever consume her body, a hunger that could not get enough of the hardness impaling her. She writhed, she arched for his kiss, hot and wet, as every rigid inch of him blasted inside her. She felt aroused, volatile, and she felt all of him, that hot, hard possession filling her to bursting and to sensual excess.

Blackburn turned molten as her long shudders began, the trembling, the muffled moan as his thumb, slick with her cream, circled her core. Then she peaked, her muscles clenching, milking him as the heat coalesced between her legs and she dissolved in his arms, her world floating away. He ground his hips against hers, still deep and hard within her, tormenting her, tormenting himself. Arms tensed, muscles coiled in response, he could hold back no longer from her tight wetness and pulsed into her with a ferocity that heated his blood. His breaths came harshly before he agonizingly withdrew and spilled his pleasure on her smooth thighs.

They didn't move for a time, damp with sweat, panting, pulses racing. But as the fire burned lower, Blackburn finally felt compelled to pull away from her to stare unseeingly at the first light of day slanting through the windows.

They lay in silence, shocked beyond words, resplendent on the wine-dark carpet, not daring to touch.

Chapter 8

"What the hell's been going on?"

Arthur Wellesley, the first Duke of Wellington, looked up from his breakfast of coffee and kippers.

In dusty riding breeches, crop still in hand, the Marquess of Blackburn appeared unceremoniously in the morning room of Stratfield House exuding a combination of anger and arrogance that reminded the Duke immediately of the dangers of cannon fire. He knew Blackburn well enough to recognize that a time of reckoning had arrived.

"You'll have to be somewhat more specific," he said calmly, motioning for a nearby footman to pour another coffee. "In the interim, can I interest you in some breakfast?"

"Forget breakfast and I can be as specific as you'd like." Blackburn glowered, striding purposefully into the room. "What exactly is Devon Caravelle's role in the *Eroica* and what is the nature of her relationship with that bastard de Maupassant?"

"Pardon me—but I thought you knew," said the Duke, his long face with its prominent nose blandly impassive.

Still standing, Blackburn twitched his riding crop sharply against his tall boots. His posture was unequivocal, giving the man who had bested Napoleon on several occasions a moment of pause. A towering individual with a military bearing, the Duke rose from the table and stepped toward the

French doors overlooking Stratfield's extensive gardens and grottoes.

"We've already given you all the information we have, Gray," the Duke explained with his back to the younger man. "You know as well as I do that Devon worked closely with her father. We surmise that she's probably as talented as he was, a brilliant mathematician and musician. We know that and Le Comte knows that. The conclusions are obvious."

The Duke turned from the window to face Blackburn. "We also believe that Le Comte is involved with republican groups in France to whom he's been funneling money."

"Explain that one to me," said Blackburn, the bright sun of the morning room etching the sharp planes of his face, made even more pronounced by several sleepless nights. "I thought his sympathies lay with the Bourbons and the reestablishment of the French monarchy."

"We're involved with a larger proposition here, one that precludes political factions with which we're accustomed to dealing," the Duke explained. "And while de Maupassant has always made his allegiance to the monarchy obvious, even during Bonaparte's reign, his leanings have been questionable."

"He wants power, nothing else, that much has always been clear," Blackburn said abruptly, suddenly tired as he blocked the jagged memories that threatened to override his better judgment. "I suppose if the conduit to that power is Bonaparte, then he can live with that."

"Currently, Napoleon is on St. Helena. In James Bay, three frigates and two other vessels are being kept on stand-by. We also have six other vessels deployed on observation duties with two of their number continually circling the island. Guard posts and gun emplacements are set up all over the island. Even Tristan da Cunha, over twelve hundred miles to the south, is garrisoned."

Blackburn smiled grimly. "All that naval power could well prove meaningless. If de Maupassant deciphers the code before we do, he could force Britain to release Bonaparte. We would have no other choice."

"All the more reason to exploit Devon Caravelle however you can," Wellington said forcefully.

"My question concerns her role in this gambit."

The Duke was a shrewd man who had known and worked alongside Blackburn for close to ten years and he detected something unusual in the timbre of his voice. "Are you holding her at Armathwaite by any chance?" he asked absently before adding guardedly, "And is that wise?" He suspected that Blackburn had ridden from his hunting lodge several miles north of Stratfield in the Berkshires.

By way of answer, the Marquess threw open the French doors and moved onto a broad balustraded terrace outside. The Duke was compelled to follow.

Leaning against the ironwork, his arms crossed, Blackburn chose his words carefully. "She is not de Maupassant's mistress as your informants led you to conclude."

The Duke raised his eyebrows in disbelief. "Don't be preposterous, man. Will you have me assume that they are living together as brother and sister?"

"Trust me in this, Arthur." A slight wind came up and the sky was a hard, unrelenting blue canopy that stretched over Stratfield's extensive gardens.

The Duke made a rapid calculation and, as was his tendency, came to an irrefutable conclusion quickly. "If she's not his mistress, Le Comte is using her for a more critical reason. We believe he has the *Eroica*—but only you and Clifton's daughter know what to do with it." He paused significantly, brow furrowed. "This is hardly surprising: He's using her to reel you in."

Blackburn paused somewhat longer than necessary, watching in the distance as the gardeners tended the hedges. "What you're saying is that he plans for me to become emotionally involved with Devon Caravelle, a beautiful, ultimately useful young woman who also happens to be close to what I want—

the *Eroica*. I think that's what they call pandering, but then that's an old story."

"All the more reason to tread carefully."

"I'm certain that Clifton didn't want her involved."

"Of course not, what father would? But he should have thought of that long ago." Wellington looked over the balustrade to the parterre beyond. "Well, she's involved now, Gray. Whether she's thrown her lot in with de Maupassant for money or because she shares his political cause, who knows? I rather suspect it's the former and that Devon Caravelle may be selling to the highest bidder. And so as long as we're in on the bidding . . ."

It took a moment before Blackburn's vision cleared, the green of the parkland and the blue of the sky coalescing for one agonizing minute. He remembered carrying her to bed early in the morning, the feel of her in his arms, the shock of learning her innocence. She lay sleeping, exhausted, leaving only a profound silence that dropped them both into a chasm of unanswered questions.

Selling to the highest bidder.

Blackburn said quietly, "Money is not her objective—I've already tried that. Which means," he said, stepping away from the balustrade to face Wellington directly, "that she's even more dangerous than we might have anticipated."

"Only if you *allow* her to become a danger to you."

The Duke glanced at Blackburn, whose countenance betrayed absolutely no emotion, the earlier anger wiped clean as if from a slate. Wellington was reassured. This was the man he knew.

"Hell will freeze over first."

"I'd rather hope so," said the Duke dryly. "And as long as you have Devon Caravelle's talents under your control, we've everything to gain. Which is why we've put you directly in her path in the first place."

"Right—the abduction," Blackburn said, irony lacing his voice.

"Le Comte thinks he set the trap, put out the bait, but we're just ensuring there's a double cross. Get in on the bidding and find out if Devon Caravelle is open to other offers."

"I don't think it's that simple and, as I've already said, I don't think money is at issue here." Blackburn leaned against the sharp edges of the ironwork shutting out the view. "But trust me, I know she'll do anything to find out who murdered her father."

"To clear his name, presumably?"

"And to keep herself out of prison. I'm sure she's convinced of his innocence and that he never traded his talents to France or England for nefarious purposes."

"Well then, do whatever necessary to get her cooperation," the Duke said curtly. "Distasteful though it may seem, manipulating her love and loyalty for her father would appear to be key. Remember there's still the distinct possibility that she's simply a traitor, working for Le Comte."

"I'm well aware that exploiting emotional undercurrents can be quite productive. However, there are certain contradictions about Mademoiselle Caravelle that are difficult to rationalize."

The Duke cleared his throat and adjusted the cravat of his morning coat. "You've never let a beautiful face cloud your judgment before. Be careful on this one, Gray."

Blackburn cut Wellington off before he could continue, a derisive, deadly lightness coloring his voice. "And you've never underestimated me before, Arthur, even those many years ago when you first enlisted my aid against Napoleon."

The Duke remembered all too well. Boredom and an insatiable greed for all manner of exploits had driven Blackburn, the directionless younger son of an old family, into offering his services to the Crown—which had jumped at the chance to profit from such reckless abandon and fine intellect. "You displayed a taste for danger, a rare talent for mathematics to rival Napoleon's own, and an even rarer talent for dissemblement," Wellington returned crisply. "Don't disappoint me now."

"I'll ignore that," said Blackburn, turning to leave.

"Where is she at the moment?" They both knew to whom the Duke was referring.

"At Armathwaite, where I want her until I can ensure her cooperation," Blackburn offered shortly.

"Then what?"

"I'll do some horse-trading with the Frenchman."

The Duke eyed him closely, testing. "Rather dangerous for her, wouldn't you say?"

Blackburn's expression didn't change. "Whatever it takes."

The Duke sat back down to a cold cup of coffee. He left the French doors open to allow a slight breeze to ruffle the sheaf of papers which he removed from the drawer of a handsome Regency desk.

Always an ambitious man, his fortunes of war with Napoleon had made him the first Duke of Wellington. And he would be England's subsequent prime minister if he could bring this next trophy home to Parliament and king.

He would do his best to rein in Blackburn. The man's dealings with Le Comte in the past could very well threaten the future of the Duke's own plans. Blackburn had never divulged the source of his personal and abiding hatred for de Maupassant, but Wellington knew the story. His informants were more than capable. He just didn't trust vengeance as a good way to get the job done.

Ordinarily, Blackburn operated on pure intellect and reason, attributes indispensable to a code-breaker and master spy. Even when it came to his own brother, he had sacrificed innocence at the altar of king and country. The Duke just hoped that Blackburn remained true to his nature, evading any snares set by the duplicitous de Maupassant and the very lovely and talented Devon Caravelle.

Wellington eased back in his chair, crossing his legs, and examined the parchment closely, the only page of the *Eroica* manuscript they had in their possession, signed in Brendan

Clifton's bloodied scrawl perhaps only moments before his violent death.

Beethoven's Third Symphony, the *Eroica*, its title revealed in Clifton's script. The Duke knew it well, a composition written in the spirit of democracy and freedom and dedicated to a man who could have been Europe's savior, but turned out instead to be its tyrant. Napoleon Bonaparte had disappointed many people.

Including Brendan Clifton—who knew exactly the nature of the encryption.

Unfortunately, that knowledge was now available to some of the most dangerous men in Europe, men who would not see Napoleon exiled on St. Helena but set loose again on the continent of Europe and beyond. It was a dangerous secret woven into the notes and rhythms of the symphony that, alas, Brendan Clifton, had not taken to his grave. His daughter still lived. And so did the Marquess of Blackburn.

Wellington slid the papers into a leather-bound dossier and took another sip of his now bitter brew. Although he was reluctant to let it out of his possession, he would have the dossier with its incriminating title page sent to Armathwaite immediately. Without doubt, Blackburn would find it useful in his deliberations with the Frenchwoman.

A wild goose chase? The Duke of Wellington couldn't afford to think so.

The prospect of Le Comte holding Great Britain hostage was as unthinkable as "this scepter'd isle" slipping into the sea.

"I find myself singularly unhappy," declared Le Comte enunciating with the kind of precision designed to strike fear into lesser mortals. "Are you two miscreants telling me that you are unable to locate the Marquess of Blackburn and Devon Caravelle? How did they disappear under your *watchful eyes* in the first place?"

They had assembled in the library where Le Comte held court at this unusually early hour, his manner as contemptuous as his dress was immaculate. His two disciples waited for his wrath to descend.

"I want them located now. Immediately. Use tracking methods, send messenger pigeons and, if you must," he paused significantly, rising from behind his desk, "extract information requiring whatever techniques you like. But I want them found and Devon Caravelle returned to me at once."

Malcolm Crosbie, large and brooding, nodded obsequiously, only stopping short of pulling his forelock. His many talents included the judicious use of thumbscrews and the rack and, most recently, he'd also been one of Blackburn's abductors.

"It won't be simple, Monsieur Le Comte," ventured Bertrand Lacan, fueling his employer's ire. "They're smart, resourceful. Look what I found in her rooms." He placed two books on the oak desk—Blaise de Vigenère's *Traicté des Chiffres* and Abbot Trithemius's *Polygraphia*.

Le Comte's eyes narrowed in contempt before he swept the books from the table in one irate motion. They thumped to the floor at Lacan's feet. "You fool, of course I know that Devon Caravelle is familiar with cryptanalysis. She's her father's daughter, for God's sake. But these old tomes won't help her and Blackburn to break the code we're after and they very well realize that."

Swallowing his anger, Lacan bent to retrieve the volumes. His loyalty to France and the Bourbons had managed to override his loyalty to Le Comte. He was already five steps ahead of de Maupassant, having taken Susannah Treadwell's advice by assigning two men to trail the young woman and the Marquess. "We checked Blackburn's house in Mayfair and there's no sign of them," he lied almost beneath his breath before returning the books to the desk.

"Do you think, Lacan, that a man as wealthy as the Marquess of Blackburn just may have other estates to which he and Mademoiselle Caravelle may have repaired to?" asked Le Comte sarcastically, his impatience clear in the thin set of his lips.

Crosbie moved into the morning light filtering in from the

one window of the library. "When we kidnapped Blackburn, she probably believed we were helping her," he sneered, his pleasure in the deception flagrant.

"That did work rather well for our purposes at the time," said Le Comte slowly, as though talking to small children. "But, gentlemen, this doesn't help us out of our present predicament, does it? Where have they disappeared to? I need to know their whereabouts and exactly what they are about."

"They are together, to be sure," Lacan tried again. "We require the Marquess in any case, as he's the undisputed specialist in complex ciphers and chemistry. Mademoiselle won't be able to accomplish much without him."

Le Comte's impatience was once again a barometer on the rise, his pale features sharpening. "Are you truly as witless as you appear?" he asked with ripping sarcasm, leaning a hip against the desk, arms crossed. "Why else do you think I brought the two of them together, if not to work on the score jointly! But only under *my* control!"

Neither Crosbie nor Lacan chose to mention the last time Le Comte had tried to wrest cooperation from the monumentally invulnerable Marquess of Blackburn. Now all of Le Comte's ambitions rested on the slender shoulders of Devon Caravelle who, with the proper persuasion, could turn the screws on Blackburn far tighter than Crosbie or Lacan ever could.

Lacan watched Le Comte pick up a fountain pen and begin twisting the delicate cartridge in his hands.

"Do you think she realizes the significance of the cipher?" he asked, not entirely clear himself as to their shared objective.

He had worked with Le Comte for years and could not fathom his defection from a noble cause, the restoration of the French monarchy. As for Devon Caravelle, she and her kind were species of the peasant rabble that had dared to usurp what had been for centuries the divine right of kings. Punish her he would, until she had nothing left to threaten the shaky throne of France. He'd learned the worst of methods from the best—Le Comte de Maupassant.

He probed carefully, "Would Clifton have told her and put his daughter in danger?"

Le Comte tapped the pen impatiently against the side of the desk. "Another stupid question. She knows more than she's willing to divulge at the moment."

"How can we trust her to stay loyal to you, Monsieur, once she and the Marquess have unraveled the cipher?"

Le Comte patted the top drawer of his desk to reassure himself. "As you'll recall, Lacan, I have her father's last letter to her. Without it, the formula will make no sense. Besides, what daughter could resist receiving that last missive from her father? Even though most of it is filled with a surfeit of sentimental rubbish."

"What about the Lady Treadwell—maybe she knows somethin'," suggested Crosbie, eager to be of help.

"Leave Lady Treadwell out of this, as a matter of fact. Permanently." Le Comte addressed Lacan directly. "I'm not sure if the hot little bitch has changed allegiances since Blackburn has been warming her bed."

Lacan managed to keep his expression blank. "One never knows, Monsieur."

"It's your business to know, Lacan," Le Comte reminded him unnecessarily.

Crosbie shuffled toward the door, wary of Le Comte's mood.

"Just find Devon Caravelle, or *I will*," the Frenchman reiterated, more to himself than to anyone else in the room. "Follow Blackburn before his trail cools and we might just end up with both of them twisting at the end of our rope."

"If we're lucky," contributed Crosbie.

"Only fools rely on luck," responded Le Comte with a sharp bark. "We must find ourselves one step ahead of them. Otherwise this whole situation explodes in our faces."

Le Comte meant what he said—quite literally. And with white hands surprisingly strong, he snapped the fountain pen in two.

Chapter 9

By midafternoon, the tavern was blue with smoke. The stench of unwashed bodies and stale wine hit Devon like a fist. Burly men lined long wooden tables, their booming, raucous talk rising in waves to the rafters.

She pulled her hood further over her hair and, edging toward a hard bench, she accepted a small cup of harsh red wine from the sullen serving girl, paying her a few coins she had found in the pocket of her pelisse.

What was she doing? She didn't even know anymore.

She had slipped from Blackburn's hunting lodge, her need to get back to London at fever's pitch, so overwhelming that she left the grounds on foot, having discovered the manor house stables empty.

Even now her hands shook, clutching the small cup and the memory of the past few hours. How would she ever forget, wipe the slate clean?

It had meant nothing to him. She was a sentimental fool if she thought that their physical coupling had in any way influenced Blackburn's plans. For him seduction was purely a means to an end.

She leaned her head forward on both her palms, for the moment unwilling to contemplate her near future. The coarse skirt she had found in the lodge's deserted kitchens scratched at her legs, but at least she'd also been able to exchange her silk slippers for a pair of overly large wooden clogs, and to grab a few chunks of cheese. Refusing to hire a conveyance, once she found the road, for fear of bringing attention to herself, she had walked along the byway toward London, ignoring the anxiety gnawing at her stomach, banishing the images that teased, the pleasant heaviness between her thighs.

Let Blackburn stay away a while longer—wherever he'd disappeared to. As the afternoon's sun had begun to strengthen, she had continued to look over her shoulder, startled by a wagon turning a corner or a goose honking its irritation.

Get back to London. It was her only hope. She could not let the two men she feared most in the world toss her back and forth between them like a piece on a chessboard.

She did not trust Blackburn nor, more important, did she trust herself around him. The morning light had stung her into an awareness of her actions the night before. She'd learned that he was a master of seduction, and she an apt pupil, but little else. The situation surrounding her father's murder was still lost to her. That she'd surrendered her body to him, that her senses had soared at his touch, she couldn't, wouldn't think about that right now.

She took another sip of the wine before pushing the hood of her cloak from her eyes, scanning the crowd. Her skin prickled beneath her woolen skirt and she looked up to see two men appear out of the smoky haze only to slide, one on either side, next to her on the bench.

She surged to her feet.

"Why so shy, don't the lady want us to join her?" Nails rimmed with dirt gripped her arm, pulling her back down on the bench. The man was bearded, his eyes small and shrewd.

"I think we can convince her, Morton," said his cohort on her left. He was younger and his breath reeked with ale, yet there was an awareness in his posture that cut through the alcoholic haze. He placed three heavy tankards on the table.

Devon's eyes darted around the room, but no one had

seemed to notice a lone woman being crowded into a corner by the unwelcome attentions of two men.

"I think we know this lady here, Hal," said the bearded one as he tried to get a better look at her face. "I think we damn found what we're looking for."

The two men edged her into the farthest corner of the bench. "You putting on airs?" Hal shook his head. "I don't think that's such a good idea," he said, pushing down her hood before she could protest.

Her hair spilled out in rich profusion. Devon swallowed hard while Hal grunted his approval.

"I think she's the one. That hair color is uncommon, wouldn't you say, Morton?"

"You're an awful quiet one, *Devon Caravelle*," said Morton, placing both his elbows on the rough-hewn table in front of him. "Maybe if we go upstairs to a private room you'll find yourself more talkative." He was clearly considering his options, some more pleasurable than others. "No use running to London. We've plenty of time."

A spark of anger crowded out the tightness in her chest. "You must have the wrong woman." Emissaries—Le Comte's or Blackburn's men?

She looked past the table with its heavy tankards foaming with ale and surveyed the pub through a smoky veil, looking for a plausible escape, a diversion.

Morton dropped a solid arm over her shoulders. "So you have a voice after all. Now I'm sure there are plenty things we could be discussing," he said, his breath heavy, "what with all the time you've been spending with important gentlemen and all."

"I think you're the one all right," said Hal, lowering his gaze to the folds of her cloak. "Why don't you just let me help you off with that there and get you more comfortable." Before she could push away his hands she saw the glint of a knife at a perfect right angle to her breast.

"You understand now, Mademoiselle?"

She nodded mutely while Morton shifted in closer. The acrid smell of sweat smothered like an old blanket. "Nobody likes a traitor, do they, Hal? And that's what we've got here with us today—a traitor."

"What do you want?" Her voice was hoarse.

"Let's see—what do we want Hal?" Morton pursed his thick lips while Hal hooked his thumbs in his belt as though giving the question serious consideration.

"We want to give the turncoat what she deserves. You think that's a fair reckoning, Morton?" Hal tested the sharpness of the knife's blade with his callused thumb for emphasis.

"I think you're onto something there. We're here to do a job, but we can always make a little extra coin, enjoy the lady and, when we're finished, deliver the goods." The two men laughed at their own dark humor, their voices lost in the din of the room.

Devon damned Le Comte and Blackburn to hell and back.

"I have money."

"You in a bargaining mood now?"

"We're wasting time, Morton. If we're wanting to be enjoying ourselves and get our pay packet, let's move on."

"I'm thinkin' you're right. Still got that knife at the ready?"

"Time to go upstairs, Milady." Hal's voice was suddenly adamant, the fumes on his breath as strong as the arm around Devon's waist. His bloodshot eyes focused on the shape beneath her cloak, the point of his knife poking through the rough wool.

She'd see them drop dead first.

"I appreciate that I don't have much choice." She tried to ignore the sweaty arm holding her close and propelling her toward the backstairs. She eyed the full tankards of ale on the table in front of her.

"Look at that," said Morton. "The lady's ready to go now. She's had a change of heart."

"Maybe she's beginning to appreciate our charm. When

we get upstairs she'll really see how entertaining we can be, won't she, Hal?"

Gritty from smoke, her throat constricted. Shutting out the sound of their laughter, she twisted from Morton's loosened grip, grabbed two of the tankards and hurled them, like cannonballs, at both men. A sheet of foaming ale arced across the table and into their faces before the metal clanged to the scarred wooden boards. Outraged, the serving girl gave a shrill cry that just managed to penetrate the clamor.

"I won't have me no fightin' in this establishment," she shrieked, dragging along a meaty barman already brandishing his fists. With barely enough time to wipe the brew from their eyes, the three men advanced on each other like boars snorting and shuffling on the ground. Hal swung first. The barman recovered quickly, but not before he was seized by Morton in a headlock from behind. Two more men jumped into the fray, their curses and grunts filling the smoky air. Toward the front of the room, another table was overturned, a fight broke out at the bar, and the serving girl took cover under the stairs.

It was all Devon needed. Crunching over broken crockery amid a river of ale, she stumbled to the exit. She wrenched open the heavy door at the back of the tavern, expecting a heavy arm about her waist, holding her back. Instead she was rewarded by the bright sunshine and a deserted road, only a few clumps of daffodils nodding in her direction.

Peering around the corner of the building she saw a horse, four-legged salvation. Just what she needed, a horse to fly her to London.

Murmuring softly, she approached the animal which was impatiently pawing the ground. He was beautiful, his saddle made of fine-grained leather, indications that his owner was wealthy, an aristocrat or both. Devon felt a stab of guilt. She couldn't walk. Impossible. Theft was her only option. Untying the reins, she was about to place her foot in the stirrup.

A hard hand covered her mouth cutting off the air to her

lungs as effectively as a tourniquet. She struggled and then she was catapulted back against a wall of muscle.

Devon knew him immediately. Intimately. His touch, his scent, his body pressed against hers, radiating an invading heat. A surge of dizziness enveloped her and she began to shake.

Blackburn had come for her. She was filled with fear and an exhilaration that recalled the agony of his touch.

She fought off panic. "Let me go!" And then his hard palm crushed her mouth once more.

Blackburn felt her struggle in his arms, the sensation sending ricochets of hunger through his body.

He should wring her neck. Instead, he tasted desire so potent that it shook his soul. He wanted to shove aside her skirts, baring the soft skin beneath and take her from behind. Here, on the dirt road outside London.

Blackburn felt her mouth go slack beneath his palm. "Let's move out while we still can," he growled. "Otherwise, we'll have your friends and half the tavern at our backs."

Devon didn't have time to argue. Already noises from the tavern were spilling through its doors and windows. A few men lurched onto the road on unsteady legs, shirts torn, ready to take the fight outside. Blackburn boosted Devon onto the saddle before he leapt behind her. The horse whinnied once as they tore toward a copse of trees, whipping up a trail of mud.

She slumped against him, defeat in every limb, oblivious to his beard raking her cheek. Her body was featherlight against his chest and, *damn*, she felt good. Aware that no one was following them, Blackburn slowed to a canter, the horse's hooves like drums of war as he navigated the woods along a path where the oak trees grew closer together. Although it was daylight, an owl hooted somewhere in the distance and a half-moon appeared against the blue of the sky.

They stopped at the crest of a hill and, without saying a

word, he slid from their mount, pulling her with him. Without releasing her, he unfastened the horse's bridle.

As soon as her feet touched the ground, Devon's breaths came in gasps. "Are you mad stopping here? They can't be far behind. Do you know what they'll do if they find us?"

"They'll head in the opposite direction, along the road. The woods are entirely unfamiliar to them." Blackburn was dressed in black, his breeches and jacket covered with dust as though from a longer ride. "Those were probably de Maupassant's men. I said he'd come for you."

"Isn't that what you wanted all along?" Her words came at him in a torrent.

"You would have been safer with me at Armathwaite."

"As though my safety is your primary concern."

"You'd have a better chance with de Maupassant with me in your camp."

"Don't test my credulity." Along with anger, he could see the wild panic in her eyes.

"What happened back there, Devon?"

"What do you think?"

They stood facing each other in the dappled light of the copse. Something caustic and corrosive burned through his stomach. He suddenly remembered the two pistols in his saddlebags. "Did they hurt you?" His voice was so low it was almost inaudible.

Devon simply shook her head. She stared at him uncertainly, poised like a deer ready to run into the brush and out of sight. Blackburn felt what was left of his conscience slip through his fingers.

"Now do you understand the ugly reality of this situation? De Maupassant will stop at nothing to get what he wants."

"And how are you any different, sir? Whether it's two strangers in a country tavern or Le Comte's bed—I don't understand the distinction you're making," she said in a strangled voice.

Her hair tumbled about her face and smudges of purple

framed her expressive eyes. She was all vulnerability, her seeming fragility even catching him unawares. In his world, there was no such thing as trust. Devon Caravelle was right not to trust him, as he was correct in not trusting her. She had never been Le Comte's lover. One night with her and he'd plunged off a steep cliff and into a free fall. Damn her. And damn her loyalties, wherever they lay.

"Sit down," he said abruptly, gesturing to the base of a large oak. He ran a lean hand along the length of the horse's neck. The animal tossed his mane in pleasurable response. "We'll give them an hour or so to get thoroughly lost. Now tell me exactly what happened."

Devon looked up at the sky as though looking for an answer in the gathering clouds. "They called me a traitor. And they were eager to mete out the punishment deserving of a traitor."

Blackburn tried to keep his next words neutral. "Are you certain they were Le Comte's men?" To quell the tightening in his chest, he sat down at the base of the tree, crossing his booted legs at the ankle.

She slumped wearily. "Who else? Either Le Comte's men or possibly yours. I didn't discount that possibility."

"Not my men—I got you back on my own." He didn't like the possessive quality of his words. "You're exhausted. Sit down." It was a command in the hushed green stillness.

Devon's lashes lowered and heat flared suddenly between them. "You want everything, don't you? And you give nothing in return," she bit out, not moving an inch toward him.

A spike of desire shot through him. Devon Caravelle didn't know what she was asking him. Ironic, that. He reminded himself that he wanted nothing, no woman, no emotional entanglement, no connection.

"You need to calm yourself."

"I don't think I'll be calm ever again. At least until this is over." She shuddered.

"They'll never bother you again." He said the words lightly, but a fire burned in his belly.

"You can't make that kind of a promise. If it's not those two men, there will be others."

"I can protect you."

Her glance was derisive. "Don't be absurd. You're the one I have most to fear. Although for the moment, I will sit down next to you. As you see—I'm absolutely confident that I won't swoon at your feet. You must think me the rankest amateur."

But even with her feeble attempt at humor, her statement rang false. She sank down onto the ground, the bark of the tree snagging the material of her skirt. She made certain not an inch of their bodies touched. His face appeared suddenly savage to her, the dark stubble of his beard throwing into sharp relief the stark contours of his face, the arrogant line of his strong nose.

"You're certainly not an amateur, Devon Caravelle," he said softly, watching as she carefully stretched beside him, arranging her skirts with anxious movements. "Your performance at Armathwaite was convincing to say the least. You had me fooled for a while."

A light flush suffused her skin, belying that she was the consummate actress, one who exploited, for her own purposes, the undeniable passion that flared between them. She had tasted and tested her power—a worrisome realization and yet he knew he could not dismiss his own role in the deception.

"I might make a similar observation about you, sir," she said stiffly, plucking at her skirts.

"But then I was hardly a virgin."

"Why should that make a difference? It's only you men who place such a ridiculous premium on purity, as though women were merely property."

"To think that I had nearly forgotten how opinionated you are."

"I don't know why we're even talking about this," she said, feeling the first drops of rain, like tears, fall on her cheeks.

Blackburn looked up at the sky and then moved with long-legged strides to his saddlebags nearby. He shook out a tarpaulin and quickly secured the ends with two good-sized rocks, suspending the remainder to the lowest branches of their tree. He worked swiftly, with an economy of movement, before sitting back down next to her.

"So what will it be, Devon?" He wiped his hands on his breeches.

Her gray eyes widened at the question and her breathing came faster. "Why do you assume that I've agreed to work with you against Le Comte?"

His gaze locked with hers. "That's precisely the problem. At this point, I can't make any assumptions."

"So you came after me—when you discovered that seduction didn't quite have the effect that you were after." Her delicate jaw was set hard.

"Believe me—I've hardly begun." His words were insulting, insinuating, a match thrown on tinder. She stiffened and inched away from him.

They both knew to what he was referring. "Our sexual interlude was both pleasurable and meaningless, Blackburn." The rapid rise and fall of her chest indicated that she was becoming increasingly agitated. Or aroused. "I understand completely the motives behind your seduction."

"I can offer you much more than de Maupassant." He leaned his head back, exposing the muscled length of his neck, the leanness of his jaw.

She raised her brows, mocking him. "Sensations more gratifying than what Le Comte could supply, you mean?"

"Can't say that I'm surprised he didn't get there first." His body tightened at the thought of her in another man's arms, in another man's bed.

Her voice dropped a few chill degrees and she buried her fists in the folds of her coarse skirt. "This is just a contest to you, isn't it? I'm no different from that godforsaken score, or possibly even less important."

Devon Caravelle was an incredibly good actress. He detected the hurt in her tone, in the soft flush of her cheeks. He noted abruptly that his breathing had become as disordered as hers and that her pupils had dilated in a combustible combination of anger and desire.

Blackburn's blood surged, searing beneath his clothes despite the dampness rising from the earth beneath them.

"Don't play the vulnerable victim with me, Mademoiselle." Arousal stirred hotly, angrily, in his groin. "You knew exactly what you were doing when you first agreed to de Maupassant's scheme to abduct and involve me in your plans. And you knew exactly what you were doing last night when you were willing to trade your body for information."

Devon stared back at him as though barely comprehending. "You dare judge me when you spend your time whoring with women like Susannah Treadwell? And when you were willing to trade *your body* for my cooperation last night?" The rain began a pointed staccato on the canvas overhead.

Blackburn saw the faint pulse in the tender hollow of her neck, this woman he neither understood nor trusted.

"I think it's a little late to be lamenting our lost innocence," he said harshly for both their benefits. He adjusted one of the rocks, securing their canopy with his booted foot, knowing they were treading on dangerous territory. His territory.

"You'll forgive me for my suspicions. You're more than a talented pianist. Over the past twenty-four hours I've seen you connive, manipulate, strategize, seduce, and escape with your life and virtue intact, all with a finesse that takes even my breath away. A finesse that could only be learned from a master—Brendan Clifton." Blackburn paused significantly, deliberately stoking the fire now. "I would have thought he'd spare you involvement in the more unwholesome aspects of his life."

"You're one to judge, Monsieur le Marquess." She crossed her arms defensively, the French inflection of her syllables more pronounced in her antagonism. "You *claim* to have knowledge of my father's work, but judging by your remarks you know very little."

Cursing the rain under his breath, Blackburn wished that were true, that he were not trapped as he was now, buried alive under a bedrock of lies that would remain, by necessity, between them until the bitter end. And the end, he was convinced, would be bitter.

A damp wind blew through the young leaves of the sheltering oaks. Wrapped in her servant's skirt, Devon appeared fragile and defenseless but Blackburn resisted the urge to touch her.

"I knew enough about his work, trust me. And, for your sake, I need to know how much you were involved in his various projects."

The wariness was apparent in the rigidity of her shoulders, the straightening of her spine. "Why would I ever trust you? All you've done is threaten me with the hangman's noose, for God's sake. I don't even know for certain that the men back at the tavern aren't in your employ. And you keep telling me that you know the circumstances around my father's murder, and yet you've revealed not one detail," she protested. "The only thing I know for certain about you is that you're more than eager to send me to seduce Le Comte." She looked away and stared into the wet copse a few feet ahead before adding bitterly, "Anything to get your hands on that damned score."

He turned toward her, their breaths mingling now, she was so close. Her hair streamed over her shoulders, pins loosening their hold in the dampness. "This is bigger than you or me, Devon." Blackburn made sure she could feel the intensity of his gaze. *Did she want to see Bonaparte escape from St. Helena?* He didn't want to hear her answer to the question. "The sooner you accept that fact, the better."

"I can't," she said in a half whisper, fighting against the drift of a simmering yearning, trying to keep her anger at him alive.

He couldn't ignore the shivery tone of her voice. "I'm the one you can trust," he said, still not touching her directly, but the flash of arousal was clear in his eyes. He sensed vulnerability held perilously in check. He'd exploited her need once before, a coldly conceived component of his own strategy, just like the wicked throb pulsing between his legs at that very moment.

Not so indifferent. Not so disengaged. And not so dispassionate.

She was close to surrender and he took one of her hands in his. Devon didn't resist the simple gesture. Her fingers were slender and strong, the palms broadly smooth, hands of a pianist. "You know I've yet to hear you play," he said in an intimate tone as the rain outside their cocoon began descending in earnest.

"I studied with my mother for years and then at the Conservatoire," she revealed carefully, combing the fingers of her free hand through her hair, the gesture all innocence, all allure. "She and my father shared a great love of music."

Devon didn't try to withdraw her hand from his larger one but turned her face away, as though afraid of where he was leading her but powerless as a leaf buffeted by a strong gale. Blackburn was well aware that the innocent stroking of his thumb inside her wrist evoked sensations that were making it difficult for her to think clearly.

"It won't work," he said in that singularly suggestive tone that was his. "You can't run from me."

"What do you want?" She jerked her hand from his, moving from a sitting position until she was kneeling away from him on the damp earth. A pin tumbled from her hair falling into her lap and she tossed it aside in frustration.

"Just give it up." His voice was darkly persuasive. "Let me help you."

Defensively, she shook her head mutely. *Need.* What did she need? Her body she had already given him, but she couldn't afford to give him anything else.

"I'm not so easily fooled, Blackburn." She crossed her arms against the firing of her senses, the flush of physical lust racing over her skin, the unfamiliarity of flesh warring with reason. "This whole situation revolves around what *you* need and I'm not prepared to share anything with you, my mind or my body."

"What if I told you why I came after you—would it make a difference?" he asked, knowing that it would, and a risk he was willing to take, adding yet another layer of lies between them.

The distance she kept between them was her answer. "Will this be the truth, or some variation on the theme?"

Blackburn's mouth widened in a smile. "You be the judge."

She was edgy and exhausted. "You're getting wet you know." He pointed to the border of the tarpaulin dripping steadily and dampening her cloak.

She eyed the chasm that yawned between them. Blackburn smiled knowingly as Devon regarded the small space between them with suspicion.

"You have my word—I won't come near you." He placed a hand over his heart, lying once again.

Wordlessly, she settled herself gingerly next to him, irrationally concerned that some part of her might make contact with him. Blackburn passed her his jacket which she accepted silently, shrugging the garment over her shoulders.

"So why did you come after me?" she asked finally.

Even as she posed the question, her eyes drifted closed against him, an attempt at shutting out reality in this makeshift shelter with the tavern brutes in the distance and Blackburn's presence a heartbeat away.

In a thicket a small animal scuttled over the wet underbrush, the rain having slowed to a drizzle.

He heard the words rumbling from his chest. "To keep you safe, safe from the truth a little while longer."

Her murmur was inarticulate, a soft exhalation from her lips. She appeared bewildered and defenseless, a hundred miles away from the detached, calculating woman he knew her to be. He could barely hear the soft rain over the hammering of his pulse.

His mouth filled with hunger. The situation was becoming untenable, bloody impossible. He had a job to do.

All he had to do was remember.

It had been another beautiful woman who had led his brother Edward into de Maupassant's trap.

Blackburn felt stirrings of an emotion he thought all but lost, feelings he couldn't trust himself to have, passions that could make him vulnerable. Better to exploit those passions and harness the *lust* to tie Devon Caravelle to him, until she was as inseparable from him as his shadow.

His dark thoughts were interrupted by her soft voice. "I don't need protection, Blackburn, particularly from the truth." Her eyes were sad.

"Are you certain?" he asked searching her face. He could see the faint creases that radiated from the corners of her eyes.

Blackburn didn't have to touch her to feel her beginnings of surrender. Her eyes were unguarded, confused. He couldn't resist brushing the high curve of her cheeks, his thumb tracing the fullness of a lower lip, conscious of the dampness of her chemise and the length of her legs as she lay against him. They rested in their small shelter, although the rain had all but stopped.

Devon ran her hand along his shirt, feeling the solidity of the bone and muscle beneath. Catching her hand in his, Blackburn brought her fingers to his lips.

It was different this time, they both acknowledged silently, a moment stripped bare of schemes and manipulations, the past and the future, leaving only the present. Devon felt heat rise deep from within her body as Blackburn traced butterfly kisses along her brow, the tip of her nose, the outlines of her mouth.

"You're all right, you're fine," he breathed into the curve of her ear. He kissed her and found that her mouth was succulent, sweet, warm, and responsive to the driving rhythm of his tongue. On a slow moan, Blackburn hotly and harshly plunged into the shreds of her resistance as if battering down a castle wall.

He knew it was weak and desperate to want anything this much, and for all the wrong reasons, but his body overruled his mind. His lips moved to the slim column of her throat, tracing her breastbone, the delicate flutter of her pulse beneath her skin. He paused to savor the darkening passion in the depths of her eyes, igniting his senses like a blast furnace.

"What is it that you do to me?" The question was torn from his throat.

Devon's reply was a faltering murmur, defenseless in the onslaught of feeling prompted by his marauding hands, the sensitive fingers that outlined her lips. Anxious to take him inside her, her mouth parted and he drove his thumb inside.

Her tongue was succulent as honey moving recklessly along the length of his fingers, sucking, nibbling, showing how much she needed him. He groaned at the lust rushing through his veins as he dropped forward to take her breast in his mouth, drawing it between his teeth, into the warmth of his mouth, sucking through the thin fabric of her chemise. Her breasts were responsive, and he parted the thin muslin with heated deliberation. The hard buds beckoned, made all the more erotic by the satin resilience of her skin. He stroked hungrily, kissing them, licking them, sucking, and nibbling while she writhed in his arms. He bent his head to both nipples, sweeping his tongue along them, quickly flicking back and forth.

Devon felt close to fainting from the sheer pleasure of his mouth. "You shouldn't be able to make me feel this way," she panted, her passion mingling now with anger at herself.

Just one more time. And then she would be free of him, she lied to herself watching him strip the black shirt from his body. His broad shoulders narrowed to a lean abdomen and hips, banded by a ridge of tight sinew and muscles.

Blackburn sensed the change in her, the tensing of her body, the focusing of her passion. Her eyes burned brightly as she ran a slim hand along the sable satin of his hair and he saw her full lips move closer to his. "Just one more time," she whispered the vow into his mouth. "And then we'll finish with this."

Clouds parted, and in the fading afternoon sunlight, she rose like a wood nymph from his arms to stand before him, resplendent in her nudity save for her rough skirt pooling around her waist. Blackburn reached for a fine ankle, his hand then encircling the elegant arch of a foot before roaming to the sensuous curve of a knee.

Resting her arms on his shoulders, she buried her face in the coolness of his silky hair, breathing in the aroma of his maleness. She wanted to absorb and annihilate him with her desire while going wild with the feel of his hands massaging the firmness of her buttocks. She felt her skirt slither to the ground as he traced the taut globes before moving to the curls between her legs.

Blackburn lay back, pulling her to a kneeling position, straddling him. Skillfully, he slid his fingers into her slick folds to feel her readiness, dancing over the core of her desire, slick with want. She moaned her pleasure urging him on with the grinding of her hips against his hands until she thought she would explode.

This was what they needed, a fire that burned so brightly it would incinerate into ashes their longing for each other. Devon felt the flames build, melding her desire and anger for this man whose embrace was so wildly voluptuous. He was good, a small corner of her mind registered, an expert of female flesh whose practiced tongue trailed between her breasts to her abdomen until she heard herself whimper for relief.

"Blackburn," she begged, "I can't endure any more . . ."

He smiled in a way that made her melt before kissing her deeply, one arm lashed tightly around her waist. "Capitulating so soon?" he taunted, his teeth moving from her mouth to graze the soft lobe of her ear as he pulled her to the damp earth.

It would always be a contest between them. A contest of wills, deceit, and passion. In the last at least, she would have the upper hand, the craving in her blood charging her determination. Her eyes heavy with sensuality, she replied with a slow kiss to his wide mouth, "Never underestimate a worthy opponent." Her hands roved to his narrow hips. Eager to explore, determined to overcome her inexperience, she unbuttoned his straining breeches. Devon felt him spring free, hot and heavy against her hand, his size overwhelming.

Blackburn threw back his head enjoying the feel of her soft hands traveling the length of him, intoxicated by her challenge.

"I'd never be so foolish as to underestimate you." And wondered why his self-control evaporated at her inexperienced touch, her untutored hands. A virgin the night before, she was demonstrating a reckless abandon, willfully skimming along the ripple of big ribs and taut muscle before taking the weight of his erection back into her hands. Hungrily, she wrapped her fingers around it and felt it twitch impressively against her palm. He heard her make a little hum of pleasure deep in her throat as she bent low with parted lips against the tightness of his abdomen and for a delirious moment he was almost certain she meant to pleasure him with her mouth. Devon was wet heat playing with him, mistress of the moment, enjoying his torment as he lay beneath her.

His body jolted upward and he thought he was going to explode. "We're not even close to finished." He vowed revenge and, grasping her by the shoulders, pulled her over him to straddle his hips. Devon's eyes widened in surprise as he slid his long, capable fingers into the heated flesh between her legs. Need cut through her like a knife as she arched beneath his hands.

Blackburn could feel her pressed hot and wet against him. "Is this what you want?" he taunted hoarsely, his free hand cradling her buttocks. His only answer was to see her expression dissolve into pleasure. He lifted her and then glided her down, inch by inch, over his pulsing erection so she could feel every thick, iron ridge.

Positioning one hand over the soft curls of her mound, he eased between her distended folds, through the warm heat, to find her hard eager nub. He brushed it once, softly, with the pad of his thumb and watched Devon begin to gasp, her breaths coming in little pants. His hand spread her wide as he lowered her completely, slowly onto his shaft.

His hugeness filled her to the hilt. Devon's body came alive with each demanding thrust, meeting each incursion with a grind of her hips. Slow, then fast. And when she thought she had all of him inside her, he pushed yet another inch into her wet tightness. Playing with her nipples with each plunge, Blackburn sent waves of sensation to her core until she lost control.

Something snapped, a roll of sensation that made her want to draw him into herself, leaving nothing except a blinding flare to mark the convulsions blasting through her body. Riding him until the earth and trees around them began to spin, she exploded in a series of undulations until gradually becoming aware that he was kissing her lips, moving her beneath him as he quickly shed his breeches before wrapping her legs around him.

Now he roused with long, slow strokes building to his own climax while murmuring hot words of desire against her neck, her breasts, the indentation of her waist. Restlessly, she began to recover, moving beneath him, making small, soft noises in the back of her throat. Blackburn withdrew from her, then drove deep inside, holding himself at a perfect angle as she dragged her pelvis searchingly against his erection.

Again, he stroked his full length into her unbelievable tightness, holding himself higher to make that pivotal contact. Sliding his hand between them, he ran his finger over her sensitive nub, his mouth capturing her whimpers with his tongue. He stroked her deep, then almost withdrawing, tormenting her again with his fingers until she rose frantically beneath him. Instinct drove hold of Devon and her hips tilted up to take Blackburn deeper still. Almost breathless, she felt herself on the brink again and, with one last rock of his hips, plunging deep, she was gone.

Driving into her with a power that robbed both of them of their breaths, he eased her legs over his shoulders, his thrusts intensifying, his breathing shallow and savage until he could no longer contain his carnal fury and came in a low, extended growl of release on her thighs, his timing flawless.

Hearts slamming in tandem and with a faint sheen of sweat covering their bodies, they lay together cradled on the ground.

Blackburn swore under his breath, pressing a last agonizing kiss to the damp skin of her neck. How could he have ever let it come to this? He wanted her again, right now, to pulse into her body, to feed voraciously on her lips, tongue, and nipples.

He couldn't control her. He couldn't control himself around her. His heart contracted against his ribs.

Devon listened to the drip of water from the leaves overhead, the aroma of the earth mingling now with the dusky scent of sex. She exulted in the seal of Blackburn's lips on her luxuriously satiated flesh, but like the oncoming night, thoughts began to intrude on her false bliss. Pleasure beyond all words, the power of sensuality, the secrets between a man and woman. A dangerous thing.

Moving from Blackburn's arms, she turned her face to the indifference of the darkening sky, willing nature to erase the recent past.

How could she have ever imagined one more time would be enough?

They had begun to dress in silence moments earlier, wisely declining to exchange words before regaining a semblance of control, embarrassed by the unaccustomed intensity of what had begun in lust and had ended in uncontrollable, libidinous mayhem. The soft air, benign now, lapped gently at the no longer useful tarpaulin.

Devon shrugged Blackburn's jacket over her chemise. She thrust her hands into the garment's deep pockets and regarded him unflinchingly.

"Don't take me for a total naïf, Blackburn." Her voice was still husky despite a growing anger with herself. "I know exactly what you're doing—aside from *protecting me from the truth.*"

"So tell me," he invited, watching her closely with a forced casualness she couldn't afford to ignore. "What am I up to?" He leaned carelessly against the trunk of an old oak, arms crossed against his chest.

Her eyes were drawn ineluctably to the elegant length of his strong legs. "You're trying to overwhelm me with your— how can I put it—*ardor* in order to steal away the last of my reason." She cleared her voice and secured the last button of his jacket with nerveless fingers. "So that I become mere putty in your hands."

Blackburn did not miss the sarcasm that infused her tone. "You can hardly accuse me of making any secret of my intentions. As you'll recall from last evening, you agreed quite strenuously to my overtures. Next thing, you'll accuse me of having corrupted a virgin." He began to fasten his shirt, every line in his body infused with athletic grace.

Devon sent him a look that could cut glass. "Don't even try to use that tactic with me. If you think that my relative inexperience in these matters will color my perception of you or the tangled mess we find ourselves in, then you're sadly mistaken." She clenched her fists in the pockets of his jacket. "But I am willing to admit that we share an attraction for one another. I also believe that this attraction is best overcome by exhausting these . . . unwholesome emotions."

Blackburn's eyes were coldly amused at the sudden primness. "I trust that I can accommodate you in that respect since I find *exhausting* those potentially unwholesome emotions, as you put it, distinctly pleasurable."

It was far too late to feign embarrassment. Devon forced herself to acknowledge that, although Blackburn had seduced her, it was hardly against her will. She had no recourse except to admit that she too played a part in the mad game of pleasure that held them in its grasp.

"Just so you understand one thing," she said, her posture rigid. "I am no man's mistress. My body is my own and only I choose how and when I bestow my favors. And as for virtue," she paused deliberately, "as one of your own countrywomen wrote, it can only flourish among equals."

If everything else was lies between them, posturings, strategies, and machinations, at this moment at least, Blackburn believed Devon Caravelle meant what she said, conviction ringing in her voice.

Devon caught the flash in Blackburn's eyes as they locked with hers. "Mary Wollstonecraft also wrote that 'we reason deeply, when we forcibly feel,' " he said. He then proceeded to tuck his shirttails into his breeches and Devon was hard-pressed to look away from his hands, large yet lean, and the easy grace with which he moved.

"I'm surprised that you admit to being familiar with her work, as most men consider her a pernicious influence."

"You should know by now that I am not most men."

As if she could ever forget. Even in the clearing among the oak trees, he seemed to take up all the space in her mind and in her emotions. It was weak of her to want him so much, a need that was fierce, frightening, and threatening to obliterate her sense of self.

Her mouth was bruised from his kisses. Every limb felt languid, boneless. A taste for the Marquess of Blackburn was a dangerous thing.

We reason deeply, when we forcibly feel. She could only hope that their intimacy would eventually purge the passion he so easily unleashed. How could she let go of her fundamental principles, her belief in loyalty and honor, swept away by an avalanche of wild emotion?

Devon moved on trembling legs toward the horse that stood patiently in the clearing. "Before I ride with you anywhere, before I stay with you one more moment, I want you to tell me what happened to my father—who killed him? What *truth* are you so eager to protect me from, Blackburn?"

His blue eyes darkened against the falling light filtering through the trees. "If I answer your question, you just might discover that you need me more than I need you."

"I'll take that risk. You still haven't answered my question." She turned decisively to leave, pretending to know which direction would eventually take her to a road. She should have looked over her shoulder because, suddenly, he stood right behind her, an inch away from pulling her back against him. The fear she kept tightly coiled in her stomach flared to life.

"What makes you think I'd let you go," he said in a low voice. And he had yet to touch her. His dark voice, deadly calm, continued. "We both want to find the *Eroica*, don't we, Devon?" he said speaking to her rigid back. "You know why your father was so interested in that damned composition, but I couldn't care less at this point. All I know is that if de Maupassant has it, it's in my interest to get in his way."

His voice moved lower. "We can find it together. Work on the score together."

She shook off the hypnotic quality of his words, resisting the urge to give in to him, to throw herself in his arms and accept his help. But it was all illusion, the promise of refuge prompted by the coldest calculation.

Did he take her for a fool? She whirled around, her eyes gray tempests. "For the last time—who murdered him?"

"The truth?"

"The truth."

Even through the dense trees they could see the sun beginning to set, burning through the last of the dampness, penetrating their thick copse of trees. Blackburn stood absolutely still, weighing his response, the most arresting, compelling man she would ever know. That knowledge hurt her heart as she listened to his next words.

"De Maupassant murdered your father. And I have the proof."

The world might have stopped spinning on its axis. The early evening was suddenly so still that Devon thought she could hear individual blades of grass move in the damp breeze.

"That makes absolutely no sense." Blackburn's strong profile flickered before her eyes as she tried to absorb the impact of his words. "It's impossible. Why would Le Comte murder my father?" she asked mindlessly. "He needed him."

"Your father," Blackburn told her flatly, "was neck-deep in espionage activities, at once in the employ of Fouché, the next moment reporting to Castlereagh, playing France off against England, helping encode the components of a weapon so destructive that it could bring the world's greatest powers to their knees." He paused for the length of a gunshot. "De Maupassant wanted in—and your father most probably resisted."

The horse whinnied nearby, impatiently pawing the earth, reminding them both that they would eventually have to leave their version of a poisoned paradise. Devon pushed the hair back from her face, her eyes glaring into Blackburn's.

"Prove it to me," she demanded recklessly. "Or is it revenge you want—a convenient proxy for the man you wrongly believe betrayed England? Why not just throw me to the magistrates as you've threatened?"

His tone hardened. "Don't tempt me. Right now I have my sights set on de Maupassant."

Somehow she believed him, although her better instincts warned her of too many danger signals. It was too simple, the two of them united against a single foe. And she would never, could never believe that her father was part of any traitorous, destructive scheme. He had been the consummate intellectual, cool, scholarly, his passion reserved for her mother and his work.

Le Comte—was it possible?

Devon continued walking toward the horse, stopping short to throw him a cold glance over her shoulder. "You say you have evidence that Le Comte murdered my father—so where is it?" She was acutely aware that she might be walking into a trap, the wet earth giving way beneath her feet.

"At Armathwaite."

"Where all will be revealed, no doubt," she said sarcastically. She turned to appraise him dispassionately, once again the mistress of intrigue that he'd first met at Blackfriars Bridge, as cold as the polar ice caps. "Very well, Blackburn," she said as if she made such arrangements every day of her life. "Show me the proof and I'll bring you the *Eroica*—along with my unadulterated cooperation. If Le Comte is in any way responsible for my father's death, I'll never allow him to unearth its secrets."

"I'm glad to hear it." Darkness was fast approaching, obscuring the angular lines of his face. He quickly took the horse's bridle.

Devon stayed rooted to the ground. "If I find out you're lying, all agreements are off," she said, demanding her own pound of flesh.

"I can live with that."

She had to look up at him, as he already sat in the saddle, the black horse snorting and skittering sideways.

"Are you ready?" He held out his hand to her, the animal beneath him impatient to be off, rearing on its hind legs, grass flying in all directions.

Against her better judgment she answered, "Armathwaite, then." And put her hand in his.

Chapter 10

It was unfashionably late to be riding in Hyde Park, but Lady Susannah Treadwell had good reason to be trotting sedately along Rotten Row. She knew she presented an elegant image, attired as she was in an emerald green riding habit, a long skirt draped softly over her polished boots. Her jacket was tight with an impossibly narrow waist and, most important, a top hat and flowing veil concealed her expression.

She had received a note earlier in the day from Bertrand Lacan asking her to meet him at the south end of Hyde Park with its four-mile-long riding route. In the seventeenth century the road was used by William the Third who had found the walk from Kensington Palace to St. James too dangerous. He had oil lamps installed instead along the path and it quickly became a stylish haunt for London's elite to see and be seen.

The bridle path was deserted in late afternoon, the ton having already decamped to pursue other pastimes. Susannah reined in her handsome hunter when she spied the dappled gray mare mincing toward her, Lacan astride. With fine-boned legs, the horse sidled and fretted, before matching its pace to her hunter's.

"Good day, Madame." Lacan tipped his hat in Susannah's

direction, slipping the reins into one hand. "So kind of you to meet with me here and at such an unfashionable hour."

Lady Treadwell played along as though they had not just spent the previous evening exhausting every last one of Lacan's libidinous inclinations. Not that he was an inventive lover, thankfully. However, the encounter did cement their relationship in more ways than one.

"Indeed, Bertrand, ordinarily I wouldn't dare set foot here in the afternoon. But then again, the dearth of society at this time of day does serve our purpose. And you do have information that simply cannot wait, I understand."

Lacan's arm flexed as he eased the reins and the two horses moved to a smooth, even pace. A new determination simmered in his eyes, the ambivalence she'd sensed at the concert having evaporated into hardened resentment. "My men did manage to find her." His voice was clipped and they both knew to whom he was referring.

"You mean with *him*—or alone?" A hint of anxiety colored her tone.

"It's rather complicated and I won't bore you with the details, Madame. Let us say that they are now together, having fled north."

Lady Treadwell's blood pulsed thick and dark. "We can't have that now, can we, Bertrand." She gripped the whip as they rounded a sharp curve by a stand of trees, the tracks of the two horses tangling behind them. The Marquess was *hers*. "He's probably taken her to that place he has in the country."

"I could *perhaps* tell Le Comte," Lacan muttered enigmatically, handling his reins softly. "But I'm not certain whether that's prudent."

Susannah glanced at him sharply. "Why not simply dispose of her?"

"Were it that simple, Madame." In the clear light of the afternoon, it appeared an appealing, if unfeasible, option. "She's too valuable to all of us. Without her, the formula remains useless and buried."

Susannah twitched the reins and the hunter's muscles convulsed beneath her. "I would prefer that she remained useless and buried." The sentiment shocked neither Susannah nor Lacan. Eliminating both a potential rival for the affections of the Marquess of Blackburn and a traitor to France was worth the trouble.

"First things first." Lacan's voice held a certain regret, along with a determination that set Susannah's nerves on edge.

"Well, then, what would you have us do?" she asked impatiently.

"The longer that bastard Bonaparte is on St. Helena, the sooner his legend has a chance of fading. De Maupassant will want to strike quickly which means he needs the formula in his hands as soon as possible."

Susannah smiled her satisfaction, understanding dawning. "After which Devon Caravelle will prove dispensable? I won't have to wait overly long?"

"*Précisément.*" The one word held a world of promise.

"But then what will you do with the formula, *if* you wrest it from Le Comte?" inquired Susannah, the words coming from behind her veil.

"Do you really care?"

Susannah wondered briefly whether Lacan's plans extended to both Le Comte and Devon Caravelle. To dispense with a peasant, a revolutionary, would be considered a patriotic duty. To expose Le Comte—well that would be potentially ruinous.

Susannah adjusted the tulle on her top hat. "No," she smirked. "I don't really care. But I do know that you'll want something from me in exchange for eliminating that French trollop and traitor. More than the usual," she said meaningfully. "What will it be, *mon amour?*"

Lacan's mare pulled away slightly, her ears pinned back.

"The letter in Le Comte's possession," Lacan said abruptly, looking past Susannah's sultry promises, now focused on his sense of obligation.

"Ah yes, the one we can't do without. The one that's necessary to completing the formula." Lady Treadwell feigned consternation, bringing her horse to a halt. "My goodness, all this intrigue, my head is absolutely spinning." But her glance was as sharp as a fisherwoman's. "You can consider it done, Monsieur. You will have your letter."

Lacan brought his mare up short, his thin torso seeming to elongate in the saddle. His rheumy eyes hardened as he took Susannah's fingers and kissed them. "And in time, you will have Devon Caravelle—*useless and buried*. You may consider it done, Madame. With pleasure."

Blackburn was usually much better at this sort of thing. Angry with himself and with the woman upstairs, he paced the drawing room at Armathwaite, gazing into the snapping fire of the grate, looking for answers in the embers. He didn't like what he saw.

The heat warmed his skin, reminding him all too readily of his freshly exposed weaknesses. Blackburn knew well enough how to identify and exploit vulnerability, a tactic that had, in turn, taught him to guard his own susceptibilities closely, to the point where he had, until recently, believed none remained.

After all, he was the man who had stood by unflinchingly and watched his brother's life mercilessly snuffed out.

And now he would stand by unflinchingly and send Devon Caravelle to the Frenchman's bed.

There was no other choice.

By nature he knew himself to be a cold and analytical man, yet even when he was physically removed from Devon's presence, he could scarcely outrun the chaos that clamored in his head. It was something he could barely admit to himself and the last thing he wanted Devon Caravelle to know.

The clatter of dishes in the hallway captured his attention. Turning from the fireplace, he turned to see Burgess balancing a heavy silver tray that held a cold supper for Devon. Soon she would be back in the drawing room, a veritable tornado, demanding he reveal what he knew about her father's murder.

Blackburn remembered the dispatch from Wellington that had been waiting at his and Devon's return to Armathwaite. Plans were on track. History would march on despite heartache, misdirected emotion, and family loyalties.

He walked over to the small stand of books on the opposite side of the drawing room, doubt still lingering in his mind. The men at the tavern, somehow he didn't think they were there at the orders of de Maupassant. It wasn't his style.

No, Le Comte would come for Devon Caravelle, to see with his own eyes the relationship he'd forged between his protégée and his intractable opponent. And by that time, Blackburn thought, reaching for the thick folio bound in tan leather sent by Wellington, a sensually satiated and emotionally bemused Devon Caravelle would be thoroughly married to the Marquess of Blackburn's cause.

And primed to cooperate flawlessly with his plans.

Cradling the folio in his hands, he thumbed through its pages, the black and white notes of the music by Beethoven seemingly innocent ink marks on sheafs of paper, but marks which had their own particular kind of power, a power he could manipulate. It was exactly the kind of strategic thinking that made Blackburn the amoral operative Wellington had counted on for years.

Blackburn knew perfectly well what he was doing, and for whom. Exploiting a beautiful woman as means to an end was hardly the worst of crimes to add to a list of sins.

Confidence restored, he saw Burgess coming back down the stairs without the dinner tray. "By the way, Burgess," he said with the gaze of a man with no limits left. "Bring Mademoiselle Caravelle to the music room once she has dined."

Blackburn closed the cover of the folio with a snap but didn't return it to its place on the shelf. He knew that music was integral to Devon's being.

And since he already had her body, now he just needed her soul.

"You want me to do what?" Devon's voice stuck in her throat.

Burgess had escorted her to a richly paneled salon where they found Blackburn casually leaning against a small upright piano and sipping a brandy.

"The piano has just been tuned, as a matter of fact," Blackburn said as though they were just passing the time in aimless conversation, "although I must apologize that it's not much of an instrument, given your talents."

Devon looked up from the piano and let her eyes drift over his black hair and his wide mouth now set in a crooked smile.

Damn him straight to hell.

It was in the air. She steeled herself, knowing that the evening would hold more of the usual duplicitous games, subtle manipulations, and irresistible seductions. What was worse, Devon had to admit Blackburn's strategy was working like a finely engineered clock, her emotions as tightly pitched as piano wire; all the while he stood before her untouched by the impact of their explosive physical intimacy. Limned by the candlelight, he was sheer male beauty, austerity marking the lines of his face saved by the wide, mobile mouth and midnight eyes. Her body contracted in response.

"I want you to play the piano for me," he said simply. His glance took in her slender form now clothed in a demure blue dress that Burgess had magically produced from the depths of a wardrobe. She wasn't looking her best, the delicate fabric hanging from her shoulders, the lace of her sleeves drooping to her fingertips.

Impatient with herself, she exhaled sharply, her gaze moving from him to the sheets of music already waiting for her at the keyboard. "Here you are suggesting that I play as though we had all the time in the world." She shook her head and tapped the piano for emphasis. "I want the proof you promised me. Now."

"And that's what I intend to do—provide you with the proof," he said, raising the glass of brandy to his lips.

"Now you're talking in riddles. What does playing the piano for you have to do with the evidence I'm seeking. And, according to you, we have no time to lose—what about Le Comte's men allegedly lurking in the bushes?"

"We can expect de Maupassant in the morning."

"And then what—the horse-trading you talked about earlier?" She couldn't keep the urgency, born of helplessness, from her voice.

"Play." Blackburn said the word with lethal softness. He took up every inch of space within the confines of the room, filling it with his presence in a way Devon found overpowering. Although she knew that she would find none, she looked to his face for answers or explanations. His expression remained inscrutable.

Sparing him no further glance, she slid onto the piano bench, cool against the silk of her skirt. She touched the yellowed keys, their tone resonant in the narrowness of the room as her gaze drifted to the sheet music in front of her, the "Sonata in C-Sharp Minor."

"Beethoven—how appropriate," she said, taken aback momentarily. "Beethoven himself called it a sonata *quasi una fantasia*."

"A sonata somewhat like a fantasy, " Blackburn translated fluently, stepping back from the piano into the shadows of the room. "I also believe a critic named Rellstab referred to it as the 'Moonlight Sonata.' "

Devon stopped herself just in time from sending him an admiring glance. "That's right. Rellstab seemed to see in the calmness of the first movement a picture of moonlight streaming over ocean waves. It's a beautiful piece. I particularly love the first movement which, instead of a usual sonata form, is an adagio sostenuto built from a romance melody over triplets in the bass."

She could hear rather than see the smile in his voice. "I can't wait to have you play it."

Devon couldn't resist the approbation in his voice, although Blackburn's opinion of her should matter no more than anyone else's. In response to her predictable weakness, she pulled herself upright and straightened her spine before touching the keys and beginning to play.

The first notes seduced her as she knew they would, their deep serenity hinting at a rich complexity to come. She was reminded of the crescent moon that had lit their way back to Armathwaite, a beacon leading her toward a deepening passion that she both craved and feared. As she neared the last notes of the first sheet, she sensed Blackburn's presence at her side as he prepared to turn to the page that would introduce the notes of a graceful and delicate allegretto.

The music began to invade her soul, the beauty of the themes bringing a flood of emotion. It was a magnificence she could never get enough of, this melding of passion and logic, a carefully preserved balance defining the mathematical and yet magical relationship between notes. The sonata was a perfect piece of music and all too short. Devon waited that instant for Blackburn to turn to the last sheet, her eyes half closed in blissful concentration.

A pulse beat later, her hands frozen above the keyboard: "What's this—" Her voice broke.

It was the cover sheet of the *Eroica*, baptized the Third Symphony by Beethoven himself before it had been baptized in blood. The name *Bonaparte* still appeared prominently on the title page of the manuscript, but its presence had been scratched over so violently that the erasure left a hole in the parchment.

The room began to spin and she grabbed the sides of the

piano bench to steady herself. She felt faint and leaned her head forward onto both palms. The manuscript screamed "violence," the stains of blood spelling out the name *de Maupassant* written in a feeble hand that had surely been grasping to keep death at bay. Fighting to keep the nausea from rising to her throat, Devon knew the scrawl was her father's.

As if through a fog, she heard Blackburn say, "Have some brandy." Devon grasped the hard arm at her elbow, but pushed away the proffered snifter. "No . . . I'm all right . . . just give me a few minutes."

Blackburn set down the snifter and sat next to her on the piano bench, pulling her toward him as the heat from his body burned through the clammy coldness enveloping her. In an attempt at self-preservation, she let her mind go blank, allowing herself to lean back onto his chest. She wrenched her glance away from the bloodied page, wanting to hide her face like a child in the solid warmth of his shoulders.

"Take deep breaths." His voice low as his palm cupped the curve of her face, his thumb brushing softly at her unshed tears. Devon had never felt so weak in her life. She turned her face into the callused skin of his hand, breathing in his scent in shaky, unsteady breaths.

For a moment they were a frozen tableau, Blackburn keeping her safe from the demons that threatened, from ugliness she didn't want to see. Yet she knew that the harbor of his arms was an illusion and slowly forced her eyes open. His arms had been warm, but his eyes were cool, filled with a strange wariness. She straightened away from him.

His calm was incongruous. "You wanted the proof—the truth I was protecting you from—so here it is. In all its unvarnished reality."

Devon took a deep breath, her mind still numb, uncomprehending. "Where did you get this . . . this horrible thing?"

"Wellington's men were right behind de Maupassant," Blackburn said, rising from the piano bench, taking his warmth with him. "They retrieved the title page of the *Eroica* from the cottage at Blois—but not the score itself—from the scene of the murder."

The image chilled. Devon couldn't bear to imagine her father covered with blood as he felt life seep from his body. Their small cottage in the countryside. She felt the room begin to tilt again and her hands gripped the bench, holding on to her sanity.

"But why? Why would Le Comte want my father murdered? He would have been more useful to him alive," she said with conviction meant as a bulwark against a fresh onslaught of emotion.

Blackburn paused for a moment, wanting to hold something back. She sensed again the drive and self-possession that would always keep him well above torturous emotions like passion and love.

"Devon, I won't keep the truth from you," he finally said, hard-eyed. "I told you earlier, your father was involved in intelligence activities and we were never quite sure which side he supported. Obviously, the day de Maupassant arrived in Blois, Brendan Clifton was unwilling to cooperate for whatever reason." As though speaking from experience Blackburn added, "Trust me—de Maupassant doesn't respond well to obstacles thrown in his way."

Still trembling slightly, Devon rose from the piano bench watching Blackburn efficiently gather the sheets of music together and return them to a leather folio. He seemed so strong, so confident, as though nothing and no one could ever touch him, move him. She envied his invincibility.

"Are you sure you're all right?" His eyes were keen and quietly watchful.

At that moment Devon doubted that she would ever be normal again, but as the numbness began to lift like a heavy fog, she recognized the fearsome outlines of the path that she would take.

"I will do whatever I must, not only to get the score away

from Le Comte, but also to avenge my father's death. I want to see him punished and my father's name cleared. Even if that means working closely with you. I can't live with myself any other way," she said, her eyes level with the perfect angle of his jaw. She didn't want to see his reaction, his triumph at her submission.

Even if it means seducing Le Comte.

"I'm glad you see reason," Blackburn said, his tone neutral. He gestured to the settee in the corner of the room, now the consummate agent, a man whose life was devoted to the work of intelligence, to the exclusion of all else. "Sit down, and I'll tell you what I know."

As if she'd been pummeled, she moved stiffly to take a seat, her head turned away from the piano sitting innocently across from her.

She felt his eyes upon her and he looked, for the briefest second, as though he might take her in his arms and carry her to the settee. She was clearly delusional because Blackburn remained standing.

"It didn't begin with evil, Devon," she heard him say, a part of her still detached from reality. "From what we understand, your father was a passionate believer in the rights of man and in the humanistic principles of the French Revolution. *That's* where it all began."

"You're not telling me something I don't already know. My father and mother lived the spirit of the age," said Devon shakily. "They had read Rousseau and Voltaire and fervently believed that a new epoch was dawning—one where equality, rather than inherited privilege, would reign supreme."

"And they were willing—particularly your father—to guarantee the success of the Revolution."

"Let's not go there again. Please."

Blackburn's eyes hooded over. "If you choose to believe that your father—the brilliant cryptographer—had nothing to do with the original code, then I won't try to convince you otherwise," he said roughly. "What I do want is for you to care enough to help me find the manuscript and decipher the formula."

"Why? So that you can deliver what we discover to Wellington? If I didn't want to find proof of my father's innocence, I would simply destroy the *Eroica* itself. The formula isn't safe in anybody's hands."

"Why didn't your father simply destroy the manuscript when he had the chance, then?" Blackburn dropped his arms to his side, backing away from her. "Believe what you want, Devon. As for the formula, in the right hands, in Britain's hands, it can be used for good." He concluded, "Perhaps as your father intended."

"Yes—as my father intended," she echoed, suddenly exhausted by all the possible permutations of truth she was expected to weigh and examine. It seemed that too much rested on her shoulders, a burden that was becoming heavier by the moment. Maybe Blackburn was right and the formula could be used in the service of good, fulfilling the idealistic aspirations of her parents, fulfilling the tenets of equality, fraternity, and liberty. Devon sank into the settee, rubbing her temples in an attempt to quell her confusion.

"Devon—look at me."

And she did, noting again the way he had of turning his dark blue eyes upon her, then piercing her through to her soul.

"Don't you want to hear the rest of the story?" His voice took on an unmistakable edge, the lines bracketing his mouth more pronounced.

Devon nodded mutely.

Blackburn rested one elbow on the piano, his stance deliberately casual, his voice seeming to come from far away. "I thought you would want to know how the formula found its way into the symphony in the first place."

"Go ahead," she said more calmly now, looking at the floor, intently studying the pattern of the parquet.

"We have reason to believe that the idea of dedicating the

symphony to Napoleon was suggested by then ambassador to Vienna, Jean-Baptiste Bernadotte. Marshal Bernadotte may have played a role in the genesis of the *Eroica*, as Beethoven became a frequent visitor to Bernadotte's salon at the French embassy."

Devon looked up. "My father said that Beethoven wrote the piece not in honor of Bonaparte's military victories, but because the first consul had produced political order out of the chaos of a bloody revolution."

"Quite right," agreed Blackburn. "Beethoven also held a degree of self-identification with Napoleon. The French ruler was barely a year older than he was. Both came from less than aristocratic backgrounds and both men hailed from provincial areas and had to go to capital cities to achieve success."

Devon straightened in her seat to face Blackburn squarely. "My father also told me that Beethoven admired Bonaparte in the role of a republican consul, but not in the role of an autocrat like Julius Caesar. Did you know that in his study Beethoven had on his writing table a small bust of Lucius Brutus, Caesar's assassin?"

"Your father must have known Beethoven very well," Blackburn said pointedly.

"But that doesn't mean he had anything to do with the formula originally," Devon snapped back, some of her strength returning.

"In any case," Blackburn continued smoothly, "we now believe that Bernadotte asked Beethoven to compose a symphony, with the help of a young cryptographer . . ."

Devon interrupted him with a dismissive wave of her hand, *"Not my father."*

"Use logic, for God's sake, Devon." Blackburn straightened away from the piano and ran a hand through his hair, his only indication of frustration.

"We are talking about my family, Blackburn—you can know nothing of that sort of devotion."

Devon saw the muscle in his jaw pulsing hard, his face

suddenly lined with fatigue and an emotion she didn't recognize.

"You're quite right," he said with a sudden cold anger that chilled the lamplit room. "I would know nothing of family or compassion. How discerning of you."

For a moment, she regretted her words but, seeing an opportunity for advantage, she pushed on and rose to pace the small salon, each step punctuating her statements. "A friendship between Beethoven and my father doesn't necessarily add up to subterfuge."

"As you wish, if it makes things easier for you."

She stopped in her tracks and looked over her shoulder at him. Blackburn once again broadcast studied indifference, the earlier flash of anger gone. He'd shoved his hands into the pockets of his breeches. "Have it your way—Bernadotte asked the composer to create a symphony in honor of the first consul with the help of *a* young cryptographer."

"What about the chemical compounds, the knowledge of explosives—definitely not in my father's area of expertise. Even if he did help," Devon managed to concede, "he probably didn't know the precise implications of the formula."

"And like any curious cryptographer, fifteen years later, he couldn't resist finding out. Probably why he didn't simply destroy the score." Blackburn knew enough not to mention the possible French and English connection.

"Are you finished?"

"Why?"

"I'm not waiting here for Le Comte to come and find me and for the two of you to bargain over what I know or don't know."

Blackburn stared at her as though determined to understand her. "You can't pull this off alone, Devon. Remember what happened this afternoon at the tavern." His tone brooked no opposition. "He's expecting us together, remember?"

"You still don't trust me, do you? That's why you want me

in the room when you meet with Le Comte, to control me, to ensure my loyalty to you."

He moved one step closer toward her in the small space, not answering her directly. "You're going nowhere tonight."

"You said yourself that we must get the manuscript. Therefore, I return to London immediately." Determinedly, Devon gathered her skirts and moved toward the doorway, hoping to skim by him. Her eyes flared with indignation. "I can't just sit here knowing that Le Comte was responsible for my father's death."

"It can wait till morning," he said as if speaking to a small child, crossing his arms over his chest.

A spike of hot anger shot through her. "You mean your sending me to Le Comte's bed can wait till morning."

The silence was thunderous, the air charged, and Devon wondered whether she should be afraid.

"I didn't say that." The words were spare, stripped of emotion, Blackburn's dark blue eyes frosted with ice.

"You don't have to," she said recklessly. "Get out of my way," she added between clenched teeth, measuring the short distance between them. "And if you're any kind of a gentleman, you'll have a carriage or a horse readied for me."

Blackburn looked about as movable as a medieval stronghold. "I said it will wait until morning," he repeated, his face dangerously impassive. She took stock of the broad shoulders, the long legs in their scuffed boots.

And then she felt a familiar flush suffuse her body, a combination of shock, anger, and frustration culminating in an unwelcome sensual charge. Inevitably her heart began to spin under his gaze, her palms gripping compulsively by her sides.

If she had learned anything about men and women, it was that a cold-hearted bastard like the Marquess of Blackburn would always win out. And whether it was the fate of nations at stake or simply male prerogative, it made little difference. The realization made her angrier at her weakness. *She still wanted him.* And she was a fool.

Her whole body blazed with resentment. "I am entirely and supremely tired of you, Blackburn. You have seduced, manipulated, enticed me, and all but held me hostage in this old pile that you call a hunting lodge. Furthermore, I know that you intend to sacrifice me to Le Comte in the space of a heartbeat, despite a certain shared intimacy that for you is simply just one more avenue of control." Devon exhaled and lifted her chin in the air. "Please move aside."

Blackburn's response was to lean back on the piano and survey her coolly, but his jaw hardened at an obstinate angle. "Now, Devon," he said slowly, choosing his words for maximum impact, aiming deliberately for her heart. "I can't help that you're devastated at discovering the true nature of your father's character."

Devon couldn't stifle a small cry, a sharp agonized moan. "You bastard," she hissed, blinding white anger propelling up her right hand to strike him.

She should have remembered that Blackburn was fatally quick, capturing her hand in a blur of movement. For a moment he held it high over her head while a slow, cynical smile carved his mouth, deepening the hard lines of his face. Then brutally, he jerked her closer, bringing her hand to his mouth, his breath hot on her inner wrist. His tongue lingered on the softness of her pulse point as Devon sagged against him.

She was lost once again in the shadows of his eyes, helpless as he exposed the flesh beneath her lace sleeves. In achingly slow motion, his tongue traced a languid trail of heat down the skin of her inner arm, thrusting her into a miasma of sensuality so powerful, she thought she would dissolve into the parquet beneath her feet. His strong hand captured her fragile wrist, his eyes holding hers with a focus so frightening that she futilely made to pull away.

"Don't ever raise your hand to strike me," he said dangerously, softly. "You haven't the slightest idea what you're letting yourself in for." Devon looked into eyes that caused her stomach to tighten in fear and something else. His mouth continued to caress her skin, the set of his jaw merciless.

"You're not going anywhere. Or do I have to tie you to the bed upstairs?" he growled into the flesh of her wrist.

In an instant of clarity, Devon saw that Blackburn was not unmoved, the muscles and tendons of his throat tight with tension, his breathing shallow. Suddenly she wanted to test him, push him further, torment him as he had done her, manipulating her emotions until her every sensitivity was open to him. She resented her irrational response to his every gesture and she was desperate for an opportunity to weaken his impenetrable façade.

Well, perhaps she had found it. She wrenched her wrist from his grasp with a slow smile, triumph heating her blood.

"That won't be necessary, Blackburn, although the idea has possibilities," she said, deliberately provocative. "And who knows, the concept might appeal to Le Comte."

His eyes hooded for a moment and for a split second, she wondered if she'd gone too far. The thought made her breathless. It occurred to her suddenly that she did have power over him, power in the brush of her breasts against his chest, power when she ran her tongue over her full lower lip. She saw his eyes darken. No—the Marquess of Blackburn was not entirely immune to the demands of his rampant masculinity.

Devon slid her body in closer, one hip leaning into his, her breasts crushed tightly to his chest. Emboldened by her newly found confidence, she let her hand drop to his crotch, her fingers casually brushing the front of his breeches.

He stood as still as a statue, only the blue of his eyes gaining intensity. "I wouldn't play with fire, Devon."

"Only you can play, is that it?" she asked, her face lingering near his, her lips parted. Power and lust drove her to skim her hand down between them. Without hesitation, she slid her fingers around the heavy bulge in his breeches, the shaft hard and hot beneath her hand.

If she'd only known. His reaction was like a match to gunpowder, his breathing jagged as he thrust himself harder against her hand. She unbuttoned his jacket and opened his outer garments wide, running her hands over the fabric of his breeches. For a moment, her palm lay quiescent on his lower abdomen, flirting with the buttons separating her from his erection.

He was as hot as a furnace and she couldn't resist trailing her fingers languidly around his waist before returning again to his navel and the taut muscle of his groin beneath.

He was hard as iron. Wanting her. She hoped it *hurt.*

"I think we've had enough *play* at the moment." Devon moved her hand away with a light caress. Playing with fire felt good. She closed her mind to thoughts of seducing Le Comte, a horror that she could not yet contemplate. Instead, with a desperation that left a metallic taste in her mouth, she wanted Blackburn to suffer, to taste a little of what she was ready to surrender.

"And by the way, Blackburn, many thanks for the lessons. Most useful." She lingered over the last words, and some devil in her made her want to push him a notch higher. "I'm sure Le Comte will be suitably impressed, would you not agree?"

Blackburn's body tensed, the muscles in his neck tightening as he fought for control, repressing the sensuality that boiled just beneath his unfaltering restraint. His answer was a look of dark challenge, carnal and rapacious. "I don't trust you. Never will."

"I suppose that's where fate leaves us then, Blackburn."

He would send her to Le Comte's bed, she reminded herself cruelly, willfully hurting them both. And she would go— but alone and on her own volition. Drunk with her power, she decided to throw him a bone in compensation.

"It is late and I will stay the night," she said, in total command for once. Her eyes raked his long, lean form insolently and the wide-set shoulders admiringly, before adding, "*Only* because I want to. After which *I* decide when and how to *manage* Le Comte."

Then she wandered from the room without a backward glance.

Devon paid a price for her pride, tossing and turning, *alone* in her bed, her thoughts a jumble of puzzle pieces vying for her attention. She burned for Blackburn, listening to every noise—from the creak of the floorboards to the groan of the eaves—imagining that he was coming for her.

Drifting into a fog of dreams, she fantasized that she heard his steps, the door to her room opening, and then the heat of his body sliding into the sheets beside her to take her into his arms. Her womb felt heavy and her breasts ached as he slid into her slowly, infinitely slowly, the hugeness of him welling up inside her.

Perhaps it was the branch of a tree knocking against the shutters, but she awoke with a start and in a cold sweat with only the silvery moonlight slanting through the mullioned windows. An hour before morning remained.

She left from the servants' entrance, already familiar to her, Burgess nowhere to be seen. There was a small kitchen garden planted with rows of burgeoning herbs and vegetables surrounded by an iron gate. The hinges creaked behind her, as she began her walk in her borrowed shoes along the gravel way lined with silvered trees—toward Le Comte and away from Blackburn.

Each step was heavier than the last but she recognized that she couldn't allow either of the men control over the *Eroica*. *Over her.*

It wasn't the sound of the breeze moving through the leaves that caught her attention, but of wheels turning and horses' hooves pounding from a short distance away. Devon looked up to the curve of the driveway and saw a small, black phaeton appear on the lightening horizon, bearing neither crest nor insignia.

It came closer, coming for her, she knew, and she could see that the shades were drawn, its driver atop his box swathed in a black funereal cape. She stopped and it slowed at her side, the door opening. The sun was rising and she squinted into the darkness of the carriage interior before the rough grip of a heavy arm hauled her inside.

At first Devon could make out nothing save a sensation of heaviness holding her down on the leather banquette. Eyes adjusting to the dimness, she felt the weight across her shoulders ease. She lifted her head to see a sconce with a single candle illuminating the man sitting across from her. Despite the warm spring morning, Le Comte's lap was draped with a fur rug.

"I must apologize for the melodrama, *ma chérie*," he murmured, lifting a gloved and apologetic hand toward Devon. "But you see, I just couldn't contain my impatience any longer." His face glowed white in the carriage interior. "How are the two lovebirds getting on?"

He directed the man, whose loutish face was familiar to Devon from the evening at Blackfriars Bridge, to relinquish his hold. "You may let her go, Malcolm. Join the driver up top, if you will."

With a curt nod to Le Comte, Malcolm slid from the carriage, the door opening and closing quickly, leaving the Frenchman and Devon sitting across from one another, alone.

Le Comte's shrewd glance appraised her quickly. "My, my, Blackburn isn't exactly treating you well, is he?" he said with a moue of distaste at her ill-fitting blue dress and voluminous jacket. "And carrying you off here in the middle of nowhere. I would have thought the Marquess would have considerably more élan. Are you certain this is where he takes all his lady loves?"

"I haven't the slightest idea," said Devon sharply, pulling herself up straight on the banquette as if facing an adversary across a field at dawn. Her body vibrated with distrust and something close to hatred.

This was the man who had murdered her father.
This was the man Blackburn wanted her to seduce.

She fisted her hands in the pockets of Blackburn's jacket, willing her features into indifference. She felt the comfort of the coat around her body, welcome armor in the face of a malevolent presence.

Le Comte casually adjusted his lap rug, peering at her through half-lidded eyes. "I trust you have moved things along with the Marquess brilliantly," he said with aristocratic inflections praising a job well done. "Although having him heave you off into the hinterlands was not part of my plan, my dear. Even made me somewhat suspicious." He smoothed the rug over his lap before glancing at her shrewdly. "But I must say, despite your curious ensemble, Devon, you do look positively radiant."

The Frenchman was delighted. The thought that Le Comte knew anything about the intimacies she had shared with Blackburn filled her with revulsion, a faint nausea curling around her. She felt stifled by the closeness of the phaeton's interior and by the cloying sweetness of his cologne, all the while trying to ignore the prurient look on the Frenchman's face.

Disregarding his comment, she bluffed coolly, "You should have trusted me, Le Comte. I even anticipated your arrival—here I am." She forced a small smile. Le Comte didn't give his trust easily, if ever.

The papery skin of his face creased into a smile. "You must forgive me my peculiarities, my dear, one of which is never leaving anything to chance. And as you can see, I couldn't wait any longer to discover where *exactly* we find ourselves in this very pleasant charade. Samson and Delilah, if you'll recall?"

"I fulfilled my part of the bargain, Monsieur," Devon said automatically, savoring the words and the chance that one day soon she would have the opportunity to undermine the

Frenchman fatally. "Blackburn is willing to work with me on the manuscript."

"So you say, so you say," Le Comte murmured, steepling his fingers in front of his face. He crossed one leg over the other, swinging his slippered foot. "But you see, I don't feel quite comfortable relinquishing the manuscript to you . . . as yet. I am a cautious man, another one of my peculiarities."

"Why not?" she asked, eyeing the door handle of the coach, fighting the urge to make a quick escape, and rapidly calculating the likelihood of eluding Malcolm's heavy grasp. What was Le Comte waiting for? Did he have the score with him? Her eyes darted nervously around the darkened interior.

The Frenchman chuckled at the obviousness of her reaction. "Alas—no score here in the phaeton, Devon, if that was what you were expecting," he said in a singsong voice. "I trust you understand, I would prefer the two of you to work on the manuscript in London, *chez-moi.*"

It was Devon's turn to laugh. "I said that I have secured Blackburn's cooperation, not his mental faculties, Monsieur. He will never agree to those terms."

"Then you will just have to make him, my dear," said Le Comte simply.

"And if I don't? If I can't?"

"Not to worry," Le Comte, interrupted, detecting the misgiving in her tone. He distractedly pushed aside the black curtain covering the small window and peered briefly outside. "Blackburn will follow after you like a stallion scenting a mare, if you forgive the crudeness of the analogy. Exactly as I'd planned."

Devon felt small wings of panic flutter against her chest, fear once more threatening to overtake her as she began to feel the phaeton roll along the gravel pathway. "Where are we going?" she asked unnecessarily.

Le Comte softly patted her hand that clutched, knuckle white, the fabric of her skirt. "To London, of course."

Which was what she had wanted, wasn't it? To keep the two men apart? Devon swallowed her panic, trying again. "And you're convinced Blackburn will follow?" The phaeton sped up, and although she had no chance to see out the window, she sensed Armathwaite—and the Marquess—receding in the distance.

The Frenchman fussed with his lap rug again. "You will see—Blackburn will follow close behind and then we will have him where we want him. It's quite simple, truly." He pursed his lips in satisfaction. "Our Englishman finds himself tantalizingly close to the score and to the only woman who can help him with the code. How can he resist?"

"I still don't understand," Devon said, not trying to hide her confusion as the carriage rocked with motion.

"I know the Marquess all too well, my dear. And I know that he'll be hard-pressed to relinquish you to me, for a variety of reasons."

Don't be too sure, thought Devon with a heavy heart. "And how exactly does that help your cause?"

Le Comte smiled mysteriously. "It helps in every way, Devon. Sometimes the circuitous route is the best. Or think of it another way, my dear. Think of this as a little test. You can hardly blame me for wanting to ensure that the two of you are working on my behalf."

"I never promised you my loyalty."

"Exactly—you see my point? I'm sure the three of us shall be able to reach a concordat over champagne and one of your inimitable concerts this evening." He leaned across the phaeton to pat her on the arm. "And besides, I promise that you will learn all sorts of things about the Marquess—useful things," he emphasized, anticipation honing his sharp features.

Devon's gray eyes widened at his last statement which rang in the air. As the phaeton rolled on in the early morning toward London, Le Comte relaxed into the banquette, appearing once again at his civilized aristocratic best, urbane, sophisticated, a fashionable ennui marking his tone.

But with a sinking heart, Devon knew better.

Back in her rooms at Le Comte's London town house, Devon listened to the quiet streets beyond her windows come to life. The morning began with a rain shower puddling the lanes and giving nourishment to the jonquils and tulips embroidering the handsome façade of the residence. Carriages splashed carelessly through the streets of the square, their occupants confidently going about their business.

It seemed as though life was normal everywhere else in London while she felt herself a prisoner, inexpressibly adrift in an ocean of conflicting thoughts and emotions. The Frenchman's last words peeled ominously in her ears. Her flesh recoiled at the thought of contact with de Maupassant, her experiences with Blackburn still too fresh, a thick cloud of sensuality in which she could too easily lose herself.

She had made love with a man who would betray her in a heartbeat. He had a lifetime's experience seducing women, a talent that he wielded all too ably and with an amorality that took her breath away. The Marquess had bound her to his bed—in order to bind her to his cause.

A half hour later, she sank into a tub of hot water in her dressing room, scrubbing away his touch, his feel, his scent. What she really needed at the moment was a clear head, and a renewed confidence that she was an equal participant in the game, a variable in the equation that Le Comte and the Marquess could not control. She plunged her hair under water before resting her neck on the edge of the tub, closed her eyes, and let the heat seep into her bones.

Through a fringe of eyelashes, she saw the two maids preparing fresh jugs of water and unfolding linen towels, their efficient movements interspersed with scraps of conversation.

"She just burst into his rooms, unannounced, just like

that," said the younger one from behind work-reddened hands, her back to Devon.

The older, stouter woman responded querulously, her expression gloomy. "Such goings-on in this household, Becky." She shook her head, jowls shaking. "Mark my words, that Lady Treadwell is up to no good."

Becky stole a sharp glance over her shoulder at her mistress slumbering in the tub before whispering carefully, "I heard them arguing, I did. The yelling . . . she sure is a highstrung one, she is." She began arranging the brushes and mirrors on the dressing table, dusting the Meissen figurines and finely spun glass bottles of all shapes and sizes.

Devon said nothing as the two women eventually assisted her from the tub, drying and then dressing her hair. They helped her into a simple morning gown of peacock blue, banded by a narrow satin ribbon tied below her breasts. When they fell silent in their ministrations, Devon turned their conversation over in her mind.

Lady Susannah Treadwell visiting Le Comte at this unfashionably early hour.

Most of London knew that the two were involved in some type of relationship, which in itself was no surprise, given Lady Treadwell's reputation for generously distributing her favors. As the young maid swept her hair into a low chignon, Devon glanced into the mirror above her dressing table without seeing her reflection. Instead, the image of a possessive Susannah the night of her concert burned into her consciousness, her prettily plump but proprietary hand on Blackburn's broad chest.

A combination of dread and jealousy, which she could scarcely justify, hauled her to her feet the minute the two servants left her dressing room. Opening the door of her apartments, she peered down the hallway, a gleaming corridor of polished mahogany. Deserted. She eyed Le Comte's apartments, the heavy doors slightly ajar.

Light on her slippered feet, a moment later, she peered through the ribbon of open space.

Lady Treadwell was beautiful. In the gray of the mid-morning light her hair, a sheen of bluish black, contrasted elegantly against a crème muslin dress with puffed sleeves and a matching pelisse in a darker caramel shade. Her scarlet lips were set in a tight, thin line and Devon guessed she was about to burst into tears, screams, or both. The voices were muffled behind the heavy door, a staccato of French and English.

"I don't believe that you would cut me off, just like that, Henri," exclaimed Susannah, twisting a delicately crocheted handkerchief between her fingers. "Even you could never be so cruel."

In his rooms fit for a king, Le Comte advanced menacingly toward Susannah who, crablike, backed her way toward the door.

"You of all people, dear Susannah, should know better than that. My cruelty, as you have so often reminded me, knows no bounds." He regarded her as if she were an annoying insect. "And *never* speak to me of money. You may directly importune Lacan," he said with a dismissive wave of his hand, presenting her with his back.

"Henri," Susannah whined petulantly, deciding to change tactics, "I have been so useful to you in the past, doing anything, everything for you."

Remaining with his back to the woman, Le Comte immersed himself in a portrait of one of his ancestors prominently displayed in the sitting area. "I won't disagree," he answered slowly, taking his time with the words. "You are a whore of the first order."

Susannah reeled like she'd been slapped, her face crumpling in outrage, her hands wringing her handkerchief. Taking an agitated breath, she drew her mouth into implacable lines, the importuning mistress transforming into a vituperative shrew in the space of a hurled insult.

"You will regret this, Henri," she spat with a toss of her head. "Remember, I have the Marquess of Blackburn at my beck and call."

Le Comte whipped around to face her, his laugh ugly. "You have had him in your bed, and I use the past tense quite deliberately, Madam," he said succinctly. "I now have something that Blackburn wants much, much more."

"You can't be talking about that shriveled bluestocking, that Frenchwoman?" Susannah hissed like a cornered cat.

Devon could feel her own breathing quicken. What had she come to, listening at keyholes? She bit her lower lip, her conscience rising to taunt her an inch from de Maupassant's bedroom doors. The smell of beeswax suddenly overwhelming, she heard Lady Treadwell's sharp cry.

"Answer me—are you talking about that bastard child of a traitor?" she asked, her voice rising an octave.

Le Comte's face was haggard in the morning light, the green of the watered silk wallpaper distinctly unflattering. "You forget yourself, Susannah. And you forget that I don't answer to *anyone*." Perhaps it was his expression that prompted a fresh whine from a woman who was accustomed to life unfolding exactly as it should.

"I *hate* you and I *hate* that bitch even more," Susannah shrieked, placing her handkerchief to her lips. "If I had known how evil you are . . ." she trailed off in a theatrical sob before grappling with her reticule dangling from a gold chain. With shaking hands, she withdrew a crumpled sheet of paper and brandished it before the Frenchman's face.

"I have it right here, that letter you're keeping from her," she taunted hysterically. "I stole it from you, you fool!"

Lady Treadwell danced away from Le Comte, her eyes unnaturally bright.

Le Comte despised weakness, and lack of control even more so. Any hint of feebleness sharpened his appetite for cruelty that was as much a part of his nature as his desire to own priceless *objets*. He stroked the velvet lapels of his green morning coat contemplatively. "Give me that letter, see Lacan for your draft, and then leave here at once," he said in a voice so low that Devon had to strain to hear.

"I will tell her—I will tell Devon Caravelle *everything*," Susannah threatened, her words building to a crescendo that all but rattled the window panes.

Le Comte moved toward her in three impatient strides, snatching the letter from her wildly gesticulating hands, and placing it on the escritoire behind him. "You will tell her nothing because I forbid you," he said in sibilant tones. "Do I make myself perfectly understood?" For added emphasis, his pale fingers closed like talons around her wrist.

Devon was sure she was going to be sick, as she could almost hear the fragile bones of Susannah's wrist begin to crack under the vicious pressure of de Maupassant's grip. His face was a mask of pure malevolence, a self-satisfied smile on his face.

Her detestation of Susannah Treadwell faded into the background like an ugly bruise. The man was a *sadist*. It was her last thought before she launched herself through the partially opened door and burst into the rooms.

"Enough." The one word exploded from her. "This is barbaric."

Her head spinning, she placed herself between the Frenchman and Lady Treadwell, who appeared as though she were about to faint. The scene was grotesque, a macabre drama set against the backdrop of luxurious rosewood and of peach and green brocade.

Neither moved and Devon could see a fine sheen of perspiration marring Lady Treadwell's perfect brow. Her eyes were ablaze with hatred, her red lips curved into a rictus of pain.

"I said—enough," Devon repeated with strength and resolve in her voice.

"I heard you the first time, *ma chérie*," said Le Comte with one of his reptilian smiles. For a moment she thought he was going to relent but, purely for her benefit, it seemed, he instead pulled Susannah's arm away from her body to twist it tightly behind her back. Lady Treadwell did not make a sound, concentrating her beam of hatred instead on Devon.

Shocked by the violence, Devon improvised madly, her voice sounding distant and hollow in the room. "Monsieur, I must insist, this behavior is beneath contempt!"

Le Comte spared her an amused glance, not bothering to register his surprise at her intervention. He let go of Susannah's arm abruptly and then fastidiously flicked down the sleeves of his morning coat. Devon watched as Susannah massaged her injured arm, faint marks from the Frenchman's grip already appearing on her fragile wrist.

"Now isn't this unimaginably sweet?" mocked Le Comte. "Blackburn's current mistress coming to the aid of his former mistress. I seem to surround myself with positively saintly women." The Frenchman watched her with the unblinking gaze of a snake.

"Although not too saintly, I trust," he mused, as though he had all morning to take in her appearance from the tips of her *peau de soie* slippers to the glow of her auburn hair. "I think that the Marquess of Blackburn would probably agree with me on that point." He watched a pale flush of color suffuse her features. "No need to be so reticent, my dear. After all, I don't really mind. I shall simply ensure that you make it up to me in some way."

Devon could only hope that it would never come to that, conscious of the ill will that saturated the room. Susannah Treadwell, galvanized by a jolt of jealousy, came back to life with an arrogant swish of her skirts, her fine features lit by savage emotion. It was as though she had forgotten Le Comte's brutality of the moment before, her fury directed at Devon with the power of grapeshot.

"You could never hold the attention of a man like Blackburn, on any level," she shot out contemptuously, her eyes alight with an unholy gleam. "How could you ever believe that the Marquess would seriously consider the daughter of a traitor and a trollop? Someone without the slightest beauty or name to recommend her?" Her words came from behind clenched teeth.

Devon fought the urge to back away from her and out the door, away from the stream of hatred enveloping the room—while Le Comte watched the exchange intently.

"Careful, Susannah. I shan't warn you again," he murmured.

"Warn her against what, Monsieur?" The rooms were cold despite the heavy velvet drapes and plush rug. The letter Le Comte had taken away from Susannah still sat crumpled and forlorn on his desk, importuning Devon somehow.

Something was very wrong. "What is it you wish to say to me?" Devon confronted the seething woman. "Never mind casting aspersions against my parentage, Lady Treadwell, or sharing your assumptions about the nature of my relationship with the Marquess."

Looking for any opening to continue her rampage, Susannah jerked her beautifully coiffed head toward Le Comte. "My God, Henri, why not tell the chit the real reason Blackburn is so keen to further an association with her?" She turned a withering gaze toward Devon, adding, "You should know by now that Blackburn doesn't do anything without *cold-blooded intent.*"

"That's enough, Susannah," Le Comte barked, his hand reaching for the servants' bell. "I shall have Lacan see you out."

Susannah's gaze shifted rapidly between the Frenchman and Devon as though coming to a decision. With a small snarl, she gathered up her gloves, pulling them on with ruthless little tugs. "Don't bother. I can escort myself out, Monsieur Le Comte," she said, spitting out his name.

Her gaze flickered over Devon contemptuously. "And as for you, Mademoiselle, why don't you ask Blackburn sometime about his deceased *brother?* One day, you may thank me for bringing his name to your attention."

She paused theatrically, her voice relishing her next pronouncement. "And if you remember anything, remember this: The Marquess would feed you to the fish in the Thames in an instant, if it suited his purposes." She pointed to Le Comte with venomous flourish. "Including feeding you to the biggest, nastiest fish of all."

She snapped her reticule closed and wound the chain tightly around her reddened wrist. "Au revoir to you both."

Devon moved out of the way, relieved to see Susannah march from the room in a cyclone of skirts and high color.

Suddenly she was alone with Le Comte.

"Cold, my dear?" The Frenchman's silken, cultured tones crept over her skin. He seemed unaware of the obvious non sequitur. "That thin muslin can't possibly serve as adequate covering."

"I seem to have forgotten my wrap," she said rubbing her arms, acutely aware of the crazy tilt of the world she had entered. De Maupassant studiously adjusted a pleat on his trousers, Lady Treadwell and the cruelty marking their previous moments all but forgotten.

"In such a hurry?" He watched her edge toward the door as though unable to endure another moment of his company. "I believe we have a few important points to cover now that our Lady Treadwell has, in the poorest of taste I might add, let the cat out of the bag." He quirked a thin gray eyebrow before picking up a fine silk shawl from the settee and draping it around her shoulders. "Now, isn't this better?"

Devon tried not to cringe away from his touch, murmuring halfhearted thanks as the silk enveloped her bare shoulders. She moved toward the door, her palm resting on the cool wood. "You're referring to Blackburn's brother, of course?" she couldn't resist asking, before facing the Frenchman again.

"Indeed I am," he intoned in a solemn, carrying voice. "A most *interesting* development in the history of Blackburn's character formation." He watched her face for any signs of curiosity. "I thought these *insights* might prove useful one day. And here we are—that day seems to have arrived."

"Useful to me, you mean?" she asked doubtfully, pulling the shawl more tightly around her shoulders.

"Let's just say that, although dear Lady Treadwell was somewhat peremptory in divulging some of the details, I thought that I might need a little something to *leaven* your relationship with our Marquess."

Curiosity warred with trepidation. *"Leaven?"*

Le Comte sighed with mock weariness. "I understand perfectly how heady passions can be, how carried away one can become." He beamed insinuatingly. "There's nothing quite as susceptible as a virgin who has just discovered sexual congress, after all."

Devon refused to look away as acute humiliation flushed her body. "And what's that got to do with the Marquess's brother?" she asked, determined to bring the conversation back around.

"What indeed," echoed Le Comte tormentingly in his overly polished voice. As though he were giving the question serious thought, he turned his attention again to the portrait, sliding his hands into the pockets of his dressing gown introspectively.

"I'm waiting, Monsieur." Devon refused to be swayed from her question.

He twisted around to face her, striving to look solicitous. "I know you are, my dear, and difficult that it may seem at the moment, you may have to wait longer for your answer." He paused with mock solemnity. "But not overly long—why not ask the Marquess to answer your questions this evening?"

"Why don't you answer my question now?" Her voice was surprisingly even.

"Remember that test I mentioned this morning, *ma chérie*? I'm sure that you do."

"Your wanting to test my loyalty, to ensure that both Blackburn and I are working on your behalf?"

"*Exactement*, well done!" Le Comte enthused, his lips thinning into a smile. "Just a little test, the results of which I'm sure will dilute your tendresse for the Marquess. Just a little reminder that he's not the knight in shining armor you may believe him to be. And just an added guarantee that you have my own—and your own—best interests at heart. I promise you, your questions will be answered."

He concluded in the silken tones he used to smooth over contretemps. "Dinner at nine in the conservatory? And you will play for us, won't you, *ma chère*?"

Chapter 11

The gown was obscene, flesh-toned and so diaphanous that she might have been wearing nothing at all.

Devon stood in the double doors of Le Comte's conservatory and took a deep breath. She felt the thin fabric move against her body like a fine mist. It was a departure from Le Comte's usual stellar taste and selected by him for good reason—to taunt the Marquess of Blackburn, to emphasize that Devon belonged to the Frenchman, his to do with as he wanted. It was the kind of gown a mistress might wear and her host made it quite clear that she should be the one wearing it.

The silk garment had been draped over her four-poster bed along with a velvet ribbon for her neck when she'd returned from an afternoon of pacing the walled garden, a walk that had been intended to quell her rising anxiety, her sense that Le Comte was intending a sleight-of-hand for the main course at this evening's dinner.

How eager the Frenchman had been that Blackburn would join them, to play his role in a convoluted scenario that he had planned down to the last line. Devon knew that she meant nothing to Blackburn, and yet she couldn't bear the thought that he would sacrifice her to Le Comte.

Perversely, she preferred to make that decision on her own. Sick with nerves, she edged the bodice of her dress a little higher as she entered the conservatory, the candlelight reflected from the room's side panel mirrors casting suggestive shadows. For a moment at least, she was alone.

The beautiful Broadwood was positioned in one corner and she felt the overwhelming desire to play, simply to lose herself in the music that for many years had been her only salvation. She had played just yesterday for Blackburn and, for some unearthly reason, it was important to her that he would always remember the moment.

The house was absolutely still. Irresistibly, she found herself by the piano, caressing the ivory keys, the image of the *Eroica*'s bloodied title page coming back to haunt her.

Maybe Blackburn was right and she hadn't understood her parents at all. She recalled her many hours at the piano in her youth, her discipline and her focus. Her mother sitting in a chair across from her, listening with eyes closed, while her father worked at his desk, the last hours of sunlight filtering over his strewn papers.

This was the world from which she came, a place where reason and discipline triumphed over chaos, where the pursuit of liberty and free inquiry were held in the highest esteem. She wouldn't allow that world to desert her now.

Blackburn couldn't matter anymore.

The nerves in her neck and back tightened. The door behind her opened and footsteps crossed the expanse of the black and white marble floor. Preparing herself for battle, she turned to greet Le Comte's entrance, her smile brilliant.

"You look absolutely charming, my dear," the Frenchman said in dulcet tones, taking in the clinging silk as though critiquing the latest creation from Paris. "I took the liberty of choosing your gown tonight, very apropos for an intimate evening."

Le Comte, as usual, was sartorial perfection, his cutaway evening coat made from dark superfine, his cravat tied in an elaborate knot. He rubbed his hands in delight, surveying the room prepared exactly to his specifications.

The candlelight could barely compete with the stars that winked through the glass dome of the conservatory and the wealth of crystal, silver, and porcelain that covered a table set conspicuously for three. Silently, a footman stood behind each seat, ready to dispense the finest wines and cuisine. A moist and heavy scent of exotic flowers thickened the air.

"And very thoughtful of you," Devon said, disinclined to rise to his opening salvo for the moment. She felt his breath on her shoulder when he came nearer, sensing his appraisal of her bared shoulders and the curves of her breasts as he led her to the table.

Devon assessed her opponent from across the expanse of china and crystal, arranging a heavy damask napkin on her lap, taking a deep sip of fortitude from her glass of wine kept full by an attentive footman. An ornate ormolu clock ticked off the minutes after nine o'clock while Le Comte played with the stem of his glass, openly relishing the coming moments. They knew exactly for whom they waited.

"Your timing earlier today was regrettable, Devon," the Frenchman began perfunctorily, deciding that this would be the first of many painful lessons that Brendan Clifton's daughter would have to learn. "That scene with Lady Treadwell was not intended to be overheard."

Despite his accusing tone, his eyes lingered on her meager bodice and she shook off a feeling of revulsion, like a clammy grip, keeping her tone light.

"Really, Monsieur? I thought that you weren't entirely displeased at Lady Treadwell's revelation. And then there was the matter of the letter she was so desperate to flaunt under your nose . . ." she trailed off between sips of wine. "You must forgive me, but I was compelled to investigate when I heard such a heated argument."

"I can assure you, Lady Treadwell will be dealt with appropriately," he responded with a veiled threat, motioning to the footman to refill his glass. "As for Lady Treadwell's taking the letter from my desk, her actions simply represented an hysterical ploy designed to raise my ire unnecessarily," Le Comte said with a sharp glance toward the Broadwood in the center of the room. "Although her mention of the Marquess's brother was actually quite fortuitous."

"Blackburn's brother," Devon stated in a reasonable voice that the Frenchman would be more likely to acknowledge. "He's involved in this somehow?"

"Indirectly—yes." Le Comte arranged his linen napkin perfectly on his lap. "Life can get so very complicated, as I'm sure you know. You see, Blackburn is under the impression that I had something to do with Edward's death."

Treading carefully, she asked, "And did you?"

Le Comte leaned forward halfway across the table. "What do you think, my dear?"

Devon focused on the gold filigree embroidering the still empty plate in front of her. She traced the ornate pattern with a fingertip deliberately circumventing his question, "In other words, you would have me believe that Blackburn hates you because he blames you for his brother's death."

The conclusion was easy enough to draw, a powerful sentiment that she could well identify with, her own loathing for the Frenchman stemming from the murder of a loved one.

"Precisely," he said clasping his hands together as though he'd just been presented with a particularly splendid first course. "But there's yet another reason that I am now eager to share this bit of history with you."

He feigned an expression of newfound intimacy, as though the two of them were about to revel in a morsel of gossip or scrap of scandal.

" 'Which if not victory is yet revenge,' " he quoted in a seeming non sequitur, yet fully aware that Devon would recognize the line from *Paradise Lost*. "Are you familiar with the passage, my dear? Of course you are. Milton, almost as great as our own Molière," he added absently.

The phrase echoed familiarly in Devon's memory, her knowledge of both French and English literature almost as comprehensive as her knowledge of mathematics and science. She grasped for a connection just out of her reach.

Le Comte's eyes narrowed expectantly. The conservatory was suspended in stillness, the footmen shadowed statues, the charade of dinner frozen in midair. Then it came to her: Blackburn was hunting for revenge.

A kaleidoscope of images descended. Blackfriars Bridge, the night of the concert, the rainstorm, their time at Armathwaite. The music room when she had lashed out at him in bitterness about her family, his cold withdrawal, quickly masked. She had sensed from the beginning an extra darkness about him, a detachment cloaked in a natural magnetism that hid a profound emptiness.

"Devon, my dear," the Frenchman interrupted her chaotic thoughts. "It's best not to be feeling too much sympathy for the Marquess."

"And why exactly is that?" she asked bleakly, forcing herself to look at her host who appeared miles away down the expanse of the glittering table.

"Because the Marquess's need for revenge is simply misplaced." Le Comte made it sound deceptively simple and placed his palms flat on the table for emphasis. "Quite deliberately, the Marquess chose *not* to save his brother's life—when he very well could have."

Over her glass of wine held in a steady grip, Devon forced herself to look straight into the Frenchman's eyes. "Why are you telling me this?"

"Because I want you to know exactly the kind of man the Marquess is, *ma chère*," he said, as though making a reasoned argument. "I want you to know that he's the kind of man who will stand passively by and willingly watch his brother writhe in pain as he is tortured to death. When, I might add, he could have prevented it."

Devon heard the words as though they were coming from a long, dark tunnel, each vowel and consonant elongated, all meaning obscured, bleached from the sentences.

A door slammed shut in her brain, leaving a nauseating void. Le Comte's voice rang in her head conjuring a vision so bleak that her unwilling mind could not absorb it.

Even now she could feel the heat from Blackburn's body, trace the cut of his cheekbones, inhale his scent—and the realization sickened her. Who exactly was the Marquess of Blackburn or, more accurately, *what* was he? If Le Comte was telling the truth, she had shared intimacies with a lover who had no soul, who for whatever convenient rationale could stand by and watch his own brother die in agony. She didn't really care what the reasons behind his decision were. They didn't matter.

Blackburn's brother and her father's bloodied corpse merged in her consciousness.

"Would you like to hear more?" inquired Le Comte with false solicitousness, raising a brow questioningly.

Devon held up a staying hand and paused to collect her wits, clutching at the damask napkin on her lap. The footmen stood quietly, seemingly oblivious to the discussion, having yet to begin serving the meal. Devon had lost whatever small appetite she had to begin with and observed Le Comte watching her with finely tuned malevolence.

"You've turned quite pale, my dear." He caressed the stem of his wineglass reflexively with tapered fingers. "So I trust my little revelation has had the desired effect."

"How can I know that you're telling the truth?" she asked bluntly, her throat raw.

Le Comte gave a Gallic shrug, his white hair gleaming in the candlelight. "Let me make it simple for you by framing your dilemma, Devon. You and the Marquess have formed an amorous alliance, as I'd intended. But from what you've learned about your lover—if it were *you* stretched on the proverbial rack—do you think that the Marquess would save you any more than he would have saved his brother, if it meant sacrificing his own interests, whatever they might be?" He paused significantly. "A rhetorical question, I know."

A question she couldn't bear holding up to the light.

Le Comte was in a disturbingly congenial mood, as though he had already tasted victory, the ruby red in his wineglass like blood against the white of his shirtfront. He turned his head toward the door of the conservatory and before she could follow his lead, her pulse began an erratic staccato.

Le Comte's next words struck sparks off the cavernous space of the conservatory, "But if it is the truth you're after, my dear, then why don't you ask the Marquess yourself?"

Blackburn stood tall in the shadows of the entrance to the conservatory, his reflection multiplied in the room's paneled mirrors. The lean grace was already too familiar to her, the candlelight revealing the face she wished she would never have to set eyes on again. And Blackburn's smile, she saw with escalating panic, didn't even begin to reach the hard blue of his eyes.

"So pleased you could join us at such short notice." Le Comte rose from the table. "I trust you received my invitation late this morning, Blackburn. As it is, it's been a while since we sat down together and dined, no?"

"The invitation did come as a surprise, as did Mademoiselle's hasty departure," he said in the dark voice that Devon was trying to forget. He presented himself like a mistral in the stale and perfumed air of the conservatory, radiating a cool but menacing power.

Helplessly, Devon traced the set of his profile, foolishly noting the strong, straight nose, the wide, deep-set eyes. He arrogantly ignored the Frenchman's offer of a chair, remaining standing, his broad shoulders and obdurate jaw reminding de Maupassant and Devon that they were playing with a still unknown quantity, one that had proven intractable in the past.

Blackburn bowed briefly over her hand, taking in her outrageous costume, her hair swept up in burnished curls that tumbled in artful disarray over her shoulders. She knew she gave the impression of luxuriant, available flesh. She could read it in his eyes.

"It *is* what you wanted," she murmured defensively and for his ears alone, her eyes meeting his with defiance, forcing her movements to be leisured and unhurried as she self-consciously adjusted the velvet ribbon around her neck.

"Don't you really mean to say that you made your choice, reneging once again on your promise?" The words were low, rich with accusation. "And wasting very little time."

How much she wanted him to believe that she would never give herself to the Frenchman. For any reason. And yet how patently, sickeningly absurd. She had always known that Blackburn would send her to Le Comte's bed, or to the hangman's noose, without a second thought.

As coolly as he had sent his brother to his death.

Yet it remained inexplicable and irrational, her desire for him coalescing into one simple wish: to dive into his arms and remain there, sheltered against the wall of his chest. They were so close that she could reach out and touch that sinfully sensual mouth that had given her so much pleasure. At that moment, she despised herself, despised herself for still wanting him, for feeling the unwelcome excitement and tension that his nearness ignited in her like a match to gunpowder.

She remembered his hot words as he took her on the floor in front of the fire. She remembered his hardness filling her to oblivion, a fog of sensuality clouding her brain.

And she hoped he couldn't read her mind.

Both men were watching her and she felt their cunning pervade the room like a scent. Le Comte dismissed the footmen, the illusion of dinner quickly disappearing under the mounting tension in the conservatory.

"You had a question you wanted to ask of the Marquess, *ma chérie*," the Frenchman interrupted, eyes narrowed. "Now's your opportunity before, of course, we get to the matter of the *Eroica*." He swiveled in his chair to address Blackburn as though referring to a mutual reminiscence. "I'm sure you do recall that evening, Blackburn, a few years ago on the coast involving your brother?"

Blackburn straightened away from Devon. His gaze flicked over the Frenchman as if he wasn't even in the room, his eyes without a glimmer of emotion. His evening dress was simple as to be almost austere, the cravat a white slash against the hard lines of his face. "You have a question for me, Mademoiselle?"

She was afraid to ask, afraid of what his response might be. And she was ashamed that it still mattered to her after what she had learned tonight.

Did Blackburn still want her to give herself to the Frenchman in exchange for the score?

She looked up at him and into his eyes, her gaze strong and unfaltering, and in the darkness found her answer.

She would forever associate the rich heaviness of exotic flora with this agonizing moment, the bouquet of moist earth and alien blossoms constricting her throat. She swallowed hard, unable to form the words that would hold all her unspoken and unacknowledged emotions. She recognized then how childish her hope had been, nurtured in a place whose existence she didn't want to admit, a hope that now foundered in the futility of emotional connection with such a man. Detachment was his survival mechanism, a way of existing in a world that required a flexibility of conscience that made her head and heart hurt.

If she tried hard, if she imagined it, she could read in his eyes an overlay of bitterness and pain, his expression holding the faintest echo of the man he may have been long ago.

"No," she said finally, softly, sadly, "I don't have a question."

Then recovering herself, she finished the last of her wine and rose from the table, pushing back the chair and leaning into it for just a moment. "I don't have a question," she repeated and, without looking at Blackburn again, walked slowly to the crimson velvet chaise a few feet away. Arranging herself on the welcoming softness, she summoned her will, which she had lost somewhere along the way, since that first night at Blackfriars Bridge.

Barely recognizing her own voice, she heard herself say, "But I do believe it's time that we all lay our cards on the table regarding the *Eroica*."

Le Comte nodded approvingly, the condescension in his tone breaking through her numbness. "Quite right, my dear, as long as you feel comfortable working with the Marquess and as long as you know for *whom* you are working."

"I do," she lied, answering without hesitation.

"And you, Blackburn?" asked Le Comte.

For a moment, it seemed to Devon that anything might happen. For the first time that evening, Blackburn turned his attention on the Frenchman and Devon was almost expecting to hear the report of a pistol, the flash of a knife's blade. She couldn't say what checked Blackburn's impulse to violence, perhaps the training of a lifetime or the stakes that were higher than she could even begin to calculate.

"Let's have this done with," he said without preamble, pressing his shoulders against the mirrored wall as though making an effort to stop himself from crossing the room to finish the Frenchman once and for all. "Your twisted machinations and baroque revelations notwithstanding, when do we get our hands on the *Eroica*?" He drew a breath that seemed to grate through him. "Anything else is superfluous."

Le Comte gave a bark of laughter that echoed off the glass dome of the conservatory. "How reassuringly rational you are, Monsieur," he said, but quickly gauged a safe distance between them. "But as it happens, and as you well know, getting your hands on the *Eroica*, as you so crudely put it, is Devon's job alone to accomplish."

Devon held her breath, afraid to look at Blackburn directly, afraid to see the acquiescence in his eyes. She wrenched her gaze back to the Frenchman.

"You're a sick bastard." Blackburn pushed away from the

mirrored wall and proceeded slowly toward Le Comte who, for a moment, must have tasted something like fear. He rose from the table, darting a quick look over his shoulder to confirm the presence of several footmen in the shadows and then recovered by averting his eyes from the gaze that had turned rapier sharp.

"What's fair is fair, Blackburn," he returned with false confidence. "I'm simply ensuring what's best for my own interests." He waved an elegant arm toward Devon on the chaise, her pink gown resonant against rose velvet. "I wouldn't want the two of you getting too close, after all, and conspiring against me. Of course, I am forced to acknowledge that you work for Wellington, so I must have some guarantee. Although I should have thought the young woman would mean something to you," he added slyly. "But then your brother didn't either, did he?"

Devon noticed her breath coming quickly, aware that she was being metaphorically passed between the two men like a parcel of goods.

"And you should indulge me," Le Comte continued, moving toward the precipice, "as you've already sampled the wares, if I assume correctly."

Devon dug her hands into the silk of her gown, her nails scraping against the sheer fabric.

But Blackburn didn't rise to the bait, his mouth curved in a grim smile instead, moored now in the center of the conservatory. "I don't have time for your perverse games, Le Comte," he said, as though bored by the whole scenario. "And I trust that you haven't invited me here to compete with you for the lady's attention. Now that she knows what there is to know about me, I think she's best equipped to make her own decision."

He turned to her, a hint of challenge flashing in his face. "When you left with de Maupassant this morning, you already made that decision." The words were hollow.

Devon would remember forever the smell of the tallow

candles burning down low, hanging in the air as her gaze raked his expression, looking for any way out. The light cut his face into even sharper angles, his expression impenetrable, giving her no ground. He stood relaxed, that elegant, long-limbed grace defying all odds multiplied in the shimmer of the conservatory's mirrors.

She allowed herself to lower her lashes for a split second in wearied acceptance. How well she remembered that night at Blackfriars Bridge and his parting shot which pinned her to the wall like a lance. Whether his thoughts this evening were driven by an underlying regret, or a lingering doubt that had nothing to do with insinuations but everything to do with a resurrected conscience—she would never know.

When she opened her eyes again, her smile was brittle. "How very civilized of you, Blackburn."

"Indeed," murmured the Frenchman drifting over to Devon's side.

"You will understand," Devon continued, dredging the words from the bottom of her soul and shutting out the intense blue of Blackburn's gaze, staring somewhere over his wide shoulders where her reflection glittered coldly, "that Le Comte and I will come to an arrangement that is mutually beneficial. And then I will inform you as to when your assistance is required."

"I understand," Blackburn mocked, a remote civility belying a ferocious anger that threatened the surface of well-made plans. He watched de Maupassant lean over the chaise and place a proprietary arm around Devon's silken shoulders while clearly enjoying an unobstructed view of her breasts.

"A worthwhile visit on your part, Blackburn, no?" declared Le Comte as he caressed Devon's creamy skin for the Marquess's express benefit. "So sorry we never did get around to dining—or Devon's little recital." He smiled triumphantly. "But I know how anxious you are to work on the score, nonetheless. You and Devon will have ample time to spend together in the very near future. I guarantee it."

The words were heavy with import and, for a moment, Devon couldn't breathe. Le Comte was testing Blackburn. What was more important to him—Devon Caravelle or the *Eroica*? She turned to meet Blackburn's unyielding scrutiny with a sharp twist of her head, only to absorb the many Blackburns reflected in the mirrors of the conservatory—the spy, the libertine, the cold-blooded brother, the even colder lover.

Whatever it takes.

If Devon understood the words he had thrown at her at Blackfriars Bridge, she understood them even better now.

Devon felt as though her heart might break. A ridiculous cliché. She sat on the edge of the bed, *Le Comte's bed*, in a suite of rooms dark with heavy baroque furnishings. She remembered the scene between de Maupassant and Susannah Treadwell with sick trepidation.

What now?

If she was to survive Blackburn and the Frenchman, her only recourse was to banish all emotion, to hold in her memory forever the moment when the doors had snapped shut behind the Marquess, leaving her alone in the conservatory with Le Comte.

Blackburn had walked away from her.

For the only time in her life she could remember, her heart was at war with her head. Why was she prepared to ignore all the evidence for the sensation of Blackburn's arms around her? The facts told the story of a ruthless man, one who would sacrifice his brother to get what he wanted. Sacrificing her to Le Comte had about as much impact on what was left of his conscience as a drop of water in the ocean.

Devon swept herself from the bed impatiently and surveyed the contents of the bedroom, the solid ornate appointments in oak and royal blue brocade attesting to generations of a powerful, aristocratic family. The Frenchman had quite deliberately escorted her to his rooms after Blackburn had departed, a heartless glow of satisfaction settling upon his face.

Her only plan was the silver pistol nestled under the heavy counterpane of Le Comte's bed. Cold but necessary comfort. She had perhaps a quarter hour before de Maupassant returned. The pain in her heart, strangely enough, focused her concentration. She began ticking off the possibilities. The score had to be somewhere in his apartments. She began with the dressing room, a small alcove lavishly decorated in blues and burgundy. She rifled quickly and efficiently through yards of clothing, checking pockets and cuffs for clues that surrendered no more than a cravat pin studded with rubies and a gold pocket watch.

The desk in the bedroom was too obvious, the contents of its lone drawer neat and unhelpful in its orderliness. Perplexed and on the edge of panic, she stood to the side of the giant canopied four-poster which dominated the apartments.

She could hear the footsteps coming down the hallway, a murmur of voices, of servants being dismissed for the night.

She wasn't ready. She would never be.

It seemed that in the next moment, de Maupassant stood a few feet away from her in his dressing gown in the center of the room. He regarded her with pale eyes and a thin smile, appraising the jewel he'd just purchased.

"I see you've waited to undress for me," he said, pulling tightly on the sash of his dressing gown before disposing himself confidently on a recamier at the foot of the bed, readying himself for the evening's entertainment.

Devon didn't move, steadying herself with one hand on the textured counterpane of the bed. "I'd rather not," she heard herself say with the flatness of apprehension. "That is, I'd prefer to see the score first."

"You don't trust me?" asked Le Comte with a raised eyebrow. "My, my . . . I'm beginning to think your obsession with the *Eroica* precludes all else and I don't know if that's entirely wise."

She clenched the brocade more tightly, moistening her dry lips. "I would just prefer it," she offered lamely, not moving an inch.

"I'm sure you would," he returned acidly, crossing his legs to settle more comfortably into the chaise. "But your choices are limited, as we've already discussed at length. And furthermore, you must appreciate the fine balance I've achieved, quite brilliantly, if I might say so. After this evening's event, you no longer find yourself overly enamored by our dashing Marquess and, after tonight," he paused significantly, his narrowed eyes taking in her outrageous gown, "he shall, against his will, desire you even more. I somehow think that our Marquess isn't in a sharing mood."

Devon's hand drifted over the counterpane, the cold metal of her pistol outlined in the heavy brocade. "I must congratulate you, Le Comte. You have concocted quite an elaborate scheme to ensure no unmanageable loyalties develop between two people whose only remaining focus is to work on the *Eroica.*"

"I'm so glad that you understand, Devon, that our becoming intimate is necessary for so many reasons now, most of all as a guarantee that the score remains permanently under my purview." He watched her with that look of cunning that reminded her of a snake's. "And I knew that the Marquess would find the dynamic of the situation irresistible—access to the score he's been after for years *and* an opportunity for revenge against me wrapped in the beautiful form of Devon Caravelle, brilliant Brendan Clifton's brilliant daughter."

"Then why the public music recitals?" she asked, her mouth as dry as sandpaper. She could feel the seconds ticking past as she waited for his next words.

Le Comte chuckled, looking inordinately pleased with himself. "To set the scene, of course, *ma chérie*," he explained. "And most important, to draw attention to you and let the world know—including Wellington, Blackburn, and their colleagues—that I had what they wanted right here in London."

He added, "And you do play brilliantly, my dear. That Broadwood has never resonated so well."

Devon's mental processes seemed to slow as she gambled for more time. A sputtering candle centered her attention and she tried to absorb Le Comte's words, his baroque scheming.

"You may be overestimating my abilities, Monsieur, musically and mathematically," she said, her voice loud in her ears.

"I don't think so—your father taught you well."

She flinched from the words, the rushing of blood in her ears making it difficult to concentrate. "Not well enough," she responded, knowing instinctively that to show weakness would prove her undoing.

"The time is over for vacillation, Mademoiselle," de Maupassant declared suddenly, impatient to get on with it, not a man accustomed to waiting. "Come now, don't stand there like a statue." Without removing his pale eyes from her, he gestured like an autocrat. "Undress."

Devon wouldn't, couldn't allow herself to think of Blackburn now. Her shaking hands hovered over the tiny, pearl buttons of her low bodice as her mind raced forward.

The Frenchman watched with a gleam in his eye, satisfaction coursing through his veins. "And dispense with the maidenly airs, my dear, they interest me not at all. I'm sure Blackburn would have found such behavior tedious as well," he remarked slyly, never knowing how close he came to reading her mind.

Devon eased the satin sash from below her breasts and slipped her arms out from under the sheer silk of the gown. The garment dropped from her hips and swished to the floor in a heap.

Le Comte caught his breath involuntarily and Devon cringed as his eyes crawled over her breasts trembling beneath the thin fabric of her shift. He lingered on the tops of her stockings where an elegant length of leg met silk and her white skin gleamed in the candlelight.

He purred with satisfaction. "The Marquess of Blackburn must be burning tonight. He knows exactly what he's missing, doesn't he, Devon?" he asked salaciously, the pale of his skin flushing with excitement. He noted the pride in Devon's graceful posture, the defiant tilt of her head and her wide gray eyes, shutting him out. A powerful, pleasurable surge of potency swept through him. To have both this outrageously beautiful young woman and the Marquess of Blackburn under his complete control—the anticipation fairly made his mouth water.

"Please proceed, my dear," he continued mercilessly, inching forward on the chaise. "And I wouldn't give a moment's lament for Blackburn. You would have discovered soon enough that his interest in you is," he paused deliberately, pretending to examine the small silver candelabra on the low table in front of him, "as compromised as mine."

Opportunity, Devon knew, would have to come from somewhere, instinctively sensing that ensnaring the Frenchman was her only hope. She redirected Le Comte's attention by toying with the thin straps of her chemise, allowing one to fall slowly from her shoulder, baring more skin.

"I'm simply a little nervous," she murmured, making sure that Le Comte was focused on the sultry curve of her seductively bared breasts. She still clutched a handful of silk to her shoulders, the gesture deliberately erotic and innocent at the same time. "And yet you now know that I will do anything to get my hands on the *Eroica*." She slowly walked away from the bed and toward him, moving closer until he could reach out and almost touch the sleek length of her legs. Her full lips were enticing, the artful tumble of dark red hair lustrous against her skin.

Le Comte was transfixed as her light scent enveloped him. Her thighs brushed his arm.

Her breath was soft against his ear and at odds with the

sensation of cold, unforgiving metal pressed hard against his right temple.

"Now where might I find the *Eroica*, Le Comte?" Devon Caravelle asked in her low voice, her small pistol, poking out from under several yards of thin silk, secure in her hand. "I did tell you that I would do *anything* to finally get my hands on that score."

If it weren't for the cold metal kissing his skin, Le Comte may have thought he was caught in a nightmare. Cold sweat broke out on his brow as he battled lust and fear simultaneously, unwilling to grasp fully that he was suddenly in an exceedingly vulnerable position. In a small part of his still rational mind, he vowed that Brendan Clifton's daughter would pay dearly for her actions.

"I'm expecting an answer." Devon nudged Le Comte, the gun still pressed against his temple, into sitting up straight on the recamier.

He struggled against her, but with surprising force Devon pushed him back down on the chaise. Still balancing the pistol in one hand, she pulled up the straps of her chemise efficiently, then quickly began making strips of her gown, the flimsy fabric rending easily in her one free hand and teeth. Exhilarated, she was thrilled to see the offending garment savaged.

"Don't dare move." She used the strips to tie his ankles around the legs of the sofa. His wrists came next, which she bound behind his back.

"You can't kill me!" Le Comte declared as the reality of the situation penetrated his brain, his anger rapidly rising to a fever pitch at being tied like a trussed pig. If he tried to move, he would fall face first with his backside in the air.

His usually pale features contorted into a mottled red. "You haven't the slightest idea what I'm capable of or you would be a quivering mass of nerves at this moment. Mark my words, I will *hunt* you down like an animal!"

"Back to my question, Le Comte, if you please. Once more,

where might I find the *Eroica*?" Devon refused to be cowed, taking great pleasure in Le Comte—ridiculous in his dressing gown and immobilized on the elegant sofa. After ensuring her handiwork was sound, she stepped away from him, one hand on her hip, the other on her pistol still cocked in his direction.

They must present an incongruous sight, a woman in a shift holding a man at gunpoint. But her head felt strangely clear, her thoughts rational and unclouded.

She waved the pistol in Le Comte's face. "What will it be?"

Le Comte's face, now drained of blood, turned crafty. "I can help you . . . save you time and effort," he offered with finely honed negotiating skills, convinced in his arrogance that he could persuade her to reevaluate her situation. "The best cryptanalysts have already applied themselves to the composition and to no avail. We've found neither a cryptographic system nor a codebook that's of any use."

Devon shook her head, her contempt evident. "Do you take me for a fool, Le Comte? My father taught me that every mathematically constructed cryptographic system presents a unique challenge, the unraveling of which requires the exercise of unusual powers of observation, inductive and deductive reasoning, much concentration, perseverance and, I might add, a vivid imagination."

"Which is precisely the reason I came to you," Le Comte tried with flattering words.

As though she would respond to such sycophancy. Her mind raced ahead, calculating how she could convince him to tell her where the score was hidden.

"I'm becoming exceedingly impatient, Monsieur," she said, shifting her weight to her other foot. "If you're expecting either divine or domestic intervention, you'll be disappointed. If I remember correctly, you informed the servants that you would brook no interruptions this evening." All the while her ears strained nervously to hear approaching footsteps outside Le Comte's apartments.

The haughty bitch. The Frenchman was near apoplexy, his bound hands quivering to fold themselves around Devon Caravelle's elegant neck until they had squeezed the last bit of air from her lungs.

Instead, he sighed dramatically in an attempt to signal a partial surrender.

"There's no reason we can't work with one another now, is there?" he asked, conciliation in his tone. "Your parents were Bonapartists, as am I. We share the same allegiances in the end. I assure you the *Eroica* doesn't contain all the answers—there's more, much more that I can provide you with. Even Blackburn won't be of any help deciphering the score without my contribution."

Devon considered him carefully, at the moment cool, chaste, and determined in her whisp of silk chemise to end the matter. "You don't have to worry about Blackburn—like you, he's no longer a factor in this equation as far as I'm concerned, Le Comte. But what you do have to worry about is this. I am going to count to three," she said calmly, "after which I will shoot you, not in the heart or head or anywhere fatal, but merely in the foot or maybe somewhat higher on your thigh . . ." she trailed off deliberately. "That way, if you give me misleading information as to where I might find the score, I can return and finish the task. And finish it I will. So once more, where is the score?"

For emphasis, she cocked her pistol and aimed at the inside of the Frenchman's thigh, now trembling underneath the rich fabric of his dressing gown.

Le Comte refused to struggle against his bonds, preferring instead to dwell upon all the horrific things he might do to Devon Caravelle once he was finished with her. To be powerless was his worst nightmare, a fear that had haunted him most of his life, the ghosts of marauding peasants, a glistening guillotine, and masked executioners always close in his dreams.

Devon Caravelle couldn't begin to know what she'd just done.

Then he felt the snout of the pistol nestle close to his right testicle. His voice thin and high, he said, "You will find the *Eroica* score in the Broadwood piano."

Could anything have been more obvious?

Wasting no time, Devon proceeded to gag Le Comte to guarantee against screams that eventually could bring servants running.

"Now how hard was that?" she asked him, a part of her regretting that she never did get the chance to pull the trigger. Spinning on her feet, she quickly doused the tapers flickering by the bedside. Le Comte grunted helplessly, and the room subsided into darkness. She was all too aware that she hadn't much time.

It wouldn't be long before the suite was bedlam, Le Comte's sputtering commands lost in the pounding of footsteps, in fumbling attempts to light the tapers. Hovering around the Frenchman like drunken wasps, the servants would fall over one another in awkward attempts to free their master.

She moved quickly, slipping from the room, leaving Le Comte behind groaning into his gag and struggling against the silken ties that bound him to the chaise. She raced through the house, wraithlike in the darkness, making her way down the deserted front hall, her feet flying soundlessly over the cold marble floors.

Before any of the footmen might see her, she ducked into her rooms and dove into her wardrobe. Tearing off her shift, she threw on the shirt, breeches, and boots, tightening a leather belt holding her pistol and money pouch at her waist. Peering around the corner, she then made her way back to the conservatory where she hoped the Broadwood still stood.

Damn. For some reason the heavy door was locked and she nearly sobbed with frustration, her cheek warm against the cool wood. She grappled with the latch, hands trembling, her body shaking as she imagined she heard voices floating down the front hall.

She tried again. Tugged harder. Miraculously, the latch gave way under her nerveless fingers and she opened the door to a slit. Candles had burned down to the last inch, dimly illuminating the cavernous space. She held her breath as she crept into the conservatory, the Broadwood piano silhouetted against the moonlight.

It seemed impossible that she had never thought to search the instrument for a hiding place that Le Comte must have chosen with the deepest sense of irony.

If he'd been telling her the truth.

Dreading the prospect of having to retrace her steps to his apartments, she began by lifting the lid of the piano bench only to find empty space, which left the piano itself and the heavy cover that fanned over the hammers and strings. Gritting her teeth against the silence and cursing the lack of light, Devon pushed open the lid to peer into the viscera of the instrument. To ensure she hadn't missed a musical folio taped up against the cabinet, she palmed the interior carefully.

Nothing. Le Comte had lied.

She bit back her disappointment, easing the lid closed with a soft thud that had the sound of finality. It would have been too bloody simple, and yet, hiding the score in the Broadwood would have so delighted Le Comte, as he watched her practice, listened to her play, hosted the toast of London—with everyone totally oblivious to the century's most explosive secret hidden in their midst.

Then she remembered. The concert. The loose pedal that had vexed her while she played. She crouched down to the floor, pushed aside the seat, and groped for the piece of brass. Ecstatic now, she wriggled it gently at first, finding it as movable as she remembered. A few more energetic tugs and the pedal came lose from its moorings.

She probed the opening carefully, finding to her astonishment that the two-foot panel easily gave way—along with a grosgrain folder which fell conveniently on her lap.

Beethoven's Third Symphony.

In her trembling hands she held the original score of the *Eroica.*

Chapter 12

Two weeks later . . .

The London home of the Duke of Wellington overlooked the entrance to Hyde Park. The prominent location of Apsley House just outside the toll gates at Knightsbridge led people to refer to the imposing residence as *Number One* London, although there was no such official designation.

On a warm early June morning the Marquess of Blackburn found himself waiting at the bottom of the grand interior staircase of Number One examining Antonio Canova's daunting statue of Napoleon portrayed as Mars the Peacemaker. This was not the first time that he had been summoned to the Duke's official residence in the capital and it was not the first time that he wondered about the perils of hubris, the overweening vanity that could bring heroes tumbling from their lofty heights.

The house had been purchased by the Duke over a year ago and he was intent on enlarging it to express his status, adding a ninety-foot Waterloo Gallery to house his impressive collection of paintings from grateful kings and emperors whom he had delivered from Napoleon's marauding grasp. Blackburn had been one of the first to admire the astonishing collection, including works by Velazquez, Goya, Rubens, Correggio, Brueghel, Steen, Hooch, Wilkie, and Lawrence.

But it was always Canova's colossal nude of Napoleon that gave him pause.

Instead of being ushered up the broad staircase to the first floor, where Wellington often entertained privately in the smaller, more intimate rooms, Blackburn was led by the butler through the vast main salon and into the dining hall which was more commonly used for hosting on a grand scale. In preparation for a state visit later that day, the table was set with Sèvres Egyptian service commissioned by Napoleon for his Empress Josephine. The morning sun glinted off the eight-foot-long silver Portuguese centerpiece which always adorned the table at the Duke's annual Waterloo Banquet, the event where the Duke entertained officers who had served under him at Waterloo and in the Peninsular War.

Blackburn himself had never been present at the ceremonial dinner. He understood his role all too well, a responsibility that had little to do with muskets and cannon fire and everything to do with deception and deceit. Disappearing was what he did best, only to reemerge as the world-weary Marquess of Blackburn intent on his tour of womanizing and other sundry debauchery that society came to expect from him.

And in the interim he lived his other life trying to ignore the consequences of treachery on the spirit and on the soul. Meeting with a French spy on a darkened Paris street, breaking a code that was assumed indissoluble, rescuing Wellington's adjutant taken prisoner the morning before he was to be executed—sometimes the exhilaration of the game called spycraft softened the jagged edges that had begun to engrave permanent scar tissue around his heart. Like the best narcotic, the exhilaration could mask the damage that was being done underneath, only to be exposed when the stakes were highest.

Waiting in the cool interior of the dining hall for Wellington, Blackburn thought of Edward's death. The stakes had never been so high as that night on the coast when he had learned how inured to real human connection he'd become. Not that he and his brother—or his parents for that matter— had ever been particularly close. Theirs had been an arm's-length upbringing marked by a procession of governesses and tutors and then, not soon after, public schools meant to harden them into stalwarts of the English aristocracy.

Whether he'd loved his conservative, reliable brother, who was particularly suited to his position as heir to the family estates, was not at question. On good days he could rationalize his murder, a *sacrifice* as it became known in his mind, for king and country and for the too many men and women who had suffered and perished in the conflagration of Europe. He had exchanged his brother's life to keep vital information from the hands of a dangerous enemy.

Yet what truly haunted him most during those dark nights of the soul was the realization that he had been able to make that decision so easily, all too ready to bring down an iron curtain on his emotions, leading him to fear that he could no longer experience any authenticity of feeling at all.

And now when he looked at his hollow-eyed reflection in the colossal mirror above the sideboard laden with silver, he wondered whether his own sense of self had survived. His dealings with Devon Caravelle had thrown his deficiencies into sharp relief once again—and he hated her for it. Not that it should matter, this numbness. It was better this way, better that Devon Caravelle had fulfilled all his cynical assumptions about her motives. Like the rest of their colleagues involved in the craft of intelligence, she had a job to do, a game to play, and she did both admirably. He had given her what she wanted, the man who had murdered her father, and in return, she had seduced de Maupassant.

Blackburn despised himself for the volcanic anger that welled in him at the memory of their last meeting. *Hell*, he'd been like a rutting stag in her presence, hard-pressed from running Le Comte through with whatever blunt instrument was at hand.

Blackburn would remember forever the Frenchman's pale hands on Devon's creamy flesh. Once again, he saw her long lashes close over her eyes, shutting out his unyielding scrutiny. And at that moment something he thought he'd lost long ago, something deep inside him that he couldn't even identify, died.

Mercifully, as it turned out. Today he felt nothing.

For the past two weeks, he'd been waiting for word that she had fulfilled her bargain with de Maupassant and secured the score for their work. Together, they would unravel the formula both the Frenchman and Wellington so desperately wanted—and they would do it cleanly and with the detached precision of professionals. He welcomed the dispassionate purpose that had honed his need to avenge his brother's murder into a finely wrought weapon.

In the interim, he was left wondering why he was cooling his heels in the dining hall when the door opened and the Duke of Wellington swept into the room dismissing his adjutant over his shoulder.

"My apologies, Blackburn," he announced with his usual accelerated cadence, "kept busy with dispatches from St. James's Palace, you know, never give me a moment's peace."

"Lady Wellington and the children are at Stratfield Saye?" inquired Blackburn politely.

"Yes, they prefer the country estate to London," the Duke said shortly, gesturing to two chairs covered in cerulean satin positioned at the west end of the massive dining hall. "And you, have you ridden in from Armathwaite?"

Blackburn realized that the Duke asked the question out of mere courtesy, as he well knew that the Marquess hadn't opened his family's London house in Mayfair since Edward's death over two years ago. He preferred to stay in the country, the isolation of Armathwaite reflecting his need for privacy, while his rooms at White's were more than adequate when he was in town.

The two men took their seats, as moments later a footman

appeared with a tray of coffee and brandy. Blackburn declined the offering.

"Have you heard anything from de Maupassant?" Blackburn rested his hands on the arms of the chair with deceptive nonchalance.

The Duke balanced his cup and saucer carefully on his knee before answering, "Not precisely."

Blackburn fixed him with a gaze that revealed exactly nothing. "You expect me to believe that, Arthur?"

"Belief has no place in the world in which you and I inhabit, Gray, I should think." The Duke looked down his long nose at one of his oldest and best recruits. "I trust you've had enough to keep even your restless mind busy in the past fortnight."

He was referring to the series of intercepted dispatches that St. James's Palace had received from France five days ago that were encrypted in a sophisticated code that nobody quite knew what to do with. More important, they spoke directly to the contents of the *Eroica* manuscript. Blackburn had been working to analyze their contents, applying both transposition and substitution ciphers. He remembered many days and nights devising and decoding limitless numbers of ciphers in the Peninsula and later in Vienna and Brussels. But the ones he had labored over at Armathwaite were of a distinctly different quality—and content.

"Find anything interesting?" asked the Duke keeping his voice neutral.

"Absolutely—and it makes our pursuit of the *Eroica* even more critical." Blackburn was not entirely pleased with Wellington's circuitous approach to their meeting. "Before we get to that, I'm still wondering why you wanted to have this conversation here in the dining hall—it's a little grand even for you, Arthur."

The Duke smiled approvingly, setting down his cup on a side table, studying Blackburn carefully. He then unfurled his body from the chair, his highly polished Hessians making long strides across the room to the sideboard. Leaning against the wall was a sword.

"Do you see this, Gray?" Wellington held up the rapier, a simply carved but deadly weapon.

Blackburn sensed rather than knew where the Duke was going with this change of direction, and he didn't like it. "You miss the battlefield that much?" he jested in an attempt to throw him off the scent.

"No, as a matter of fact, I do not." Wellington turned the sword first one way and then the other, studying it as though it were a curious museum object. "I simply keep Napoleon's sword close by as a constant reminder as to what we were— and are—fighting for."

Blackburn swore silently before wiping a palm over his eyes. "I'm a little too cynical for what you're about to say next, Arthur. Best save it."

"We rescued the world from a tyrant." Undeterred, Wellington pushed on, putting the sword back in its resting place. "It's that simple—and we're continuing the fight, particularly right now, or had you forgotten, Gray?" The question echoed in the air between them, the face of Devon Caravelle shimmering in front of Blackburn's eyes.

What did the Duke of Wellington want from him? He drummed his fingers impatiently on the arms of his chair. "You can hardly accuse me for turning my back on the cause, Arthur." And what he really wanted to say was that he had given up his whole life for a cause he wasn't entirely sure of. Unbidden, he remembered an incident just a few days before the battle of Waterloo. It was the night he had rescued the Duke's top lieutenant who had been taken prisoner by the French behind enemy lines. Dressed as a simple soldier, he had slipped by a young sentinel, probably not much more than a boy. Their exchange had been brief, the youth's devotion to his cause and for his General Bonaparte, the symbol of a Revolution, something that Blackburn almost coveted.

"*Liberté, égalité, fraternité,*" the boy had murmured as Blackburn slid past him in the flicker of torchlight around the encampment. The sentinel could not have possibly known about the battle that would soon snuff out his passion and very probably his life.

Perversely, at this moment in Apsley House, Blackburn envied him.

"I'm not faulting you for anything."

The words wrenched him from his recollection and he saw the Duke facing him down the treasure-filled length of the dining hall. "I'm just reminding you that our very way of life was at stake—is at stake. And that's not simply my opinion," he added, gesturing widely to the contents of the room. "I now possess a collection of art and furnishings unrivaled by any of my contemporaries, the result of grateful nations and private citizens. Don't forget the two hundred paintings from the royal collection of the kings of Spain that I recovered from Joseph Bonaparte after the Battle of Vitoria in 1813. And don't forget that after King Ferdinand was reinstated as monarch, he asked me to keep the paintings as a gift of thanks."

"You'll be lecturing me on the existence of good and evil next, or worse still on the existence of God," Blackburn said, leaving his chair and walking over to the window that overlooked the back garden. He stared at the trunk of a tree, away from Wellington's treasure chest which, at this moment, glittered falsely. "Even you can't perceive life as being that simple, that black and white."

"It certainly helps at times—which is all I'm saying to you."

Blackburn turned away from the garden and looked at his old mentor. There was recognition in his eyes that were as astute on the battlefield as off. "You don't have to bludgeon me over the head, Arthur. I understand what's at stake. But I also understand what's been lost."

"You're speaking of the thousands of lives lost."

"I'm also speaking about the valuable principles of Rousseauian ideals that have been lost."

Wellington snorted contemptuously. "The world isn't run on idealism, for God's sake, Gray! It's run on power—military, political, and economic. You're worrying me."

Blackburn inclined his head in agreement, but the pause before he spoke was significant. "Thanks for the reminder, but let's move on. These types of conversations tend not to go anywhere useful." And made him damned uncomfortable, as though he were revealing too much. "I was summoned here for a purpose, so could we proceed?"

Pleased that he had set the right tone and the right course, the Duke nodded and sat back down in his chair, gesturing to Blackburn to do the same. "Very well," he said, helping himself to more coffee and pouring a cup for Blackburn. "What did you find in the dispatches?"

"Some extremely volatile messages, and I mean that literally," supplied Blackburn with his customary directness, beginning to relax, at ease with the world of ciphers and codes. "From what I could glean, we're dealing with a type of explosive, a substance or device capable of producing a volume of rapidly expanding gas that exerts sudden pressure on its surroundings."

"Like gunpowder."

"Better than that. By a thousandfold."

Rarely was the Duke of Wellington at a loss for words. He leaned forward in his chair, urging Blackburn to continue.

"We know that blackpowder, the first chemical explosive, was invented in China some one thousand years ago. It's a mixture of saltpeter, sulfur, and charcoal and it must be ignited by flame or intense heat." Blackburn's voice was bone dry. "But we're looking at something far more powerful here."

Wellington loosened the collar of his military jacket. "We suspected it was a new type of explosive. But what exactly do you mean by more powerful?"

"We're dealing with a highly unstable mix that has explosive implications. And once again, I mean that literally. Other than that, the dispatches gave us no clue as to the chemical compound or mixture. That's what we need the *Eroica* for."

The Duke had lost all his color against the martial red of his coat. He jerked from the chair, expanding to his full height with hands behind his back in military fashion.

"*Bloody hell*—we'd better get our hands on the *Eroica* score quickly," he snapped. "If we don't uncover the actual formula and secure it for Britain, I shudder at the thought of what a revolutionary faction in Europe might do with it. They could force the instant release of Bonaparte."

"Wasn't that always the plan?" asked Blackburn slowly, watching closely for Wellington's reaction, not quite certain whether it was panic that he was witnessing. He leaned back in the chair, his eyes narrowing suspiciously. "Now it's my turn—what have you heard from *chez de Maupassant et al*?"

"That's the problem—we've heard nothing." The words were clipped.

Blackburn inwardly recoiled at the image of the Frenchman and Devon reveling in their newfound intimacy. He let out a short, painful breath before saying sarcastically, "I suppose the lovers have other things on their minds. And as long as it's not the score, we can buy some time for ourselves. We know that de Maupassant is planning to offer the formula to the Bonapartist camp."

Looking momentarily out of his depth, a rare occurrence, the Duke answered with uncharacteristic vagueness, as though he had more important matters to attend to. He rested his hands on the back of his chair. "And you were going to do something about that, Blackburn, as I recall."

"Were it that simple," said Blackburn. "Whereas I *have* accomplished three objectives, Arthur. First, I have secured Devon Caravelle's cooperation in exchange for evidence that de Maupassant murdered her father. She promises to work with me against the Frenchman. Secondly, these dispatches reveal that the *Eroica* won't give us the entire picture. Le Comte must have in his possession the link that will make the formula complete."

Wellington's eyes sharpened. "You mentioned the unstable nature of this compound."

Blackburn nodded. " 'Unstable' means that it would prove useless in the battlefield because it couldn't be transported safely without the possibility of it exploding at the wrong time. Which is where de Maupassant comes in and the reason why he's confident about letting me work on the score. He has the final piece of the puzzle, without which the formula is useless to England or anybody else for that matter."

"Do we have any idea where we might find it?"

"Absolutely none. You can be sure that de Maupassant will be playing those cards very close to his chest."

"What about chemists, scientists. Somebody must be familiar with this stabilizing compound."

Blackburn shrugged. "I know a man from my Paris days who may prove useful—Ascanio Sobrero. But let's get at the *Eroica* first."

"And what's the third objective you've accomplished?"

Blackburn paused for a second. "According to the dispatches, Le Comte is late on delivering on his promise to liberate Bonaparte from St. Helena." It was something he didn't want to understand, the Frenchman's reluctance to relinquish the score to Devon Caravelle. Perhaps his lust had overcome his reason. Recoiling from the thought, Blackburn continued, "The Bonapartists would pay dearly for such leverage. Imagine holding Europe and England hostage with the threat of explosives that could detonate instantly, releasing the rapid expansion of hot gases to cause a highly destructive blast."

As though torn from his considerations, Wellington's voice became firmer, taking on the booming tone that Blackburn was accustomed to hearing. "No—I don't care to imagine it at all, Gray. Which is why we must act with the greatest haste."

"De Maupassant needs me to decipher the code." Blackburn's eyes were hard.

"Unfortunately, it's not up to Le Comte," said Wellington, straightening the collar of his military jacket.

"What's the problem?" Blackburn asked, his suspicions growing. He pushed himself from the chair until he was facing the Duke directly.

"Le Comte no longer has the score, we fear."

"Then who does? I can't imagine that he'd let it out of his sight," said Blackburn, suddenly listening to the pounding of his heart.

The Duke of Wellington knew when he'd won and he knew when he'd lost. There was no use holding out for reinforcements in this instance.

"We think we know who has the score."

"Who?"

"Devon Caravelle." The Duke looked Blackburn straight in the eye.

"What do you mean? De Maupassant has given it to her to work on, correct?"

The Duke took a deep breath, a catastrophe of epic proportions looming on his horizon. "You don't understand, Blackburn. We discovered today that Devon Caravelle has left London—she's disappeared and we believe she's taken the *Eroica* with her."

Blackburn swore in every language he knew as he catapulted from Apsley House to his rooms at White's. Damn. She must have seduced the Frenchman, then made off with the century's most explosive secret and gone back to France. He felt it in his blood that she had returned to the country of her birth.

Devon Caravelle would have friends there, contacts there. Better still, she would know where to hide, which would give her time to work on the formula. While she was a superb musician and mathematician, she lacked the scientific or military knowledge to make sense of what she might discover. Thank God for that.

Whether she would destroy the formula ultimately or deliver it to the Bonapartists was anybody's guess, including his. Because as he'd discovered, he didn't know Devon Caravelle at all.

He threw his greatcoat to the butler who stood patiently in the hallway at White's. The club on St. James's Street numbered close to five hundred members, including some of society's loftiest aristocrats, from the earls of Cholmondeley, Chesterfield, and Rockingham to Blackburn's own family, including both his late father and brother. He bypassed the bow window where the inner circle often held court, placing wagers in the betting book, gambling on everything from matters of life and death to such trifles as whose wife would be the first to beget an heir, who would marry or die first, and which debutante would succumb to the charms of various club members.

Instead of repairing to his rooms, he ordered a brandy and threw himself into one of the deep leather chairs in the library. His was a cool head which dictated that he not go running off to France without first knowing where to look. Her father's old house outside Paris in Blois was too obvious, and she wouldn't go back to the Conservatoire, the first place anyone would look. Wellington's men knew nothing about her whereabouts. Until two days ago the damned fools had believed she and Le Comte were simply comporting themselves clandestinely within the walls of the town house on Berkeley Square.

Two weeks—and the tracks were as cold as an arctic winter. Blackburn slammed the crystal tumbler on the satinwood table at his side, attracting at least a few curious glances from club members. He would leave tomorrow for Calais, but first he had to find answers to a few questions.

A half hour and an anonymous hackney cab ride later, he

inhaled the tangy air of the docks as he strode through the debris-strewn streets, the murky corners only occasionally lit by torchlight revealing a sailor bobbing on liquor-drenched legs or a streetwalker, eyes gleaming for her next customer. Striding through the darkened streets, Blackburn thanked his inner demons which had dictated that he hire his own man to keep track of de Maupassant's comings and goings. He had learned long ago that the wheels of bureaucracy, particularly St. James's Palace's, ground exceedingly slowly.

The gamey odor of the ludicrously named White Swan was a combination of too much tobacco and sweat layered with scent purchased by the gallon and liquor distilled in the backroom. The tin lamps swaying in the threshold brought Blackburn back to countless nights spent in uneasy exchanges with hardened criminals who had information to sell and not much else. Although most of the customers were busy drinking or playing dice, it always paid to slant a newcomer a look, to take stock of his considerable height, the quality of his clothes, the confident gait.

Blackburn sat down at a table by the fire where a buxom waitress, her wide face liberally rouged, immediately threaded to his side, ready to serve him drinks and whatever else he wanted. He thought it wise to forgo the brandy and ordered a whisky and a gin instead.

"Is Simon around tonight?" he asked. The waitress pursed her lips, leaning one elbow on the table to ensure Blackburn got an eyeful of her charms displayed by her low-cut dress.

"Sure is—but yer sure ye wouldn't be wantin' to spend some time with someone else tonight?" She puffed up her round cheeks looking hopeful. Blackburn smiled and stuffed a few coins into her apron pocket, sending her on her way for his order and for Simon.

He'd lost too much time in places like the White Swan, looking for men like Simon. He surveyed the soot-stained painting over the mantelpiece depicting a mighty fleet of ships on a storm-tossed ocean, the Union Jack flying proudly on the mastheads. Britain's heroic fleet that had helped turn the tides against the French and Napoleon. If it had only been so easy, so clean and decisive as history would make it. All the subterfuge and the ambiguity, the lies and the ugliness, would be swept away, leaving a narrative that was as undemanding and satisfying as a painting hung over a fireplace.

Out of the din and the pall of smoke, Simon materialized and slid unnoticed on the bench opposite him.

"It's been a real while, guv'ner," he said, his grin revealing a few missing teeth despite his comparatively tender years. His hair was either blond or dark brown, hard to tell from too few baths and too much soot from smoky backroom taverns.

He eyed Blackburn speculatively, taking in the brooding glance and the dangerously restive mood. Simon had seen enough in his time to know Blackburn was never a man to be trifled with, particularly, he sensed, tonight. "I've been keepin' an eye on that Frenchie like you ordered and tryin' to stay out of sight of those other gents," he said helpfully.

Wellington's useless men. Blackburn's fingers tightened around his glass.

"Not much to report, though. Jes the usuals comin' and goin'."

"What about the young woman, with the dark red hair?" Blackburn found himself describing Devon as he would any other prospect he was tracking.

"Didn' see much of her, jes once or twice," answered Simon, a grin spreading his face when the waitress appeared and dropped a tumbler of gin in front of him. "Thanks, guv'ner."

Although knowing what the answer would be, Blackburn continued, "When was the last time you saw her?"

Simon's head bobbed up and down as he gave the question serious consideration. "Mebbe a fortnight ago . . ." He took a serious draught of his gin. "When you was last there, come to think about it. After you'd left early in the morning, I was standin' in the corner of the square, you know, by the mews. An' there was this terrible tumult, footmen running around like with their heads cut off."

Blackburn tensed, inhaling deeply from the thick tavern smoke. "But no sign of the woman." Devon Caravelle had disappeared into thin air, his worst fears confirmed.

Simon squirmed on the hard bench, wishing he could provide more details. "There was another woman, though. You know, the dark-haired one, Lady Treadwell, leavin' the house in a high dudgeon she was, earlier that afternoon."

Leaving his whisky untouched, Blackburn pondered that last nugget. An angry Susannah did not bode well, leading him to think that she and Le Comte might have had a falling out. But over what? He doubted very much that the Frenchman would share information of even the remotest value with the sometimes useful but always volatile Lady Treadwell. He passed a few gold sovereigns to the young man at the table, his muscles twitching to get back to White's and off to Calais. He'd learned no more than he already suspected.

"Good work, Simon," he said with a grim smile, shrugging on his greatcoat. "Keep on the lookout—I'll be away for a time, but you can send me messages via my club."

He left as swiftly as he had come, leaving his scout a few pounds richer and happily nursing not only a gin but also a whisky. He exited out into a narrow, unlit alley, closing the door behind him. A light rain slicked his hair as he walked toward the light at the nearest end of the laneway. There was nothing else he could do but follow his instincts and set out for Paris, and once there, hope his contacts had seen or heard of Devon Caravelle. In his worst moments, he wondered whether she was now working with a new partner or had allied herself directly with a member of the Bonapartists.

Not bothering to draw the collar of his greatcoat around his face to offset the rain, he considered walking back to St. James's Street. The road was heavy with fog and thickened by a steady downpour.

He looked up for sympathy to the black sky when out of the dark three men appeared, vaulting over a low wall in the alleyway. Shadows coalescing in the dark, they hurled themselves at him a split second later.

Blackburn dodged. Then a fist smashed into the side of his face. Pain slashed through his head and neck and the world swam blackly. The dancing lights that temporarily blinded him didn't slow him down when another man grabbed him from behind to give his arm a brutal twist. The pain jolted him to a new level of awareness as he spun around and hit him in the stomach, just as the third man's hands went straight for his throat.

Blackburn forced his body to relax for the slightest of seconds and lean into his assailant before launching both his fists in a series of lightning moves that pummeled the man into the ground. Breathing heavily, he turned to the two remaining men in a rush of movement, kicking one to the gravel next to his partner, and then grabbing the last one, already dazed from the fusillade of blows, by the neck.

"Who the hell are you and what do you want?" he growled, hauling him up against the low wall. He banged the man's head against the whitewashed stone for added emphasis. "Talk."

Upon closer inspection the face appeared familiar, with the big beefy look of one of de Maupassant's henchmen—Malcolm, was it? Last time, the trio had success abducting him outside Susannah Treadwell's residence.

Tonight, however, was an entirely different matter.

Reluctantly, Malcolm opened one eye and stared uncomprehendingly. He shuddered, not at the fire of pain coursing through his body, but at the coldest pair of eyes he'd ever seen. In his greatcoat, Blackburn looked like the grim reaper ready to take him home.

Perhaps his luck was turning after all, thought Blackburn, ignoring the pain pulsing under his right cheekbone. He gripped the man's face between his hands, pressing his gloved fingers into his purpling skin.

"I want a straight answer—what does that bloody bastard of a Frenchman want?" he ground out.

The response was a dry whisper. "Devon Caravelle ... Mebbe you're together with her ... ye know her whereabouts ..." He coughed and sputtered as Blackburn released him, sparing a shaky glance at his cohorts lying motionless on the ground of the alleyway.

Blackburn shook his head menacingly, the droplets of rain like crystals showering from his hair. "Why don't *you* tell me where she is?" The hopelessness began to close in on him again.

Malcolm didn't answer. De Maupassant hadn't a clue where Devon had gone either.

Fuck.

Somewhere in the dark a cat mewled. Blackburn pushed back from the wall allowing Malcolm to stagger to his full height. The man looked like he was barely capable of finding his way home.

"I have a message for Le Comte," said Blackburn, stepping over one of the men at his feet as he turned to exit the alleyway.

"Tell him that if he knows what's good for him, he'll not go after Devon Caravelle. She's mine now—along with the *Eroica*." His face was splattered with rain, sweat, and blood. "And tell him one thing more. Tell him that there's more to come. I'm only just getting started."

As if to underscore his words, the downpour intensified, pelting the bodies in the alleyway with brutal disregard.

Paris in the springtime, but Blackburn was in no mood to take in the low hills and the winding Seine with its beautiful bridges. He recalled a time when the French capital was the most dangerous of places after the first years of the Revolution, when a gray haze had masked the city in a permanent mix of wood smoke and mist.

But in these first weeks of June, he was surrounded by whitewashed walls, pale stone, and a profusion of church spires reflecting their light back into the sky. At night the streets were lit by thousands of tallow candles, a wonder to many eyes accustomed to the pitch darkness of overcast nights.

Following a quick two-day passage from London to Calais by boat and then Paris by horse, he established himself prominently in apartments borrowed from an old friend near the Luxembourg Palace. In the twenty-four hours that followed, he sent out messages to his old contacts, setting up meetings to discover whether any of them had seen or heard of Devon returning to Paris.

After another fruitless rendezvous that surrendered no new information, Blackburn found himself riding by the Concergerie on the Île de la Cité in late afternoon. Silhouetted against an uncommon blue sky, the medieval building recalled a Paris that he had only heard about, a time when the fortress's more famous prisoners included Marie Antoinette. During the Terror, the Conciergerie regularly housed the prisoners slated for execution and it was also one of the sites for the gruesome September massacres in 1792. Earlier that afternoon he'd met a former contact near the newly rechristened Place Louis XVI, during the revolutionary era better known as the Place de la Révolution and the home of the guillotine that ultimately executed the king. Blackburn had been told that in the final stages of the Revolution the ghastly mechanism had moved to the Faubourg St.-Antoine because the residents along the rue St.-Honoré could no longer tolerate the stench of blood.

It made his brother's death insignificant in comparison.

On the fourth day, he decided to abandon his strategy and simply wander the area around the Faubourg St.-Victoire, strolling by the Conservatoire on rue St.-Cecile. From the upper windows came the sounds of violins, lilting and sweet, drifting down to the street below. He stood on the corner, looking for a lithe figure, burnished hair covered by a hood or buried in a pelisse. Blackburn would know her instantly, the turn of her head, the tilt of her chin, the flash of gray eyes.

From a distance came the strains of a piano, wafting on the breeze of the chestnut trees like the scent of early summer, a simple cantata. And then in the innocent sunshine, it occurred to him—the one thing Devon could not live without, even in hiding: a pianoforte.

There had to be thousands in a city with a population close to one million. Blackburn began with the best, Sebastian Erard. He sent two of his premier contacts to do the frontline research, questioning the great man himself, the designer who'd won favor not only from French piano buyers, but also from Louise XVI, from whom he was granted a license to produce pianos.

Then it was only a matter of footwork. Interestingly enough, Erard in the last month had sold two pianos, one in the area of Faubourg St.-Michel, the other on St.-Jacques. Blackburn placed two men in front of the identified addresses, both of whom came back to him empty-handed.

It was too simple, he argued with himself, pacing the salon of his apartments near the Luxembourg later that evening. Amid an unaccustomed splash of silks and satins, he rifled through the disparate facts that he knew about Devon, hoping that some pattern would emerge. He remembered her playing the piano at Armathwaite, on the old pianoforte that she had made sound like magic. He also remembered her concert at de Maupassant's. Of course, the Frenchman would have nothing but the best for his protégée, and the best piano in England was the Broadwood, a name associated with innovation and quality.

He moved toward the windows overlooking the ordered beauty of the Luxembourg Gardens suspended in twilight stillness. The calm beckoned, inviting him to recall the opening bars of Beethoven's *Eroica*, the triumphal crash of chords, the soaring rhythms that for him would always conjure the worst associations.

And then he remembered.

Just two years previously, somebody, somewhere, at some tedious reception mentioned that Broadwood had built a special piano for Beethoven with four strings per note, for extra volume, in the hopes that the almost deaf Beethoven might be able to hear it.

Blackburn turned away from the window and allowed his mind to wander. It was an educated guess, nothing more, and he resumed his pacing. And yet, the idea was gaining ground, becoming more viable with every impatient step he took. Devon would try to find a Broadwood—not only to play, but also to help unravel the code buried in Beethoven's *Third Symphony*.

And how many English Broadwoods could there possibly be in Paris—particularly after the blockade of English goods that lasted for close to fifteen years?

Thirty-six hours later Blackburn stood in front of the Place des Vosges with its fragrant linden trees and symmetrical lawns. Hidden in the shadows of one of the arabesque arcades, he watched as Devon Caravelle, in a somber brown pelisse, made her way up through the courtyard of one of the seventeenth-century *hôtel particuliers*.

As unexpected as a rapier's thrust, white hot desire knifed through him, cutting through the cold, bursting through the numbness.

He wanted her. Instantly. Fiercely. Wildly.

And this time, on his terms alone.

A surge of fire suffused his body, the heat contrasting with the cool marble interior of the building. A quick look told him that it was divided into three flats. An old woman stood perplexed in the domed entranceway, hobbling her way slowly down the last steps of the spiral staircase.

"Mademoiselle Caravelle?" he asked rapidly, aware of the raisin-sharp eyes assessing him shrewdly. The elderly lady shook her head, pulling a scarf closer around her neck despite the warmth of the June day.

Burning with an impatience that gnawed at his nerve endings, he bypassed her on the stairs, taking three steps at a time, pulling first on one bell rope, then on another. If he had to, he would knock down every single door until he had Devon pinned in his arms, writhing beneath him.

He was breathing like a pugilist, a pent-up and unpredictable mix of lust, anger, and revenge fueling his blood. He heard the thud of his boots, the rasp of his breath. Then a door opened a fraction on the third and top floor, revealing a face that was all eyes widening in disbelief.

The reality of seeing Devon again was like an explosion going off in his head.

He shouldered his way through the open door.

Shock tightened the lines of her body, ramrod straight, as she stood in the corridor of the apartment. "Get out of here . . . I don't want or need you here," she said in her low throaty voice.

The sun filtered through a pair of thick velvet curtains, dust motes dancing in the light. He took in the tension about her full mouth, the shadows around her eyes and in their depth.

Ignoring her words, Blackburn advanced into the room, slamming the door behind him with his booted foot, never taking his eyes from Devon. Stripping off his greatcoat, he threw it on the pink marble floor, closing the distance between them while she backed her way into one of the narrow hallways connecting the rooms of the apartment.

"I said get out of here," she breathed, lacing each syllable with defiance.

"You seduced him, didn't you? You used your body to get the score, didn't you?" Blackburn ground out, the words foreign to his ears. Every bone, muscle, and sinew in his body seethed outrage as he grabbed her by the shoulders, the fine bones fragile underneath his hands.

She tried to wrench away from his grasp, her hair tumbling from her simple chignon to her shoulders, her words coming from behind clenched teeth. "That's what you wanted me to do, you callous bastard. From the start, you were ready to send me to Le Comte like Salome to King Herod." Her eyes glittered with unshed tears. "Good God—why do you even *care*. You sent your brother to his death with less thought. Why would something as basic as sexual bartering trouble what's left of your conscience?"

"You're right." His eyes flamed fury. "My conscience isn't what's in question here. Yours is. Although I don't even care about that. What I care about is that you gave something away that is *mine*. Mine alone."

Devon looked at him as though he were mad, pushing at him as he blindly propelled them past the salon where, in the far corner, stood a Broadwood. But it was the next room which caught his attention, a room with a four-poster bed.

"What's *yours*?" she echoed hysterically, her voice raw, her face inches from his now. "You are outrageously arrogant. What's mine is mine to give—do you hear me? It has absolutely nothing to do with you!"

Turning, she spun out of his grasp and into the bedroom, tumbling onto the bed as his arm grasped her waist. Blackburn grabbed a handful of her brown serge dress, hearing the fabric rent as he pulled her closer. "Let go of me," she muttered, her face pressed toward his, her warm breath sweet.

With the kiss he meant to destroy her, his lips open, violently possessive, feeding on her tongue, on her mouth and on her lips. He meant to obliterate her and the uncontrollable reactions that she set off in him like pyrotechnics exploding against the night sky. If he could only get enough of the feel of her, the scent of her, that indefinable voluptuousness that was hers alone.

Heat and flame engulfed him, burning up every last rational thought. With a low groan, Blackburn dragged his mouth over hers, then surged inside again. Hotly, wildly, he plunged into her, somewhere in the back of his still conscious mind wondering what he was unleashing.

Blackburn felt the dampness of angry tears on her skin as Devon's mouth first softened and then opened hungrily against his. With a hot greediness, her hands skimmed along his sides, up under his shirt, searching for taut muscle. Her hair had come loose, longer, fuller than he remembered, entangling them both in a web of desire.

In a smooth motion, he rolled her fully onto her back and dragged himself over her, the muscles in his arms tensing. He pulled at her gown, making short work of her stays while his fingers slid through her luxuriant hair, drinking in the honeyed scent of freesia. He drew her full lower lip between his teeth, listening to her low moan of pleasured pain. Responding with an almost feral groan of his own, he continued to plunder her mouth, a sensual assault on her being. His need was fierce, frightening and wholly unlike anything he had ever known. He was as intent on stripping her gown from her body as he was intent on baring her soul.

She grabbed his cravat, pulling, unwinding, until it billowed to the floor. Half-sitting on the bed he struggled with his shirttails, hands suddenly clumsy, as he watched her impatiently shrug out of her bodice, popping several buttons of her shift beneath. She sat in a slant of sunlight, her full high breasts bouncing and shifting as she tugged her dress to the bottom of the bed.

Blackburn remembered the feel of those breasts in his hands, the hard nipples tormenting the tip of his tongue. Devon slanted him a look and it was nearly his undoing.

He had to admit it. She had the power, the power in her hands, and for the first time in his life, he couldn't resist and he couldn't control. Instead he rammed his surging body against her as he began the serious seduction of her breasts.

Her body liquefied underneath his caress at the touch of his hot tongue against her taut nipple. He felt her lean into him with an incoherent murmur and then suddenly, startlingly move away, heaving against him, rolling away from him to crawl on her knees across the bed.

"Nothing should be that easy—not even for you, Blackburn," she said hoarsely, her hair tumbling over her shoulders. "You come in here like some kind of medieval marauder and expect me to play along with you, no questions asked. Isn't that just like a man?"

Sitting back on his haunches, he slowly opened the buttons on his breeches until his granite hardness was exposed. His eyes locked with her wild ones and he thought that the last thing he wanted to do was talk. But, he began counting slowly to ten; if she wanted to play games, he was the undisputed expert. In one big hand he held the impressive weight of his erection; with the other he slid his palm down to cup her silken buttocks, feeling her melt into his hands. "You're right, it's just like a man," he said, letting his fingers part her pantalettes and slide into the slick folds of flesh between her legs.

Her eyes held his with a startling intensity, but instead of protesting, she eased her creaminess into his long, skillful fingers, her peach nipples puckering into hard buds of desire. And then she turned the tables and with a sly smile she watched as he watched, her head tipped back, her mouth parted, as her hands came up to caress the long tips temptingly.

In the dim shadows of the bedroom, eyes half closed in delirious pleasure, they held each other hostage. Blackburn braced his knees on either side of her thighs, his fingers still stroking himself, still stroking her. He drew his hand down the length of his shaft once more and then gently pushed Devon back into the softness of the bed, mesmerized by the play of her hands on her nipples.

For a moment her fingers stilled, her gaze enveloping him in their mutually, explosively sensual stand-off. His eyes were dark blue, his hard jaw heavily shadowed, tensing for control as he loomed over her. Slowly, he shunted aside the last of her gown until she lay naked under him, her long legs sheathed only in stockings. Roughly, Blackburn parted her thighs as he felt her hands clutch at his buttocks and hips. His muscles tensed as she urged him hard against her, rolling her hips seductively until he thought he would explode.

He probed at her slick entrance, her body open with readiness to take him, every granite inch. One look at her thrusting breasts and he couldn't wait. He drove into her wildly, then again and again, pushing himself tightly against her to slake her thirst with his heat and hardness. Pulling her silk-sheathed legs over his shoulders, he tilted her hips to take him further still. She writhed restlessly beneath him, making soft noises in the back of her throat at the fine torment. Again, Blackburn dove deep inside her, then withdrew, holding himself at an exquisite angle, dragging his hardness against her feminine flesh.

"Now," she panted, throwing one silky leg around his waist and dragging her pelvis against his erection. "I can't wait . . . Blackburn."

Blackburn looked down at her and laughed, a low growl. "I thought you weren't going to make it easy for me, Devon," he taunted as he stroked his full, hard length into her moistness and withdrew tauntingly, leaving her open and wanting.

In response, she clutched the bedclothes with her hands, her head thrashing back and forth on the pillows. She was open like a flower to him as, slowly and lightly, he ran his finger over her sensitive core as she began to whimper. He tongued the delicate shell of her ear as he leisurely drove back into her, one inch at a time. "Spread your legs, Devon. Push tighter, harder . . ." he murmured against the soft rotation of her hips. He found once again her aching, agonizing point, and he slid and rocked against her as she moaned and grasped his hard arms.

Deliberately tantalizing, tormenting, Blackburn brought

her to the edge of the precipice, his strong hands spreading her wide as he drove mercilessly inside. He rocked back and then into her again, their hot flesh melding together as he worked her deeply.

"I can't ... I can't ..." she breathed, her hands sliding from his arms to the taut muscles of his chest.

"You can, let go ... let go ..." He grasped her thighs and ran his hands upward to her buttocks and lifted her higher against the thrust of his erection. He could feel her tense, shuddering with pleasure as she was swallowed up in a hot rush of ecstasy coursing through her body to a crescendo. Blackburn shut his eyes as he pounded against her, lurching against her, covering her with his body, as though he could not get enough and he couldn't take any more. Then he flexed his hips into one massive thrust and moaned against her lips, before erupting in a long, shuddering release, pulling out just in time.

Devon's body felt weightless and limp, as though she had just emerged from an exquisite, erotic dream. She was spooned with her back against Blackburn and she could still feel him, hard and deep within her. Devon slid her hip against his long, muscular thighs, aware of him beginning to move within her once again. Mindlessly, she savored his wickedly erotic mouth against the soft skin of her neck, pleasured by the slow slide of his lips.

She was happy to be facing away from him. She didn't want to meet the glittering dark blue of his eyes and the questions she would be forced to answer. So for the moment, she lost herself again in his deliberate caress, reveling in his hand cupping and stroking her buttocks lightly, before he slipped his fingers into the erotic shadows and downward to lightly tease her swollen, sensitized flesh. She wriggled her hips, inviting further exploration, knowing that he would more than gratify her with those skillful hands that knew just where to linger.

A deep sigh escaped her as his fingers smoothed into her

velvet folds to her moist core, already prepared for him. She parted her legs, inviting him entrance.

"I can't get enough of you . . . I can't keep my hands from you . . ." The words were harsh, desperate like the hot length of his body burning into her back. His other hand moved to her breast and he began lightly moving his thumb across her pointed nipple while she arched closer, closing her eyes against the sensation of his rhythmic thumb. And then she felt the heat of his tongue, hot on her taut tip, as he began rubbing and sucking simultaneously.

She relaxed into the spiraling tension that moved to a fever pitch against the strumming of his hands and tongue. She felt the heel of his hand on her pelvis, his fingers working magic as he sucked at her turgid nipple. Pulsing, flexing, she felt him move within her, brushing against her buttocks with his aching length. Pushing her onto her stomach, he grabbed her around the waist to bring her to her knees.

"That's it," he murmured, stroking her waist, her swaying breasts. He pulled her tighter still toward him, smoothing her trembling thighs as he rocked against her buttocks, one hand playing with her nipples, the other splayed against her mound. Whispering hot words in her ear, he pushed aside a swathe of her hair, and gently nipped the side of her neck. And then there was nothing but the heat and his relentless pumping as he bore down on her, grinding himself into her from behind as her whole body heaved toward explosive pleasure.

Blackburn drove deep and hot, the long, elegant line of her back and shoulders, the tumble of her hair, his only focus. Devon bit her lip against the onslaught, against her desire to scream from wanting him. He coaxed and teased with short bursts, then longer incursions, his hands wandering languidly from her breasts to her aching core until she could bear it no longer. Suddenly everything was feeling, eddying to a final culmination, a melding of his hardness and her softness.

At the same time, she felt him drive deeply into her, plumbing the depths of their shared desire. She felt him stiffen, his hands gripping her waist, as he shuddered violently at the tip of her womb. And then, her body gave in to his hot, hard possession of her, as the last wave took them both and pulled them deep into waters of sensual oblivion.

"Good God." Devon finally caught her breath as he rolled away from her. Blackburn lay with one arm over hers, staring straight up at the ceiling. She drank in the sight of his long body, sprawled heedlessly on her bed, the man that, despite her best intentions, despite the dictates of her reason, she could not deny. Drawing the bed's coverlet over her body, she forced herself to swallow that unpalatable fact, the bitterest medicine.

Running a hand through the tangled mass of her hair, she wiped perspiration from her brow, her breathing steadying. In one corner of her mind, a troublesome doubt arose, a pebble dropped into the calmness of a millpond.

Devon stared at the hard wall of his chest, watching his breathing even out into the cadence of sleep. He had accused her of seducing Le Comte in exchange for the score, and it was only anger and lust that had fueled this latest exchange. Making love had changed nothing. It never did between them.

She rolled her head away from him, surprised at the tears burning in her eyes. It was only then that she sensed Blackburn wasn't asleep. He moved his arm and levered up on one elbow to look into her face.

She could barely endure the scrutiny of those hard blue eyes.

"I owe you an explanation," he said without emotion, without preamble. "I want you to know what happened to my brother."

"You don't owe me anything." They had both won in the dangerous game they played; both were well pleasured, she thought with a newfound cynicism. She inched farther away from him on the bed as though the distance might help.

Blackburn sensed the tension in her body and in the arm

that she threw despairingly across her eyes. In an unexpected gesture, he reached for her hand, drawing it to his mouth to kiss her open palm lightly. Her eyes flew open, pupils dilating in bittersweet pleasure and pain at his caress.

"I want to tell you," he said quietly. "I need to tell you." He rolled from his side to his back, refusing to relinquish her hand. Devon sensed he was telling the truth, and that the truth weighed heavily upon him in a way that she couldn't begin to imagine.

"Edward was older than I was by two years, the scion of the family groomed from the first day to assume the title Marquess of Blackburn." The words were dispassionate, like he was reciting a story not his own. "Serious, committed, cautious, and conservative, he was everything that I was not. Six months before he was set to marry a suitable heiress, Edward met a woman in London. She was beautiful, cunning," he paused briefly, "and a French *émigré*. My brother thought himself hopelessly in love and insisted to my parents that he wanted to marry her."

"An impossible misalliance, of course," said Devon, fighting an urge to turn toward him in the bed.

"A dangerous one as well, it turned out. For the first time in his life, Edward disobeyed my father and planned to elope with the Frenchwoman. The night of the assignation, he was found hanged in an old barn just outside Portsmouth."

The silence in the room was deadening.

"That's where you found him," whispered Devon into the crisp sheets redolent of starch and lavender, barely able to form the words.

Blackburn stared at the ceiling and continued tonelessly, "Moments before Edward died, excruciating moments before he died, de Maupassant offered me a way out." He exhaled hard. "My cooperation in exchange for my brother's life."

And you refused. The hush in the room completed the horror story.

Devon didn't know how many minutes passed before she asked, "So what's changed?" His strong hand holding hers felt good, too good. "Why did you agree to Le Comte's proposal to work with me on the *Eroica*? If you couldn't bring yourself to cooperate with him then—why now?"

The next words cost Blackburn considerable effort. "I don't understand it entirely myself, that's part of the problem. But I do recognize that I was younger, more arrogant then. And that I could never contemplate capitulating." He stopped and swallowed hard. "I also admit that on most days I compensate by lying to myself. Telling myself that I did what I did purely for patriotic reasons. But what's closer to the truth is that my sin was simply and crudely a matter of pride."

Devon gripped Blackburn's hand more tightly. The image of Blackburn, Le Comte, and Edward swam in front of her eyes. And her father. How did one ever go on, forgive oneself?

"And why didn't you publicly accuse Le Comte of murder?"

"There was too much at stake. Which de Maupassant knew all too well. If he'd been thrown into Newgate, we would have never gotten our hands on the score."

"So now you see the chance to set things right." Devon's voice constricted. "You want a reprise, but this time to see it through to the end, to annihilate Le Comte, assuage your guilt, and of course, to save the world." She didn't try to keep the irony from her voice. "This is complicated."

"Revenge always is," he said. "As a postscript I should add that my parents died soon after my brother. They couldn't stand the shock, you see, particularly the shock of my inheriting the title." A sliver of humor entered his tone.

"I'm not surprised." Devon rolled toward him, her hand in his now resting between his hard chest and her soft breasts. "The rarefied air you aristocrats breathe doesn't leave much room for choice."

"Careful, *Citoyenne Caravelle*, your republican sympathies are showing."

"I didn't think you'd notice."

"I notice everything about you." He encircled her with an arm and drew her closer. "I notice the way your eyes turn color when you're angry, the texture of your hair, soft as silk." He smoothed a curl with his fingers. "The way we're united in our quest for vengeance."

"Against Le Comte."

He raised his head from the pillow so he could look into her eyes. "For different reasons perhaps." He gave her a smile, but it faded much too quickly. "I have no right to judge you, as I did earlier today."

Her heart skipped a beat. "You accused me of seducing Le Comte in exchange for the *Eroica*."

"I believe you if you say that you didn't seduce him. In any case, as you pointed out, it's none of my concern. De Maupassant is deliberately using you to ensure I do his bidding, in the same way he tried to use Edward. I didn't allow him to succeed the first time and I won't let him succeed this time."

None of his concern.

"I didn't seduce him." The words were intended as a declaration. Her gaze moved over his face looking for signs of trust, as elusive and impermanent in their relationship as patterns in the sand.

He let go of her hand. "I believe you."

Devon lay on the bed, wasted and spent. They were good at lying, both of them. Sensing her mood, Blackburn wrapped his arms around her when she made a move to rise from the bed.

"Stay here . . . with me," he whispered as she let her cheek rest back against his chest. "Don't analyze so much. Don't think so much." Devon felt the change, the watchfulness and pain giving way to the red hot urgency that quickly flamed to life between them. It was their way of escaping, avoiding the exigencies of plot and counterplot, and the wreckage of the past they could not ignore. As for the future, the dangerous future, that was for another day, another hour.

Devon could smell his desire, felt it scorch her as he pushed her back into the pillows, grasping her arms and pressing them over her head.

Pulling down the sheet, he traced her outthrust breasts with a finger, his voice darkly persuasive, his lips suspended over hers. "Enough talk . . . now that we know all there is to know about each other," he murmured with heavy-lidded eyes as he kissed her wickedly. "Perhaps it's time for you to make it easy for me again, Devon. And for me to behave just like a man."

Devon purred her agreement, going along with the lie.

Chapter 13

Devon doubted that she would ever learn everything there was to know about the Marquess of Blackburn. In the following days she became convinced that she knew him less than ever, despite a growing but fragile understanding that was based more on an intense physical relationship than on any solid foundation. For better or worse, she had decided to work with him on the score, to allow him access to one small important part of her, the element that she had compartmentalized as belonging solely to her father and his vocation.

A gamble to be sure, but she had little choice. When she had left London and de Maupassant behind, she had also relinquished her innocence, the simplistic belief in black and white, loyalty and disloyalty, right and wrong, justice and revenge. Her world had become an infinitely more complicated place in which a man like Blackburn suddenly felt right.

They had reached a curious détente, still wary, still circling one another carefully, yet keenly aware of their mutual need, personal and professional.

Sitting at the Broadwood as the sunlight streamed in through the windows, she absently chewed the tip of her fountain pen, surveying for the tenth time her transcription of the *Eroica*, from orchestral to piano. It was painstaking work that led her to believe that her transcribed notes might yield some insight, however slight, a glimpse into a pattern or theme that would disclose the music's dangerous contents.

Devon heard the footsteps on the stairs outside the rooms she had borrowed from an old friend at the Conservatoire who was now living in Vienna. Her shoulders tensed. Le Comte had yet to find them. She recalled Blackburn's reassurances that the Frenchman would not close in until enough time had passed for them to have analyzed the encryption.

Even so, Blackburn made sure to return daily to his apartments near the Luxembourg Palace to give the impression that he was still searching for the elusive Devon Caravelle.

The front door to the apartments opened and closed quietly in a way that was becoming familiar to her. A few moments later, she felt Blackburn's hands on her shoulders, the weight simultaneously comforting and arousing. She swiveled around on the piano bench, pretending to throw her fountain pen at him.

"You scared me," she protested, amazed as always at his startling masculinity, his broad chest and strong arms, the intense blue gaze that looked into her eyes searchingly, always watchful, never quite trusting.

"I didn't think you frightened too easily." He grinned at her, running one hand over her cheek in a gesture of concern. Devon fought the urge to bring up her hand to touch that mouth, that hard jaw, feeling herself flush at the thought of their extreme physical intimacy.

Their never quiescent desire hung over them like a sensual fog. Over the past two days, they had coupled in all five rooms of the apartment, disinclined to restrict their passion to the night. In the salon she had shamelessly enticed him to sweep aside her skirts and take her bent over the settee. In the music room he had driven her over the edge to madness with his mouth as he knelt between her legs. Last night they couldn't survive through dinner—and Devon stopped herself short, embarrassingly aware of his nearness and the knowledge that Blackburn knew exactly what she was thinking.

She rose from the piano bench, brushing against him as he shrugged off his greatcoat. "I said that in jest. Of course, I'm not frightened." She put down her pen next to the inkwell to rifle through their papers on the nearby oak table to cover her mortification.

"You are justifiably worried about de Maupassant," Blackburn said perceptively, his gaze taking in the faint trembling of her hands as she made an attempt to stack several reference books. Without waiting for a response, he withdrew a package wrapped in brown paper and string from his satchel and set it on the table.

"Shouldn't I be?" She had told him about her close escape from the Frenchman's town house two weeks earlier. "I don't think I'm on the best of terms with Le Comte right now."

"You took an incredible risk," he said with what she interpreted as reluctant admiration. "I don't believe de Maupassant will ever recover from the humiliation, not to mention the fact that you managed to prize the score from him." With deft hands he began to untie the strings of the brown package. "I thought you might be hungry," he said. "Bread, wine, and thou may help us press on with the work at hand."

Devon smiled her thanks, watching him spread the bounty on the table.

His next question seemed to come from nowhere. "What about Susannah Treadwell? I have good information that she's involved in Le Comte's machinations."

Devon tensed. She hated hearing the woman's name on his lips. "I won't bother asking whether the lady herself is your source of information," she said dryly.

He ignored the insinuation. "They are no longer on the best of terms, she and de Maupassant." It was a statement, no emotion.

"There was a horrible scene," Devon recounted flatly, "which I unfortunately witnessed. She'd taken a letter from his desk and refused to return it. He managed to get it back."

Blackburn looked at her from across the table. "Any idea regarding the contents?"

Devon shook her head. "Absolutely no idea. I can't imagine that Le Comte would take her into his confidence."

"I agree, but nonetheless, no one, not even de Maupassant, can afford to have a loose cannon about."

"Particularly a loose cannon who seems to be enamored of you." The words sounded waspish even to her own ears. Annoyed at her feelings of possessiveness, she disappeared briefly into the butler's pantry returning with several plates, two wineglasses, cutlery, and linen napkins. Because she couldn't dare exposure by hiring a servant, they had been making their own arrangements.

"I shouldn't think that's a worry," he said, taking over the tray she carried. "Susannah knows enough to take her relationships lightly."

"Even the one she has with you?"

Blackburn smiled at her. "Are you actually jealous, Devon?"

She bristled, distributing the plates and cutlery. "Absolutely not. I'm simply trying to uncover every possible motivation. Who is to say that both Le Comte and Lady Treadwell aren't close on our trail, perhaps for different reasons? After all, *you* managed to find me."

She stood behind a chair, resting her arms on its high back and watching Blackburn decant and then pour two glasses of wine. "Le Comte could just as easily."

Blackburn placed a piece of cheese and bread on her plate before helping himself. "You had your friend François order the Broadwood for you—that was your mistake. But from this point onward, you can trust me to keep you safe from Le Comte."

Trust. A term they threw about far too easily.

"It's not so much *me* you're trying to keep safe," Devon said, a cynical curve to her lips. "I think the *Eroica* is uppermost on your mind."

He came around the table to pull out her chair. "The men

I've placed around this building are not simply here to play sentinel for a manuscript."

Devon sat down, her appetite suddenly gone. "I suppose I should be grateful."

He didn't try to contradict her. "We've been through a lot together. Maybe you expect too much, Devon. From me and from yourself."

She pinched her lips between her teeth. She couldn't look at him. She focused on the plate in front of her until he moved far enough away across the table, and only then did she trust herself to speak.

"I know . . . I know what we're here for."

Two mornings ago Blackburn had begun asking questions, rapid-fire. He was fiercely and unrelentingly focused with an intellect as sharp as a rapier's blade. He didn't allow her to generalize anything and left no nugget unmined, no detail unexplored. And she had gone along with the interview, allowing him to delve into the corners of her mind like no one else before. It was the only way, as Le Comte had long recognized.

And now she watched as Blackburn speared a piece of cheese with his knife.

"We have made progress in the little time we've had," he said.

"I don't know if you can call it progress." She frowned at the food he had placed on her plate.

"You should know better than anyone that cryptanalysis is painstaking work. Going over the same ground again and again, it's part of the process." Blackburn's voice was calming. He just sat back in his chair, eyes blue-black. Devon used the lengthening silence to once again appreciate the subtle way he made himself completely unreadable, totally unapproachable.

"All right then, let's go back to the beginning and review what we know about the score," she said tightly. She was suddenly tired and furious with him at the same time. He never failed to remind her of their purpose, heartlessly reinforcing the contingent nature of their relationship.

"Go ahead."

"We know that the symphony has four movements—the Allegro con brio, the Marcia Funebre, the Scherzo-Allegro vivace, and the Finale-Allegro molto. We also know that the music was first performed on April 7, 1805, in Vienna."

Blackburn took a strong bite of cheese, chewing thoughtfully. "That's all pretty standard when it comes to symphonies, you've told me. Four movements—fast, slow, minuet, fast."

Devon nodded. "And yet the *Eroica* marks the turning point in symphonic writing—it is twice the length and complexity of either Mozart or Haydn symphonies as it continually builds upon new ideas."

Blackburn's fingers played with the stem of his glass, turning the facts over in his mind. His concentration was as focused as a beam of light.

"Given what we know now, it's entirely appropriate that with the two opening chords of the symphony, Beethoven thrust aside the old classical order, with its precise rules and opened the door to something else."

Devon rose from the table and began pacing. "In other words, what you're saying is that there's a reason for all that sound, fury, and inordinate length, that break with tradition. It's a metaphor for what the code contains."

Blackburn rose from the table, whether out of politeness or a shared disquiet, Devon wasn't sure.

"I've already told you what we're probably dealing with— an explosive, a substance or device capable of producing a volume of rapidly expanding gas that exerts sudden pressure on its surroundings." Blackburn strode to the Broadwood to stare at the black and white musical notes of Devon's transcription.

"What we're looking for then is a chemical formula." She threw her hands up in frustration. "I understand music and mathematics, but haven't a clue when it comes to the intricacies of elements and compounds."

His eyes bored into hers from across the room. "Try to remember, Devon. You must have been at least familiar with your father's projects—can you recall anything at all that had to do with chemical reactions or explosives?"

Devon shook her head, pressing fingers to her temples. "I know what you're thinking"—she faltered—"that I don't want to look reality in the face. But that's simply not true."

Blackburn gathered up her notes and spread them on the table as evidence. "There's so much at stake here. I don't need to tell you that," he said, with only the length of mahogany between them. "Don't let your personal illusions get in the way of a far greater imperative."

His eyes had turned obsidian and she couldn't hold back the words that tumbled from her mouth. "You didn't let your personal illusions get in the way with regards to Edward. And let me ask you—how does it feel now?"

A new tension filled the room. She saw the grim set of his uncompromising jaw that had nothing to do with the challenge facing them. "You're numb to the world," she continued without stopping, her breaths coming quickly. "You've watched your life turn into a wasteland of meaningless assignments and relationships. Was it worth it?"

If she was expecting a reaction, she didn't get one. Blackburn leaned one hip against the table with deceptive nonchalance.

"Unlike you, I've long since faced the fact that much of what we do is unforgivable," he said with the briefest flicker of anger in his eyes, quickly banked. "I'd say it's time that you dispensed with your illusions and grew up, Devon. Your prevarications are simply another form of cowardice."

Devon sucked in her breath and put her hand on the chair to steady herself. "Cowardice? My intent is to clear my father's name and to avenge his death! In order to do so, I also have a great stake in discovering what the score holds." She paused as he continued to regard her with a steady gaze. "I'm not holding anything back, damn it! We share the same goal. It's merely the intent that's different."

She turned away from him, then spun back and said recklessly, "And watch whom you call a coward!"

Blackburn gave a ghost of a smile. "Thanks for reminding me. I seem to have forgotten you have a way with pistols."

They had reached another uneasy truce. To fill the silence between them, Devon began clearing the table, moving restlessly to pick up a knife only to set it down again. Judging by the light slanting through the curtains, it was early afternoon. Blackburn carried the remainder of their lunch into the pantry while she picked through her papers, fanning through them with growing agitation.

"Ready to begin again?" Blackburn asked moments later, pulling out a chair for her.

Their eyes met and Devon was struck fresh by her incredible need to touch him. He had again made clear that once they had unraveled the code, their relationship was entirely dispensable. How often did she need to be reminded?

She sat down slowly, refusing to acknowledge how his nearness affected her. "This is incredibly frustrating."

"What is?"

Something flared in his eyes. They both knew that she wasn't just referring to the code.

A sudden smile quirked his mouth as, within the folds of her skirt, he clasped her hand and threaded his fingers between hers. Devon's chest constricted.

"That's why I prefer cryptanalysis to the vagaries of passion, an extreme battle of wits, intellect, cunning, and mathematical prowess." Devon was acutely conscious of his booted leg next to hers beneath the table.

"Also very cloak-and-dagger." She glanced sideways at him from under her lashes.

He grinned wickedly, "And we know how much fun that can be."

Mesmerized by the suggestive timbre of his voice, Devon looked away quickly to study the notes in front of her. She disentangled her hand from his. "Lest we digress, Blackburn . . ." she said, all too aware of where the mood could lead.

She felt the intensity of his gaze, like a caress, on her cheek. "Once we've wrestled this thing to the ground, I swear, Devon, that I'll take you to bed for a week."

Crossing her legs beneath the table, Devon let the toe of her slipper slide over Blackburn's muscled calf above his boot. "Is that an incentive?" she asked, reaching for her quill.

"Damn right," he growled, his eyes sparking with desire. "So let's get this done."

Two hours later, the front of her dress spotted with ink, Devon rubbed her eyes.

"Right—we have two strong introductory chords before the cellos open to the principal subject," she recited obediently from her notes, for the third time. "The violins then enter with repeated high notes, clouding the harmony and resolving to the second subject brought in by the clarinets and oboes. This lengthy section introduces a new melodic passage which keeps us waiting for the recapitulation of the principal subject."

Blackburn listened attentively, his eyes following the notes spread out before them.

Devon continued, "The horns then bring out the tonic key over soft dominant chords. The principal subject is restated and the harmony once again is clouded. This resolves into a completely different direction and the two keys that follow are in complete contradiction to the tonic."

Blackburn shifted in the chair, crossing his arms. Devon couldn't help but admire the pull of the fabric across his broad chest, the dark stubble beginning to appear along his jaw. "Just wanted to ask a quick question," he said. "Have you compared the original manuscript we have here with any number of the copies circulating out there?"

"I have—I had François order me two different sets with two different publication dates."

"And?"

"So far the only discrepancies I could detect come in the second movement."

Blackburn quirked a dark brow. "The Funeral March in C-minor."

"Exactly—what are you thinking?"

Blackburn pushed back his chair to cross his booted legs at the ankle. "I'm just wondering—this movement is a funeral march. Metaphorically speaking, it does speak musically to the dire implications of the code. What was the discrepancy you found?"

Devon frowned, tapping her pen against the side of the table. "The length of the sections results from a long principal subject, but what I found to be different was the series of afterthoughts extending the length of this theme to almost the size of the whole movement."

"What you're saying is that the afterthoughts were not included in subsequent editions of the symphony."

"Exactly." Devon examined her ink-stained fingers as she looked for her notes on the fourth and final movement. "I also found that the finale is a synthesis of sonata, rondo, and variations in E-flat major. Essentially, the introduction begins in a distant key that is later corrected in an abrupt manner." She looked up to find him watching her closely. "I should also add that, without doubt, this coda is one of the greatest Beethoven ever wrote. And I can say unequivocally that this is a symphony that will change music forever."

"That's a clue if ever I fell over one. But it's still much too general. Let's look at the specifics. You said it's a synthesis of a sonata, rondo, and variations."

The fingers of her right hand tightened around the pen.

"That's all I have at this point. I really don't know where to go next."

Blackburn rested his hand on her arm for a moment. "We'll get there, don't worry. Let's try it from another angle," he proposed, taking several sheets from his leather satchel. "Here's what I've been working on, taking your transcribed musical notes and arranging them simply as nonmusical letters," he said. "I then applied a simple substitution method."

"The Caesar cipher, you mean," said Devon, referring to the encryption method that followed two routes—either by replacing words with other code words or by replacing letters within the message with other letters or symbols.

Blackburn nodded, pointing to his papers with a pen. "Substitution can be simplified by deciding on a specific key. As you well know, the key is what defines the method combined with an algorithm which specifies the letters or symbols which are used in the substitution in a specific order."

"So if we knew what the key and algorithm happened to be, we could generate the cipher."

"Precisely. Then we could simply apply frequency analysis which involves calculating the percentages of letters of a particular language in plain text, calculating the percentages of letters in the cipher, and then substituting the symbols for the letters which have an equal percentage of occurrences."

Devon looked up from his papers expectantly. "So what did you find?"

Blackburn leaned forward, an elbow on the table. "Using another route, I've confirmed what you've already pointed out—that there are distinct patterns in the second and fourth movements which differ from the rest of the piece, and more important, differ from subsequent editions."

She pulled the paper closer to her, her brow furrowed. "Did you try the substitution method in English or French?"

"Both—I know your father used both languages in his encryptions."

"Which code words did you use to try to unlock the algorithm?" She forced her attention back to the text, refusing to be sidelined by mention of her father.

"I tried the most obvious—Napoleon, Bonaparte, in both the French and Corsican spellings, along with Bernadotte and Beethoven." He replaced the pen in the inkpot for the moment. "With no success."

Devon rubbed her eyes with her palms as exhaustion threatened to overwhelm her. "The key could be anything: Rousseau, *liberté, égalité, fraternité* . . ."

"Which one do you want to take?" Blackburn asked, reaching again for the pen in the inkwell. "We've got some work ahead of us."

For two hours, they toiled steadily, only the scratching of fountain pens in the silence of the room. As the light began to fade, Blackburn lit the lamp on the table, amid the rapidly growing pile of papers covered with letters and numbers. One after the other, they rejected the key words without so much as a disappointed murmur. Blackburn worked relentlessly, at one point loosening the muslin of his cravat, and opening the top buttons of his shirt.

Her leg muscles beginning to cramp, Devon rose from the table and stretched her arms over her head, letting out a groan of frustration. "We're getting nowhere with this. At this rate, we'll be here for the next year, and that's time we haven't got."

Blackburn threw down his pen, pinning her with his blue-black gaze. "So what do you suggest that we do?"

"You still think I'm holding something back, don't you?"

Blackburn frowned. "You knew your father best. What might have he been thinking all those years ago, a word or key phrase, that may have had resonance for him?"

Devon placed her hand at the tight knot at the back of her neck and began massaging. "I couldn't say," she said helplessly, "I was a young child at the time." Unbidden, images began to float before her, their rooms in Paris, and then later, their small cottage in the countryside near Blois. Her father at his desk. Her mother at the pianoforte. Passionate discussions about democracy and the rights of man. And always and again, her mother and father together, perhaps more in love with one another than the day they had first met.

Then the realization struck her. A wave crashing over her head. Of course—her mother, the woman who had brought the Revolution and its tenets to her father. The one person who meant everything to Brendan Clifton, who had convinced him to leave England to forge a new life in a country balanced on the precipice of radical change.

The smell of ink and paper hung in the air, bringing her back to the present. She was aware of Blackburn watching her quietly. She forced her gaze to focus.

"Try Madeleine," she said simply, her hands clenched at her sides. "My mother's name."

Brendan Clifton's lover, Devon's mother, held the key.

Blackburn sat at the table, picked up the pen, and reached for another sheet of paper. Devon paced the room, her nerves stretched to the breaking point, unwilling to contemplate what he might find. Her mother's sweet smile, the blaze of intelligence in her eyes so much like her own, her arms enfolding her in an embrace, her slender fingers stretched over the pianoforte keys—a collision of images unspooled in her mind.

Devon walked over to the windows to close the heavy velvet drapes against the darkening sky. She leaned her forehead against the coolness of the glass, aware that Blackburn had put down his pen and that his eyes were boring a hole in her back. After a brief moment, she took a deep breath and turned to face him.

"So?" she asked quietly.

"Thank you, Devon." The words seemed sincere, but his eyes gleamed with excitement. "I know this must have been difficult for you."

Devon refused to look away, her arms crossing her chest. "All for the greater good, right?"

Blackburn took in the rigidity of her posture, the stubborn line of her jaw. For a moment, he looked as though he meant to cross the room to stand by her, but then something changed his mind. Instead, he pushed back his chair and ran his hand through his hair as though combating his own frustrations. "I'll make it fast," he said. "I found it in the concluding movement as you specified—the synthesis of the sonata, rondo, and variations."

Devon put a hand at her throat, leaning against the window, as though hoping that the velvet drapes would soften the coming blow.

Blackburn continued, his mind working quickly. "I found three distinct references to glycerol, nitric acid, and sulfuric acid."

Devon looked at him uncomprehendingly. "What are we talking about here . . . combustible materials?"

Blackburn looked at her admiringly. "Exactly so. As a matter of fact, they're so combustible that the reaction which follows their combination is highly exothermic, generating heat and a type of explosion we've never seen before."

"Just as we suspected." Her voice was barely audible.

Blackburn moved from the table and began prowling the room, and Devon was reminded again of another type of unleashed power. "There's more to it than that, however. This combination is extremely sensitive to shock and it is difficult to predict under which conditions it will explode."

"That decides it then. We should destroy the manuscript and the formula goes with it." Devon wanted nothing more than to sweep the offending paperwork from the table and from her life entirely.

"And what about your desire to clear your father's name and avenge his death?"

Devon glared at him, her ambivalence apparent in every tense line of her body. "Maybe I should just forget about all of that. I could disappear—"

"And be forced to look over your shoulder for the rest of

your life?" asked Blackburn sharply. "You know that's no answer."

"What's your answer then?" She made her voice light, but panic closed like a fist around her throat. "I'd quite forgotten, revenge is still obviously high on your list."

Blackburn was silent for a moment. "There's no turning back, Devon. We've got to end this situation definitively."

"Which means what?"

"Ensure that we get the formula into the right hands, expose de Maupassant in his plot to help Bonaparte escape from St. Helena, and prove his involvement in your father's and my brother's deaths. That's why he so desperately wants this formula. It's the ultimate ace of spades that can bring down any government like a fragile house of cards. Think of it—with the right combination of substances he has a lethal weapon that has the potential to devastate or even annihilate great tracts of Britain and Europe. Would you want that on your conscience?"

"No, thank you—I already have enough on my conscience as it is." She looked away from him and studied a faded print of a pastoral scene on the opposite wall.

"Stop blaming yourself for something your father did almost twenty years ago." Blackburn strode around the table to stand by her side, forcing her to gaze up at him.

"I can't," she said, an unexpected lump in her throat. "It doesn't bear thinking about what he did . . . what they did . . ."

"Then don't think. Act," he said with a level voice, low and intense. He raised her chin with his hand. "The sins of the father don't necessarily pass to the sons and daughters. And you have an opportunity here to right a wrong."

Her lips trembled with effort as she fought the urge to lay her cheek on his hard chest just inches away. "But that's the problem. I don't know whether it was a wrong, whether my father—my parents—were simply doing what they thought was best in protecting the hard-won gains of the Revolution."

His hand moved up to cup her cheek, a brand on her cold skin. "You may never find the answer to that question, Devon, and maybe you should stop trying."

"Perhaps you're right," she said, softly, feeling even more bereft as he dropped his hand and moved away from her. She cleared her throat and straightened her shoulders. "So what do you suggest we do next?"

His smile was brilliant. "We've been caged up in this room all day. I suggest we need some activity, something to get the blood flowing."

Devon slanted him a suspicious look. "Lovemaking isn't going to solve all our problems."

"Is that what you think I was suggesting?" he asked in mock horror, a hand held over his heart.

"Then what are you suggesting?" she asked impatiently, watching as he dimmed the light of the lamp.

"We're going out. Where's your pelisse?"

"Going out where?" she asked exasperatedly, following him into the hallway.

"We need a little cloak-and-dagger so we're going to break into somebody's home here in Paris."

"Are you quite mad?" she asked, as he slipped the pelisse over her arms and did up the frogged clasps that ran down the front.

Blackburn looked at her for a moment, finishing with the last clasp. "I've never been saner in my life. Now, let's go."

Chapter 14

Blackburn heard the satisfying sound of tumblers clicking over as the deadbolt slid open. Securing the lock picks in the pocket of his greatcoat, he pushed open the door with Devon following close behind.

The entranceway was dark as he knew it would be, the home's occupant conveniently in Italy. He lit a small torch by striking a piece of flint against the stone of an interior wall.

Following the narrow aisle of light that led the way, Blackburn ignored the rooms to his right, including a small spiral staircase leading to the second floor. He'd visited Ascanio Sobrero near St. Sulpice many times in the past and was familiar with the layout of the Sobrero house.

Devon glided behind him. Blackburn made sure they weren't followed to Sobrero's. The last thing he wanted de Maupassant discovering was that they had need of a laboratory. It would have been far easier simply to have the analysis completed by scientists back in London, but he wasn't ready for that quite yet. He didn't want Wellington involved until he'd had the chance to exorcise his own personal demons.

Moving quickly to the rear of the house, past the small kitchen and outside toward the stables, Blackburn made a sudden left and stopped in front of a low door. He tried the latch which gave easily under his gloved hand, but the door failed to move.

"Damn, Sobrero—did you have to bolt it from the inside?" he murmured to himself.

Devon touched his elbow. "There must be an entrance from the stables. We could try from outside."

Blackburn shook his head. "I don't want to attract any more attention. Let me see what I can do here." He traced the outlines of the door, watching the damp wood give way. "It's quite rotten . . . shouldn't take much." Using his shoulder as a battering ram, he threw his weight at the entry, listening for the splintering of wood. The door trembled beneath the force of muscle after two attempts before opening with a short groan.

"Sorry about that, Sobrero." Blackburn kicked aside a few splinters littering the floor.

Devon's eyes dilated in amazement as Blackburn shone the small torch into the room: Sobrero's laboratory. From floor to ceiling, the space was covered with shelves and drawers, immaculately labeled with brass plates gleaming in the torchlight. The focused beam revealed a long table topped in ceramic tiles and covered with boxes of tubes and burners, neatly organized in boxes by size. Wooden clamps and jars, tuning forks and ear trumpets, and lodestones lined every available space. The smell of sulfur hung in the stale air.

Blackburn lit a small paraffin oil lamp. Devon's cloaked figure threw a gigantic shadow on the wall.

"Don't tell me," she said throwing back her hood, "we're looking for glycerol, nitric and sulfuric acids."

Blackburn surveyed the shelves and drawers quickly. "Not exactly. Actually, that's the last thing we want."

Devon's expression was intense. "Then what are we here for? You didn't exactly explain earlier."

Randomly opening and closing drawers, Blackburn scanned the room. "Your father's knowledge about this explosive was very likely theoretical. These three compounds mixed together are very unstable. To be a useful explosive, a substance has to withstand, without detonating, the jolts and bumps of manufacture and transportation. This compound of glycerol, nitric and sulfuric acids—let's call it nitroglycerin—is not viable on its own." He stopped his search abruptly. "In other words, what we're looking for is the last piece of the puzzle."

Devon smoothed her hands over the folds of her cloak anxiously. "Which means that we're looking for a substance that when combined with this nitroglycerin is capable of stabilizing it."

"Precisely. I found the name of the substance in the second section of the *Eroica*."

" 'The Funeral March'—how appropriate."

Blackburn smiled briefly before resuming his search, opening and closing drawers and peering at brass plates. "The substance is called kieselguhr, a German word for clay, from what my admittedly rudimentary command of the language tells me. Where it comes from I haven't a clue. I thought my old friend Sobrero, who dabbles in sciences of all kind, might have a sample and a convenient description on hand."

"It would seem he has just about everything else," said Devon, picking up a jar which glowed green in the lamplight.

"Without this clay, the nitroglycerin is useless and far more dangerous for the user than the enemy," Blackburn continued, running his fingers through a powdered substance in a lower drawer. "We're talking about instantaneous destruction and rapid expansion of hot gases that result in a highly destructive blast. One advantage that nitroglycerin has is that no form of soot or smoke is produced when it is detonated. A smokeless powder offers an incredible advantage to artillery or naval gunners whose field of vision doesn't become obscured during battle by clouds of billowing smoke."

"It just keeps getting better," said Devon, setting the jar back down as though it were highly breakable crystal. "How do you know so much about explosives—or should I even ask?"

"I learned about it by default during my years of intelligence work. It wasn't really much of a stretch, the leap from mathematics and cryptanalysis to chemistry. The concepts are much the same, generally speaking, sciences based on formulae."

Even to his own ears, the explanation sounded hollow. What had begun as a simple lark, a challenge to a restless young man had ended as a millstone. To see a youth blown apart by a musket shot and streams of men felled by cannon fire could not help but make something as abstract as the formula for gunpowder blazingly real. Purgatory wouldn't end here, now that there was nitroglycerin to add to the fearful arsenal of warfare.

His thoughts were becoming too dark, and they had work to do. Despite the minutes racing by, he wondered what Devon was thinking—about him. She was rifling through a box of tubes, her delicate profile revealing only focused concentration. The past few days with her had been a revelation, forcing him to acknowledge unfamiliar emotions that threatened the uneasy peace he had made with himself.

The intensity of being with her transformed his perception of the world from shades of gray to brilliant scarlet, an experience that wasn't always welcome. The way she moved, the quickness of her mind, her iconoclastic opinions, always strongly held, the way she felt in his arms, sometimes he felt that this most unusual woman had been made expressly for him. It was a concept that made him distinctly uncomfortable, exacerbated all the more by the fact that he didn't really know, much less trust, her.

And he'd been prepared to send her to de Maupassant's bed.

The evidence still didn't look good. She confessed to radical political beliefs. She'd worked alongside Europe's foremost cryptographer who happened to be her father. She managed to secure the *Eroica* score, something that had eluded the best intelligence-brokers on the continent.

She had relinquished her virginity in exchange for a dubious agreement.

Watching her flick through a dusty file, he wondered whether she still was working for de Maupassant. He should not have revealed the formula for nitroglycerin to her earlier that evening. It would have been far simpler—and safer—to have kept the discovery to himself, but something about her vulnerability, the hurt in her eyes, had convinced him of a genuine distress.

It seemed only fair. In exchange for her mother's name, what else could he do but offer her something in return, to make her feel as though her capitulation had been worth the steep price.

Maybe Wellington was right and he was losing his judgment. He skimmed a gloved hand over a light dusting of powder silvering a piece of ceramic tile. So far no sign of the kieselguhr. He tried to get his mind back on track. It was the key to the puzzle, a substance without which the explosive was as useless as a one-legged cannon on the battlefield.

Where in the world—literally—could this clay be found or mined? And did de Maupassant already know the location of the source?

Blackburn had barely finished the thought when he heard a faint scratching of metal. Before he could turn his attention to the sound, he glanced at Devon over his shoulder and slid his pistol from his pocket. He saw her curse silently, feeling bereft, no doubt, of her small silver revolver. He aimed at the door as it slowly swung open.

Three men stood on the threshold. Like dancers in some macabre ballet, they trained their guns simultaneously on Devon who remained rooted to the flagstone floor.

Blackburn took quick stock. He recognized only Lacan. The two men flanking the Frenchman were large, over six feet and well fed. But then again, they probably couldn't move very quickly. He tried to ignore the fact that their firepower was focused on Devon.

"I don't think this interruption wise, Monsieur," he addressed the Frenchman, with a restless glitter in his eyes.

"As though what you think matters at this moment, Marquess."

"I don't care to recall our last meeting outside Lady Treadwell's several week's ago," he continued. "You may find this encounter ends quite differently."

"Overly confident as always." Lacan's high forehead shone in the torchlight. "Although your confidence might be misplaced given the situation you and your companion find yourselves in this evening. As you can see, we've come fully prepared."

"Aren't three guns in this case excessive?"

"Always with the questions, Marquess, always with the questions." Lacan scanned the laboratory quickly before coming back to rest on Devon.

"Here we have her, the woman everyone's been looking for. Why so quiet, Mademoiselle? One should think that you would have the good manners to acknowledge my colleagues here. But then again, given your peasant background, good breeding was never your strong suit."

Blackburn shot Devon a second glance. Only he detected the fear, the slight trembling in her voice.

"The threat of rape does impact one's volubility." She addressed Lacan directly, anger and fear shimmering in the air.

"That encounter in the tavern was unfortunate. Hal and Morton here certainly feel their meeting with you ended prematurely."

To emphasize Lacan's words, the man with the heavy beard narrowed his eyes into slits and tightened his finger on the trigger.

The men from the tavern outside Armathwaite. The chill of the flagstone floor seeped into Blackburn's body. He had never felt so cold. Or so calm. He would see all three men dead. Tonight.

"I've since learned about the incident," he ground out. "Unfortunate in more ways than one."

"You think so, sir? The woman you are consorting with is

a traitor, as you well know by now, and is deserving of nothing less than the harshest treatment."

"Trust me, we'll get to that later."

Lacan waved his pistol with dramatic flourish. "While your feelings of protectiveness stem from some chivalrous inclinations to be sure, they are misdirected. This woman is a Bonapartist, prepared to see that *bâtard* Napoleon released from his island nightmare and unleashed upon Europe and England once again. For the sake of both the English and French thrones, this should give you pause, sir!"

"You're not here on de Maupassant's behest then, I take it."

"As with Bonaparte, the man is mad with the desire for power. He must be stopped."

Blackburn shrugged, diverting Lacan's interest from Devon. "We share a common cause, then, Monsieur."

Lacan peered at him through watery blue eyes. "You'll forgive me if I'm not entirely convinced. In any event, I won't allow this conspirator," he gestured with a jerk of his shoulder, "and the formula to find its way to the republicans here in France."

He took a step back and gave a small nod to the two men whose pistols snapped to attention. "Stand aside, Marquess, as you are about to witness an execution."

Blackburn's body stilled and his insides turned to ice. "Without her, the score is useless," he said. "Worse still, you'll have me to contend with." He made a rapid calculation of how many bullets it would take to end this scenario definitively. From the corner of his eye he saw Devon come alive against the rows of Sobrero's drawers and cabinets, now a flesh-and-blood target for Lacan's henchmen.

"You'll never get the formula from me." She faced her executioners, repeating the words in French for emphasis. Her hair glinted fire by the torchlight. Raw anger had trumped simple panic.

She swung her gaze to Blackburn, eyes darkening with fury. "Give them nothing."

"I don't intend to," he said calmly, keeping his aim squarely on Lacan, the most dangerous of the three men. "And you certainly didn't expect me to carry the code with me?"

Morton bared his teeth in a snarl. "Open your coat. Now— or we shoot the *mam'selle*." He took two steps closer to his target.

"If you insist," said Blackburn coolly, as he slowly and deliberately shrugged off his coat, his right hand, and then his left, still steady on the trigger. "But I wouldn't injure the mademoiselle here." He felt the tightening at the back of his neck and he sensed that Devon was focusing her anger.

Now is not the time, he warned her silently.

"I think what we have here, gentlemen, is what's called a stand-off in English. You shoot Devon Caravelle, and I *kill* you. Doesn't make much sense." He kept the tone conversational.

Hal's eyes quickly skimmed Blackburn in his shirt and breeches, deciding that the code must be buried in his greatcoat. "Very slowly, if you know what's good for you and the *mam'selle*, slide the coat over to me," he snarled.

"Don't do it, Blackburn." He heard Devon's voice coming from behind him. She realized full well that neither of them carried the information. With his finger still on the trigger, he slid the coat across the wood floor toward Morton. The man picked it up quickly, patting the fabric looking for telltale bulk.

"Bah—nothing!" he spat, kicking it aside with his foot.

Lacan twisted his head toward Devon with an almost personal hatred for her seeping from every pore. "And what about you, Mademoiselle. Your pelisse, *s'il vous plait*."

"You will find nothing. *Rien*," said Devon, with a challenging glare, but she refused to remove her coat.

"You would prefer that we shoot you first?" asked Lacan, his question clipped as, with a twitch of his pistol, he motioned to his men. "It looks as though mademoiselle needs help with her pelisse, if you would. For some reason she seems reluctant to let us have a look at it."

Morton moved closer, an arm's-length away from Devon. A moment's indecision and she jerked out of her cloak a second before she hurled the garment at Lacan and over Morton's outstretched hand where his pistol dangled momentarily.

Time collapsed.

The voluminous fabric sailed over the Frenchman's shoulders to settle around his body in an entangling net, tying his limbs, obscuring his vision. Blackburn instantly leveled his own pistol at Morton just as a shot ripped through the room. Too late, he saw Devon grab her arm as she flung herself at Lacan, knocking him to the ground. He thrashed like a fish caught in the enveloping folds of brown wool. His pistol skittered across the floor.

Blackburn's finger pulled back the trigger and fired at Morton. He collapsed to his knees. Blood spurted from a charred hole in his greatcoat. Undecided whom to shoot first, Hal squinted in Blackburn's direction before a slug of lead burrowed deep in the side of his neck. He fell backward on the laboratory table, jars and tubes clattering to the floor.

In two strides, Blackburn removed the smoking pistol that was still clenched in Morton's hand and strode over to Devon. He brought up his arm and swung the butt of his pistol at Lacan's skull. Save for the stench of blood and the pall of gunpowder, the room was quiet.

"Christ—you shouldn't have done that." Blackburn pulled Devon to her feet. "Let me see your arm."

"I think I'm fine, it's nothing serious." Her face was deathly pale. "There's not even much blood." She pulled back the scorched fabric of her dress to reveal a small wound. "I think the bullet must have just missed me."

Blackburn's vision blurred and he pushed back the emotions threatening to overtake him, hoping the ice tightening around his heart wouldn't melt. Not yet. Resisting the urge to pull Devon into his arms, he instead motioned to Hal and Morton lying a few feet away. "I'll finish them off." His words were harsh.

Devon shook her head, cold without her cloak, pulling her arms close to her chest to ward off a chill. "I can't . . . This was horrible enough," she faltered, looking away from the blood that was beginning to drip from the laboratory table.

"Turn your back then." He picked up his greatcoat where it lay on the floor, placing it around her shoulders. His hands lingered possessively and he blocked the thought of what might have happened to her had Lacan's bullet hit its mark.

Every nerve was exposed, ready, eager for any excuse to annihilate the men who had tried to take Devon from him.

"Are we any better than they are if we summarily play judge and executioner?"

He didn't want to think about that right now. "I'm not here to wax philosophical. Just remember what nearly happened at the tavern outside Armathwaite."

And remember that I promised to keep you safe. The words reverberated painfully in his skull.

"For a long while you thought I was a traitor. Perhaps you still do." Devon's voice was faint as though coming from across the room. Suddenly she looked as fragile as a child, lost in his greatcoat, and thoroughly unlike the woman who moments earlier had turned the tables so deftly on the three men.

"Our relationship has never been simple," he said refusing to examine her statement too closely. He simply wanted to hold her and fought an intense desire, almost an instinct, to gather her in his arms. Instead, he began turning up his sleeves. "Wait outside and I'll finish up."

She made no move toward the door. Looking down at Lacan, she asked, "Do you think Lacan told de Maupassant where the apartment is?"

Blackburn raised his shoulders in a gesture of supreme unconcern. "It won't matter because they aren't going to leave a trail for anybody."

Devon suppressed her revulsion by holding herself stock-still, ignoring the throbbing pain shooting down her arm. "We can't leave these men to bleed to death."

"Flesh wounds as far as I can tell." Blackburn lied without glancing at the bodies strewn around the laboratory. He would have his men throw Lacan and his cohorts into a dark hole until they could be dealt with at Newgate. Although a bullet to the brain would have been simpler—and infinitely more satisfying. "I'll bundle them in the coach house so there'll be less mess for Sobrero."

"I thought I saw some rope in the cupboard by the door earlier." Devon's face gained some color. She was about to move toward the exit when the bundle that had been Lacan twitched under her pelisse.

"Don't move, Lacan—nothing's changed," Blackburn said, his fingers shifting slightly on his pistol, itching to pull the trigger. A shaking hand pushed aside the folds of wool ob-scuring his face. The Frenchman was breathing heavily, his skin as bleached as the floor. He opened his eyes to stare at Devon.

"You traitorous, treasonous bitch," he said lying as still as a corpse, only his whitening lips moving. "You betrayed your country, your king."

Blackburn watched closely for Devon's reaction, unwilling at the moment to examine his own conscience. She stopped in her tracks, slowed down by the heavy stillness of the air and by the thick venom of Lacan's accusation. Any trace of the fragility he had detected moments ago was gone, and re-placed by solid determination.

"So you remain true to your cause, Monsieur," she said, "and you fault de Maupassant for abandoning his."

"The rabble will never prevail." Lacan's voice cracked from the effort. "And you shall not go unpunished . . ." He swallowed noisily, a gurgling deep in his throat. "Don't trust her, Monsieur Le Marquess, you do so at your peril—"

"Let me worry about that, Lacan. My view of the world isn't as simple as yours." Blackburn made certain the Frenchman felt the nudge of his boot in his ribs, suspicion giving rise to a question he had to ask. "Is there anyone else working with you, for you?"

Lacan gave a gasp or a laugh, he wasn't sure. "You should know better than anyone that the battle never ends."

Menace looming on the horizon. Blackburn was intensely aware of Devon at his elbow, listening, her eyes fixed on the man at their feet.

"This battle just did, Lacan," she said. "In addition to being a traitor as you claim, I am also a radical who believes that all people will one day have the right to fraternity, liberty, and, above all else, equality."

Lacan turned his head away from her words, blood easing from the gash at the side of his head. "Loyalty always . . ."

"Loyalty is a strange thing," Devon continued with steely reserve, the toe of her boot resting by his head. "And we French should know above all else that loyalty to the wrong cause never yet broke a chain or freed a human soul."

She hesitated for a fraction of a second and then turned to Blackburn. "I'll get the rope," she said.

They made their way quickly back to the apartments near Place des Vosges. Blackburn bundled her into the bedroom, forcing her to sit at the edge of the bed. He efficiently undid the fastenings of his greatcoat and then disappeared briefly to get linen, scissors, and brandy.

"Drink this—it will help," he said, putting the glass in her cold hand when he returned. Devon took a welcoming sip, surprised that she was still shaking. The warmth of the brandy spread through her just as Blackburn cut the sleeve of her dress.

"Try to hold still because I can't promise this will be painless," he said tersely. She lifted her left arm and winced at the sudden pain knifing through her nerve endings. "Can you shrug out of the dress or does it hurt too much?"

Devon grimaced in response, but together they managed to slip the bodice off her shoulders. From the tray at his side, he picked up a clean linen pillowcase and cut the fabric into strips. "You were quite angry back there at Sobrero's. I was wondering whether it was genuine or whether you were trying to create a diversion. Regardless, you're fortunate that the bullet missed you," he said dipping the cloth in a small bowl of brandy before pressing it to the wound on her arm. "It doesn't look too bad."

"I'm not good at these things," she said, desperate to hold nausea at bay. "The sight of blood tends to make me queasy."

"No need to apologize. It does take some getting used to," he said without emotion.

"And yes to both questions. I was both genuinely angry and intent on creating a diversion."

Devon concentrated on keeping her gaze on his dark head bent over her arm as he sat next to her on the bed. Her own head had stopped spinning, but the throbbing in her arm seemed to be getting worse. She watched as he took the first cloth away and splashed more brandy on a fresh strip of linen, then dabbed it on the wound. The throbbing turned to fire. She sucked in her breath and closed her eyes, but all she saw and heard was Lacan, on the floor of Sobrero's laboratory.

"Almost done." Blackburn's deep voice was soothing as he wound strips of linen around her arm. "All you need now is some sleep and let's hope no infection sets in."

Devon's eyes flew open, the pain suddenly forgotten. "Sleep? We don't have that option. We accomplished exactly nothing at Sobrero's laboratory tonight and we're no further ahead at discovering what kieselguhr is all about and where to find it."

"I didn't say *we* need some sleep. I said that you could use some rest. And we did accomplish several things. We discovered that one of de Maupassant's lieutenants had an agenda of his own."

"Lacan, you mean."

"He's clearly not enamored of you, Devon." She detected an element of concern behind the words.

"You of all people should know that it's often difficult to discern friend from foe." Devon had intended to keep the statement neutral. She watched his hands, strong and elegant, securing the linen in place. Resisting the urge to stroke back the hair falling over his brow as he bent over her shoulder, she felt a pang like a stab wound in her side. There was still so much doubt and distrust between them.

Blackburn straightened, his gaze fixed on her, dark like moonlit water. "Those are the times in which we live, unfortunately," he said, as though unwilling to complicate things further.

"You're still not entirely sure."

"Sure of what?"

"Whether you can trust me or not. I saw you tonight and the way you reacted to Lacan's accusations."

"I might ask the same of you. Do you trust me?"

"Another stand-off." Devon smiled weakly. "So what do we do next?"

"While you get some rest, I'm going out."

Devon jumped up so suddenly that the brandy spattered on her lap, pain slicing through her arm. "Not without me. And where are we going?"

Blackburn rose from the side of the bed, staring down at her. He touched her arm gently. "You'll be of no use whatsoever if an infection takes hold. It makes much more sense to rest."

Devon set down the glass on the floor. "I wouldn't be able to sleep anyway, so what's the point? That's part of our agreement—we work on this code together. And we still need to find out about this stabilizing substance. If what you say is true, it's the key."

Blackburn at least nodded. "Without it, the substance is just too volatile to be of any military use."

"Le Comte probably knows what it is—it's what he's been holding back," said Devon with a flash of insight, "to ensure that once we've deciphered the code, it remains useless to us." She glanced at him speculatively. "You already knew that, I suppose."

One more thing he'd kept from her.

"It's a challenge. We have the formula and the Frenchman has the missing link that will make it practicable."

"Lacan's presence here indicates that he already knows where we are in Paris." Devon spoke her thoughts out loud, the throb in her arm momentarily forgotten. "So why play this waiting game? Let's lure Le Comte to us."

Blackburn's face was unreadable. "I don't like what you're suggesting."

"I shall invite him to a private concert at the Conservatoire where I'll promise him the formula in exchange for my exoneration. He won't be able to resist the symmetry—to see finished what began at the conservatory."

"I don't see how that would help as he'll be under no pressure to provide you with the kieselguhr information."

"I'm resourceful. I'll think of something."

He was silent for the length of a pulse beat. "Absolutely not. It's too dangerous and who says that de Maupassant will play along and divulge anything?"

"I shall convince him."

"We'll find the source of the substance another way. In the interim, I won't be long," Blackburn said with customary arrogance, dismissing Devon's plan with a lingering hand on her arm. "Forget the private concert. I'm going to return to Sobrero's to see if anything else turns up. He may have some literature on the substance that we might have overlooked. There were masses of notes and books we didn't even touch before we were interrupted."

Devon rose unsteadily to her feet, shaking off his arm, suddenly suspicious. "There's something else you're not telling me."

"You think so?" Blackburn gave her a small smile.

"I absolutely do."

"You're right."

Amazed at the easy victory, she pressed on. "I'm going with you so you may as well tell me."

Blackburn pressed for advantage. "If I tell you, will you stay here and rest instead?"

She hesitated the merest second before nodding her acquiescence.

It was Blackburn's turn to look suspicious. "I don't believe you, but nevertheless I want to return to the laboratory to see if anyone else may have followed us there."

Devon's eyes darkened with worry. "Followed us there? Lacan did say the battle wasn't over. I wonder whether he was referring to Le Comte, although that wouldn't make any sense."

"We don't know at the moment, but I'll take a closer look around."

"It's all too important to me—I'm going with you," she declared, suddenly bouncing up from the bed.

Blackburn crossed his arms over his chest. "Promise forgotten so soon?"

"I've not come this far to turn back now. If we can discover who's behind all this and, even more important, where the clay is stockpiled, we can undo some of the damage that"— she swallowed hard returning Blackburn's gaze—"that my father wrought."

"If I find anything, you'll be the first to know," Blackburn said, pushing her gently back down on the bed.

"And once we know, what do we do?"

Blackburn turned back the covers. "The code tells us what we should be looking for is a location—a store of the purest kieselguhr, an ingredient necessary to transform nitroglycerin into an horrifically efficient weapon. We destroy the stock-pile—and so we destroy the weapon."

"And Le Comte?"

Blackburn's eyes were chips of black ice. "You leave that to me."

The thrum in her arm increased a notch. "He murdered my father. I have a stake in this, too. The concert that I'm suggesting—"

"I'm fully aware of your situation, Devon." He stared down at her, a blatant urge to destroy in his gaze. "What we need is *proof* to expose the man for the murderer and traitor he is. He wants a blueprint of this explosive to give to Napoleon's supporters in exchange for the power his family lost during the Revolution. No court in Europe will acquit him once that fact comes to light."

Devon shook her head, her nails digging into the bed linens.

Blackburn's words were cynical as he moved around the room turning down the lamps. "The throne in France will never be as powerful as it once was, something de Maupassant knows all too well from the lessons of history. Now, the Bonapartists are a different story." Blackburn's face became starker still in the dimming shadows of the candlelight. "Two years ago when de Maupassant murdered my brother, Napoleon was still in power. The opportunities the emperor of all Europe could offer were vastly superior to anything that the neutered Bourbons ever could." He snuffed out a candle at the bedside, plunging the room into near darkness.

"And that's why Le Comte was desperate enough to use your brother to try to get to you," Devon whispered more to herself than to Blackburn. Only the light of two wall sconces illuminated the now familiar blue-black eyes, the generous mouth, the thick black hair. She felt as though she knew him, could trace, blindfolded, the lines of his face and body. But his mind and his heart were an entirely different matter, still closed to her, sealed with a thick coat of cynicism and guilt.

Gathering her strength like a cloak around her, she rose to move to his side. They stood at the end of the bed together. "I'm sorry about it all. I hope you know that," she said quietly in a moment of complete openness.

Blackburn bowed his head in acknowledgment, taking her hand and kissing her palm. He smiled slowly with a disarming recognition of his own limitations, his eyes lighting up with something that reached out and touched her. Warmth spread through her body, from her breasts to her womb, heating her blood to a low simmer.

"We both know about loss," he said, "and regrets and the folly of loyalty too lightly given." Blackburn drew her closer until they touched, his breath on her forehead, her breasts skimming his chest. "Where we go from here is the question."

Exhausted emotionally and physically, Devon dared to lean her cheek on his shoulder, breathing in the elixir that was Blackburn. "Could you ever give it up?" she whispered into his shirtsleeve.

Something rumbled in his chest, his heart perhaps, and he said, "I don't know what I'd give it up for, Devon. Ironically, the work I do, of which I'm not proud, is all I have."

Devon lifted her head to look up at him, his eyes distant once again. She didn't want to lose their momentary intimacy, a closeness that between them was as elusive as gossamer. "We're both much alike in so many strange ways," she murmured, her arms drifting from his shoulders to loop around his neck. She winced at the pain but her need for Blackburn blotted out all else. At the sound, Blackburn kissed her forehead in what was meant to be a chaste caress, but the softness of her skin enticed him onward, to her cheek, the spot where the nape of her neck met the rich cascade of her hair.

"I think you've been right all along in accusing me of thinking too much," said Devon, feeling heavy and hot. His muscles relaxed under her palms. "I could say the same of you."

She kissed him then and for the slightest moment he resisted. Then he cradled her face with his hands and devoured her, his mouth hot and hungry. His fingers in her hair pulled gently at the pins until her chignon dissolved in wild disarray around them. His erection throbbed against her stomach instantly, hard and imperious and she heard him murmur, "You're injured—we shouldn't be doing this." He tongued the pulse point above the open collar of her chemise before tracing a path back to her lips.

She smiled against his mouth. "If anything is guaranteed to make me feel better, this is it." Devon tasted brandy on their lips as he cupped her jaw, his palm enclosing her throat before he kissed her below the ear, making her ache with pleasure. His other hand slowly slid down her body, brushing between her breasts, lingering at her waist. Like several small miracles, the tapes of her skirt were undone, the laces of her chemise dispensed with until the fabric pooled around her feet. She felt the cool air on her nakedness.

"Not fair," she said helpless as his hot gaze ran over her body. "You're still dressed."

Transfixed, every nerve ending in flames, Blackburn tore away his cravat and tossed it aside. "You can have my shirt, too, if it makes you happy," he added, casting aside the offending garment.

Devon stood back and surveyed the beauty of his finely muscled chest tapering to narrow hips that met his breeches. "What do I have to do to earn these breeches?" she asked coyly, flicking her fingers over his bulging erection.

Blackburn's eyes were fathomless as he watched the candlelight caress her ivory smooth body. She picked up the glass by the side of the bed and took a small sip. She then cradled the glass close to his bare chest, watching the liquid trail in cool rivulets across his taut skin. She began licking the brandy from his neck.

Blackburn's voice was hoarse. "You've handily won my breeches." His head was tipped back in a kind of blind ecstasy as she smoothed her hand over the taut fabric, his hardness straining for release. She tipped the glass once again as the brandy dribbled down his chest to follow the indent of muscle all the way to his tight stomach. Devon couldn't resist dropping to both knees to run her tongue along the wet path to the opening of his breeches.

"I believe I've won much more," she stated, glancing up at him, her storm-gray eyes darkening as he impatiently shrugged out of the last of his clothing. Her Adonis.

"You won't get any argument from me," Devon heard him rasp in sensual delirium as she drew him deep into her mouth.

Devon felt hot, as if her body were on fire. She tossed at the bedclothes enveloping her like a winding sheet, cutting off her breath. In the space between being awake and asleep, she reached for Blackburn, her limbs thrashing in the bed only to find empty space.

He was gone. But this was just a dream, as was the cloud curling through the already darkened room toward her. She longed for sleep to overtake her once more, to drag her down like an anchor into blissful ignorance where only she and Blackburn existed in a simpler, more innocent world.

She half-opened her eyes watching the cloud become thicker, a dense fog constricting her throat, making her cough and sputter until she was sitting bolt upright in the bed.

The intense odor was unmistakable now. Fire—announced by the thick veil of smoke coiling around the edge of the bedroom door like a deadly serpent. There was a roar in the background, a monster that waited to devour her in an inferno of flames. Devon was now instantly awake, the burning in her eyes matching the ache in her injured arm.

With shaking hands, she hurriedly lit a candle by the bedside, registering again that Blackburn was not with her. She called out his name hoarsely, and then in panic, envisioning him trapped in another section of the apartments.

Hysteria fueling her blood, she leapt from the bed and pulled on her clothes still lying in a heap on the floor, calling his name until her voice was raw. Smoke licked around the edge of the door and in terror, she flung water from the pewter jug by the bedstand over her pillows and stuffed them around the cracks. Running to the window she wrenched back the shutter, cursing the lack of a balcony.

Peering onto the street below, she could see the fire truck carrying tubs on a runner and the beginnings of a bucket brigade. It would be too late for her; they would never make it to the third floor in time. She swallowed hard. This was no time for panic. She must think.

Already the pillows at the door were steaming, charring from the heat. The heavy wood door had begun to bubble with blisters when she decided to break the window. She was just about to heave a chair at the opening when the glass plane shuddered and then shattered into a million shards.

She opened her eyes as Blackburn was shaking her. "What happened, what are you doing here," she asked incoherently, unconsciously holding her breath against the noxious fumes. "Where did you go?"

"Never mind that now." Splinters rained from his shoulders. "Let's get out of here."

Some part of her mind registered that he was fully clothed and that he had come from the outside, through the window. Blackburn tied a rope around her waist and shoulders and pulled her toward the casement. The streetscape yawned below, the fire brigade already hauling buckets to tame the roaring flames.

"This is impossible!" Her heart was pounding and her arm throbbed with renewed force as she surveyed the sheer drop. Without balconies, the only leverage they would have going down were narrow windowsills. "There's no way we'll get out of here."

Blackburn took her shoulders, his grip firm but surprisingly gentle. "I got up here with no trouble and I'll get both of us down. Simply hold on to me and I'll do the rest."

Smoke was seeping in through the bedroom door. She tried to stem a spasm of coughing as she frantically looked for other possible exits. And then she remembered—the *Eroica* score and their work, spread out carelessly on the table in the dining room.

"Damn it. We've got to go back and get the score. After all this we can't just let it burn. We might need it!"

With the thrust of his booted foot, Blackburn impatiently cleared the last of the glass shards clinging to the casement. "Don't worry—I've got it safely stored away."

"What do you mean?"

"I took it with me when I left here tonight."

Devon didn't know which was worse, choking on the thick smoke snaking its way into the room or on Blackburn's revelation. In the background, licking closer, the fire roared, building to a crescendo. "I don't understand why you would take it with you," she began, suspicions beginning to swirl in her head. The room spun around her as she fought for breath, her questions dying in her throat. Seizing the opportunity, Blackburn's eyes shone with intensity as he secured the rope around her waist once more and took her in his arms, placing one leg out on the windowsill. Devon squeezed her eyes shut, the roiling sense of nausea overwhelming her.

Blackburn's voice called to her: "Don't think for once and save the questions for later. Trust me, I'll get us down."

Trust me. Trust me. Trust me. This man with a heart of ice. This man who would have given her to Le Comte. Yet she put her arms around him as she felt the tug of the rope around her waist. Although they were outside, the air smelled of smoke and she could hear the crackling of the fire as it devoured the bedroom they left behind. Feeling like a coward, hiding her head in his chest, she sensed that she was spiraling down, unwinding, spinning as she tried to get purchase where none existed. Only Blackburn existed, the hard chest, the steady beat of his heart against her ear, as he flexed his leg muscles in a steady rhythm while her feet flailed in the darkness.

Inexorably, they made their way down until she felt a hard edge strike her injured arm, catapulting her into sharp awareness. She dared open her eyes and turned her head from Blackburn's chest to find herself on the corner of the street where he had carried her. A clutch of people raced by, shouting, carrying buckets. She looked up at the building, the flames spilling from the window of her apartments where the fire had originally started and now threatened to devour the rest of the building with an omnivorous hunger.

Devon took great gulps of air, barely aware that Blackburn was still holding her, her gaze transfixed by the inferno.

"Has everyone been led safely out?" she asked hoarsely.

She felt him nod. "Of the three apartments, only two were occupied. The older lady was, mercifully, staying with her sister this past week."

"This was not an accident," she said to no one in particular, her voice hoarse from the smoke that clung like a poisonous blanket. In her delirium she could make out the faint outlines of the truth. "Somebody deliberately set fire to the apartments." She coughed again, her mind grappling with the disaster and its malevolent implications.

She discovered that she was trembling as Blackburn gently wiped a streak of soot from her face. Lifting her in his arms, he carried her unresistingly away from the inferno, his arms a gentle cocoon where she wished she could stay forever.

"I think I know who. But this isn't the place or time," he murmured into her hair, wrapping her in his warmth. Devon closed her eyes in weariness, surrendering to the velvet voice even though it was madness, a folly for which she knew that she would pay dearly.

Blackburn signaled for his rented hansom which appeared out of the early morning darkness. In the confines of the coach Devon had no difficulty feigning sleep, reluctant to confront the possibilities, one more unpalatable than the next. The knot in her stomach twisted and mortification burned to the surface of her skin. It was a craving, this addiction that allowed Blackburn to entrap her in sensation, envelop her in passion, and wipe out the last shred of reason she might still possess.

Despite her myriad of misgivings, one worse than the next, her blood surged in response to his nearness just as every roll of the coach stung her pulsing arm. She peered out from under half-closed lashes at Blackburn sitting across from her, his grace undiminished, self-control and strength evident in every line of his body. He had saved her life.

Or had he?

She also believed that *she* had seduced him earlier that evening. Her suspicions took no time to grow, multiplying like weeds in her mind. He was a panther, he was a thief, adept at slipping from their bed after she had fallen into an exhausted slumber, perhaps to return to Sobrero's laboratory without her or perhaps to rendezvous somewhere entirely different?

With the score tucked conveniently—and with purpose—in his well-worn leather satchel.

Devon felt the hansom lurch to a slow stop.

"I know you're awake."

She opened her eyes. She had no idea what emotion lay beneath the intense glance he gave her. The sole candle wavered and danced, throwing the planes of his face into harsh relief. He moved forward in his seat, deliberately putting himself in shadow so she could not see his face.

"I'm leaving you here at my apartments in the Luxembourg. You'll have discreet but determined protection from my men. I promise you." Gone was any semblance of warmth or protectiveness, as though he'd turned a corner. His tone was clipped, professional.

"That's what they were supposedly doing at Place des Vosges," she said, watching him warily, aware of the change in his mood. "Obviously they're not invincible as somebody slipped by them. But who?" She allowed her suspicions to emerge, one by one. "Le Comte wouldn't want to watch the *Eroica* go up in flames along with the only two people who know what to do with it. Lacan and his men were back at Sobrero's."

She was waiting for an answer. His answer.

His next words emerged from the silence of the hackney with the ricochet of pistol shots. "It wasn't de Maupassant or his men."

Devon clenched her hands in her lap, her arm throbbing. She was almost afraid to ask the question which she sensed would bring them to the edge of an abyss. She was afraid to look down into the chasm when, worse still, she knew she would have to jump. Spinelessly, she played for time. "Another of Lacan's cohorts, then? Don't expect me to believe this was a random act or an accident."

Around them, she could hear the early morning sound of the streets, the clatter of horses' hooves, the scrape of iron-bound carriage wheels.

His words were shadowed. "One of my men caught sight of a woman they had never seen before entering the building shortly after I exited. She came alone, was extremely well dressed, a brunette. Of course, she didn't arouse any suspicions."

"Did they recognize her?" Devon's voice sharpened.

Blackburn gave a grim smile in the darkness. "No—but I did when I was given a more detailed description. The woman happened to be Susannah Treadwell."

Her breath caught, ragged and painful. That the revelation could cause her to ache came as no surprise. Devon pressed her hands over her burning eyes. Of course, the *other* woman Blackburn was involved with, as if she could ever forget. The Marquess knew Susannah Treadwell so intimately that he could identify her from only a verbal description.

She remembered the brittle, volatile woman the night of Le Comte's recital, disheveled, sexually satiated, her possessive hand on Blackburn's arm. She remembered the vitriol in her words, the barely suppressed violence as she lashed out that afternoon in Le Comte's town house. It wasn't inconceivable that the woman was mad, obsessed with the Marquess, but mad and obsessed enough to set a fire with the intent to snuff out lives?

She dragged her hands from her face and stared at Blackburn in the shadows of the carriage. "That last meeting with Le Comte—she was livid, threatening him with betrayal. It's a wonder that he didn't take her seriously, that I didn't take her seriously." She stilled her hands in her lap. "I think she wanted you desperately. And if she couldn't have you . . ."

Blackburn eased back into the cushions of the carriage, his face once again revealed by the candlelight. "This is all purely speculation. The only way we can find out whether Susannah is behind this is to ask her. Which I'm intending to do."

"Of course you know where to find her." Devon didn't try to keep the pain from her voice.

His gaze was as remote as ever, reminding her of the man she first met at Blackfriars Bridge. "She always stays at the Hôtel de Vendôme when in Paris."

"I'm sure she does," murmured Devon, refusing to picture the two of them together. "And while you're on this mission to find Lady Treadwell, I'm expected to remain here," she said mechanically, glancing out the window onto the grand *hôtel particulier* across from the Luxembourg Palace. "Well, for once, I will agree with you, Blackburn. The last person I want to see is Lady Treadwell. You may have that privilege all to yourself. And while you're off with your lover, I won't wait for Le Comte to find me. I'll go to him."

In the shadows of the carriage, Blackburn's eyes were cold and hard. "There will be no meeting."

"The man murdered my father."

"I'm well aware of that fact and the fact that he killed my brother as well."

For a moment she couldn't bear it. Devon leaned closer,

grabbing him by the arm. Blackburn felt her strong grip through the cloth of his coat, tight with desperation. Every line and angle of her body had become familiar to him. The scent of her skin, the tempo of her breath.

"We've come this far. I can't stop now."

His voice slashed at her. "I said no."

She let her hands drop and then made a small sound. "You still don't trust me, do you? Well, that's unfortunate. Because you can't stop me and you won't stop me—this is our only chance of getting what we need from Le Comte." An edge hardened her voice. "It's your chance at vengeance, Blackburn."

The brief hard look in his eyes made her stomach tighten.

"If you trust me at all you'll give me your word that you won't meet with him."

"A strange request coming from you. As though my word would mean anything to you."

"Or mine to you." He leaned forward. He was breathing hard. "I don't want to see you hurt, Devon. I *won't* see you hurt."

Devon slowly braced her hands against his shoulders. She searched his gaze as always, looking for something she would never find. "You should have thought of that a long time ago, Blackburn," she said finally, moving away from him. "In the interim, the best of luck with Lady Treadwell."

Devon made to rise from the carriage, every muscle protesting. Blackburn grabbed hold of her hand. "It's not—and never was—what you think," he said.

Devon shook her hand from his hard grasp, shaking her head wearily. "No need to embarrass either of us with explanations. The last thing I need is any more revelations tonight. The facts speak for themselves. You left me tonight and took the *Eroica* with you." She took a deep breath. "Those are the facts and they will never change."

Perhaps she had gone too far. She would never know. And that was their tragedy.

Chapter 15

An hour later Blackburn strode into Lady Susannah Treadwell's hotel room on the rue Madame, his dangerous mood held perilously in check.

She received him in a voluptuously resplendent black lace dressing gown, reclining theatrically on a recamier couch. Her eyes took in the sight of him resting against the door, languid menace in every line of that lean, gorgeously handsome body. She all but licked her full lips—she always did find anger particularly arousing.

"Darling, I've been waiting." She pouted and with hips swaying seductively, she rose from the recamier in a whisper of lace. She had missed Blackburn keenly since their last rendezvous in London, missed his expert touch and dangerous carelessness like the most addictive opiate.

It was a game they had often played. Wordlessly, she snaked her arms around his torso, her hands sinuously exploring the contours of his muscled chest, tapered hips, and rock-hard thighs.

But this time, he didn't seem interested in playing, his eyes a hazardous blue-black, sharp as a knife point. "You go too far, Susannah."

Her eyes widened in feigned surprise. "You usually like it when I come straight to the point," she murmured, deliberately misunderstanding, her arms still draped over his shoulders. "I thought *aggressive* women appealed to you."

"This morning I make an exception."

"It upsets you that I followed you to Paris from London? That I missed my lover—and you are a wonderfully inventive lover, darling—missed him enough to follow him to the ends of the earth?"

He unlooped the arms around his neck. "I believe there's more to this than simply your proclamations of undying love, Susannah."

"Believe me—you are the only man I would *ever* follow across Europe." She deliberately fingered the lace at the deep cut of her dressing gown. "But don't worry, darling. I know that you despise possessive women, so rest assured that I have no designs upon you whatsoever—other than that which you willingly and so brilliantly provide."

"You're missing the point, quite deliberately." The hint of reprisal in his voice belied the blandness of his words. "We both know why you're here in Paris. And," he said, pausing fractionally, "we both know why I'm here."

Her lids lowered over her shrewd glance. She'd never seen Blackburn in this mood before, a hot, violent edge evident in every controlled word and gesture. She moved slowly toward the bed, seduction very much on her mind.

"De Maupassant stopped paying you." His statement burned in the stillness of the room.

"What do you mean, darling?" She glanced at him over one half-naked shoulder.

"De Maupassant decided you were more trouble than you were worth and decided to cut off the funds. That's what I mean."

She replied lightly, "I believe you have the wrong woman."

Blackburn took a step toward her. "I don't think so. Just as I believe you ensured that I was picked up several weeks ago by de Maupassant's people." He smiled in a way that didn't reach his eyes. "Not the best way to treat your lovers, I shouldn't think."

Susannah sat daintily on the edge of the bed, examining a large cabochon diamond on her hand before answering pointedly. "Darling, I can't help feeling that you would be better directing your accusations at someone else. If there's anyone playing two men at one time, I would say it's that redheaded Frenchwoman, Le Comte's current mistress. Before you accuse me of subterfuge—"

When she looked up again, he towered over her. She was forced to sit farther back on the bed. Suddenly, she was afraid and not in the usual, game-playing way that marked her sexual exploits.

His words were toneless and his expression bleak. "You tried to kill her tonight."

Susannah knew enough about self-preservation not to bother denying the accusation. But she wasn't about to gamble her trump card yet either. "You mean she isn't dead? And what if I did? These sorts of arrangements fall entirely within your purview, if I'm not mistaken, darling," she parried, smoothing a silk-clad thigh. "Your conscience on these sorts of matters is hardly pristine, after all."

The menace of his body so close to hers pulsed heat. "You're absolutely right. I could kill you right here and now," Blackburn said almost conversationally. Only the strong hands, the deadly strength of tendon and bone which he flexed by his sides, indicated his struggle with restraint.

"It wouldn't be the first time you killed, now, would it?" Susannah asked huskily, the idea arousing her lust. She wondered what it would be like to have him take her violently, having all that power unleashed, aware that any moment he could use those hands that gave so much pleasure and apply the right amount of pressure around her throat. . . . She shivered at the thought.

Blackburn caught the glitter of desire in her eyes and responded by deliberately stepping away from her. He had always known that the rapaciously greedy Lady Treadwell had been in the employ of de Maupassant, providing him with useful tidbits of information gleaned from her dealings both with the crème of London society and the demimonde. But he never suspected she'd go this far.

"At this moment I want something more than the feel of your broken neck in my hands. That's why I am willing to enter into an agreement with you instead."

Susannah caught his dark blue gaze for a stark, frightening moment. Her mind worked deviously, cataloguing Blackburn's libidinous proclivities, all of which she could more than flagrantly satisfy. She wet her lips in anticipation and rose from the bed, ready to walk into his arms.

And stopped. His expression warned her to go no farther.

"Either you tell me what your true motivations are with regard to de Maupassant and Devon Caravelle or I can assure you, Lady Treadwell, that you will never see daylight again."

Susannah looked at him with disbelief, reaching out to him with a scarlet-tipped hand. "Why, darling, you can't be serious," she stammered. "What possibly useful information would Le Comte have shared with me?"

"I've had enough of your prevarication. Don't waste my time." Blackburn's mouth hardened.

Beneath her façade of frivolity, Susannah was a woman who always knew how to put her own interests first. From her marriage to a wealthy man old enough to be her grandfather, to forging other equally profitable relationships outside the marriage bed, Susannah was at heart as practical as a fishwife.

Except when it came to Blackburn. His reputation as a fantastic lover had preceded him when she first took him to her bed, and then there was the added benefit of Le Comte's stipend to sweeten the connection. What Susannah hadn't expected was her growing addiction to the Marquess, a craving that, she had discovered, a dozen men couldn't satisfy.

To have Le Comte summarily and simultaneously cut off

both her financial recompense *and* her association with the Marquess was more than her carnal cravings or her pride could bear.

And all because of that devious redhead, Devon Caravelle. At the reminder, a wave of jealousy washed over her and she watched Blackburn with drawn brows and an angry mouth. "If you weren't so besotted with her, there would have been no need."

"No need to kill her." She didn't care for the flicker of guilt in his eyes reflecting disappointment in his failure to protect the slattern. He clearly worried about the bitch and the knowledge cut her to the quick.

"For God's sake, Blackburn," she lashed out with a tilt of her head, "what makes her so different? Why do you even care? You've bedded dozens of women in the past for nefarious purposes without any one of them staining your conscience. And you were quite prepared to share her with Le Comte."

Blackburn's gaze wavered for the briefest second. He recovered just as quickly, the clenching of his jaw the only indication of his inner turmoil.

"I'm not here to discuss Devon Caravelle. I'm here to finish a job. And how it finishes is your choice."

How fortuitous for her. Although Susannah always had made sure that she had a way out. Her survival demanded it. She regarded Blackburn for a moment, her eyes lingering on that hard, clean profile, the lean, well-muscled body. He was a prize and he should have been hers.

Alas, there was no room in her life for sentimentality—there never had been. In a moment's decision, Susannah turned away from him in a swirl of black lace. She disappeared briefly into her dressing room, returning quickly with a look of cold purpose in her eyes and an envelope in her hand that she threw on the bed contemptuously.

"Be careful what you ask for, darling." She curved around the back of the recamier.

He walked over to the bed and picked up the envelope, his expression blank as he took in Brendan Clifton's now familiar handwriting. "Where did you get this?"

"From Le Comte, of course. Although he didn't want me to have it. I can't imagine why," she said, her tone acid. "So I simply *had* to help myself, you understand, darling, as extra insurance. Le Comte was too busy with his *protégée*," she bit off the word, "to realize that I'd revisit his rooms, with a little help, as soon as his back was turned. The besotted fool."

Blackburn's eyes narrowed. "You're very good at helping yourself, I've noticed."

"I did have a little assistance from friends. Bertrand Lacan, for example, who is as disappointed in his former employer as I am."

"You set the fire?"

"Don't be absurd, darling." She flicked a dismissive hand his way. "I merely asked Lacan to locate the two of you, after which I just had to see your cozy love nest with my own eyes. You understand, I wasn't entirely convinced that he could dispatch that bitch with your hovering about."

"You hired someone to start the fire?" Blackburn continued as though she hadn't spoken.

"Of course. But I did stay and watch."

Blackburn exhaled, a harsh sound in the quiet of the room and Susannah wondered if he would kill her now.

"Why give me this letter?"

"Won't you kill me if I don't?"

"I didn't ask for it specifically which makes me suspicious. What's in it for you?"

Susannah crossed her arms drawing attention to her dramatic décolletage framed by decadent black lace. "You'd be surprised, darling. You really would," she said, not bothering to hide her annoyance at his indifference. "On the surface, the letter is simply sentimental twaddle, Clifton rattling on to his bastard daughter. Except for one little thing..." She trailed off, her gaze feline. "There's mention of their cottage in Blois, a place that seems to have been extremely important—not just to Clifton, but to Le Comte as well, or so I've discovered."

Blackburn pocketed the letter without looking at it, his face set with a sudden intensity.

"I can see you're interested also," Susannah said slyly, tasting venom on her tongue. It would be a shame to lose Blackburn, but then if she couldn't have him, she'd prefer that nobody else could either. Let him gallop off to Blois. She would make certain that Le Comte would be waiting.

What delicious irony to have the two men destroy each other.

And she would make sure that Devon Caravelle would be part of the explosion.

Under a heavy sweep of lashes, she watched him turn to leave, a man who had no time left for discussion, or anything else. "Deserting me so soon, darling?" she asked with the brittleness of porcelain. Blackburn stopped with his hand on the door handle. He swung around to acknowledge her question, his face tense but his eyes had the light of the chase.

"Happy you didn't have to dispatch me?" She could see herself reflected as a monster in his dark blue gaze. But then again, who was Blackburn to point a finger?

"If you knew me you wouldn't have to ask." His voice was rough and he looked as if he had her fixed in the crosshairs of a pistol. "But you didn't answer my earlier question. What's in all this for you?"

She laughed throatily. "You'll just have to find out, won't you, darling?" She devoured him with one look, hunger in her eyes. She undulated her hips, her breasts jutting forward suggestively. "Unless, of course, I can change your mind in the interim . . . I won't ask again, you know."

Blackburn looked at her with a combination of pity and disdain. Susannah would have preferred his anger. She didn't bother to swallow the hysteria that rose in her throat.

"Get out of here, then. Go." She spat. "I just hope you're smart enough to figure out that that trollop of yours is as capable of treachery as the rest of us. Too bad she didn't die in the fire tonight. It would have saved you much trouble, Blackburn, as you'll soon discover."

She wanted to hurt him, wound him as he had managed to hurt her like no other man had ever done before. She saw the rage flare in his eyes, quickly extinguished, his protective armor revealing nothing. Susannah forced her lips into a rictus of a smile at the small victory. There would be more victories to come.

Blackburn said, "I don't want to have to make good on my promise, Susannah. Don't even think of going near her."

She laughed shrilly, a woman with nothing to lose. "Don't worry, darling. I won't have to."

When Devon awoke it was already noon. For a moment she was disoriented, the fog of sleep threatening to overtake her again. She peered at her strange surroundings through gritty eyes. Sunlight was streaming through the curtains of the French doors, suffusing the chamber in gold that only served to highlight the opulence of the gilt furnishings. She felt dwarfed in the huge bed set in the middle of an even larger room, the whole effect discomfiting, as if she suddenly found herself at Versailles.

Then she remembered where she was. After the disastrous fire at the apartments near the Places des Vosges, she and Blackburn had returned to his lodgings near the Luxembourg Palace. Devon recalled a bitter exchange of words before finding herself overcome with pain and exhaustion, welcoming forgetfulness in the form of a down-filled comforter and the oblivion of sleep.

Carefully, she pulled herself into a sitting position, leaning against the abundant softness of carefully arranged pillows, gingerly supporting her stiff arm. Someone had changed the bandages and dressed her in a fresh nightgown. Only the slightest scent of smoke lingered in her hair. She was as weak as a sapling, unable and unwilling to rise from the bed.

The room felt empty without Blackburn. Why, she would never know—but she missed him, missed his strength, his dynamism, even the tension of his betrayal that filled the air when he was near. Alone in the middle of the big bed, she forced herself to admit that her feelings were misplaced. Swept along into an emotional wilderness, she was now hopelessly lost.

Her vision blurred. Her body felt numb and cold. Tears spilled down her cheeks and she was helpless to do anything else but sink into the softness of the enveloping bed. Her thoughts were a jumble of painful images.

Blackburn and Susannah.

Blackburn deserting her, taking the *Eroica* with him.

Blackburn holding her prisoner here in his apartments, ready to relinquish her to the British authorities the moment he returned to London.

A moan escaped her throat, gripping her chest and pulling painfully at her injured arm. The tears flowed and she did nothing to stop them. She thought about her parents, remembering the last time she'd seen her father, waving to him from the carriage as it pulled away from their small cottage. She saw her mother again, her gracefulness as she sat at the pianoforte, her infinite patience as she helped small hands maneuver the ivory and ebony keys. Their values and beliefs that she had assimilated with her baby's pabulum and yet, many years later, she was still painfully learning the bitterly personal consequences that accompanied commitment to an ideological cause. It wasn't just about philosophy and the Revolution. It was personal and it was breaking her heart.

And it all came down to a simple fact—that she was in love with a man whom she couldn't trust, who had used her once and would use her again.

A dam burst inside her and she buried her head in a pillow,

the tears dampening the fine sheets as she allowed herself to lose control. This was it. This was how it ended, in a flood of tears that she wished could wash away all the ugliness, the subterfuge, the uncertainty that would leave fissures on her heart for the rest of her life. *Her very soul craved Blackburn.* She was swept away in a fresh tide of weeping.

Devon didn't know how much time had passed, but when she finally lifted her head, her face swollen with tears, she felt enervated and immeasurably calmer, cleansed. With an unsteady hand, she slid her fingers through her hair and wiped the moistness from her cheeks.

She loved Blackburn.

If only the truth really did set one free. Moments later she rose shakily from the bed, her body stiff with regret. She poured water from the fine porcelain ewer into the matching basin and splashed her face. The water felt cool on her heated skin, a balm for her overwrought nerves and her embattled heart.

Everything had changed and yet nothing had.

Her throat still raw from smoke, Devon reluctantly moved to the doors of the elaborate wardrobe and pulled her nightgown over her head, wincing at the pain in her arm. She then chose the simplest dress she could find, struggling with the bodice that was closed by a myriad of tiny silk-covered hooks. A fine wool wrap completed her borrowed and hastily assembled ensemble.

She stood in the center of the room, shoving her hair into a rough chignon, her movements gaining speed along with her thoughts. She was empty, dried of emotion, as though admitting her love for Blackburn allowed her to think clearly, rationally, for the first time in weeks. Remaining here was not an option and her only hope was getting as far away from Blackburn and as close to Le Comte as she could.

Her gaze rested on the heavy door, its elaborate hinges, wondering if it was locked. If she could get to the Conservatoire, she could send a message to Le Comte's Paris town house.

Making her way down a wide hallway that, mercifully, seemed familiar despite the tumult of the previous night, she turned right and nearly collided with a young man at the entrance of what looked like the morning room. He bowed correctly, but not before Devon could see the suspicion etched on his face. She hesitated a moment and then said crisply, "I have need of a hansom or carriage. Please have one sent around."

"That's not possible, Mademoiselle." The gold epaulettes on his uniform glittered dully. "The Marquess of Blackburn asked me to ensure that you remain here and asked me to see to your every comfort."

The irony of the words pierced her heart. "I'm most appreciative of the Marquess's concern. And a carriage right away would see to my comfort, I assure you."

The young man cleared his throat awkwardly. "My apologies. That's not possible."

"You mean I'm to be kept prisoner here?" Devon shot him a damning look, her resolve quickly replacing any lingering weakness. "I'm certain that's not what the Marquess had intended."

He could not have been more than twenty, she estimated, and he had the good breeding to look uncomfortable. She was unable to see what waited for her on the street below, but she wagered that the Marquess would have distributed her jailers discreetly. No need to draw unnecessary attention.

Ten minutes later she found herself in the back of a hansom. Those too highly born had little understanding of the workings of a household. She smiled. Having stripped her princely bed of its linens, she had marched out the servants' entrance undetected under a mound of laundry.

Above the blue roofs of Paris, the sky glowed a brighter azure as the carriage clattered along the Faubourg St.-Germain, up the rue de Varenne, and past the Invalides. It was a trip she had made many times, but this journey had the poignancy of a farewell. She hardened her heart. Too soon, the horses hauled to a stop outside the Conservatoire on the rue St.-Cecile and Devon leapt from the carriage as if she wanted to leave herself behind.

Those heavily carved wooden doors, they seemed even more massive than she recalled, holding memories that she wasn't sure she wanted to relive anymore. Somebody was practicing scales on the piano, the notes melding discordantly with the strings of a cello one floor above, but the untutored sound was music to her ears. Afraid of lingering further, she stepped into the darkness of the foyer.

It was midafternoon and Devon skirted past the small reception desk with a nod to the concierge and up the steps to the main concert hall, the marble stairs beneath her feet polished perfection. It all felt too familiar and yet she needed to see it again, needed to see the rows of mahogany seats, and the raised dais with its coveted Erard pianoforte. Sentimental, perhaps. But the missive intended for de Maupassant could wait for just a moment.

The doors to the hall were ajar releasing the scent of beeswax and lingering perfume that was vaguely familiar. Tall narrow windows banked the high-ceilinged space with empty seats like blank notes waiting to be played. Her palms dampened in anticipation as she stepped into the room.

A sense of unease settled over her shoulders like a mantle. Her muscles tensed. A voice, distorted by cavernous space, echoed from somewhere near the dais. Devon squinted into the distance, nerves jumping.

"How absolutely predictable you are."

Devon stepped farther into the aisle and heard a growl of wind rattle the glass panes above her head. At the same moment she remembered her pistol lying, now too far away, in the charred ruins of the apartments near the Place des Vosges.

The scent *was* familiar. Musky perfume mingling with the intense odor of roses that were lavishly arranged in huge vases throughout the hall. And posed dramatically against a Palla-

dian pillar with her back to the door, Lady Susannah Treadwell waited. Devon could see the beautifully curved figure,
languorous and relaxed, as though Lady Treadwell were expecting her lover.

Devon advanced into the hall, her heels staccato in the
heavy silence. "How did you know I'd be here?"

Blackburn's mistress slowly turned around, a goddess from
Olympus seeking vengeance. Even from several feet away,
Devon couldn't miss the fire that leapt from her eyes.

"Well, I couldn't very well storm the Fortress Blackburn
could I?"

A tremor ran through her. "You tried to kill me earlier. In
the fire."

Lady Treadwell leaned over gracefully to pluck a long-
stemmed rose from the vase next to her, well aware of the
dramatic picture she presented. "Indeed, Blackburn gave me
the news that you had survived. How unfortunate." She
plucked at the velvety blossom. "However, I knew it would
only be a matter of time before you left the apartments at the
Luxembourg to return to the womb. As I said already, hopelessly predictable." Mocking triumph laced with hatred.

The woman had tried to murder her several hours ago and
Devon felt a prickle of sweat break out on her neck at the
thought of how important a second or two could be when it
came to life or death. That she had been together with Blackburn, that they had been together . . . Devon could not complete the thought.

Lady Treadwell's mouth curved into a smile fraught with
danger as she tossed the rose aside. "Are you looking for the
Marquess, perhaps? You might have discovered him with me
had you come last night," she said archly, drawing out each
word with relish. "Although I must say, do you think it wise
running after a man who has so clearly finished with you?"

"I'm not here to see the Marquess, nor do I care that he
spent the night with you, Lady Treadwell," Devon said evenly,

refusing to rise to the bait, sealing her mind from images of the two together.

"Oh, but I'm sure you do. I wouldn't want to lose as magnificent a lover as the Marquess."

"I'm waiting for you to tell me why you're here."

Lady Treadwell rambled on as if she hadn't heard her last words. "You didn't actually think you could hold on to a man like Blackburn, did you? Poor child. It took you long enough to realize that he was simply using you. The Marquess has an unfortunate history, as you've probably discovered, what with the business of his brother. Not to mention all the other women in his past that he's collected and discarded like so much currency. Why would you be any different? Why would you mean anything to him—a Bonapartist, for God's sake."

The woman spoke the truth. Devon felt the pressure build in her chest and it was a long moment before she responded. "You're wasting time, Lady Treadwell, with your less than helpful information. If you're planning to do away with me, you've chosen a relatively public spot. You had to see the concierge downstairs to gain entrance."

"Do away with you?" She raised a perfectly arched and plucked brow. "How perceptive of you, Mademoiselle, although what I had in mind was more of a metaphorical rather than literal death."

Devon could hear a door closing in the distance and footsteps walking away. They were quite alone. "You were unsuccessful with the former and are hoping for better luck with the latter?" An edge hardened her voice

Lady Treadwell pursed her lips and picked absently at the ecru lace edging her crimson *peau de soie* gown. "How to begin . . ."

Devon leaned into the back of a chair, the wood biting into her hip. She was strangely impatient, eager to force the denouement that Lady Treadwell was torturously withholding.

"Why not begin with the letter you tried to steal from Le Comte."

"*Tried* to steal?" She sauntered toward Devon like a dark cloud, the pianoforte silhouetted behind her. "My dear, it was never about trying. I always get what I want."

Devon held her ground, fighting the urge simply to back out the door and break into a run. But a sickening desire to hear more kept her cemented to the spot as if she were shackled hand and foot.

Lady Treadwell stopped and waved her hand airily. "You, on the other hand, should never have tried playing Le Comte for a fool. Nor Monsieur Lacan." She flicked her a contemptuous look. "Not a good idea at all for a woman of your limited physical attributes."

"What about the letter?"

Lady Treadwell shook her head disparagingly, the black hair a glossy blue in the natural light. "You still haven't the slightest idea, do you? Which makes it doubly delightful for me to have kept the letter from you for as long as possible."

"To make me suffer?"

Lady Treadwell stared down at Devon with a mixture of contempt and reluctant admiration. Resting against a seat with her arms outspread, she allowed a small smile to play on her lips. "And why not? Why not make Devon Caravelle suffer? You *are* quite the clever girl."

Aware that she was dealing with a mad woman, Devon said nothing more, her silence encouraging her to go on.

"Now, let me think," mused Lady Treadwell, tapping her laquered nails on the mahogany of the bench beside her. "Why would a daughter want a letter from her father, his last communication to her before his death? And what would a man like Le Comte or the Marquess want with such a letter?" She sighed theatrically. "I wonder? . . ."

Devon interrupted, keeping her voice steady. "Obviously, there's an important piece of information my father wanted me to have, but you probably don't have a clue to its import."

"I wouldn't make the mistake of underestimating me, Mademoiselle." The blaze in Lady Treadwell's eyes was like a slap. Devon could feel the animosity burning from every pore. "Since you're so clever—and I'm not—why not uncover the letter's contents by simply joining the two men at the place where it all began. Ask them directly, face-to-face—what a delightful idea!"

Devon's hand clenched around the back of the seat that was supporting her. Her chest tight, she forced back the nausea in her throat. "You are speaking in riddles."

"Of course, you believe it all began here." Lady Treadwell waved her arms to indicate the Conservatoire. "But think again."

Where it all began. A puzzle, the pieces never quite fitting together. Beethoven, her parents, the code, the search for kieselguhr, she and Blackburn, Lacan, Le Comte and Lady Treadwell—where had it all started? Images shifted like fragments of a montage and she felt faint.

Lady Treadwell chuckled throatily, the tendons prominent in her slender neck. "You still don't understand, do you?" She rose with the grace instilled from childhood and strolled toward her. For an instant, Devon thought she meant to do her bodily harm, to reach into her bodice and extract a pistol or a knife. Then the older woman stopped in her tracks, hands on her hips, evaluating her with something like pain in her eyes. "I truly don't understand what he sees in you," she murmured.

It was an illogical statement, throwing Devon off center, but she held Lady Treadwell's gaze. "I told you that I didn't come here to talk about the Marquess."

"Of course you didn't," said Lady Treadwell, with something like anguish in her voice. And strangely, Devon felt her own torment rise to the surface to resonate with hers like discordant voices reaching for the same note. For a moment, they were two women longing for a man neither could ever have.

"I wouldn't want to talk about it either," said Lady Treadwell, collapsing theatrically onto a seat before arranging her gown carefully. "To have your lover so eager to share you with another man in exchange for a few bloody secrets." She looked at Devon with something close to pity in her eyes. "That's where he is right now, you understand, meeting with Le Comte, ready to thrust you aside to ensure that damnable coveted formula doesn't make it into the wrong hands. But then that explains men, doesn't it, always the political animals. Always hungry for power. And prepared to use anyone to get it."

"Blackburn's motives are no concern of mine." Her voice cracked and it seemed to have slipped beyond her control. Tears burned behind her eyes, saline and bitter.

"Perhaps his motivations should be of concern? Particularly, if your life depends on it, Mademoiselle," Lady Treadwell continued, relishing every word. "Please allow me to enlighten you. After all, I heard it from the Marquess's own lips last night. Didn't I warn you that our Blackburn has a heart of stone?"

Devon's nails dug into the mahogany.

"You can't be too surprised that he's willing to make a trade with the Frenchman. And from what I've gleaned, Le Comte should prove quite eager to negotiate, as he has some unfinished business to settle with you, Mademoiselle. I understand your departure from London was somewhat hasty."

Devon shut out the pain that cut at the corners of both her mind and heart. "Did you give Blackburn the letter?"

"Why don't you find out for yourself? And for that matter, find out why Blackburn is so particularly eager to wrest that little shred of evidence from my grasp."

"Evidence?" Devon took a step back, bumping into the

sharp corner of a pilaster. The vase, with its flourish of roses, trembled.

"You didn't think it was just about politics? These things do tend to get out of hand, spilling over into the most unsavory of personal relations." Susannah stared at her like a duelist ready to let the fatal bullet fly. "To have one's lover murder one's father—very Greek, very tragic, wouldn't you agree?"

The nightmare flared to life, smothering her, cutting off her breath. She wanted to scream, her mouth working silently, but no sound came. Reality contracted to one sharp point, focused on the fury in Lady Treadwell's eyes.

The past invaded the present and Devon anticipated Susannah's next words before they even formed on her crimson lips.

"We all come full circle eventually, it would seem," the voice echoed, as Devon feared it would echo in her mind for the rest of her life. "Where it all began—of course, at your little cottage near Blois, outside Paris. The day that the Marquess of Blackburn murdered your father in cold blood. It's all in the letter, my dear—which your former lover is so desperate to possess."

Chapter 16

The medieval town of Blois was nestled in the heart of the Loire Valley. With its fairy-tale castles rich in courtly gardens and Renaissance detail, the area had played host to kings and their mistresses for centuries. It was a destination far enough away from the intrigues of Paris, a place of beauty and refuge with its verdant forests set amid the winding Loire River and its tributaries, the Cher, Indrois, and Indre.

A small spume of smoke leaked from the cottage chimney, the decree sealing Devon's fate. Le Comte and the Marquess of Blackburn had arrived well before her, as Lady Treadwell had ensured, a carriage and half a dozen horses now ringed the property. Resolute and dry-eyed, she slipped from her horse, tethering the mare to a nearby vine, already dripping with the heaviness of green grapes that would ripen into sweetness in the coming summer months. She would not permit herself to think that far ahead.

The bright sunlight stung her eyes as she walked toward the cottage. The short path was familiar to her, a strawberry bush to her left, the remnants of a vegetable garden at the back, and all of it hemmed by tall hedges, neglected now. Her legs carried her inexorably to the front door as images unspooled in her mind, rehearsal for what was to come. She had no plan, only to cut the binds that tied her to a man who had come to mean everything to her, a man whose hands were stained with her father's blood.

She loved Blackburn—it was the bitterest of truths. Devon stared at the unblinking shutters drawn over the cottage windows, her imagination wandering down darkened paths. She clenched her fists, shutting out the scene where the knife had separated the flesh from the spirit, removing her father from her life forever.

Taking a ragged breath and shielding her eyes from the afternoon sun, she regarded the cottage with its steep mansard roof, the green shutters closed against the world, the atmosphere seemingly idyllic and untouched. If life were only that simple. She'd always known in her soul that Blackburn would exploit her to the last. Whether it was revenge fueling his motives or a misguided patriotism, whether it was his brother's or her father's blood staining his conscience, Blackburn could no more resist the lure of intrigue and treachery than the earth stop spinning on its axis.

Le Comte had understood the Marquess of Blackburn far better than Devon ever could. Fiendish, perverse, he had stoked the fire, stirred the cauldron and then poisoned the relationship that grew between them. Those eyes had seen everything, keenly recognizing that the Marquess would stop at nothing to possess his mistress, to steal her away along with the *Eroica* itself.

He had recognized her vulnerabilities, not only her love for her father, but also the passion that would lead her unwisely and recklessly to throw away first her heart and then her talent. Her head would never have allowed her to work with Le Comte, but her passion had opened the door to a relationship with the Marquess.

The truth had been revealed in all its ugliness and she couldn't look away. She was no longer afraid, no longer torn by conflicting loyalties and could walk boldly through the cottage's front door and narrow hallway, arming herself from memories that threatened to vanquish her calm, glacial control.

The letter was all she wanted. It was the least, and the last, thing she could do for her father.

Because the windows were shuttered against the afternoon light, it required several moments to adjust to the dimness. The air was close with mildew and voices that drifted from the salon. Turning the corner, she saw five men arrayed against her with Le Comte at their center.

"I was expecting you, *ma chère*." He was a ghost amid the sheet-covered furnishings, but his eyes gleamed in his sharp-boned face. "You've come prepared to do battle perhaps?"

Devon waited for her own reaction, like an unfolding experiment, to this man she hated for so many reasons. She counted the pulse beats in the back of her neck. A small kernel of emotion, hot and cold at the same time, blossomed, threatening to overwhelm her. She would nurse it carefully because right now that hatred was all she had.

His movements slow and deliberate, Le Comte unbuttoned his coat and looked at his watch chain while gesturing nonchalantly to his lieutenants. "Tie her."

As if they had stepped out of a canvas, three of the men dropped their weapons and advanced upon her. Hands grabbed her shoulders, another pulled her head back. A searing pain shot through her neck. She was towed backward off her feet, and dragged across the floor. She tried to twist out of their grasp, the hands coming from everywhere, but one of the men snapped her head back again. Lights exploded behind her closed eyes and in the next moment she was shoved onto a wooden chair. One of her mother's kitchen chairs. Rough rope snapped over her wrists and ankles, pulled tight.

Already she could feel the pulsing against the restraints, the blood draining from her limbs like sap leaving a tree. A prickle of sweat trailed between her shoulder blades and yet she was cold.

"Painful, isn't it? You'll discover in due course that it will get much worse. I promise you." Le Comte's fine features twisted, his memories of that last night in London fueling his sadistic tendencies.

"This won't do much good." Devon tried to breathe normally despite the rope around her waist that was cutting off her breath like a tourniquet. "You won't get what you want from me using your usual methods."

Le Comte chuckled but it was not a pleasant sound, then clasped his hands behind his back as though to contain his zeal. "As I'll recall from our last meeting, you gave me very little consideration, Mademoiselle."

"You gave me little choice."

"And you'll receive even less today."

The rope binding her wrists burned. "I won't give up the formula quite that easily," she challenged on a shallow breath. "You may just have to look to Blackburn for that."

Le Comte's smile was all the more sinister, emphasized by the cut of the high collar framing his face. "I'd rather believed that the two of you would arrive together—the Marquess delivering you to my door or, should I say, your father's door. One needs a bargaining chip, after all, even our Marquess."

He strolled over to the small pianoforte protected by a dustcover. Thrusting the linen aside, he idly struck a few keys as though deep in thought. Devon recoiled as his hands caressed the keys her mother had touched.

"Well, we're in absolutely no hurry," he said at last. "You and I have a few scores to settle before the Marquess's arrival, would you not agree, *chérie?*" He drew out the words, savoring each one.

She swallowed the fear and hatred at the back of her throat. "My proposition is a simple one."

"As though I would even give you a hearing." He closed the lid on the piano with a snap. "I don't really care what you *willingly* have to offer, dear Devon. Rest assured, I will get what I want before the day is out. With the help of the Marquess of Blackburn, I might add."

Devon couldn't and wouldn't think about Blackburn. She had cauterized the pain, the wound that would never heal, refusing to allow the ache to crush her. The letter was what mattered now, a piece of vellum that encapsulated it all—revolution, murder, betrayal, and the possibility of much worse to come. Blackburn still needed her to reveal the letter's message. As did Le Comte.

She had no illusions left.

Her mouth was dry and she was painfully aware of the hulking presence of Le Comte's men. But instinct told her she shouldn't wait any longer. "I know about the letter," she said, throwing down the gauntlet and at the same time wondering whether it would have been wiser to keep silent.

Le Comte whirled away, then spun around to face her again. "The letter to you from your father, you mean? Now that's an old story, my dear."

Fed by a false courage, Devon spoke quickly. "Give me the letter and I'll give you the formula, down to the last detail. I have it in my memory."

"Oh, please, dear Devon. I can't believe that you would be willing to divulge the formula in exchange for a sentimental missive from your father." Le Comte arched his brows, the look incredulous. "Forget about this exchange that you're so foolishly offering. As I said just a few minutes ago, you and I have a few scores to settle first."

Le Comte's eyes glinted with triumph, like a cat who had been playing with a mouse just long enough and was ready to move in for the kill. "Are you quite comfortable? No? Let's see if we can do something about that."

Three men stepped from the corners of the room and the rough hands descended again, pulling, tightening the ropes until she couldn't steal a breath. Pain pulsed into her hands and legs in giant waves. She swallowed hard, listening to a soft wind blow through the eaves. If she closed her eyes she could imagine her father's footsteps in the hallway and hear the ripple of her mother's laughter from the garden.

Pain screamed through the wound in her arm. Her eyes flashed open, her breath coming in smaller gasps.

"Enough for now, gentlemen." With one last wrench on the rope securing her wrists, Le Comte's men backed away from her. "We don't want our Devon Caravelle compromised," the Frenchman said, smiling at her clouded eyes huge against her bloodless skin. "I'm proposing nothing rash, you understand. You are irreplaceable after all, with skills that are unique and quite in demand. Once *we* give Napoleon what he needs to secure his place as emperor of Europe, and England, I might add, there will be many more assignments for such a nimble brain as yours."

Le Comte's future unfolded before his eyes. "How beholden the emperor will be to me."

Devon felt the blood drain from her face as much from lack of oxygen as from proximity to the Frenchman's madness.

"So you will understand that I am the one who has a proposition *for you*, my dear Devon, one which will neatly solve my dilemma."

"And what dilemma is that?" It was hard to speak. The words came out more slowly than she'd intended.

In reply, Le Comte held out his palm into which one of the men placed a knife, beautifully encased in a jewel-encrusted sheath. Taking his time, he admired the casing, running his hands lovingly over the rubies which glittered evilly in the daylight. With malicious delight, he slowly extracted a thin blade.

"My dilemma is twofold," he said, gesturing carefully, the knife marking the air. "Firstly, to right a wrong which takes us back to that evening when you so ungraciously fled my protection in London. And secondly, of course, to extract from you the details of the formula you and the Marquess uncovered together. Not too much to ask."

The tension in the room thickened. "By the way, *ma chère*, have you any experience of pain under the knife?"

Black spots danced in front of her eyes and Le Comte's voice seemed far away. The bite of the rope cutting off her scream was her only reality. Pain. More hurt to come. How could it be any worse than what she'd already endured, what she'd already lost? Images tormented her like devils at the gates of hell. She tried to lock herself away, away from the monstrous sadist whose eyes gleamed in rapt anticipation. Still caressing the knife, Le Comte did nothing to hide his appetite for inflicting agony.

His breathing came more quickly now. "As I promised, nothing rash. You'll still be useful to us even with a disfigured face and body. After all, I must have some satisfaction for the way you threatened me that night in London. What was it you said—you wouldn't kill me, but merely shoot me in the foot or maybe high on my thigh? I have a very good memory, my dear."

He came closer—the pall of his cologne smothering her. She concentrated on the searing burn of her injured arm.

"It's never a good idea to threaten your betters despite the tenets of the Revolution that you hold in such esteem, Devon."

Suddenly, her vision cleared. Le Comte stood over her. He held the wicked blade at her throat and then slipped down, almost playfully, to the wool wrap covering her shoulders. Skillfully and almost delicately, he cut through the fine fabric. Devon listened to the thunder of her own heartbeat, cursing this sudden clarity, as the knife point played with the fastenings on her bodice. She heard first one, then the second, bounce to the floor.

Cool air. Then Le Comte's fingers on her naked skin.

"Such a pity." A thin sheen of sweat coated his brow. His gaze singed her flesh. "I almost hate marring such beauty."

Devon closed her eyes, holding herself rigid, and conjured

Blackburn. She felt the tip of the knife pierce her skin, mortifying her flesh, and suffered again the pain he had caused her. Grief like she had never known closed her throat.

She was done with Blackburn forever, but something flared in her, uncontrollably, blotting out the world like an abstract force. She saw his face, felt the raw wound of betrayal, a vise that would not loosen its grip.

And then she heard his voice:

"Some habits die harder than others."

Devon was afraid to open her eyes, petrified that she had fallen from terror into madness. As the room came into focus, she saw Blackburn standing nonchalantly in the doorway by the small bookcase that had held her father's collection of Diderot, Rousseau, and Voltaire.

"Is this truly a productive use of your time, de Maupassant?" he asked, moving into the salon, seemingly unconcerned about the men circling around him like vultures, their pistols cocked. "One would think you'd learned your lesson. As a means to an end, torture doesn't always produce results." His voice stayed casual, even a little amused. "But then again, you do love wielding a knife."

Le Comte shook his head imperceptibly, as though coming out of a fugue state, his face contorting into a sneer. His eyes glittered wildly as he slid the blade gently up Devon's chest to where her pulse beat at the base of her throat.

She was sure that if her contorted breathing accelerated even slightly, she would soon taste her own blood.

Afraid to move, her eyes glued to the blade that could sever an artery with the flick of a wrist, she heard Le Comte say, "You, above all others, should know just how much, Blackburn. I'm simply teaching our Mademoiselle Caravelle a little lesson, nothing too serious. But then again, you must think this is a pleasant reprise of our last meeting under similar circumstances."

There was a buzzing in her head and she floated on an

angry sea, balanced precariously on the edge of reason. Which man should she fear more, her father's murderer or this sadist wielding a knife? Fighting against the numbness, she twisted her head the tiniest fraction to see Blackburn shrug carelessly, a hint of sarcasm darkening his voice.

"Your peculiar strategy didn't work with Edward and it certainly won't work with Devon Caravelle. Besides which, isn't she more valuable to you alive?"

Le Comte looked at Devon and then back at Blackburn. "Don't be absurd. I've no desire to kill the woman—simply a settling of accounts."

"Are you sure she's even worth the trouble?" Blackburn was perfectly calm, his presence overtaking the room as though he hadn't a thought for the four pistols that snapped to attention. For the first time since his arrival he spared Devon an indifferent glance, Le Comte's blade still poised at her throat.

"The ever useful Lady Treadwell must have told you where to find us. Now there's a woman who isn't worth the trouble."

Blackburn didn't look surprised at the abrupt change in topic. "You're none too popular at the moment. Bertrand Lacan is as disenchanted with you, almost as much as Lady Treadwell."

"I'd wondered where he'd disappeared to. He was never the brightest man, which might explain why some of us are slower to recognize opportunity when it is on the horizon." For a moment it was as though Le Comte wasn't conscious of the cold metal blade he pressed against Devon's skin. "I'll get to Monsieur Lacan in good time," he promised ominously, a tic beating erratically under his left eye. "But, in the interim, Marquess, we have Devon Caravelle to attend to."

Blackburn smiled congenially. "You're wasting your time."

The buzzing in Devon's head became louder. He spoke as though she wasn't even in the room.

"She may once have proved useful, I'll admit, but less useful than either of us would have suspected. She still has no idea of the full import of the formula. I would suggest that she's quite irrelevant to me and to you at this point."

"In your opinion, perhaps, but then you have yet to hear exactly what I have planned for Mademoiselle Caravelle."

Blackburn flicked a quick glance at the knife the Frenchman held like a religious relic in his hand. "She's certainly not the highly trained intelligence operative I was expecting when you sent her to me that night at Blackfriars Bridge. You could have done better surely?"

Le Comte straightened slightly, but still clasped the knife almost delicately. "She's disappointed you?"

Blackburn shrugged before turning to the piano. "Her experience is altogether limited to arcane knowledge which proves useless other than as exercises in the schoolroom. Aside from that," he sat down on the piano bench and folded his arms over his chest, "she's simply a musician."

Devon struggled to remain mute, aware of Le Comte waving the knife over her head as his pale eyes narrowed with suspicion.

"Why is it that I feel you're overstating the case? We're speaking about the daughter of the great Clifton who raised her as his acolyte." Le Comte clenched the knife more tightly and Devon could see the whitening of his knuckles.

"That may be so, but I've worked closely with her and will tell you that her knowledge of cryptanalysis is rudimentary at best."

Le Comte smiled knowingly, balancing the knife playfully between his thumb and finger. "We'll come back to your assertion in a few moments, although I must ask, It doesn't bother you to see the woman who you so recently held in your arms suffer under my blade?" Le Comte's words were taunting, testing. "I thought at the very least you might offer me an exchange to help mitigate any damage I might feel compelled to commit."

"Ah yes, the exchange." Blackburn rose from the piano

bench and shoved his hands in his pockets. "I hadn't considered Devon Caravelle as part of that particular equation."

Every limb and every muscle in her body stiffened. Even if the ropes crucifying her to the chair were removed, she would lock herself away, erect a barrier against what was happening, what she was hearing.

"What you do with her, I'd rather not know and I really don't care. The unfinished business I have is with you."

"You *are* a cold bastard." The words were tinged with admiration. "Let's see just how deeply the ice runs." To underscore his words, Le Comte turned back to Devon and pressed imperceptibly on the blade at the base of her neck where immediately a small red pearl appeared. She heard a strangled sound and realized it came from her own throat. Strangely, she felt no pain, watching as the Frenchman smeared the blood on the blade and held it up for Blackburn's approval.

The room was deadly quiet. Time was suspended for several heavy heartbeats. Not one of them breathed.

In the next moment the world in the salon shifted and coalesced into a blur of motion. Blackburn lunged at the Frenchman and threw him to the floor, grabbing the wrist that held the knife. And twisted. Le Comte gave a grunt of pain. The knife flew in an arc, the rubied handle glittering before clattering uselessly across the floor. The two men rolled on the ground, crashing against the stone fireplace, the sounds of flesh and bone giving way. Booted feet thudded on the floorboards, smashing into her mother's embroidered ottoman, ramming it into the grate. Devon struggled against her bonds, scraping her wrists together, raw pain shooting through her arm.

Something snapped in her mind as she twisted around to see three of Le Comte's men bear down on Blackburn who was raining blows on the Frenchman as though driven by an internal machine, his fist a powerful and horrifyingly accurate piston. Blackburn gripped Le Comte's throat with both hands—the sound of choking and flailing boots.

She waited for the whistle of a bullet, but none came.

Le Comte strained helplessly, his face purpling against Blackburn's superior strength. The Frenchman's body spasmed against the wood floor sending dust motes spinning into the air. Unwillingly, Devon caught his gaze with her own. His eyes began to cloud and she could hear the scrape of his breath.

Sprawled on the floor, Blackburn tightened his grip on the Frenchman's throat, easily evading the hands that clawed at him. Cold fury was written in every line of his body, his loose-limbed elegance transformed into lethal savagery. Nausea filled her throat and she shut her eyes to blot out the image, just as she felt cold metal biting into the back of her head.

"Leave off, Blackburn, or the bitch dies," barked one of Le Comte's lieutenants, the snout of his gun tangling in Devon's hair. The words conjured some kind of perverse magic and suddenly all was preternaturally calm. Miraculously, the men were able to pull Blackburn off the Frenchman, hoisting him roughly to his feet, his arms twisted behind him. Devon couldn't bear the look in his eyes, wild and dead at the same time.

Breathing heavily, his shirt torn and bloodied, Blackburn watched as Le Comte was helped to stand and, hunched over in pain, as he was led carefully to a settee.

Her father's favorite wing chair was dragged next to hers. No longer struggling, Blackburn's arms were viciously strapped behind him with his ankles bound to the chair legs. She wanted to say something, anything, but could only stare silently at his profile, which was turned resolutely away from her.

Le Comte strained to rise from his seat and, ironically, the action transformed his entire demeanor, despite the bruise purpling his forehead and the red welts on his neck. He seemed taller, his slight frame broader, his gaze deadlier.

"Keep that pistol trained on Mademoiselle Caravelle," he wheezed, weaving a few steps, "until, that is, I retrieve my *blade.*" Immediately, one of the men scooped up the knife and returned it to him.

Devon's chest hurt as if it had been pummeled black and blue. She couldn't afford a glance at Blackburn, but felt the intensity of his pent-up rage, a hot energy that filled her with a strange exhilaration. Rational thought came flooding back and with it a renewed sense of purpose. Energy swept through her and she was frightened by a fragile hope.

Yet a dark voice told her differently, whispering the truth in her reluctant ear.

He risked his life *for the code.* Not for her.

Her head pounding, she focused on the monster moving toward them, watched as his thin hands gripped the edge of her mother's pianoforte for support, his knuckles white. She almost forgot the cold muzzle of the gun buried in her hair.

Brandishing the bloodied knife, Le Comte gave an insanely satisfied smile. "You just made the biggest mistake of your life, Blackburn. Just as I had planned."

"Fuck you." Shadows danced around the creases of his mouth.

Le Comte ignored the imprecation. And Devon noticed how Blackburn studiously ignored her, his eyes chips of black ice.

"Wonderful how this has all turned out, *n'est-ce pas?*" the Frenchman continued addressing Blackburn, now helpless before him. Drawing a handkerchief from his pocket, he mopped his brow, swallowing a groan at the same time. A strange triumph blazed from his eyes.

"Why did you do it, Blackburn, stop from killing me, that is? Particularly since that's what you've been wanting to do for a long time. You have the formula. You could have had vengeance. And you could have had Devon Caravelle, and all she knows, swept from the face of this earth with simply one bullet."

The circles under Blackburn's eyes were deeply etched, like

granite scored by dark fissures. "Why don't you tell me, de Maupassant, as you're clearly eager to."

Le Comte nodded approvingly, delighted to continue. He was clearly drunk on his omnipotence, condescension lacing his words, his voice liquid with sarcasm. "Essentially, I relied on an acute understanding of your character, Blackburn. I knew that you wouldn't be able to resist the dalliance that Devon Caravelle presented and I also recognized that you wouldn't turn down another chance at the *Eroica*—particularly since that unfortunate incident with your brother must still rankle." The Frenchman's hooded eyes were bloodshot, but he managed a smile at his own understatement.

"You really aren't as complex a man as you appear. I knew that either you would succumb to Devon Caravelle's charms and save her from the likes of me—in exchange for your knowledge of the code, of course. Or more likely, you would take what opportunity you could to exploit her to get what you wanted from me—the *Eroica*. I couldn't lose." He looked down at the knife in his hand, bemused by his own cleverness. "So—checkmate, as the English say."

Blackburn's muscles bunched, pulling at the seams of his shirt. The worn leather of her father's wing chair protested. "Spare me any more analysis."

"I shall spare you *nothing*, Blackburn. Particularly Devon Caravelle, as you have obviously developed a tendresse for her."

Something shifted in Blackburn. She couldn't bear to wait for his answer, focusing instead on the powerful set of his shoulders, unbending and impervious to emotion.

"*I have the formula and you can bloody well have it. Let her go.*"

Devon stopped breathing. The words dropped like a rock into the stillness of the room.

Le Comte flushed with triumph. Turning on his heels, he eased himself onto a sofa covered by a dust sheet. "You are a sentimental bastard, after all, just as I'd suspected," he crowed. "But I wouldn't want the game to end so easily."

Tension so tight it nearly sliced through her. Devon's confusion blotted out the heavy numbness in her ankles and wrists and she tried to focus on what Le Comte was saying.

"I not only want the formula, I also insist on having the letter, the one Susannah Treadwell so craftily stole from me and, if my assumption is correct, passed along to you." His eyes narrowed. "You know the one. For me, it has always represented extra assurance, you understand, in case our Devon proved unnaturally recalcitrant under my ministrations."

Devon saw lights dancing before her eyes, skin pricks of sensation traveling up and down her spine. She screwed her eyes closed and saw Susannah Treadwell dancing away from Le Comte in his rooms, taunting him, the letter crumpled on the escritoire between them.

The Frenchman paused significantly, one hand stroking the red welts on his neck, his formerly highly starched collar a shambles. "As he was dying, Brendan Clifton actually pressed it into my hand, can you imagine? Although who knows how aware he was at that point, what with all the blood he'd lost."

The words rammed against Devon's ribs, her heart. The room dimmed and a chasm of rage, shock, and grief opened before her. She wanted to shout, something wild and keening, but she fought for control like never before. With a shuddering breath, she focused on the burn of the pistol still buried at the back of her neck.

"You can keep your damned letter." Her voice lashed at her father's murderer, the way her fists would have if they only could. "My father would never have wanted it to be used this way."

The Frenchman rose stiffly to stand by the pianoforte. The men behind him shifted as he turned to her with a gaze that froze her flesh. "Your problem is that you're far too loyal,

Mademoiselle. Unlike myself—or your father, for that matter—you don't see the usefulness of changing sides upon oc-
casion."

It was like a fist to her face. "You sick, evil bastard . . ."

Devon choked back more words, barely noticing Blackburn's interruption, his move deliberately drawing Le
Comte's fire from Devon. "And that's something I don't quite
understand about you, de Maupassant," he said. "Throwing
your lot behind the Revolution that cost your family both
their name, their lives, and their position in France?"

Le Comte rested heavily against the pianoforte before giving a snort of contempt. "Your understanding of power and
politics is sorely lacking, Blackburn. And unlike you, I prefer
not to wallow in sentiment, in what is long past. Why ever
would I throw my lot behind the shaky throne of the Bourbons when one of the greatest emperors in the history of the
world is just a hair-breadth from returning to conquer Europe, ready to restore my family's power tenfold in return for
my assistance? Even you and that ineffectual General
Wellington can't be that naïve."

Blackburn's voice was taut with control, as if the overwhelming threat in the room meant nothing to him, and as if
he couldn't see Devon's wide gray eyes locked in revulsion on
the Frenchman's face. "No, you can't accuse us of that," he
said with perfect irony.

"Which brings us to the ending of this story, Blackburn, an
ending which could be a beginning for you."

"I await with interest." Blackburn sat impossibly relaxed
in Brendan Clifton's chair, only the muscles of his legs and
shoulders bunching against the restraints. His earlier rage
had dissipated seemingly into the ether. Lines were etched
into the planes of his face, but he was once again a master of
control.

"Not that I will forgive this earlier incident," said the
Frenchman, as though clearing up a simple misunderstanding,

"as you shall soon learn." He glanced at Devon, who met his narrowed eyes like a swordsman ready to do battle. He shot her a look of purest poison before turning back to Blackburn. "In the interim, Marquess, I am sure you will see reason when you learn what I have in store for both you and the lovely Mademoiselle Caravelle."

Now was not the time. To calm herself, Devon looked away and focused on the pianoforte, the fireplace, and the tarnished silver candlesticks on the mantel.

The Frenchman continued speaking directly to Blackburn. "It comes down to this—you and Devon are too valuable to let slip through my fingers. Of course, you didn't bring the score with you today, but I will have the formula before the day is out."

He clasped his hands behind his back before continuing portentously, "More spectacularly, I see such potential for the future with the two of you *bound* to my side. After all, the lovely mademoiselle is French on her maternal side while you, Monsieur le Marquess, recognize both expediency and opportunity when it presents itself. A man of action and a man of intellect—a winning combination."

"What you're proposing is impossible." The cold in Blackburn's eyes cracked like a sheet of ice. Underneath lay a white-hot rage that went soul deep. For a moment, Le Comte tasted something like fear and remembered the evening in the conservatory in London, remembered the night with Edward on the coast. He shook off the feeling.

"Do you goad me?" he gestured meaningfully with the knife, waving it in front of the man who was securely bound hand and foot.

Blackburn shrugged, tense muscle moving beneath the straining linen of his shirt. "Let's cut to the quick. You're asking me to choose France over England, Napoleon over a duly elected Parliament and a king. Hell will freeze over first."

Le Comte laughed. "I may have influence in that matter.

Furthermore, I believe I can convince you, and I think Mademoiselle Caravelle might be instrumental in your decision." He deliberately placed the knife on the keys of the pianoforte, a slash of red on ivory.

Blackburn judged the mood in the room carefully. "And do I have a chance to think about this?"

"Absolutely." The Frenchman was feeling magnanimous now, despite a bruise that was blossoming on his forehead, courtesy of Blackburn's fist. "I shall simply take Devon Caravelle with me while helpfully providing you with quill and paper to record for my benefit—and Napoleon's eventually—the details of the *Eroica* code."

"I can't do it alone. I need Devon's help to reconstruct the formula," Blackburn said. "You will leave her here with me for the duration."

"And the letter?"

"I have it, but then the contents are meaningless to you and to me without Devon's help."

Le Comte's brows drew together before a new malevolence lit his eyes. "That Brendan Clifton was too clever by half. The goddamn formula is nothing without the information contained in the letter to his daughter." He paused speculatively. "You have a point, Blackburn. I'll spare you two hours and then I demand the *completed* formula. I should say that the time will also give you the singular opportunity to renew your acquaintance, which, I am sure, will make my proposition to you all the more meaningful."

"A proposition." Blackburn's voice was neutral.

"Must I paint the picture for you—and such an ugly picture?"

The silence was as heavy as the boom of cannon fire.

Le Comte trailed his fingers along a few of the piano keys, a hopeless melody. The discordant notes echoed in the room. "If you insist, Blackburn, I'll tell you what I envision: your working for me against England."

Devon could see Blackburn's hands clench and unclench behind his back. His laugh was harsh. "A good try, de Maupassant."

"Let's not be rash in making our decisions, Monsieur le Marquess." Le Comte casually picked up the knife where it lay on the keyboard. He tapped the edge against his open palm as though enjoying the prospect of pain. He smiled meaningfully at Devon. She refused to look away.

Le Comte gazed past her at Blackburn, turning toward him as quickly as his protesting muscles would allow. "My proposal is a simple one," he said.

"I seriously doubt it."

Le Comte could afford to be generous. "Judge for yourself, then."

"You can be sure." Blackburn's gaze was trained on the Frenchman. Devon had never seen eyes so cool and intense at the same time.

Le Comte gave a shout of laughter that sent chill fingers up her spine. "Still so arrogant, but not for much longer," he said. "As for my simple proposal it runs like this: You choose Napoleon, or you will find yourself watching Devon Caravelle beg for mercy, scream for salvation, beseech me for release, not just today . . . but again and again." Le Comte played with the knife's sharp tip, scoring his own skin until a fine crimson line appeared.

"*Until hell finally does freeze over. And it will.*"

For the first time in his life, Blackburn knew terror. Left alone with Devon, four of Le Comte's men guarding the door to the salon and more positioned around the house, he felt the adrenaline of fear—for the woman he loved.

She was still sitting in the chair where they had bound and then untied her, ropes now lying limply on the floor. She sat looking away from him at the fireplace mantel, the cameo of her fine features always so vivid, now drawn in defeat. Something inside him broke at the sight, anger, bitterness, and guilt burning away at the scar tissue choking his heart, leaving nothing behind but a shattering realization: that he loved Devon as he had never loved anyone before in his benighted life.

He'd been lost from the first night at Blackfriars Bridge.

Images coursed through him with startling force: her luminous eyes, sharp with intelligence, looking at him over a silver-mounted pistol. Her pale body outlined against the richness of an Aubusson rug. The determined set of her shoulders as she'd launched herself at Lacan and his men. The scent of her skin, the fullness of her hair, the cadence of her breathing. Every curve and angle of her body was familiar to him now.

But it was the sight of de Maupassant's knife at Devon's throat—his hands flexed to feel the crush of the Frenchman's bones—that had forced him to admit that he couldn't live without her. Vengeance, pride, the desire for the Frenchman's blood were suddenly and completely meaningless to him.

In two swift strides he moved quickly to her side and, kneeling, took her into his arms. His mouth caressed her hair and his hands moved over her back and shoulders to reassure himself that she was really there. Her scent, her warmth, filled him with dread that was going to send him over the brink. For a moment she held herself rigid, then she made a choking sound and buried her face in his throat.

"I'm sorry," she said, her voice muffled in his shirt. Her fingers gripped the fabric, tight with desperation. He rested his chin on her head, feeling her body shake.

It was too late, too late to tell her how he felt. "Devon, if we get out of this . . ."

She lifted her head to meet his gaze, the gray eyes as beautiful and unreadable as a night sky, the fragile skin beneath stained with the shadows of fear and exhaustion. "Don't, Blackburn . . . I can never thank you for what you did and maybe I can never forgive you either. I'm not worth handing over the formula to Le Comte."

All he could do was reach for her again, holding her against his body. She struggled for a moment like a small animal, but then she stilled in his arms. Again and again he stroked her hair back from her forehead, hoping his touch could make her believe what he was about to say, willing her not to turn away from him.

"Devon, I love you. And it's not too late."

He felt her stiffen and she pulled back her head. He saw the tiny mark on her smooth neck, and tamping down the rage that threatened to blind him, he kissed the spot gently.

"Blackburn," she whispered, "you don't have to do this." But he felt the softness of her hands in his hair.

"I want to do this. I *need* to do this," he said releasing his breath in a harsh sigh.

"No, you don't." A simple response, low and numb against his shirt front.

Blackburn fought for the right words. He felt unsteady, as though he'd been forced to abandon the familiar script that had become his life. "Sweet Jesus, Devon, all those years of manipulating truth, twisting ideals, burying myself in lies until I didn't know which battle I was fighting. It's over. I can't go back now. " His voice cracked. "I don't even know who I am anymore."

"Until today?" she whispered almost fearfully. The words contained a raw pain that he knew too well. "Is it just Le Comte's threats against me that are making you feel this way?"

His lips moved to the red marks on her wrists, kissing them. He smoothed her damp hair back from her temples, and then his eyes locked onto hers, chiding her for her foolishness. "I'm a little tougher than that, Devon." He didn't have to tell her that he had seen shattered skulls, corpses still twitching and groaning on smoking battlefields. And he didn't have to tell her that the moment he'd seen de Maupassant with his blade so close to Devon's throat . . . The fury, the fear. It was as though everything in his life had telescoped to that one instant in time, a beam of light illuminating what was truly important to him. He cut off his thoughts abruptly.

"I love you." The words were brusque, ruthless in their intensity. "I recognize what I feel for you. I don't care if your mother was a radical and I don't care whose side your father played. I don't care that they were not wed. What I know is that I love you. I want to live with you. I want us to be lovers, equals and friends."

Blackburn felt it, her trembling, this sudden fragility in a woman whom he knew to be as strong as finely tempered metal. He took her hand, the slender fingers powerful and delicate at the same time, and brushed it with his lips. "Say it—I want to hear it."

She tried to slide her hand out of his, but he kept hold of it. "Blackburn, for God's sake, I can't . . . I don't deserve this." He laced his fingers through her own. Her eyes were dark with confusion as she looked at their intertwined fingers. She buried her face in his shoulders and he felt the hot wetness of her tears.

"What is it?" He held her as he tried to kiss away the dampness of her cheeks, a man who had faced down executioners and torturers but who, at this moment, couldn't bear the thought of Devon Caravelle in pain.

"I didn't trust you," came the muffled sobs that rent his newly bared soul. "I doubted you when you believed in me. Susannah Treadwell, the letter, Le Comte . . . I thought you had murdered my father . . . I thought that you . . ."

"You thought I would use you as I had used everyone else." He groped for the right words: that it didn't matter, that she'd had every right to distrust him, that he'd given her every reason. But words weren't necessary when they had something else that could dispel the doubts and mistrust.

He caught her face in both hands and began to kiss her, deeply, thoroughly, and unfairly, searching for any shred of resistance, pitiless in his objective. He wanted them both

strung tightly on desire, his lips on hers hungry and possessive, a commanding caress from a ruthless man who would
win.

Devon softened beneath him, clinging as if he was her only
port in the eye of a storm, letting him chase away her doubts,
sweep away her lingering remorse. His kiss was endless,
rough and gentle, dominating and sensual.

His blood thundering, he set her away from him and
looked into her face.

"Devon—say it. I want to hear it," he repeated.

She pressed her fingers to her mouth and then she stroked
his shoulders, his hard arms, and the tight muscles running
down his back. She was still shaking, her lashes spiked with
tears. "I love you—despite my better judgment." Her eyes
turned luminous.

"I always said that you think too much." Blackburn grinned,
a joyous smile that Devon had never seen before stretching
across his face. He held out a hand, the elegant fingers strong
and competent, and helped her to her feet. Drawing her close
for another second because he couldn't resist, he pressed a
kiss to her forehead. "Now that we have the rest of our lives
together, it's time to get out of here."

Devon couldn't stop touching him and threw herself back
in his arms unwilling to face the impossible. "Damn it,
Blackburn. Le Comte's men are right outside the door and
surrounding the cottage."

He held her even closer to him, murmuring into her hair.
"I'll get us out. For the first time in a decade I have something
to live for and I don't plan to have it ripped away from me.
From us."

"You really are sentimental." She laughed, the sound
music to his ears. She wiped her damp cheeks, beaming. "So
where's the rabbit you intend to pull out of your hat."

"You're expecting a sleight-of-hand?"

She reached up and caressed the hard line of his jaw, her
trust in him now inviolate. "I expect nothing less."

His breath brushed her skin as he framed the words. "We just have one more added complication."

Her eyes widened at the bluntness of the statement. "I want to hear it," she said. "There should be no more secrets between us."

Blackburn now knew himself to be totally vulnerable to her wishes. He moved from her palm to her lips, kissing her lightly, trapped by every beautiful curve of her face. Then he said calmly, "I have wired this house with nitroglycerin."

She froze. "That's impossible." She faltered, taking a step back and sitting carefully down in the chair. "How could you accomplish that without blowing yourself up, without the kieselguhr?"

He looked at her for a long moment, his gaze dark and opaque. "I took a risk."

Devon's fingers clenched the folds of her dress. She stared back at him, unable to formulate a response, as though picking through a foreign language. "My God, without the clay as a stabilizer, we don't know when the fuse will detonate."

Fear and tension thickened in the room. Blackburn regarded her, arms folded across his chest.

"You did it for me, didn't you?" she asked simply, the guilt clear on her face. "You could have finished it all, if I hadn't been in the cottage."

Blackburn stared into the shadowed gray eyes. "You deserved as much, Devon. You had your own loyalties, to your parents, to a cause. I judged you unfairly while not judging myself enough."

"Blackburn." She could feel the forgiveness in the force of his words.

He pulled her from the chair and into his arms. "I thought you were safe at the apartments in Paris," he said, feeling her head fall into the hollow of his shoulder. "Knowing you as I do, I probably shouldn't have been surprised to see you arrive here in Blois while I was outside with the nitroglycerin. I came quickly to the conclusion that you had decided to take matters into your own hands." He frowned. "While we were caught inside, I also hoped that nobody was fool enough to fire their pistols. That would surely detonate the fuse."

She pulled away, shaking her head. "Dear God, you have the formula and you have the letter from my father. What else did you need? You should have blown the place heavenward with Le Comte and his hideous lieutenants inside."

And with her inside.

Blackburn's blue eyes burned. He turned her face up to his, his voice rough. "I needed you, Devon. *I need you.* Nothing else matters but that."

He felt the shock go through his body and read the sudden recognition in her eyes. Devon realized that he was talking to her completely openly for the first time.

And then he walked purposefully around the room, looking up at the high ceiling, checking out the smoldering grate of the fireplace.

They had to find an escape. The words screamed in Devon's mind as she kept Blackburn in her sight, never wanting to be away from him again. Miraculous though it seemed, he loved her and she believed him.

"You lived here for a time, Devon. Is there an attic?" He moved with calm efficiency, already estimating the size of the crawlspace above them. Unable to resist, despite the minutes that ticked away, she slipped her arms around him, feeling the unyielding strength under her palms and pulled him close. If she only had a short time left on earth, she wanted to be touching the man she loved.

"It's very small and only accessible through the two bedrooms at the back," she said, breathing in the scent that was his alone.

"Not what I wanted to hear." He bent his head to hers, his breath warm on her cheeks. "There's got to be another way."

"But even if we do get out—there are men surrounding the cottage." She shifted against him.

Suddenly, Blackburn grinned like a madman and kissed

her hard on the mouth. "You're brilliant, absolutely brilliant."

"What did I do?" she asked startled, stepping away from him.

Blackburn tracked her with his eyes, his gaze coming to rest on the gaping hearth of the fireplace. "De Maupassant's men are *surrounding* the house as you point out. But I would wager my last sovereign that there's nobody on the roof."

Two minutes later, they had tied the dust covers—which had been used to hold them prisoner—to form a rope. Blackburn quickly rent a dust cover in half, which he fastened over her head and then his own. Devon followed his ascent, crawling upward like a scuttling crab, as he edged up the fireplace chimney, still warm from dying embers. At one point the opening narrowed enough to make panic clutch her throat. This was what it would be like to be buried alive, thick earth threatening to invade mouth and nostrils. She hesitated in the cloying darkness, nerves hideously exposed, every loose pebble a harbinger of the explosion to come. She wriggled free and, despite her throbbing arm, pulled herself after Blackburn to the top.

Devon watched as he struggled with the screens enclosing the chimney, the metal gouging his hands, leaving rivulets of blood which he wiped impatiently on his shirt front. She saw rather than heard the metal grillwork give way, the blue sky now a welcoming beacon. Blackburn's head and then his body disappeared and she heard a dull thump as he rolled onto the pitched roof. Then an arm gripped her beneath the shoulders and pulled her into the welcome light of dusk.

Motioning her to lie flat, Blackburn pulled the cloth from his head signaling for her do the same. He then skimmed to the edge of the roof and looked over.

Devon could tell from his expression—Le Comte's men waited in the small courtyard below.

Choking, soot stinging her eyes and lungs, she desperately held back a cough. On her back, she felt the tiles bite into her skin and she could see the perfect blue of the sky and briefly wondered how much time they had before her parents' cottage exploded beneath them, taking them away into the cerulean horizon above.

She would not, could not, let that happen.

The cottage had only one level, so they could easily survive the twenty-five foot jump to the mercifully overgrown and cushioned garden below. She rolled onto her stomach and crept to look over the side. The green made her dizzy, the world tilting around her.

They were as trapped on the roof as they had been in the cottage—if they jumped they would be leaping into the arms of Le Comte and his men.

Devon squirmed her way to Blackburn's side, her injured arm on fire. Ignoring the stabbing pain, she scraped the hair back from her face and once again peered over the side of the roof where she counted five of the Frenchman's sentinels at their posts. Craning her neck further, she could make out the small road leading to the cottage where de Maupassant's barouche sat with its ancient coat of arms. She pictured him in the brocaded interior, counting the minutes on his gold pocket watch until he would return to the cottage and demand his pound of flesh.

She almost hoped the cottage would explode first.

Blackburn turned to her, his eyes the fierce blue of the sky. "I'm going to jump down here, at the front of the cottage," he whispered hoarsely, his face as still and hard as granite. "It will create a diversion and they'll surmise you're still inside. That's your chance to crawl down into the garden and then run like hell."

Disappointment rushed through her. She grabbed his arm in protest. "Are you mad? I'm not leaving without you."

Blackburn was all business now. "There's no other option." He burrowed into his shirt pocket, now dark with ash, as though looking for something that would convince her. He withdrew a white envelope. "It's your father's letter."

Devon made no move to touch it, shaking her head. "I don't want it." The words even surprised her, but they were true. "I no longer need it."

"Are you sure?" The vellum trembled between them on a current of air.

She nodded, the absurdity of the truth staggering. "And I'm also sure that I won't let you sacrifice yourself for me," she said violently under her breath. "I'm not about to lose you." Her hands tightened around the sharp edge of a tile.

The words were barely out of her mouth, drowned out by the rumble of wheels. An elaborate carriage appeared over the crest of the small hill, its four horses dancing to a stately rhythm, the plumes in their bridles moving in the light breeze. It was an incongruous sight, not seen since before the Revolution, such elaborate excess in the heart of the simple countryside.

The conveyance swung to a halt on the cottage's curved path and the door swept open. Alighting with the help of four burly footmen, Lady Susannah Treadwell emerged blinking against the bright light. Her gold striped gown and matching redingote fell gracefully about her, her hair looped and curled and pinned, her ruby earrings gleaming from beneath her wide-brimmed hat. Her gloved fingertips rested lightly on a muscled arm holding the horses steady.

She surveyed the little cottage like a queen, sweeping the crooked footpath and the overgrown garden with disdain. "My amusements have rarely taken me anywhere as hopeless as this poor little place," she said to no one in particular, holding herself close as though fearing contamination. She continued imperiously, "Now where are they, the Marquess and Le Comte?"

She swiveled around to take in the men with their pistols who, for a moment, let down their guard. Ignoring them, Susannah began walking toward the cottage, pulling off her gloves in time with her mincing steps. "Do tell Le Comte that

I am ready and willing to return something of value to him— for a price, of course."

With a silent nod to her, Blackburn grabbed Devon's arm, sliding them back up the slope of the roof, feet and hands scraping over the tiles until they were behind one of the clay chimney pots. They remained there, frozen as gargoyles on a cathedral, watching the drama unfold twenty-five feet below. Seconds later, Le Comte emerged slowly from his barouche, his expression unreadable.

Aware of the stir she was creating, Susannah stopped at the front door of the cottage, the bright gold of her dress clashing incongruously with a clutch of gently nodding lilies nearby.

Devon was mesmerized. Next to her, Blackburn leaned forward, his presence a touchstone. She let herself meet his steadying gaze for a moment before turning to the voices below.

"What now, Susannah?" Devon heard Le Comte ask wearily, as Lady Treadwell slowly and dramatically turned around to face him. Le Comte had changed his linen, his cravat returned to its former impeccability. "You do appear at inopportune times. Is it more money you want?"

Lady Treadwell's scarlet lips opened in mock horror, eyes widening in a perfect imitation of amazement as she took in the bruise purpling on his forehead. "And *what* happened to you, Monsieur? I might guess that you and the Marquess have already begun your discussions." She sighed theatrically, teetering on the delicate heels of her silk slippers. "I hope you didn't start without me?"

Le Comte tugged at one cuff and then the other cuff of his shirt, clearly beyond patience. Signaling his annoyance to his men, he said, "You have no business here, Lady Treadwell. I shall see you escorted from the property—permanently. Something I should have done long ago."

Immediately, one of Susannah's men appeared at her side, pistol conveniently cocked and aimed at the Frenchman.

Like a carefully choreographed dance, Le Comte's men followed suit surrounding Lady Treadwell in a perfect circle, their guns clicking in concert. Absolute silence, other than the occasional hum of crickets.

"Now look what you've done, Monsieur," Susannah's voice broke the stillness, admonishing in her little girl's tone. She clutched her velvet reticule to her chest in mock fear. "Let's have all these men put their toys away, just for the time being, of course."

Devon looked first to Le Comte and then to Lady Treadwell. Perhaps the Frenchman was learning not to misjudge the weaker sex. His face impassive, he gave an imperceptible nod. Devon saw the men lower their arms and slowly move away, but they were still encircling Le Comte and Lady Treadwell.

"Make it swift, my dear," ground out Le Comte, his polished Hessians gleaming in the sunlight. "You never quite caught on as to whom you're playing with, Susannah. Careful that you don't find out."

Lady Treadwell smiled sweetly, slapping her gloves in her palm. "Maybe you're the one who's in too deep, Monsieur. And always underestimating me—I am tiring of it. You didn't even know that you had a traitor in your midst. And I'm not talking about that Frenchwoman." She tilted her bonnet against the sun, careful of her complexion. "Bertrand Lacan proved more useful to me than to you, Monsieur."

Le Comte didn't deign to respond, while Susannah looked up at the cottage disparagingly. Devon sucked in her breath, hoping she wouldn't look up to the roof line.

"So this is where that little French slut lived. Can't say that I'm surprised. How positively rustic. Wonder what the Marquess thinks of her now?"

Devon felt Blackburn's body tighten next to hers, but he did not so much as glance at her.

Le Comte crossed his arms, his lips thinning. "Let's move things along, Lady Treadwell. If it's about the letter you stole from me, the Marquess maintains that it is in his possession now. So where exactly does that leave you?"

"Why right here on your doorstep, Monsieur." She smiled, coquettishly swaying her hips. "How do you know that the Marquess is telling the truth? You don't, do you? And before you resort to any of your proclivities with the intention of forcing me to do your bidding, I did ask my solicitors to deliver a document—in the event of my demise—to St. James's Palace. So none of your little tricks, Monsieur."

Le Comte bit back a hoarse laugh. "And why would anyone believe the scribblings of a whore?"

Susannah played with her gloves, her cat eyes narrowing dangerously. "I know more than you think. For the last two years, I've consorted with some of the most dangerous men in Europe, including you. I knew about your interest in the *Eroica*, but I didn't know about, shall we say, its *explosive* contents? But after stealing and then reading Brendan Clifton's letter to his bastard daughter, and after a few invaluable conversations with your loyal factotum, Bertrand Lacan, I now have a better idea what all you men are so bothered about. But none of that is really important to me. Not really."

"You're begging the question, my dear." Le Comte fairly spat the words.

Lady Treadwell took a deep breath, her eyes glittering. "First Blackburn and then you reject me. There are consequences in life."

Le Comte had paled with each of Susannah's successive volleys. He stood rooted to the spot, right next to the rose bushes Devon's mother had planted years before.

"All right, then," he said in a soft voice. "What is it that you want?"

Susannah gave an approving smile. "That's better. What I want is probably much the same as you do."

"Get on with it, Susannah."

"Firstly, to watch you make that slut and Blackburn suffer—as only you can. And secondly, a *modest* fortune in exchange for *a copy* of the letter. Because you guessed right, Monsieur, I did give Blackburn the original last night."

"And why was that?" A pulse leapt wildly beneath Le Comte's left eye.

She shook her head condescendingly, adjusting the brim of her hat once again. "To provide the catalyst that would have you and Blackburn finally destroy each other. What better way to salve a woman's bruised ego, Monsieur?" She pivoted on a delicate heel, her plump hand on the cottage door. "Now, let's go inside so I can watch you fulfill the first part of our bargain."

Devon forced down the scream that welled in her throat. She clung to the chimney pot paralyzed, watching Lady Treadwell, Le Comte, and their men file inside the small cottage.

They had about five seconds.

Then Blackburn's breath came hard and ragged against her ear. *"Now. This is our chance."*

Intuitively, Devon followed his lead as they rolled their way toward the back of the cottage. Blackburn was quicksilver, pulling her with him, her skirts snagging and pulling on the sharp edges of tile. Poised at the edge of the roof, he let go of her arm and then, with the sinuousness of an athlete, he leapt noiselessly to the ground.

For once, Devon didn't think. Grateful for the open arms waiting for her, she clambered to the edge of the roof and pushed off, sailing into the air to collapse into Blackburn's hard warmth.

After that everything was chaos. She heard the shouts an instant later, the staccato of gunpowder, and felt Blackburn's arms around her as he half-dragged, half-pulled her away and into the thicket behind the cottage. Her lungs heaved as they dove into the tall grass just as the first explosions ripped the air.

The ground moved beneath them, the tremors threatening

to cleave the earth asunder. It was the Apocalypse, the end of the world, the wrath of the most vengeful god. And then the blue sky turned white, showering them in the hot ash of the past. Her past.

Devon buried herself in Blackburn's chest that smelled of cinders and sweat. She wanted to sink into him forever and never come up for air until, it seemed, eons later, the madness stopped.

She rose in his arms, reborn. She sat amid the crushed weeds, heedless of the wreckage around them, only desperate never to let go of the man by her side. She tried to speak, choked, tried again.

As if reading her thoughts, Devon felt Blackburn's hand reach for hers, locking their fingers.

"Devon—your parents . . ." He seemed to be looking for the words, the things that had to be said. Above his stained collar and ripped shirt, his face was marked by indelible shadows. "I wish this didn't hurt you so much, that I could take away some of the pain."

She refused to look over the thicket where she could see the billows of smoke and fire arching up to the sky. She shook her head gathering strength from the man beside her. He was beautiful, Blackburn, and he was hers.

"There's a strange justice about all of this," she said finally, her voice hoarse with grit and emotion, bracing herself against any attempt at false comfort. "Le Comte destroyed in a web of his own design. Susannah strangled by her own greed and vanity." She looked into the eyes that she'd always suspected could read her soul. "Remember what you told me that night at Armathwaite—that I must grow up, put my parents in the past where they belong? To remember only the good?"

Reaching out to caress his brow, she brushed a layer of soot from his eyelashes. "That was the best advice."

He grimaced at the irony. "As if I'm one to give counsel." He smoothed a stray wisp of hair from her cheek. "All I know is that I love you."

She smiled at the words, delirious to hear them again. "We can put all this behind us. But I have to do something first."

His chest was lean and hard under her fingers as she removed her father's letter from his pocket. Now that it was torn and smeared with dirt, she held it for a moment before tearing it first in half and then into progressively smaller pieces, tossing them in the air and watching as they floated to the ground along with the dust that still hung in the afternoon light.

"Now only you know," she said enigmatically, sweet relaxation spreading through her limbs.

"And that's the way it will stay." He shifted against her, settling her more comfortably against the curve of his body.

"No regrets?" she couldn't help asking. "No overwhelming desire to run to Wellington with your discovery? Did the letter not contain information about the location of that last piece of the puzzle—the location of this magic clay?"

He didn't answer her directly, but cupped the fine bones of her face in his large palm. "You once told me that I was all intellect, dead to true emotion, enthralled by devious plans, impenetrable ciphers, and the endless stimulation of danger."

"I had no right," she interrupted, twisting in his arms.

"Perhaps. But you *were* right. And because of you I've had the opportunity truly to do the right thing—not for king and country—or for revenge. But for humanity, to ensure that the formula for this nitroglycerin stays hidden for as long as it possibly can. The last thing this world needs is another weapon of destruction."

"What about the letter Lady Treadwell sent to St. James's Palace?"

"It's useless to Wellington without the formula."

Devon looked up at him, loving the slant of his cheekbones, the strength of his nose, the sensual curve of his lips. "You are a wonderful man," she said simply. "But I have one more question that I'd like you to answer."

"And what would that be?"

She forced a touch of lightness into her voice. "Does uncontrollable passion lead to love?"

He smiled wickedly. "There's only one way to find out."

Epilogue

Six months later . . .
London

The audience was ecstatic. Covent Garden was filled to the uppermost balconies that evening, with even the Prince of Wales in attendance. However, all eyes were not trained on the Royal Box, but rather on the pianoforte center stage, bracketed by rich velvet curtains and gleaming candelabra.

At the foot of the podium sat the Duke of Wellington, the Duchess, and the Marquess of Blackburn waiting with as much anticipation as the rest of the audience. The ton had had barely enough time to adjust to the perennially elusive Marquess taking a wife—and such a wife—the former musical protégée of the Le Comte de Maupassant. Much more unbelievable was the open and unseemly delight that the Marquess took in his bride, encouraging and supporting her musical interests and even setting up a foundation for a new music conservatory in London.

Not that they spent much of their leisure paying attention to the Season. It would seem that the couple could not find enough time alone together, disappearing for weeks into the countryside with nothing more than nature and an inexhaustible passion for each other to sustain them. Quite unusual among married couples, and almost a miracle, given the Marquess's history with women.

As for his former rival, Le Comte de Maupassant, the man had disappeared into the wilds of Europe, taking with him, the gossips wagged, Lady Susannah Treadwell. It was quite the scandal, however much peace it offered the ailing and aging Lord Treadwell.

This evening's concert was being given in Beethoven's honor, although the musician was too ill to travel from Vienna to attend. The Marquess of Blackburn and his new bride had taken their honeymoon in Austria and spent some time with the genius, quite understandably, given their predilection for the man's music. This evening's concert featured his Moonlight Sonata and, most surprisingly, a pianoforte version of his *Eroica* symphony.

The chandeliers glimmered and the audience hushed as a figure emerged from the back of the stage. Dressed simply and shockingly in unrelieved black, the pianist seemed to glide to the piano, the burnished glow of her hair smoothed into a sleek chignon. She paused for a moment and glanced over the seats in the hall before her gaze came to rest on the front row, directly beneath the podium.

Devon Caravelle glowed and even those sitting in the very back rows could feel the passion she radiated for the tall man whose eyes, heart, mind, and soul locked with hers. Then the Marquess of Blackburn gave her a smile that, for the rest of his life, would be reserved for her alone.

The woman he'd been waiting for.

AUTHOR'S NOTE

What is fact and what is fiction in *Explosive?*
The *Eroica* is one of Beethoven's most famous symphonies, originally intended by him to be dedicated to Napoleon Bonaparte. Beethoven had admired the ideals of the French Revolution that were seemingly symbolized by Napoleon, but when the general crowned himself emperor of France in 1804, Beethoven was so troubled that he erased Napoleon's name from the title page with such force that he broke his pen. The manuscript copy of the *Eroica* is now in a museum in Vienna. In the main title, the name "Bonaparte" has been scratched out so violently that the erasure has left a hole in the paper.

Nitroglycerin and dynamite succeeded black powder, the first chemical explosive invented in China, as the newest explosives in the nineteenth century. An Italian chemist, Ascanio Sobrero, discovered nitroglycerin in 1846, but with one major disadvantage—its unstable nature. The man who solved this problem was the Swedish chemist Alfred Nobel. To make the handling of nitroglycerin safer, Nobel experimented with different additives, including a type of clay called kieselguhr, which turned the liquid into a more stable paste. In 1867, he patented this material under the name of "dynamite."

If you liked this story,
you've got to try
THE BLACK SHEEP AND
THE HIDDEN BEAUTY
by Donna Kauffman,
available now from Brava.
Turn the page for a sneak peek . . .

Elena backed down the ladder from her loft apartment over the outer stables, yawning deeply and wishing like hell she'd remembered to set the timer on the coffee pot the night before. The sun was barely peeking over the horizon and last night the temperatures had dipped down a bit further than they had recently, making for a chilly late spring morning. She shivered despite the long underwear top she'd donned under her overalls this morning. Teach her to be a smartass and offer up a dawn class. But then, she hadn't really expected him to take her up on it. He struck her as more of a night owl than an early bird. Serve her right if he stood her up. Her luck—Rafe was probably still tucked in his nice warm bed. Which was where she should be. Well, not in Rafe's bed, but . . .

No way could she stop the visuals that accompanied that little mental slip. It wasn't a shot of warm coffee, but it did have the added benefit of getting her blood pumping a little faster. Of course, if she were in the same bed as Rafe, she wouldn't need any coffee, just . . . stamina.

"Morning."

His voice surprised her, making her lose her footing on the last rung. An instant later two strong hands palmed her waist and steadied her as both feet reached the ground. She could have told him that putting his hands on her was not the way to steady her at the moment, but she was too busy trying to rally her thoughts away from imagining him manhandling her like this while they were both naked amongst tousled sheets.

Then he was turning her around, and she was getting her first look at a scruffy, early morning Rafe. And whatever words she might have found evaporated like morning mist under a rising sun.

Goodness knows, her temperature was rising.

He had on an old, forest green sweatshirt and an even older pair of jeans if the frayed edged and faded thighs and knees were any indication. It was standard weekend morning clothing for most men, but, until that moment, she'd have been hard pressed to visualize it on him. Of course, on most men, that combination would have given them a disheveled look at best. In fact, she was feeling incredibly disheveled herself at the moment. Rafe, on the other hand, without even trying, looked like he'd just stepped off the pages of the latest Ralph Lauren ad. She'd resent the ease with which he made scruffy so damn sexy, except she was too busy fighting off the waves of lust the look inspired.

"So," she said, her tone overly bright. "You ready for lesson number two?"

"As I'll ever be."

She led the way down the aisle toward Petunia's stall. "It's been a while since your first lesson, so keep in mind that you'll probably need to reestablish your report with Petunia."

"Check." He said nothing else, just followed behind her.

She stopped at the tackroom door and went inside. "I haven't set anything out, so we need to get her saddle, pads, bridle, everything."

He followed her into the smaller room. "Just point to what we need."

She could feel him behind her, her awareness of him as finely tuned as her senses were to the animals she worked with. Except with him, there was all that sexual energy jacking things up. She cleared her throat, maybe squared her shoulders a little, then made the mistake of looking back at him before reaching for the first of the gear.

Something about the morning beard shadowing his jaw, the way his hair wasn't quite so naturally perfect, made his eyes darker, and enhanced how impossibly thick his eyelashes were. And she really, really needed to stop looking at his mouth. But the ruggedness the stubble leant to his face just emphasized all the more those soft, sculpted lips of his.

Her thighs were quivery, her nipples were on point, and the panties she'd just put on not fifteen minutes ago, were already damp. The morning air might have been head-clearing. Her body hadn't gotten the message at all.

"You take the saddle there," she said, trying not to sound as breathless as she knew she did. Dammit. "On the third rail," she added, pointing, when he kept that dark gaze of his on her.

"What else?" He didn't even glance at the rack.

"Grab one of the pads. Same kind that we used last time. I'll get the halter and bridle."

"Okay."

She waited a heartbeat too long for him to move first. He didn't.

So they were officially staring at each other now. The silence in the small space expanded in a way that lent texture to the very air between them. The room was tiny, the temperature warm, with little ventilation. The sun hadn't risen enough to slice through the panels on the roof, leaving the room deep in shadows, with thin beams of gray dawn providing the only light. There was a light bulb overhead, but she'd have to reach past him to get to the switch.

He stepped forward. "Elena—"

"Rafe—"

They spoke at the same time, both broke off.

He paused. "Yes?"

She really wanted to know what he'd been about to say,

before she potentially made a very big fool out of herself, but went ahead before she lost her nerve. "I can't—I mean, not to be presumptuous here, but I can't—don't—mix business with pleasure."

"Are we?"

She didn't back down. She might not be the most experienced person in the world when it came to relationships, but she knew the way he was looking at her wasn't of the innocent teacher-student variety. "It feels like more than a simple riding lesson to me." *There. She'd said it.*

He took another step closer, and her breath suddenly felt trapped inside her chest. So much for being brazen.

"It is a simple riding lesson," he said. "Not a corporate merger. So what if there is more? I don't really see a conflict of interest here."

"You're a close friend of my boss."

He stepped closer still. It was a small room to begin with. He was definitely invading her personal space. Again.

"And you're not planning on staying here long term anyway, right?"

"What is that supposed to mean?"

"Meaning that as potential conflicts go, that one is temporary at best. As is anything that may happen between us. No commitments, right?" His voice was all just-rolled-out-of-bed rough.

"What are you saying, then?" she asked, tipping her chin up slightly as he shifted closer. She felt the bridle rack at her back. "What is it you want?"

"I just want to learn to ride." His lips curved then, and her thigh—or more accurately, the muscles between them—suddenly felt a whole lot wobbly.

His eyes were so dark, so deep, she swore she could fall right into them and never climb back out. And that smile made it dizzyingly clear that horses weren't the only thing he was interested in riding.

It was too early in the day for this. She couldn't handle this kind of full-out assault on her senses. Or on her mind. Or . . . hell, what part of her didn't he affect? He muddled her up far too easily. Muddled was definitely not what she needed to be right now.

But when he lifted his hand, barely brushing the underside of her chin with his fingertips, and tipped her head back a bit further . . . she let him.

"I think about you," he said, his voice nothing more than a rough whisper.

Her skin tingled as if the words themselves had brushed against her.

"Too often. You distract me."

"And that's a bad thing."

"It's . . . an unexpected thing."

She wasn't sure what to think about that. And his neutral tone made it impossible to decipher how he felt about it. "So, this is . . . what? An attempt to exorcise me from your thoughts?"

His smile broadened as his mouth lowered slowly toward hers. "Either that, or make all this distraction a lot more worthwhile."

She had a split second to decide whether to let him kiss her, and spent a moment lying to herself that she was actually strong enough to do the right thing and turn her head away. Who was she kidding? Her body was fairly humming in anticipation and it was all she could do to refrain from grabbing his head and hurrying him the hell up.

Like he said. It was just a kiss. Not a contract.

His lips brushed across hers. Warm, a little soft, but the right amount of firmness. He slid his fingers along the back of her neck, beneath the heavy braid that swung there, sending a delicious little shiver all the way down her spine at the contact.

He dropped another whisper of a kiss across her lips, then another, inviting her to participate, clearly not going any further unless she did. She respected that, a lot, even though part of her wished he'd taken the decision out of her hands. It would make all the self-castigation later much easier to avoid. Given his aversion to commitment, somehow she figured he knew that. They were either in it together, or not at all.

He lifted his head just enough to look into her eyes, a silent question in his own. *Will you, or won't you?*

She held his gaze for what felt like all eternity, then slowly lowered her eyelids as she closed the distance between them and kissed him back.

Don't miss Jill Shalvis's
STRONG AND SEXY,
out this month from Brava . . .

"Why do you look so familiar?" His mouth was close to her ear, close enough to cause a whole series of hopeful shivers to wrack her body. He was rock-solid against her, all corded muscle and testosterone.

Lots of testosterone.

"I don't know," she whispered, still hoping for a big hole to take her.

"Are you sure you're all right?"

"Completely." *Except, you know, not.*

"Because I can't help but think I'm missing something here."

Yes, yes, he was missing something. He'd missed her whole pathetic attempt at a kiss seduction, for instance. And the fact that she was totally, one hundred percent out of her league here with him. But his eyes were deep, so very deep, and leveled right on hers, evenly, patiently, giving her the sense that he was always even, always patient. Never rattled or ruffled.

She wanted to be never rattle or ruffled.

"Am I?" His thumb glided over her skin, sending all her erogenous zones into tap-dance mode. "Missing something?"

"Yes. N–no. I mean . . ."

He smiled. And not just a curving of his lips, but with his whole face. His eyes lit, those laugh lines fanned out, and damn, that sexy dimple. "Yeah," he murmured. "Definitely missing something."

"I'm a little crazy tonight," she admitted.

"A little crazy once in a while isn't a bad thing."

Oh boy. She'd bet the bank he knew how to coax a woman into doing a whole host of crazy stuff. Just the thought made her feel a little warm, and a nervous laugh escaped.

"You're beautiful, you know that?"

She had to let out another laugh, but he didn't as he traced a finger over her lower lip. "You are."

Beautiful? Or crazy?

"You going to tell me what brought you to this closet?"

"I was garnering my courage."

"For?"

Well wasn't that just the question of the night, as there were so many, many things she'd needed courage for, not the least of which was standing here in front of him and telling him what she *really* wanted. A kiss . . .

"Talk to me."

She licked her lips. "There's a man and a woman in that first office down the hall. Together. And they're . . . not talking."

"Ah." A fond smile crossed his mouth. "You must have found Noah and Bailey. They've just come home from their honeymoon. So yeah, I seriously doubt they're . . . talking."

"Yeah. See . . ." She gnawed on her lower lip. "I was hoping for that."

"Talking."

"No. The *not* talking."

Silence.

And then more silence.

Oh, God.

Slowly she tipped her head up and looked at him, but he wasn't laughing at her.

A good start, she figured.

In fact, his eyes were no longer smiling at all, but full of a heart-stopping heat. "Can you repeat that request?" he asked.

Well, yes, she could, but it would make his possible rejection that much harder to take. "I was wondering what your stance is on being seduced by a woman who isn't really so good at this sort of thing, but wants to be better . . ."

He blinked. "Just to be clear." His voice was soft, gravelly, and did things to every erogenous zone in her body. "Is this you coming on to me?"

"Oh, God." She covered her face. "If you don't know, then I'm even worse at this than I thought. Yes. Yes, that's what I'm pathetically attempting to do. Come on to you, a complete stranger in a closet, but now I'm hearing it as you must be hearing it, and I sound like the lunatic that everyone thinks I am, and—"

His hands settled on her bare arms, gliding up, down, and then back up again, over her shoulders to her face, where he gently pulled her hands away so he could see her.

"I saw the mistletoe," she rushed to explain. "It's everywhere. And people were kissing. And I couldn't get kissing off my mind . . . God. Forget it, okay? Just forget me." She took a step back, but because this was her, she tripped over something on the floor behind her. She'd have fallen on her ass if he hadn't held her upright. "Thanks," she managed. "But I need to go now. I really need to go—"

He put a finger to her lips.

Right. Stop talking. Good idea.

His eyes, still hot, and also a little amused—because that's what she wanted to see in a man's eyes after she'd tried to seduce him: amusement—locked onto hers. She couldn't look away. There was just something about the way he was taking her in, as if he could see so much more than she'd intended him to. "Seriously. I've—"

He turned away.

Okaaaay . . . "Got to go."

But he was rustling through one of the shelves. Then he bent to look lower and she tried not to look at his butt. She failed, of course. "Um, yeah. So I'll see you around." Or not. Hopefully not—

"Got it." Straightening, he revealed what he held—a sprig of mistletoe.

"Oh," she breathed. Her heart skipped a beat, then raced, beating so loud and hard she couldn't hear anything but the blood pumping through her veins.

His mouth quirked slightly, but his eyes held hers, and in them wasn't amusement so much as . . .

Pure staggering heat.

"Did you change your mind?" he asked.

Was he kidding? She wanted to jump him. *Now.* "No."

With a smile that turned her bones to mush, he raised his arm so that the mistletoe was above their heads.

Oh, God.

"Your move," he whispered.

She looked at his mouth, her own tingling in anticipation. "Maybe you could . . ."

"Oh, no. I'm not taking advantage of a woman in a closet, drenched in champagne." He smiled. "But if she wanted to take advantage of me—now see, that's a different story entirely."

He was teasing her, his eyes lit with mischievousness and a wicked, wicked intent.

"I'm a klutz," she whispered. "I might hurt you by accident."

"I'll take my chances."

She laughed. She couldn't help it. She laughed, and he closed his eyes and puckered up, making her laugh some more, making it okay for her to lean in . . .

And kiss him.

Don't miss
ANY WAY YOU WANT IT,
the newest title from Kathy Love,
available now from Brava . . .